MOLLY BOWES

Val Scully

2nd Edition 2023

First published in 2016

Cover Design by Tom Carr

Front
Gibside's Column to British Liberty by Tom Carr
A Young Beauty with Flowers in Her Hair by Albert Lynch

Back
Detail from *Massacre at St Peter's* by George Cruikshank

All images licensed by Creative Commons

ISBN: 9798375883533

Chapter 1

Charlotte was born in a weaver's cottage in Middleton, Lancashire on 14th February 1819 and I loved her utterly and completely from the first moment she was laid on my breast. I was back at my loom the following day, with my baby safely strapped to my body. In moments of rest I would bend my lips to her shiny golden pearl of a head and inhale her scent. She was mine and mine alone. For now, there was safety among these good, warm-hearted, hard-working people, though times were terribly hard and dark shadows hung over the cottage industry that gave them their living.

Five miles distant was Manchester, a smoke-shrouded hell-hole suffocating under blackening fumes, as though a great gash had split open the earth, sending jutting towers of black rock and shrouds of smoke billowing up to block out the sun.

I feared and dreaded the place. Why did I not listen to my instincts? Why did I agree to go with them? I could have said no: I had a small baby, they would have understood. But I felt I owed it to them: they had taken me in. How Fate must laugh at such decisions.

That August, as we descended from the gentle hills, skeins of smoke coiled across the clear blue skies as though the town were sending out tentacles to draw us in: my very soul shrank from entering that blackness, and I clutched Charlotte more closely to my breast.

Joseph had fallen silent, and even Hannah had ceased her chatter as we observed the foul streets and the evident poverty all around us.

The cart rocked to a halt and Joseph jumped down without a word. Hannah stayed still, her face grim, until Joseph let down the back of the cart, took off the bag and helped us descend. I saw the mouth of a narrow alleyway between the houses, and Joseph disappeared into it, leaving us to mind the cart. All around us, wordless bent figures shuffled past, their faces pinched with hunger.

Close by my shoulder, Hannah whispered, 'Look at that,' and I turned to see a faded and tattered bill-post stuck to the blackened brick behind me. Dirty as it was, the message was still clear and the words shouted their warnings: *"ILLEGAL MEETING. Whereas it appears by an advertisement in the Manchester Observer paper of this day that a PUBLIC AND ILLEGAL meeting is convened for Monday the 9th day of August next, to be held on the AREA NEAR ST PETER'S CHURCH, in Manchester; we, The Undersigned Magistrates, acting for the Counties Palatine of Lancaster and Chester, do hereby caution all persons to abstain AT THEIR PERIL from attending such ILLEGAL MEETING."*

'It's out of date, Hannah, shall I pull it down?'

She looked around fearfully before she said, 'No, I wouldn't. They have spies everywhere.'

'Spies?'

'If you pull down the magistrates' words, there are some as would report you. Leave it to the authorities.'

'Even though it's out of date? It's the 15th today.'

'Leave it, Molly. Here's Joseph back now.'

He had emerged from the alleyway, his face even grimmer. Taking Hannah to one side, he whispered briefly in her ear, then planted a firm kiss on her forehead. Turning to me, he said, 'Take care of each other you two, and I shall see you on Monday. If there's any trouble, you know what to do.'

'Aye, don't worry about us, Joseph, your folks'll look after us. You get on back now.' Joseph kissed her cheek, reached out to squeeze my hand, briefly touched Charlotte's sleepy head, then climbed back into the cart and turned for home.

'Is he not staying even for a drink?'

'He wouldn't touch the water here Molly: he's a flask from home if he's thirsty,' which of course left me wondering what that meant for us, left here for a whole night. I resolved there and then that I would not stay in this midden any longer than was necessary.

The narrow alleyway opened into a foul-smelling yard with lines of grimy washing slung from hooks. Ducking under the low wooden lintel, we were noisily welcomed into a crowded, smoky, filthy kitchen the like of which I had never seen nor hope to see again.

The Fallons were kindly people though their lives were harder than any I have ever witnessed before or since. When I first stepped into that room holding my baby, I recoiled from the dank airlessness and crowded bodies: it instantly took me back to the prison cells and my heart shrank. Hannah, clasped in an embrace by two of Joseph's cousins, looked over with wide eyes and hastened to free herself from the melee.

'I think we shall go for a walk to stretch our legs and get our bearings. We'll be back in an hour. Come on, Molly.'

As we emerged from the alley onto the main street, the air seemed brighter, and I remarked as much to Hannah.

'It's dreadful in there, isn't it? No doubt they are used to this foul air, but I could never be. It's just for one night and will teach us to count our blessings, Mol! Come on, let's stride out. St Peter's Field – at least that sounds like there should be some grass!'

But of course there wasn't, so hot and dry had been the summer that when we finally found the area where the meeting was to be held, we were sorely disappointed to see it was a parched brown wilderness, strewn with rubble and dry timber.

'This is no field, not as I understand it!'

'I suppose it's what must pass for a field for these people.'

3

We had entered from the north and stood at the corner of Bootle Street. The area was a large rough rectangle, perhaps a hundred and fifty to two hundred yards each side, bordered by houses and criss-crossed by shallow trenches, perhaps the start of some drainage works.

'Where will the speakers stand?'

'Last time Hunt spoke, in January, the hustings were over there,' she gestured to the opposite side of the square, 'backing onto Windmill Street.'

'Were there many here then?'

'Joseph reckoned about ten thousand.'

'Ten thousand people?' I looked around in wonder. 'I can't picture them all fitting!'

'Joseph reckons there'll be ten times that number tomorrow!'

'Ten times? A hundred thousand people? No, surely that's not possible.'

'Well, Bamford's done the sums. He says four people can stand in a square yard, but having seen the state of these poor people, I'd say more'n that. Double, even.'

I surveyed the area doubtfully, and the conviction grew upon me that it had been a mistake to come. I certainly did not want to bring Charlotte to such a place and be squashed in amongst all these filthy people. I would find a way out of it, even if it meant lying to Hannah. What harm?

'Was there any trouble at the last meeting?'

'No, the cavalry watched but there was no bother.' Her eyes twinkled. 'Oo, come to think of it, I hope there's some handsome soldiers here tomorrow. All those heroes of Waterloo in their fine uniforms. I do love a man in uniform, don't you?'

An old man who we hadn't noticed standing nearby suddenly spoke, muttering darkly, almost to himself. 'There's too many soldiers about for my liking.'

Hannah giggled, nudging me playfully, 'There can never be too many soldiers for me and Molly, eh Molly?'

The old man looked hard at her, his toothless mouth a hard line. 'Ye'll regret saying that, to my mind. These are not local men. It's Hussars. They've been sent up from Lunnen to squash us, you mark my words. There's guns an' all. Big uns. Watch out, that's all I'm saying.'

'There'll be no trouble.' Hannah was nonplussed. 'Mr Hunt has expressly forbade it. The marchers will have no weapons. What does it say on his posters? Bamford read it out. What did it say, Molly?'

But I was already hatching plans to be elsewhere. I had experience of soldiers and I felt nothing but fearful. And if there were guns, too, maybe even cannons...

'I remember now: "Come armed with no other weapon but that of a self-approving conscience" – that's what it said. Pretty turn of phrase, that. I'm looking forward to hearing him speak: he's quite an orator, they say.'

'You'll be lucky if you can hear him if there's going to be a hundred thousand here.'

'Yes, that's a point. Let's have a think. Where shall we stand?' She looked around speculatively, and I saw her eyes alight on the high stone wall over to our left, behind a few stunted oaks. 'What's that wall?'

'That's the Quaker burial ground, behind there.'

'Lord, that's a high wall, must be all of ten foot! We couldn't climb that.'

'Ye could from the back. If you go round to the Friends' Meeting House on Dickinson Street and walk across the graveyard, soil's banked up on the other side of that wall, and it's only three or four foot high.'

'There you go, that's what we'll do. I reckon we'll be good and safe on that wall and we'll be able to hear Henry Hunt across the heads of the crowd.' She linked my arm and set off at a jaunty pace across the field, calling over her shoulder, 'Thanks for that, old man. And for your warnings. We'll be careful. Byee!' To me she whispered, 'Come on, let's go and find some soldiers to look at.'

Charlotte was tied in a sling across my body, and I pulled a face to Hannah, indicating with a rueful glance that I was hardly likely to attract the attentions of a soldier, except for the wrong reasons.

As it turned out, I was about to attract unwanted attention, and from an unexpected quarter.

When we got back to the dwelling of the Fallons, both of us taking deep breaths as we entered the alley, there was a younger man we had not seen before. He was clearly one of them, having the prematurely grey hair and thick dark eyebrows that made the men of the family so distinctive: he was, however, taller and better-nourished than any we had yet seen.

'This is Declan, a cousin from Stretford. Declan, you know Hannah, Joseph's wife from Middleton. This is her friend Molly.'

'And this?' He indicated the baby sleeping on my shoulder.

'This is Charlotte.'

'And where are your menfolk, Hannah and Molly?'

Hannah was taking off her shawl, her eyes alight with mischief. 'My Joseph is at home all alone. Or so I hope.'

'And you, Molly? Where is your squire and protector?'

There was something about the way he said it that tensed the muscles in my jaw, and I didn't reply at once, but instead laid Charlotte down on the mat in front of the empty grate and watched her stretch out her legs and arms with an extravagant yawn. It was a relief to both of us, for the heat of the day and the exertion of the walk had made the flesh between us sticky. The coils of her red hair were pressed flat against her scalp like gold coins. I knelt down beside her and busied myself in loosening her clothes and blowing her face. She chuckled toothlessly and her fists gripped my hair, pulling me down.

When I felt a sudden gentle pressure under the middle of my backside, I jumped, startling Charlotte, whose shoulders and head were lifted when I pulled back. I sat back on a booted foot. I had thought it an accident in the crowded room, but when I knelt up so the foot could be removed, the pressure was renewed briefly and then withdrawn. I stood up slowly, holding the squirming Charlotte before me like a shield. When I turned round, he had moved away and was standing in the doorway, looking out. Then he turned, winked at me and was gone.

By the time he reappeared with the other menfolk, it was dark and the children were all asleep. We had heard deep voices coming down the passageway and when the door was opened, a great cloud of beery breath billowed before them and suddenly the quiet room was full and loud. I had stood up as soon as I heard them and I took my leave, slipping away and softly climbing the narrow wooden staircase to the attic, where I laid Charlotte on the sacking where we were to sleep. There was no air in the room and the acrid smell of the hot, unwashed bodies of five or six children made me swallow to stem the nauseous feeling of being smothered.

I fell asleep instantly and knew nothing until suddenly a weight was upon me, beery breath in my face, wetness of lips and tongue, hands rummaging, pain as my arm was twisted back and pinned under what? A knee? I burst into wakefulness, pushing the heel of my other hand hard into his shoulder, digging my nails in, wrestling my knees up, twisting sideways, biting the hand that gagged me. It swung back and slapped my face, not hard, then locked again across my mouth, thumb spread wide and digging into my cheek. I bit down hard on the stretched flesh and my teeth met. With a yelp, his other hand grabbed my hair and yanked my head back, hard. Charlotte, where was Charlotte? Sounds now from the children, woken by the scuffling and thudding of heels on the wooden floor, and surely by his yelp. Still now, beery breath, panting hard in my face, weight on my legs, pinning them sideways, hot wetness smeared across my cheek, the metallic taste of blood in my mouth – his or mine? Teeth sinking into the lobe of my ear, but gently, like a caress, and then a light kiss of the neck beneath, that sent hot chills down my shoulder, then a voice. 'I'll have you, slut. Another time.'

And then he was up and off and gone. Charlotte. Feeling, bare boards, rough sacking, straw spikes, splinters, fingers softly scrabbling. Where is she? And at last, a sound, a snuffle, a whimper, fingers find her soft hot flesh, cup her plump cheek, scoop her up and clasp her to me and the two of us sob and sob and sob as the bewildered sounds from the older children turn to questions, reassurances, some disgruntled tutting and then subside into silence.

When I woke again into the airless attic, the sun was up, thrusting swords of yellow light through the cracks in the slates and a whey-faced girl of about ten was looking down at me. 'Yer've cut yer face,' she said, and vanished.

Charlotte still clamped to my belly, I struggled to sit up, dazed by heat and pain. My shoulder hurt and a small tear at the side of my mouth seeped sticky blood; I ached and the back of my head felt bruised, but otherwise I counted myself lucky. I would get out of this house as soon as I could and I would get out of this filthy town and I would never come back. At that moment I cared not one jot for the welfare of anyone under this stinking roof and would cheerfully have taken a knife to that bastard Declan.

That's my father in me.

Nevertheless, I must pass muster, get some food in my belly, steal some if I could, and get away unnoticed. Sod the march and sod the lot of them, these were not my people, I had no people, nor did I want any. People could not be trusted.

But when I came down into the living room and saw that the men were gone, and there was Hannah in her white dress, her eyes alight with excitement, I could not for shame leave her. She and Joseph had done so much for me since they found me in my distress. So many times I had thanked the fates that brought them to me, a warm group of Irish newly arrived at Holyhead, who instantly understood my situation, never judged, never asked questions, just took me along with them to join their promised new life among the weavers of Lancashire. But she has all these Fallons, I told myself, and renewed my resolve to get away. Only she came to me and gave me a piece of bread and honey and a sprig of laurel for my hair and I could not leave her.

And so, when we heard music in the distance, we took our leave of the other women and children and took to the streets, for we must not miss the arrival of the Middleton contingent, nor any of them, for didn't they all deserve a cheer?

We burst out of the alleyway like fish from a sewer pipe and joined the great shoal of humanity, the great rolling river of marching, singing, smiling people pouring in from the hills with their sunburnt faces and their banners and flags, their flagons of water, their shared laughter and the exhilarating beat of those drums. And I have never in my life felt such a feeling, before or since.

We marched down Peter Street to the tune of 'See the Conquering Hero Come', and as we emerged into the great open space of the field, we saw others doing likewise from the four corners, great rivers pouring into a desert, and that soon the rivers would converge and cover the desert with a great sea of people.

8

And all of them, it seemed to me, all the men women and children, were in their Sunday best if they had such a thing, many of the women in white, and it seemed such a celebration of togetherness, of a common purpose, that I felt myself quite carried away in the thick of it.

As our contingent spread apart and the press of bodies lessened, Hannah drew near to me and hooked her arm through mine, and together we made for the eastern side, where the great wall stood, and we could see that there were already a few people sitting on it. But the press of people was becoming greater, all gathering in the centre, and so we skirted the edge and at last came to the side of the wall and then we went faster, for that was surely the best place and quickly, we must get there before others took our places. I was not so fast as Hannah, for of course I was carrying my baby and although I had said nothing about the events of the night, my knee was sore and hindered me somewhat, so I called out to her, for she was already ahead, 'You go on and save me a place!' I saw her nod and then push on through the throngs who were surging towards the hustings.

When I at last achieved the street, I had to step off the path to work my way towards the gates of the Friends' Meeting House, and I was thankful that Hannah had had the foresight to show me the way on Sunday. As I turned in at the gate, I closed it behind me, although a man following me pushed it open again immediately and shoved past me on the path through the neatly-kept gravestones.

As I rounded the building, I saw how the earth had been piled up to make a level surface, though the land sloped steeply on the outside of the wall. And there was Hannah, waving and shouting, 'Molly! Molly Bowes! Molleeee! Over here! Quick! I think our people are coming! Look, look over there!'

I reached the wall where she sat and I stood next to her and looked where she pointed. 'There, see? That's Bootle Street, that was to be their route. There's our banners! See? And that's Bamford, I'm sure it is! See how they're marching in lines of six? That's how they were drilled. Joseph's in the second row. Is that Joseph? Joseph!!'

She shouted and waved and then jumped up onto the wall and I held her skirts for fear she would fall, though I had to do it one-handed until a kind lady beside me said, 'Here, I'll hold your baby,' and then I could grasp Hannah round the legs with both my arms, for she was jumping and shouting and waving and I really feared she would fall in her excitement, and when I looked over and saw how high the wall was, I felt sick.

The lady holding Charlotte was much older than us, perhaps forty, and she had a kind face, and when she saw my fearful look, she pulled sharply on Hannah's skirt, and she said in a firm voice. 'Sit down, dear. They cannot hear you. Sit down and calm yourself.' Hannah sat down like a chastised child and even said thank-you.

I said to the lady, 'I cannot sit on the wall holding my baby, for fear I will faint in this heat.'

She smiled, and her eyes were the palest blue. I remember that.

'You sit next to your friend, my dear, and I shall stand here behind you, holding your baby safe. She is such a little beauty. What is her name?'

'Charlotte. Her name is Charlotte.' And I did as I was told.

We watched as the field filled up in the fierce midday sun. To protect Charlotte's fair head, I wrapped my handkerchief around it and tied a loose knot below her chin, placing a tender kiss on the rosy button of her nose. The wall was filling up, and we had to shuffle along a bit, and then I could not see so well for a branch of one of the oaks was in front of me. Charlotte was asleep again, and when she saw me looking, the lady said, 'Don't worry, she is safe with me.'

I have held onto those words.

I remember she had a basket at her feet and in it a stone water-bottle and some apples, tiny and wizened but doubtless sweet. A kind lady, I was sure of it. I am. I did not see her speak to anyone else, and I do not remember her clothes. Perhaps she was a Quaker, although when I asked the next day, no-one said they knew her.

I had to ask Hannah what was happening, and she told me that she could see the hustings, two wagons lashed together, and they were where they had been in January, just as Joseph had predicted, on a bit of higher ground over near Windmill Street on the opposite side from us.

'And are there any officials on the hustings? Magistrates or anyone?'

'Not that I can see.'

The wizened little man next to me, whose bony thigh was uncomfortably pressed against mine, said bitterly, 'Not them. They'll be watching but in comfort, you mark my words.'

The woman on the other side of him said, 'They met at the Star Inn this morning, and I've heard they're now in Mr Buxton's house, over there, on the corner of Windmill Street. They'll have a good view from his upstairs. Oh ay-up, what's this?'

'What?' said he, with his view likewise hindered.

'Marching men coming onto the field, two columns, uniforms, looks like they're carrying cudgels.'

'It'll be the constables,' he said and spat copiously onto the ground beneath, narrowly missing a young woman whose bonnet was decorated with springs of laurel like Hannah's. 'What they doing?'

'Looks like they're lining up, making a channel, like.'

'How do you mean, a channel where?' he said, rocking dangerously towards her in his efforts to see.

'They're all standing in two lines now, facing each other. There's hundreds of them. Must be four hundred, easy. It stretches from the house nearly to the hustings. Oh, ay-up!'

'What? Bloody hell woman, yer driving me mad. Swap places, I can't see nothing.' Whereupon the old woman seemed about to try to climb obediently back into the graveyard, but finding after some unseemly shuffling and writhing that there was no room for her to swing her legs round, the grumbling old man had no alternative but to submit to her account of events.

'They've all but disappeared now, the constables. They must be still there, yes, they are, but seems like the people have squeezed in amongst.'

'Course you know what that's for, don't ya? That's so they can send an officer from the magistrates to arrest Hunt. That's to make sure, you mark my words. They'll 'ave 'im as soon as 'ee opens 'is mouth.'

'Ha! They're pushing the hustings deeper into the field!'

'Who are? The constables?'

'No, the people. They must be wise to it, like you said. It's just like you said, ower Billy,' and she gave him an affectionate nudge, though it nearly had the effect of knocking him off the wall, had he not been so securely wedged between us.

'So can you see Hunt?'

'Yes, well I can see a white top hat. That's what he wears, isn't it? There's a lot on the hustings, women too. I can see women in white dresses, in amongst all the men. Oo, what's afoot? Shhhh!' And indeed, all across the packed field, the sound of collective shushing whispered like the wind through a field of corn. A field of corn about to be mowed. And threshed.

But I get ahead of myself.

So the miracle of silence descended on the field, though it can have lasted but moments, for surely so many cannot hold silence for long, and then the voice of Henry Hunt himself drifted across their heads, just as Hannah had hoped it would. He was so far away, and the susurration of movement and noise impeded our hearing, but I have read the text of the speech since, insofar as it was delivered, and here it is:

'My friends and fellow countrymen – I must entreat your indulgence for a short time; and I beg you will endeavour to preserve the most perfect silence. I hope you will exercise the all-powerful right of the people in an orderly manner; and if you perceive any man that wants to raise a disturbance, let him be instantly put down, and kept secure. For the honour you have done me, in inviting me a second time to preside at your meeting, I return you my thanks; and all I have to beg of you is, that you will indulge us with your patient attention. It is impossible that, with the utmost silence, we shall be able to make ourselves heard by this tremendous assembly. It is useless for me to relate to you the proceedings of the last week or ten days in this town and neighbourhood. You know them all, and the cause of the meeting appointed for last Monday being prevented. I will not therefore say one word on that subject; only to observe that those who put us down, and prevented us from meeting on Monday last, by their malignant exertions have produced two-fold the number today.

'It will be perceived that in consequence of the calling of this new meeting, our enemies, who flattered themselves that they had gained a victory have sustained a great defeat. There have been two or three placards posted up during the last week with the names of two or three insignificant individuals attached to them. One Tom Long or Jack Short, a printer – '

Here he broke off, for he had discerned, as we now know, a disturbance on the edge of the field. And true enough, our commentator at that moment called out, 'Soldiers! Galloping onto the field! Wait, they've pulled up under the window of the magistrates. '

Excited, the old man leaned forward precariously. 'Soldiers? Their uniform? Tell us quick, woman!'

'Blue, sky blue. Funny-shaped black hats.'

He slumped back, disappointed. 'Pah! Soldiers? They're not soldiers. Now if you want to see proper soldiers, you only have to go to Pickford's Yard. Them's real soldiers. Some of them's been at Waterloo. That lot, sky blue ye say? That's just the local yeomanry. Not a soldier between 'em. Them's just pretend, for anyone with a bit of money and a nag can be a yeoman. They just like dressing up. TOY SOLDIERS!' he bellowed into the branch that blocked his view. Disgruntled, he chewed on a wad of tobacco. 'And they're pissed. I saw 'em, them and their hip flasks, admiring each others' shiny boots and toasting the king.'

But the woman was taking no notice, mouth agape, and beside me Hannah had stilled. Across the field, we faintly heard three cheers, but before the final hooray had sounded, the thunder of hooves and the wall beneath us seemed to shake.

What happened then? Oh what indeed? How can I convey the minutes that followed and the irrevocable impact on the people who were there? A storm hit that sea of people and swept their lives away.

There had been optimism and companionship, laughter and music, families and communities gathered in the sunshine, basking in the simple hope that their lives mattered, that this famous man come from London would see them and hear them and speak to them and listen to them.

That he would take their plight to the parliament and explain that things must change, that people could not live like this, that a Christian country cannot want to feed its honest working folk into the mouth of machines. That every man deserved a vote, and yes the women too. That we worked hard, we paid our taxes and our voices deserved to be heard. That laws passed in London that made people poorer and food more expensive were causing people to starve and sicken and weaken and die, yes even die, in this rich and fertile land.

And into that sea of hope, of upturned faces, singing and cheering in the sunshine, the magistrates sent a brutal storm of thundering hooves, slashing sabres and merciless cruelty, vindictive, deliberate murder.

No matter what they feared, what insurrection they thought they must prevent, no matter whether the Riot Act was ever read, for they swore it was, though no-one heard it, no matter. None of it matters. None of the reasons why. There can be no reason for what was done that day. None. Those people were defenceless. There were many many women in that crowd, and children too. And they knew it. They all knew it, the magistrates and the men who slashed and trampled and beat the innocent people into the ground.

My story of pain and loss is just one of many.

So first there was the thunder, and the wall seemed to shake. Then those who could see shouted out in shock and disbelief, their hands clasped to their mouths. And before they could answer the questions of those who could not, the thunder was pierced by the shrill crack of screams, shrill, sharp, staccato, multiplying: then thuds and cracks and wailing voices on a dying fall. And rapidly grew to a great wall of noise, voices indistinguishable, a great roar of fear and pain rose up and grew nearer, and before it came a great stampede of people and beneath our feet the crowd thickened and pushed out air in a great sigh and then the voices beneath us distinct, 'Hold back! Hold back! I cannot breathe!' and we looked down and there were suddenly too many people pressed against the wall, beneath our skirts and as I watched, I saw the girl's bonnet in the crush of heads like pebbles on a beach and then it disappeared beneath the sea of heads and a hand reached up, not hers, a man's hand, and gripped my foot and pulled.

And that's all I know.

I can tell you no more about what happened to me in the immediate aftermath. I have read reports in newspapers and handbills, and some time later, in another part of the country, I heard that Bamford had written his own account in prison, and it took a long time for me to get hold of a copy but I did in the end, and here is what he wrote:

"In about half an hour after our arrival the sounds of music and reiterated shouts proclaimed the near approach of Mr Hunt and his party; and in a minute or two they were seen coming from Deansgate, preceded by a band of music and several flags.

Their approach was hailed by one universal shout from probably 80,000 persons. They threaded their way slowly past us and through the crowd, which Hunt eyed, I thought, with almost as much of astonishment as satisfaction. This spectacle could not be otherwise in his view than solemnly impressive.

Such a mass of human beings he had not beheld till then. His responsibility must weigh on his mind. The task was great, and not without its peril. The meeting was indeed a tremendous one.

Mr Hunt, stepping towards the front of the stage, took off his white hat, and addressed the people.

We had got to nearly the outside of the crowd, when a noise and strange murmur arose towards the church. Some persons said it was the Blackburn people coming, and I stood on tiptoe and looked in the direction whence the noise proceeded, and saw a party of cavalry in blue and white uniform come trotting, sword in hand, round the corner of a garden wall, and to the front of a row of new houses, where they reined up in a line.

"The soldiers are here," I said; "we must go back and see what this means." "Oh," someone made reply, "they are only come to be ready if there should be any disturbance in the meeting." "Well, let us go back," I said, and we forced our way towards the colours.

On the cavalry drawing up they were received with a shout of goodwill, as I understood it. They shouted again, waving their sabres over their heads; and then, slackening rein, and striking spur into their steeds, they dashed forward and began cutting the people..."

"Stand fast," I said, "they are riding upon us; stand fast".

The cavalry were in confusion: they evidently could not, with all the weight of man and horse, penetrate that compact mass of human beings and their sabres were plied to hew a way through naked held-up hands and defenceless heads; and then chopped limbs and wound-gaping skulls were seen; and groans and cries were mingled with the din of that horrid confusion.

Many females appeared as the crowd opened; and striplings or mere youths also were found. Their cries were piteous and heart-rending, and would, one might have supposed, have disarmed any human resentment: but here their appeals were in vain.

In ten minutes from the commencement of the havoc the field was an open and almost deserted space. The sun looked down through a sultry and motionless air. The curtains and blinds of the windows within view were all closed.

The hustings remained, with a few broken and hewed flag-staves erect, and a torn and gashed banner or two dropping; whilst over the whole field were strewed caps, bonnets, hats, shawls, and shoes, and other parts of male and female dress, trampled, torn, and bloody.

Several mounds of human being still remained where they had fallen, crushed down and smothered. Some of these still groaning, others with staring eyes, were gasping for breath, and others would never breathe more.

All was silent save those low sounds, and the occasional snorting and pawing of steeds."

My ribs were cracked, of that I was sure. The skin of my back was lacerated. Bruises blossomed on my arms and shoulders. Something had happened to my hip, a boot perhaps. I don't know.

I don't know who tended to me. I don't know who lifted me. I don't know where they left me. I don't know how I was taken to the infirmary. I don't know anything. I didn't know my name when first I woke. I must have said her name, for the next I remember was a cold wet cloth held to my forehead and woman's voice whispering 'Charlotte? Charlotte? Open your eyes, Charlotte. Can you hear me, love?' The voice seemed far away and then suddenly in my ear. I could feel hot breath against my cheek, and then the crack of pain, a deep shuddering breath and my ribcage knifed my lungs.

I could not speak. Memories crowded in, my head bulged with pain. I know I whispered, 'My baby,' and tears burned.

'You have a baby, love? I'll go and see. There are babies here, don't cry. What's his name?'

'Charlotte. My baby is called Charlotte.'

'Will she answer to her name? How old is she, sweetheart?'

'Six months. She's only six months. She has red hair.' I was calm. I do remember that. When I look back, I wonder that I did not scream out and panic but my senses were dulled and all the wheels of my being faltered.

'I will go and see if there's a baby without its mother. I'll be back soon. You try and stay awake now. I want you to drink some water. Two minutes.'

I knew she would not find her. I lay on my bed of pain and let the tears and the life seep out of me. Tired. So tired.

The next thing I remember was the sharp jab of pain as she slid her hand under my neck to lift my head, then water on my lips, cold wetness trickling down my chin. And so much pain. My back, my breath, my heart. Oh let me die.

But this woman would not leave me be. 'Come now, try to sit up, love. It'll hurt, but you might find you're better sitting up. From the state of your back, you'll have broken bones I think. Let's see what you can do. Come on, together. I'm not leaving you love, never fear.'

I know I lolled against her like a broken doll, lapsing into sleep, breaking awake to yelp at the sudden burst of knives through the aching wilderness of pain, but we did it. On the edge of the bed, my feet on solid ground, the room bucked and swayed and I know I vomited though there was nothing in my stomach.

When Hannah found me, neither of us could speak, but wordlessly held hands and cried. I did not have to ask – her eyes were full of the fear that I would.

When finally I found the words, I could only whisper, 'No news at all?'

Her eyes downcast, the shake of her head was barely perceptible.

'And Joseph?'

'Unscathed. We are all fine. You are the only injured one of all of us. The men are everywhere asking after Charlotte. The Quakers...'

'Yes?' I clutched her arm, harder than I knew I could. 'Is there hope? Is there news? That woman...'

'No real news, only rumour. There is such shock, Molly. So much anger. It's chaos out there. Only...'

'What? Tell me, Hannah.'

'Joseph was talking to a Quaker in the grounds of the meeting house who reckons that woman came from York. He says he thinks she travelled here for the meeting. That no-one knows her except those she travelled with, and they've already left for Liverpool but she wasn't with them. If it is her.'

'Then no-one's seen her since?'

'No, no-one that we can find. Joseph has pinned a notice to the door of the Meeting House. We're making notices to put all over. She'll bring her back safe, Molly, I'm sure of it. She looked a good woman. She's probably looking for you right now. It's chaos out there, but the word is spreading that there's a baby missing. People have their own worries, but everyone cares that a baby's missing. And her hair, you know...that'll help. Such a mite, but little coppery curls, there's not many babies like that. She'll come back to you, don't you worry.' Her eyes expressed a doubt and a fear that she tried hard to cover. 'Meanwhile, we've got to get you well. To be ready to give her a great big hug when you're reunited.' But her chin buckled as she said it.

It took three days before I could walk unaided, and even then I had to depend on Joseph's hawthorn stick, for a sharp pain shot down my leg with every step I took and I often felt faint because my breathing was of necessity shallow. For two days, I sat on the step by the gates of the Friends' Meeting House until the sun went down. Every babe in arms borne towards me caused a flare of painful hope to ignite in my breast, and every time it was extinguished I slumped a little lower. Joseph's notice still clung to the door, bleached now through five days' exposure to fierce sunlight. I asked every single person who passed whether they had seen a red-haired baby with a dark-haired woman. It was hopeless.

18

As the amber sun slipped below the blackened chimneypots on the second day, and I heard the key turn in the great wooden door behind me, it seemed the loss of all hope and I wept. Footsteps approached and faltered, then a white-haired gentleman I'd spoken to earlier sat down beside me.

'My name is Abraham. I am sorry for your pain. Perhaps tomorrow you would like to come inside and join us. There is comfort to be had.'

I turned my damaged and beaten face towards him. 'I cannot. I must stay here. In case…'

'I think that if the woman you are waiting for intended to find you, she would have done so by now, child.'

It was the first time anyone had addressed my deepest fear and I felt a surge of something like hope.

'What do you think I should do?'

'Well, if she was looking for you, this would be the natural place to come, if only to leave a message. If we accept she is not looking for you, there can be only two reasons. One is that she has assumed you are dead, but that is unlikely and would not adequately explain why she has not appeared asking for you or your relatives. The more likely explanation is that she wishes to keep the baby for herself.' He studied my face in the dim light. 'What are your thoughts?'

'It is what I fear. She was so quick to offer to hold her. The way she looked at her. Rapt. The more I think about it, the more it seems likely that she wanted her for herself.'

'She was completely alone, you say?'

'I cannot be sure, but yes, no-one approached her or stood with her.'

'Describe her for me again, please.'

'She was of my height, slender, perhaps forty years old. She had pale blue eyes and dark hair with I think some strands of grey. Her face was not lined and her cheeks were rounded. She looked healthy, I think. She wore dark clothes and a white bonnet. She carried a lidded basket in which were apples and a stone bottle.'

'Her voice?'

'Low, gentle, a kind of lilt…' I faltered.

'Local?'

19

'I...I cannot tell. Certainly of the north, with perhaps a touch of Irish.' Though he did not speak, his brow raised a question. 'I am from the south, though perhaps you cannot tell.' I looked into his kind eyes and relaxed into the need to be known. 'I seek to blend in.'

His nod was slight and gone in an instant. He seemed to consider what I had said and for a few moments neither of us spoke.

'There is a possibility, but you must know it is only a faint possibility, that she is the woman who travelled here from York, sixty miles hence.' I hardly dared speak lest he thought better of it. 'A group of Friends travelling in the ministry arrived here on Sunday, and with them was a woman whom none of them knew. She had asked to join them when they stopped at York, saying her travelling companion had turned back to Darlington through illness but that she wanted to carry on to Manchester. Those Friends have now moved on towards Liverpool, but she was not with them.'

'She has not been seen since the meeting?'

'No, I have heard no-one say they had noticed her.'

'And does no-one know why she was in Manchester? Did she mention relatives?'

'No. When your friend first appeared here asking after the woman and the baby, one of the group told him that it sounded like the woman who had travelled here with them but that she had kept her counsel on the journey. They knew nothing of her or her circumstances. And of course, you must remember, my dear, that it might not be the same woman.'

'But it's all I have!' I started to move compulsively, not knowing whether I intended struggling to my feet or wringing my hands or clasping his. I hardly knew myself.

'Calm yourself. Sshh, there now. Breathe deeply.' He waited while his words took effect and then he spoke again. 'Here is what I think you should do. I must emphasise that I suggest this only in the absence of another plan and in order to raise your spirits. It is important in all our lives that hope should spring eternal. I can see that your spirit has suffered a devastating blow, but it seems to me that you are a strong young woman. Am I right?'

'Yes. I am strong.' And as I said it I remembered that it was true.

'Well then. You have friends here, the news has spread and if your child is brought forth, she will be taken care of and news will find you as long as you lay a trail. I suggest you follow the possibility that this woman is on her way back to York or Darlington. Do you have the means to sustain yourself?'

'Yes, I have some earnings. It is enough.'

'A family of Friends are planning to leave Manchester for York on Monday morning. I shall arrange for you to travel with them. Be here at 8 o'clock in the morning.'

Chapter 2

My spirits lifted as we left Manchester, though my bones protested at the rocking of the cart. As the sun rose over the distant hills, it dazzled us into silence. The family knew my circumstance and the mother, a tall woman of middle years and bent before her time, sat in companionable silence beside me holding my hand.

In my heart I was torn: at last I was doing something which felt positive and an act of hope, but I had such a sense that I should not be leaving that several times I thought of asking them to stop so that I could climb down. Perhaps I tensed the first time it came to me that I must not leave: whether by sixth sense or not, she seemed to know it and she released my hand, only to pat it with a soothing, repetitive motion. I brought Abraham's face to mind and held onto his belief that I was following my baby, not leaving her behind.

At the coaching house where we spent the night, I saw the elders of the family making murmured enquiries before I had even got down from the cart. The groom and the innkeeper gave me curious looks, as did their womenfolk when we entered the inn, but there was much shaking of heads and sorrowful sighing. I suppressed a feeling of irritation with all this discretion and pity. I wanted to know what they had asked: I wanted news of any baby who had passed through here, not just one with coppery curls. Who was to say the woman had not hidden or coloured Charlotte's hair, disguised her as a boy or even concealed her altogether? I made my own enquiries, regardless of any feelings I might hurt, but it came to naught.

At York, I laid down my bundle on the narrow bed in the attic room, but then hastened back downstairs, where I declined the offer of soup: I wanted to go straight to the coaching inn and make my enquiries, for it seemed to me likely that she would have travelled on public transport or mail coach.

One man did give me hope: a woman with a baby had arrived late one night a few days ago, but he was sure she had been accompanied by a man. I made no effort to keep calm: gripping his wrists, I bombarded him with questions: her height, her age, her luggage; had he seen the baby's hair? What age would he say the child had been? Was she crying? And here my voice broke. Sudden weakness in my legs made me sway and hold him tighter. Helping me to a chair, he stood apart, somewhat embarrassed, and waited until I could collect myself.

Had he noticed which direction they had walked in? Towards the marketplace, he said, so off I went, asking, asking. But I could offer nothing beyond dark clothes, a basket, a baby. Everyone here was dressed in dark clothes, and babies were everywhere.

By nightfall, I must have appeared as a madwoman. I had hardly imagined that she would be there waiting for me, holding Charlotte up so that I could fold her in my arms, but I had, I now realized, felt sure there would be some firm sighting, some clue, something to give me hope that I was nearer to her now than I had been in Manchester.

It was as dark as pitch by the time I admitted defeat and the knock I gave on the front door was weak and tearful. The mother opened it and helped me into a warm parlour without a word. I ate the soup and bread with gratitude then climbed the stairs with heavy heart to sink in to a restless sleep.

The following day, I made posters and pinned them up around the town, talking to shopkeepers and clergymen and constables as I went.

As that fierce summer mellowed into a golden autumn, I began to take notice of the quiet people in their sober dress with whom I lived, and I wondered at their kindness, their unquestioning patience. In the evenings, instead of staring, lost in my own thoughts, I began to listen to them talk around the fireside and I heard so much that gave me hope for the world. These Quakers with their old-fashioned speech, their lack of adornment, their plain home and quiet ways, had seemed so unworldly and asked so little of me that I had barely given them a passing thought, but now I began to attend to their conversation, though I never engaged.

At breakfast one morning in late October, one of the daughters mentioned that she was going to a meeting which was to be addressed by Elizabeth Fry. I had heard them mention that name before, somehow linked with Newgate, but had taken no notice: I had revealed nothing of my background, let alone that I had been born and brought up in a prison. When I did speak in the house, which was

23

rare, I still affected the soft Irish lilt I had acquired in Holyhead. Even the Fallons had learnt nothing of my true story when I absorbed myself into their group. We were settled in Middleton working at our looms before it became clear that I was pregnant, and they never asked.

'Elizabeth Fry? I have heard of her, I think.' If they were startled by my question, no-one showed it.

One of the daughters, Sarah, answered me: 'Yes, perhaps in connection with her prison work. She was shocked by conditions when she visited Newgate, which is in London. I first heard her speak last year, when she toured the prisons of England and Scotland. She established Associations in every town she visited: we work to educate and support female prisoners. The conditions in which many are kept are inhumane. She is about to present her findings to a Committee of the House of Commons. No woman has done this before. We are privileged to have her here in York. If you would be interested to attend, Molly, you are welcome to come with me.'

I did not answer, looking down at my bowl of porridge in my customary sad silence, and the conversation soon resumed around me. I loved this about them, and for a few moments, gratitude for their acceptance threatened to overwhelm me.

For the first time in my life, I felt perfectly safe and surrounded by real strength and goodness. These people were comfortably off: that had a bearing, of course it did. Amongst the Lancashire weavers, the fear of hunger and injury made everyday life precarious. The knowledge that I was an unmarried mother had made my social status uncertain, and I was conscious in the streets of being eyed with suspicion or lust: I was clearly considered by some to be easy game. It would have been simpler if I had pretended to be widowed, but some private code of conduct prevented me from taking that route. Let it be known that I had a child out of wedlock: I would be judged by no-one.

But here, amongst these people, I was in danger of letting my guard down. I had always wanted to be free, but was that determination masking a desire to belong? Was it a way of dealing with the fact that I belonged nowhere?

24

The dream of a home with my aunt in Ireland had been shattered, for had not she said, 'Keep yourself pure'? She was a Roman Catholic, my mother had explained, and for her the concept of sin was central. I was no longer pure, and though it was no fault of my own, I had known she would not see it that way and I could not bear to confront the injustice of her judgment upon me. And so, I had not gone to Ireland.

I knew nothing of religion beyond what my mother had explained of Catholics and sin. Whether she had ever followed a religion, I knew not. My notion of God was hazy: the idea held no interest for me. But these Quakers and their concept of an inner light caught my attention: naive and untutored as I was, I felt we had an affinity, for was not the dark house of my mind lit from within? Their way of being drew me.

I could stay here. I could make myself useful and stay here; I could live from day to day in peace, holding within me that hope that one day a russet-haired child would look at me in the marketplace and we would know each other.

Chapter 3

Once upon a time was a little girl who lived in a prison. She didn't know what a prison was, because it was her world. She had a mama who was an angel and a father who was a devil, but she didn't know that either.

Here are the things she remembers: the patch of dusty light which moved across the floor, sometimes bright, sometimes faint, sometimes strong enough to warm the stone, sometimes so weak that only her mama could see it.

The pigeons who cooed and bowed to each other on the outside of the bars.

The smell of washed air after rain.

The burning smart of a slapped cheek.

The soothing cool of stone.

Stories that began, 'Once upon a time…'

A cherry in the palm of her hand. The wonder of it. How it drew the light to itself and if you looked carefully into the glow of its outer curve, skin stretched tight, you could see the reflection of a sliver of sky with a single bar reduced to the width of a hair.

The indentation in the top of the cherry where a bead of moisture nestled.

'Taste it, Molly. With the tip of your tongue, like this.'

The teasing sweetness, gone too soon.

Mama giggling. 'Like the bead of water in your belly button. You remember?' Her sudden seriousness.

And above my palm another bright bulb hanging from a thick thread. 'See this one? This is the stalk or the stem.'

'Can you eat it?'

'If you were a horse you'd eat it, that and the stone in the middle of the cherry. But it doesn't taste nice to us. Like wood.'

I remember she studied my face for a moment and then laid her cool hand against my cheek. 'It's the part that connects the cherry to the tree while it's growing.'

I probably sensed what she was going to say next, but I wanted more of the sweetness and bit my cherry, transfixed by the burst of colour in my mouth.

She took her hand away, murmuring, 'Time enough. You'll understand soon enough.'

Those were the quiet times before the boys were born, when it was mostly just me and Mama in the one room. Papa must have visited, of course he must, but I have no memory of him from those days. Else I have shut the door on it.

I picture the inside of my head like a big house. There are locked rooms upstairs. I tremble when I walk past their doors. I try not to go upstairs at all, but sometimes it seems I have no control at all over where my thoughts go. That happens mostly in dreams. The hanged man. If I find myself on the dark landing, a door creaking open, or worse, already slightly ajar, I wake myself up sharpish. I stay downstairs in the brighter rooms where I can open doors and windows as I wish, even open and close them in one motion, on a whim, just because I can.

Sometimes, going about my business, a sight or a smell will bring a creak on the floorboards upstairs. If that happens, I freeze. Breathe deeply. Will it into silence.

Sometimes, as I pass the foot of the stairs, I cannot help but look up into the blackness. There are eyes up there, looking down at me, but I will not meet them.

As I get older, I hope to learn to stare them out.

My father was a man of shadows, smoke and mirrors. He's dead now. What shall I tell you of him?

I'll tell you about the man I knew when I was a little girl. As I say, we rarely saw him when I was little because he was very busy and very important and he had important business at the courts. Soon after the cherry, when I was five and Jack was a tiny mewling baby, we moved into a different room and it had a door that Mama could sometimes open by herself but only when she'd heard the key turn on the outside and his heavy footsteps walk away, then the creak of a bed.

When that happened, she would hasten and hush us, lay Jack on the mattress and tell me to lie down next to him and keep him quiet. Then she'd leave us for a while, softly closing the door and turning the key.

I'd lie there, obedient mostly, and look into his scrunched up little fist of a face. If he looked as though he was going to start his mewling, I would blow gently on his eyes and his forehead. He used to like that, and if I was lucky, he'd be quiet. Sometimes, if he did that thing with his mouth that meant he wanted Mama's breast, I'd give him the crook of my little finger to suck on. He could suck hard for such a little fellow, and if that worked, it was nice to see him chomping away and falling for my trick. If he started proper squawking, I'd pick him up and pat his back like mama had taught me.

Once, nothing I did could stop him and he howled and yelped and made my ears hurt, so I got up and walked across to the window with my fingers in my ears, shouting an angry lullaby more and more loudly to block it out. I didn't hear the key turn or the door open, but when Papa's voice from behind me bellowed, 'Hell's teeth! Can a man get no peace?' I spun round just in time to dodge a blow - it fell instead on the corner of the nightstand. His anger redoubled; he grabbed me by the arm and flung me towards the mattress where the baby lay screaming.

Memory is such a strange thing: sometimes it's as clear and sharp as the moment itself. Sometimes we can summon up a clarity we might not have felt at the time. My imagination will not stay confined, even now, but seeps into reality whether I allow it or not. Here is what I think I remember:

Jack was instantly silenced.

I know not whether it was anger or fear that made me do it, but I sprang up and stood facing Papa, jaw jutted and eyes blazing. You see, there's a devil in me, too.

He was standing stock still, eyes wide. It was the only time I ever saw him lost for what to do or say.

There was a keening sound from behind me. I choose to believe it was Jack.

Father went out then. I heard him shout something I couldn't understand, then the boards creaking under his heavy feet as he gathered his clothes and dressed, then the key clashing in the big lock in the outer door, then a slam which rattled the bars, then silence.

I don't know how long I must have stood still, staring at the cold moon.

In my memory there was no sobbing, but I think perhaps there was.

Jack wasn't even in my mind: I do know that. Nor was he my first thought when I came out of the trance into which I had fallen to find my mother's hair tickling my face and her tears wetting my brow.

The next thing I remember was sensations of heat and cold – a burning in my shoulder and the back of my head, the pain of icy toes. I started to sob, and felt my mother gather me into her arms and lay Jack across my chest. Still. She carried us into the other room and lay us for the very first time in a real bed. A high bed, big enough for two grown-ups to lie side by side, pillows, softness beneath my back, warmth.

I never saw Jack again. I asked once, and Mama told me a kind lady had come in the night to take him away to a house where everyone had a bed of their own and he would want for nothing.

The next time I saw my father, there was no mention of what had passed, in fact he neither looked at nor touched me, but after that, if he was out, Mama and I slept alone in the big bed and I counted myself blessed to have her to myself once more.

The bed came with us when we moved again, this time to what Papa called 'a sweet of rooms.' The next baby, Nathaniel, was crawling by then, and there was another new baby, a girl this time. Our room was very much like the old one, but bigger, with two barred windows and two narrow mattresses on the floor. The big bed was on the other side of a door again, and the trunk was in there too. At the other end of our room was a door that we could sometimes open ourselves and look into the next room, where there was a long table with six chairs. There was a door at the other end of that room. We weren't allowed into the room with the table. We just glimpsed it sometimes, and often there were men in there with Papa. We'd hear their voices, deep and rumbling, but not what they were saying because the cold stone walls were so thick and the door was made of rough oak that could scratch your cheek and Mama would be anxious if I tried to listen and pull me away and whisper, her face close to my face and her eyes wide. She had very long pale eyelashes.

Mama said that the men who visited Papa were lawyers and explained that he had very important business in the courts and that our futures depended upon it. For a long time, I thought he was a lawyer too. Which is funny when I think about it now.

My job was to help her soothe the little ones and make them go to sleep on the mattresses, though my bony ribs offered little in the way of comfort. Once we'd experienced the soft snufflings and burrowings of sharing the big bed with Mama, we all yearned for it every night. Perhaps it would have been better if we'd never tasted such pleasure.

The night sounds were rumblings and murmurs, sometimes sobbing and sighs. Mice scuffled in corners. When Papa was there, the night sounds had a harsher quality, banging and creaking and grunting and muffled cries. I don't like to think about that. No.

As I grew, I began to be more troubled. I behaved badly. And then I wished I had my mother's sweet nature, not my father's wickedness that made me sometimes despise her.

I'd look at her, shining in her sweetness like a diamond in a dung-heap, and I'd imagine she was an angel fallen from heaven. Lost and abandoned by all the other angels, condemned to live out her life in the midden of humanity. And my heart would ache for love of her. And then I would run to her, cling to her, press my face into her soft neck, breathe her in, wordless, soundless, powerless.

When the darkness was on me, I'd squat in the corner like a grimy gargoyle fallen off a gutter. I'd watch her through hooded lids, hating her, hating her complacent serenity and wanting to spurt venom out of my eyes to obliterate her. And the longer I sat, the greater my hatred, and the more she ignored me the more the hatred grew, until I felt I must explode with rage.

That's my father in me, you see. Can't get away from it.

But the thing is, what I'm not telling you is that at the same time, I was crying in my head. What I most wanted in the world was for her to get up, put down the baby and come to me, huddled in my corner. I wanted her to crouch down beside me and put her arms around my stone shoulders. I wanted her to press her face against my hair and breathe against my neck until the stone melted to lava. I wanted her to seep into me and make me better.

When I say baby, it wasn't any particular baby. I don't want you to think I hated the babies. We were all babies once. I used to think good, here's another one like me. We're all in this together. The more the merrier.

Chapter 4

Autumn. A sunny day. A corner of the grey prison yard lit gold. A small thin child drawn to the light and warmth. A pile of leaves, moist from the night's rainfall. The unexpected beauty of the reds and golds and greens, the veins and serrated edges, the delicate stems through which the tree had fed life into the leaf. The textures, some waxy and flexible, others older, more careworn, fragile and brittle. Curious fingers rustling into the pile, lifting, examining, rustling deeper. Suddenly encountering dry solidity, rough, sharp, warm. What is it? Fingertips softly exploring, the slow prick of spines. Gently scooped and brought out into the sunlight. What is it? I've never seen such a thing as this.

Held carefully, no more spikiness. Softly cupped in two hands, gently turned, underneath a snout, a face, bright dark eyes peering and blinking. It is a wonder of a thing! And how did it come here? There is no grass, not even a weed. These leaves have whirled in from a tree unseen, out there beyond the walls. What can it eat? How can it live?

I will keep it: it will be my pet. I will take it inside, show it to my mother, keep it safe.

But no, I cannot. It would not be fair or kind. It would be a prison indeed for the little thing, this creation of bark and leaves. A stirring of conscience in my young breast, imagining the life of this other creature and wanting the best for it. A new feeling, I will examine that later.

But now, take it to food and safety and save it and make it happy. I know the place. The marshal's garden, where there are bushes and green grass and sometimes flowers, where there are worms and beetles and moisture and things for this little creature to eat and where he'll be safe from the cinders and the boots and the hardness.

And taking him there, swiftly, slipping through the gate into the greenery and the softness and the moist fecundity of an autumn garden. And choosing a place with care, and putting him down on the soil and digging fingers into the earth and finding a worm and lifting it to show him. Look! Eat this and you will live and grow strong! And he did. And I stayed there and watched him snuffling and burrowing and sniffing and scoffing until the afternoon waned and the sky darkened; until, sated, he scuffled into a warm ball and went to sleep. And feeling happy, a happiness that came out of something I'd done for a fellow creature: a happiness that stayed with me and warmed me.

It was that, the excited telling of the tale of the hedgehog, that made my father give me the book. I had my letters by then, for sure: my mother had begun to teach me as soon as I could hold the chalk. She did it so well, when I think of it, with the small means at her disposal. We had a fine piece of slate, though it got broken in half one day, but even then, though I raged at the brother who'd done it – those boys were so clumsy and bangy – she turned the tragedy into a blessing, for couldn't we now have two pieces of slate, one of my very own and one for the teaching of the others, so much smaller and further behind?

The first words I copied were those of her lullaby, words I already knew: "Rock-a-bye, baby, thy cradle is green, Father's a nobleman, mother's a queen."

'Letters are a kind of key,' she said.

I knew about keys, of course: it was the right thing to say. By knowing the sounds these shapes made, I could work out new words, she told me.

'Look! Baa baa black sheep, have you any wool. Here is the word sheep. See? Sh-ee-p. Here is the word wool. W-oo-l.'

'But what is sheep, mama?' I never thought before. 'It is a thing, then?'

'It is, my lovely. It is an animal that lives in freedom on the hills. It is about as tall as you and it has four legs. It has rough hair all over its body and that gives us wool. This is what it looks like.' She quickly drew a cloud, gave it two dots for eyes and four sticks for legs. It was the first drawing of an animal I had ever seen and I will never forget it. Somehow, its likeness to a cloud gave me the impression that sheep floated over the hills, those four helpless legs hanging down towards the earth, a thought that still makes me smile.

She wet the rag by dipping it in the small pot and started to wipe away the words.

'Stop mama, I want to look at the sheep!'

'Hush, child, I will not wipe the sheep. See here, I have left him. And two words beside. What are the two words I have left?'

Indignant, my voice rose. 'Why sheep and wool, of course, mama!' I was always quick-tempered.

'And so....I am going to write a new word and using those two words as your key, you are going to tell me what the new word is.'

When she passed me the slate, I remember feeling scornful: I hardly needed to look. Instead of saying the word, I wet the tip of my little finger and wiping away the sheep's round black eyes, I drew in their place two tiny bowl shapes and turned it to show her. I remember her surprised and joyful gasp of laughter: 'Why, you clever little thing! We will have you reading your Bible in no time!'

But we had no Bible, which is lucky for me, for the book that was first put into my hands was to become the only Bible I ever needed or wanted.

The fabric of our world provided mama with rich material: we had woollen blankets and horsehair mattresses, cotton shifts and a tortoiseshell comb. The walls were of stone that had been dug out of the earth, but not here in London. She held up the rough-hewn piece of chalk, which worried me by growing smaller by the day. I looked and saw for the first time how it passed the softness of itself onto the slate, and thence to the rag, and from the rag to the water to turn it white. 'Where do you think this came from, Molly?'

'From the earth?'

'Yes!' she delighted, always, in my quickness. 'The earth in London is made of chalk. In Essex, where I come from, it is sandy and gravelly. In other places, the rocks are limestone, soft like chalk, and in those places, rains and rivers wash the soft rocks away, though it takes years and years to shape the valleys and hills and caves and cliffs. In some places, the earth is red and made of clay, and clay can be used to make pots like this bowl. But there are places in the north of England where your father comes from, where the rock is hard and nothing can wash it away. Nothing.' Her face, at first flushed with excitement at our subject, had suddenly clouded.

Where my father came from was a matter of no interest to me, though little did I know it was to become an obsession. The fabric of my world had suddenly shifted into focus: each object in it had taken on a life: each thing in that room had been part of another thing, once upon a time. The shape my mother drew next, like a fat lady sitting, she said was England. This very slate, she said, probably came from Wales, on the fat lady's tummy, or perhaps from Cornwall at her pointy feet. 'We are here,' mama said, 'under the fat lady's bottom.' We laughed to think of it, Mama with her hand over her mouth as she had been taught. That was manners.

She drew a ball floating above the fat lady's knees. 'Papa grew up here,' she said, 'that's Ireland, another country. When he was young, Papa came over the sea on a boat with other soldiers, and they marched all about, wherever the King wanted them to go. And they went to here,' and she pointed her chalk at the back of the lady's neck. 'That's where Newcastle is.' She looked up at me, a long and level look, but then she saw that I was impatient to get back to the things, for suddenly, the room was full of ghosts.

There were horses and sheep and people combing them and bent over mysterious work, fashioning their hairs into blankets and mattresses. Ghostly shapes bent to the ground and lifted aloft bowls and jugs. Across the floor there shambled a giant tortoise, and this last gave me pause for thought, for I suddenly understood that though the horse and the sheep could live without their hair, the tortoise had given up an essential part of itself to make mama's comb. I had studied slugs, which Mama said were like snails without their shells, and I felt fear for the fate of the tortoise..

And the chalk that had come to us from the ground to give of itself in our service and dissipate itself upon the air and the water, where had it gone? No longer a solid thing of use and substance, but a thing of dust and liquid, to sail out through the bars and seep down through the ground. To escape. It was the first shape-changer I ever apprehended.

I was to become one myself.

Let me think of the animals I had seen by the time I found the hedgehog. From the tiniest, the spiders and ants and beetles and bedbugs, to the mice and rats we encountered in the worst stages of our incarceration, to the pigeons who were our friends. Mama had a habit that fascinated and frightened me in equal measure: she would go to the window and hold a piece of dry bread or a split pea in her lips, then push her lips out as though to offer kisses and the pigeons would peck the food from her lips. I never knew them hurt her. She tried to teach me but I would not countenance it. For a blackbird, I might have risked it, for they were always my favourite with their glossy feathers and fierce yellow beak.

Once a butterfly flew in, fluttered pitifully to the corner and hung, trembling on the wall. I was torn between wanting to keep it and wanting to see it fly away. I kept it and it died.

Besides the animals with whom we shared our air, skin, blood, dried bread and split peas, we briefly had a room which overlooked the street and then, from my mother's arms, I saw a horse clopping past. I viewed the horsehair mattress with more fondness after that.

There was a period when we had some degree of liberty within the prison bounds, and that was when the hedgehog came into my life. That small encounter was to have a lasting effect, for if my father and his friend had not heard me excitedly telling my mother about the hedgehog, and if he hadn't been in one of his benevolent moods (for the court case was going well, I heard him say) he might never have given me my book.

Father's trunk was a large, impenetrable object that I had never seen opened. Each time we moved apartments, it took four men to lift it. What was in it, I never saw, but whenever a new object appeared in his hands or on his table, I knew the trunk had given up a treasure in the night, in secret.

Mama's tortoiseshell comb had come from there, and the first time I ever saw my own face, it was in a silver hand-mirror decorated with an intricate design of twining vines. I loved it when Mama said that. 'See the beauty of the craftsmanship, Molly. Such an intricate design of twining vines.' She did not tell me at the time, but when I knew my letters and briefly saw the mirror again, I saw the letters MEB.

36

Silver was a metal. The shiny bands around the trunk were metal too, but that was iron, which was not precious but very useful and used to make swords.

The trunk was used to store plates and linens, many of them also bearing the initials MEB – the maker's mark, Mama said.

When he heard us talking of the hedgehog, I remember how he cocked his head to one side like a blackbird listening, though not nearly so handsome. He was an ugly man, my father, especially from the side, with his hooked nose and sneering nostrils from which protruded tufts of grey-brown hair. I did not like to look at him.

But now he beckoned me over. 'Come here Molly, I may have a thing for you. Sit there whilst I rummage.'

Always delighted when he showed us any kindness, my mother went to stand beside him as he bent to turn the key in the great padlock on the trunk. 'What do you have for the child, Andrew?'

'I think I have in here a book with drawings of animals. You-know-who has never had her greedy hands on it, mind.' And here I saw him turn a gleeful and somehow wicked smile on my mother. He often looked like that when he spoke of this mysterious She. 'It arrived ready bound and I nabbed it swift.' He saw me looking and threw me a brief and leery smile: 'If it's still here, you shall have it, young Molly, and Mr Bewick shall show and tell you all about Mr Hedgehog.'

I believe he thought me still a child, though I was nigh on eight at the time and scornful of childish talk.

'Ha! Here it is! No, that's not it. Quadrupeds was bound in the Bowes colours. What the hell? Well, I'll be damned, it's gone! Confound that Peacock, he'll have stolen it when my back was turned, or some bastard's come in the night and had it away!' His voice was rising dangerously, and I saw my mother's face blanch when she turned to me, and with a flick of the eyes, bade me make myself scarce. I'd just stood to go when he suddenly subsided, and turned to me, holding out a brown object tied up in purple ribbon. 'You might as well have this, Molly. It's unbound, just trussed between boards, but it's useless to me and She doesn't even know I've got it, so where's the fun in that? Here.' And he tossed it onto the floor at my feet, where it landed with a thud and sent up a cloud of chalk dust into the air.

Chapter 5

How to convey to you what that book meant to me, to the little girl that I was and to the woman I became?

To imagine it, you must think yourself a child of eight winters whose eyes had seen nothing of the world beyond the looming black brick walls of the King's Bench Prison. Whose sooty sky was far away and bound by borders, studied through bars. Whose birds were pigeons mainly, though distant glimpses of migrating geese or swooping swallows merely meant more cold was coming, or more stifling heat. Whose water came in pitchers and bowls, whose young eyes had never seen it flowing, not even sluggishly between the slimy banks of the foul-smelling Thames.

I don't remember the act of opening the ribbons, nor even where I was, whether I was observed. I would certainly not have heard if I had been spoken to. I remember the feeling though, and can conjure it still, the whole of my being focused on the object in my hands. Stroking its edges, wondering at the smooth texture of the covers. Smelling for the first time the musty paper and board, unwrapping tenderly the weighty purple ribbons and laying them in my lap to keep them safe. I cannot remember where I sat, how I carved out a place and time where I could be alone. I picture myself sitting cross-legged, perhaps facing the corner where a shaft of light would fall across my lap.

I carefully read the title page first, I know I did, because once I had read it, I felt the book to be more securely mine.

Not only was it the first page of print I ever saw, but it also held the first drawing I ever saw that was not made by childish hands with chalk on slate. It excited me beyond description, though I understood it not at all, nor did I question how it had been made.

It occupied a position just below the centre of the page and had no borders, no boundaries, simply inhabiting the space it required. It was roughly oval, no more than two inches in height, perhaps three in breadth. The central subject was a block of stone, perhaps a gravestone, sorely tilted, and on it a shield with four white turrets. Behind the gravestone, giving the impression of natural support, was a bush or a stumpy tree, with two types of vegetation, one frondy and pale, the other dark and dense and profuse, but all swept back by the wind. I imagine I must have gasped, for never had I imagined that wind could be conveyed in a drawing, but yes, there it was, evident in the long plume of smoke from a distant chimney.

I love the wind, always have. Even now a windy day excites me, but then I loved it as a starving man loves food, as a thirsty dog loves water. In the cramped cells of the prison where the stale air festered and stank, even the northerly that brought the fetid whiff of the Thames was welcomed. I had so few chances to go into the prison yard that I know I was yet to experience what it is to have your whole being caressed by the movement of fresh natural air.

The chimney having drawn my eye, I let it rove along the far horizon and there beheld tiny windmills, and below the windmills fields and hedges, and below the fields a dense profusion of boats whose sails billowed in the same wind, and on this near shore, three tiny human figures walking bent into the wind. And then I understood that the artist had been sitting on the ground close to the gravestone to draw it and its friendly supporting vegetation and that the men and boats and windmills were in the distance and so had appeared tiny to him. To Thomas Bewick. Worker of magic.

It was a miracle of creation. I apprehended the fact, though I could not have put it into words, being content to sit in mute adoration of his work.

Raising my eyes to the text, I studied the composition of the page, so pleasing to the eye. The letters were all block-capitals, perfectly formed, some solid, some composed of lines so closely-made and parallel as to be another miracle.

"History of British Birds by Thomas Bewick." A history! And there must be so many, for the book had many pages! More birds than I had even known existed, for Mama could think of so few. Her description of a swan and an owl had charmed and delighted me, but how could it be true, for how could the neck of one be so long or that of the other rotate so far? I had nodded and smiled at her simple chalk outlines but secretly felt the reality of their existence to be unlikely. But here was possibility…

"Volume 1. Containing the History and Description of Land Birds." Land birds? What could this mean, for birds surely were of the air?

"The figures engraved on wood by Thomas Bewick." I stared at these words, blank with incomprehension. What could it mean? They were drawings, surely. Agitated, I moved on, seeking firmer ground. Below the picture was the one word: "Newcastle"

Newcastle Upon Tyne! I knew where that was on the fat lady map. And father had lived there!

"Printed by Solomon Hodgson, for Beilby & Bewick: Sold by them, and G.G. & J. Robinson, London. Price in boards." I understood none of this, but no matter: I had already noticed the date and my heart jumped. 1797 – the very year of my birth! This surely must be a sign: it surely sealed my ownership of this book?

I remember being tremblingly alert then. Alert to the fear of a boisterous brother with grasping hand, a toddling baby with puke and worse on its hands. But also alert to choice and possibility. I could read the words – I could see that at a glance, for that word father had said – quadrupeds – leapt out at me on the next page. It meant four of something, I knew. I would deduce the rest. But should I look at the pictures first? "Introduction" it said. I would read this first, or at least begin to, until my impatience to look at the pictures got the better of me.

I was glad I did, for by the second paragraph I knew that here was not only a description of all the land birds of Britain, but the secrets of life and how to live it. "Instead of the large head and formidable jaws, the deep capacious chest, the brawny shoulders and sinewy legs of the quadrupeds..." - here was my father and all the other shouty men! – "...we observe the long and pliant neck, the gently swelling shoulder, the expansive wings, the tapering tail, the light and bony feet; which are all wisely calculated to assist and accelerate their motion through the yielding air..." *The yielding air.* My heart raced and swooned – this was poetry – the words spoke directly to my heart. "Every part of their frame is formed for lightness and buoyancy; their bodies are covered with a soft and delicate plumage, so disposed as to protect them from the intense cold of the atmosphere through which they pass; their wings are made of the lightest materials, and yet the force with which they strike the air is so great as to impel their bodies forward with astonishing rapidity."

Here were words of transformation, possibilities of a world turned on its head: a vague apprehension animated my heart: physical weakness could bring a different kind of strength: adaptability was the answer, and oh the joy of imagination – the thought of moving freely through the yielding air! From then on, my dreams would be of flying.

I would read no more words. This was food enough. My mind alight, I wished no more than this. I picture myself staring rapt at the walls and ceilings and seeing through them for the first time: through the concrete binding world to the world of air and light and swift movement, the world where the swallows went when they flashed past the square of sky that was visible to me. It was what I now know to be an epiphany: the sudden apprehension that there really was a whole world beyond these walls. I would have struggled to imagine how it looked had it not been for Mr Bewick.

The next I saw of his astonishing skill with what I still took to be a pencil was another dense little picture only a couple of inches in depth. Above it, a strangely shaped wavy line I thought must have been an accident. It endeared the drawing to me before I looked at it, for hadn't I too made many such smudges and lines on precious pieces of paper? But when my eye fell on the drawing itself, I was struck with awe, for I could never make a picture like this. Again, the more I looked, the more I saw. It showed a cluster of buildings: in the centre, the largest had a pointed roof and three large birds flying up the wall, or so it seemed to me in my innocence. A smaller building adjacent had a ladder leaning against it, and towards the ladder was walking a man bent nearly double   under the weight of a sack of something. Grain? A woman in a long dark dress with a shawl and an apron was tipping something from a round sieve and all around her feet teemed birds of different shapes and sizes, birds with no tails and extravagant tails, with tiny beaks and long beaks, webbed feet and spikey feet and no feet at all – I suddenly understood that they must be on water, and yes, see the shading – horizontal lines quite different from the lumpy ground – Mr Bewick had drawn a small pond, some ducks still in it and some walking out of it towards the woman and the seeds.

And look! A pig and its litter of six piglets, all turned toward the woman and whatever she was tipping onto the ground, and in the foreground a small heap and on the top of the heap was a small black cat, curled up and asleep. And around this charming scene of teeming life, ramshackle fences and low walls made of patterned stones, pretty walls over which you could see into the next place, and a roof with a chimney out of which coiled a wisp of smoke. Oh how I yearned to see inside that small cosy house with its fire waiting for these people when their day's work was done.

And behind the roof, trees at a great height with leaves and branches of all kinds, some dense and dark and some with branches visible, fine lines tracing their shapes against the sky, and in the sky - of course! Not a squiggle but a flying skein of what? Geese, maybe, it didn't matter, for I had understood what it represented. Mr Bewick had seen birds flying far up, too far to see, and he had drawn them as a line, and I had seen just such a things as that, a dark line of I knew not what kind of birds. And it didn't matter, it was a connection between us.

That farmyard was the first scene of rural life that my eyes ever saw, but oh what treasures were to follow! This Tyne! Such a river I never could have imagined! Verdant and winding between low banks, fringed with trees, its shallows fished and paddled by children, who sailed small boats and frolicked with perky dogs; its deeper waters waded by men on stilts and horseback, and rowed by oarsmen, crossed by beautiful low bridges and rickety boats. Its horizons dotted with windmills and castles and turrets and factory chimneys. Its inhabitants housed in cosy cottages with coils of smoke twining into the white air when pristine snow lay on the ground.

And the stories these pictures suggested – the man deliberately relieving himself against an elegant wall, the other losing his hat as he led his packhorse though the water. What happened to the owner of the abandoned crutches? Where had the traveller been who was greeted with such emotion by the old man emerging from the tumbledown cottage?

Others made me laugh – the giant snowman, twice as big as the boys who had made him, his outlandish pipe as long as the arm of the boy balancing on a rickety stool who reached up to place it there while a horse looked on in amazement. The man riding a giant pig while his dog ran alongside, laughing. The pictures were full of laughing dogs, so different from the bony, craven ones who scavenged a living in the prison yard.

The daily dramas, the gaggle of daft lads scaring themselves in the runaway cart, the woman in the clean white apron throwing up her arms in alarm under the sign of a crescent moon. The sheep caught by its fleece in the thorny thicket.

And the darker side, too. The wiry devil with his lashing forked tail brandishing his whip over a man in a cart, going backwards towards a gallows. The man digging a grave while a cat looked on, impassive, and a tiny bird perched at the top of the picture, out of reach of anyone.

The hanged man. My eyes flicked away when first I saw this drawing. I turned the page: I could not look.

I should explain. I had seen a man being hanged, seen him kick and twitch. Heard the jeering crowds cheer. My heart had shrunk with fear and he had haunted my dreams.

But here, Mr Bewick showed me a different kind of hanged man. This man had laid his stick on a high fertile bank of a calm alcove of the River Tyne. The tree in the centre of the picture was like none I had ever seen, wide and gnarled and knotted, but the top must have cracked and snapped through age. But new growth, slender boughs grew horizontally from the blasted trunk. He had strung his rope from a bough overhanging the river, and he had stepped out into space. Only his little dog, sad and bewildered, stood on the bank to witness his master's leave-taking. The river flowed calmly on. Nothing changed. The new branches carried on growing. The little dog would find a new master. The man was free now. And I felt a new peace.

And then there were the birds....

And just as the hedgehog brought me my book, my book brought me to the attention of Mr Palmer. It is a wonder to me, when I look back over my tale, how one thing led to another.

My world was my Mama, my book, the birds who visited and my little brothers and sisters. We barely saw our father and only knew he was in the other room when the deep voices rattled the locks. Usually they just rumbled on into the night like distant thunder, sometimes cracked through with shouts and curses. Raised voices in the night usually meant drink, and those were scary times when Mama would huddle us close on the mattresses together like a litter of puppies. As the eldest, I began to feel it my duty to stay awake with Mama, for until the voices were silent she never knew whether he would come for her.

The men who came in the daytimes were usually much less frightening, though often their voices were raised and they waved papers in Father's face and thumped the table. Once, one of them thumped him instead, for he staggered into our room with a bloody nose and sat cursing whilst Mama tenderly wiped away the blood.

None of these men ever took any notice of us, except Jesse Foot, who was with Father often: Mama said he was a doctor. He once examined me, listening to my chest with a stethoscope (I liked to get new words, especially big ones). At first I lay quietly, well apart from the wheezing in my breath, but the more I looked up his nostrils and wet lips while he listened and tapped my chest, the more I wanted it to be over. His breath stank of porter and his nails were long and yellow and curved like the turnkey's toenails.

One afternoon, I'd been helping Mama teach the little ones a nursery rhyme while Nathaniel sat drawing on his piece of slate. We had eaten our bread and cheese, and we were just preparing to settle them on the mattresses for their afternoon nap. Mama signed deeply and swept the hair away from her brow with the back of her hand. I knew by then that there was another baby on the way and she was tired.

'Why don't you have a sleep too, Mama? You could go into the big bed. Father's not been home these two nights.'

Immediately, Nathaniel sprang up, 'Yes, Mama, let's all go in the big bed! It's so soft and we can all cuddle.'

One of the babies was already asleep, so we carried them through into Father's room and they didn't stir. Mama was asleep in an instant, Nathaniel soon followed, and I had an hour of peace with my book in the yellow light of a stump of tallow.

I was just immersed in deciphering a tailpiece when I heard the key in the outer lock and then men's voices, one of them Papa's, in the room beyond. The surge of annoyance nearly choked me. I slid off the bed, still clutching my book and tiptoed to the door to tap softly.

It was opened by a gentleman I hadn't seen before with a bright white cravat and kindly blue eyes which crinkled when he saw me.

'Hello, little miss, and what is your name, pray tell?'

'Molly Bowes, sir.'

The gentleman looked quite astonished, though his eyes were still kind. 'Bowes, eh?' He straightened his back and looked over his shoulder to where Father was standing with a decanter in his hand. 'I'll say this for you, Mr Stoney, you've a cheek.'

'Bowes is my name now and it shall stay, divorce or no.'

The gentleman's face was turned to me while Father spoke and he was unabashed to show me the curious smile that crossed his face. Then he winked. 'And what's that you've got there, Molly Bowes?'

So fearful was I of anyone taking my book away from me that without thinking, I put it behind my back and held it there with two shaking hands, for now my father was standing behind the gentleman.

'It is only my book, sir.'

'Yes, quite. And what is the name of your book, if I might enquire, Molly Bowes?'

To my own surprise, tears sprang to my eyes. 'It is just a book of birds, sir. Father gave it to me.'

Seeing my tears, the gentleman clearly divined the source of my fear, and he resting a large warm hand on my head, he turned to speak to my father. 'Kind of you, Stoney. Mr Bewick's excellent volume, I take it?'

'Yes, my property of course. Bowes property.'

I had stopped crying. This was interesting.

There was a pause before he answered. 'Well, whether it is your property is a moot point, I think, but I'm sure Lady Strathmore would not begrudge this child the pleasure.'

Lady Strathmore. Was this the name of the mysterious She? He turned back to me, saw that his words had strengthened me on the instant, and gently cupped the back of my head in a comforting hand.

Father's expression was a picture: I could see the two halves of him fighting to decide which would speak. Finally, the charmer triumphed, and pulling a chair from the table, he sat down to look at me, his mouth smiling but the devil looking out of his eyes.

'Come here Molly, come and sit on my knee.' He had never laid a finger on me since the night Jack disappeared. I didn't move, couldn't move, but the presence of the gentleman gave me strength and I forced my feet forward.

I could play a part too. Meekly, I said, 'Yes Papa,' in a voice not my own, and laying the book on the table out of his reach, I climbed onto his knee, where I was instantly engulfed in the reek of alcohol and tobacco.

'A bonny child, Mr Stoney. Her mother has red hair, I take it?'

'No, the Suttons are all blonde. There's red hair in my side, though not as curly as this mop!' He roughly ruffled my hair, as if with affection.

'How old are you, Molly?'

'I'm nine, Nathaniel's five, Patricia's four, the twins are three and the new baby is coming soon. I hope it's a girl.'

Abruptly, my Father stood up and tipped me off his lap. 'Enough of this, Palmer, let's to business. Molly, leave us.'

But Mr Palmer spoke gently, 'Perhaps Molly would like to sit at the table and read her book. It is unbound, I see. We must take care of it, mustn't we, Molly? Mr Bewick's work is so very fine, I think, and I'm sure Molly agrees. Do you have a favourite bird?'

'The blackbird is my favourite, Mr Palmer, but I chiefly love the tail-pieces.'

'Do you indeed? I too! They are a wonder, are they not? Do you know how they were made? No? Perhaps if your father and I agree to work together on his case, I shall see more of you, Miss Molly Bowes, and we can talk about clever Mr Bewick. You can show me your favourite pictures and tell me all about them.'

Now that I recollect this conversation, I understand the reason for my father's civilized behaviour, for it turned out that Mr Palmer of Gray's Inn was not of the usual class of father's lawyers, and his coming was to signify a change in our circumstances. First there was some celebration, some win in the courts that made my father jubilant. He celebrated for a week, and all his old cronies came out of the woodwork to take part in his good fortune.

The mood changed abruptly, however, because seemingly news had spread and men to whom he owed money came banging on the doors. One of them, Mr Peacock, had once been his friend but it seemed he had turned into his mortal enemy. I never saw him, heard only his voice bellowing on the other side of the door. Mama and the little ones were terrified, so to distract them and Mama, I began to whisper a fair imitation of Mr Peacock's accent, which I knew showed he was from Newcastle. 'Aah'll get ye yet, Bowes ya bastard! Divvn't worry, ye'll get yer cumuppance!'

It wasn't long after that that news came that the mysterious She was dead, a cause of great jubilation because it meant that we were free to live outside the prison walls. Father took a house in Lambeth Road, St George's Fields, within "the rules" of the King's Bench.

There at last the trunk was opened, and more treasures poured forth: plate and candlesticks and napkins and bedding. I was given a pillowcase and a fine linen handkerchief embroidered with the initials MEB in silk thread. I asked Mama again what they stood for, and again she professed to believe they were the maker's mark. Young as I was, it seemed doubtful to me that the same maker would work in silver and also in silk.

47

I have often wondered since then whether my mother actually knew what the initials stood for. It is perfectly possible that she did not, for she was only seventeen when father took her, and as far as I know she never was part of a conversation with anyone but Father and occasionally Dr Foot. I did ask her once whether the things had belonged to Lady Strathmore, and I remember she looked at me startled, but if she knew the truth, she must have been a great dissembler, for she answered without hesitation, 'Why no, my little sunflower, for then it would say LS, would it not?'

Chapter 6

While we lived there, we received a visit from Father's sister, a beautiful lady with a lilting voice and wavy auburn hair. She took me on one side one day and whispered to me. 'Molly, if I had had a child, I think she might have looked like you. You and I have a special bond, I think, and I shall write to you when I get home to instruct you in the ways of the Lord. Keep yourself pure, my dear, and do the Lord's work at all times, and perhaps one day there will be a home for you with me in Ireland.'

She did indeed write to me, but the letter was full of religious talk I did not understand. I memorised the address, however, and folded the letter into the cover of my book, for who knew what the future held?

Despite no longer living in the prison, our father went into a steep decline, though it did not stop his excursions, few visitors ever came and he often drank alone, becoming more and more self-pitying as he grew older, his mood only lightened when first he started drinking or gambling, or caught sight of a pretty woman passing by.

Finally, he stopped getting up in the morning, calling instead for a jug of porter. My mother had to fetch it for him: by then we had only a scullery-maid who told me she only stayed with us because she had nowhere else to go.

'But what do you mean, Becky? There must be other houses far happier than ours! You are free to go, unlike us.'

'Can I ask you something, miss? I don't understand, never have.'

'What don't you understand, Becky?' She was a simple girl with a wide flat nose like an ox.

'I was brought here from the workhouse, miss, I know naught else. I know this house belongs the prison, but what have you done?'

'We have done nothing, Becky, but our father owes money to many people. He has been most unlucky.'

'Gambling, miss?'

I gathered myself to my full height. I may be low, but I was above poor Becky and did not wish to invite too much confidence.

'No, Becky, business. Father's business dealings are what brought him to the debtor's prison. And a wicked woman to whom father was married and who ruined him out of sheer wickedness and greed.' I lowered my voice. 'She was a madwoman.'

'But you, miss? You did nothing wrong?'

'No, of course not Becky, but we belong to our father and therefore have to stay with him.'

'And your mother? Was she too a prisoner?'

'No, Mama was not a prisoner, but her father was, so...' Suddenly, I saw something clearly for the first time, and I was so shaken that I went straight to find Mama.

'Mama. What will happen to us when father dies?'

Accustomed to my directness, she blinked once and then answered thus: 'To be honest, Molly, I do not know. The thought of it makes me very fearful.' She went back to her darning.

'Talk to me, Mama. You were only a little older than me when first you met Papa, weren't you? Is that what will happen to me? An old man will lock me away in prison and have babies on me?'

I saw in her eyes that the thought had already been in her mind. Her answer was unconvincing. 'No, Molly, I shouldn't think so. But you must remember that there are worse fates for a young girl with no protector.'

'But how is it to be prevented?' I grasped her shoulders and forced her to look at me.

'And what of the little ones?'

Her eyes were full now and she put down her darning. 'I don't know, Molly, I have cast all about in my mind to think who can help us. You mustn't tell your father, but I have written letters.'

'Who? Who have you written to?'

'To his family in Ireland and to mine in Essex.'

'And received replies?'

'No, none. I hardly know what has become of my family since my father lost his land. My mother used to write but I have not heard from her for over ten years now. I think she must be dead. For...' and here she faltered, 'I am, you know, a fallen woman.' She gathered herself and sat up straight. 'There are homes for fallen women, of course. It need not be the workhouse.'

'The workhouse! You cannot mean that, Mama! Becky came from the workhouse! And we must go there? To pluck hemp for our keep? No, no, I shall never...'

'Molly, my child, it is you I worry about most. You are ... of all of us, I should say, the one who will be in the most danger. Your hair ... it draws men's eyes. I have seen them. I fear for you losing the protection of your father.'

It was one of those moments when everything changes. *The protection of my father.* I stood up and looked down at my mother's upturned face. I suddenly felt that the roles were reversed. When only three years older than me and though no fault of her own, she had been plucked from her comfortable life like a delicate flower pulled up by the roots. All her strength had left her then, and in her weakness, my father had seen her and wanted her and taken her. And ever since, for all those long years, over twenty of them, she had submitted to his will and made a world for her children. She knew of nothing else.

I, on the other hand, born on a stone floor in a prison cell, had needed no roots. I could adapt to anything.

I cropped my hair off that very day.

'I could sell that for you, miss,' said Becky when she came upon me with my plait in my lap.

'Could you, Becky? Who would buy it?'

'The doll-maker in Covent Garden. Customers pay a lot for a doll with real hair. And your hair is a marvel. I never saw the like.'

I had never even held a coin in my hand, though I had seen plenty heaped on Papa's gaming table. 'How much would it get?'

'I don't know, miss. I can ask if you want, next time I go to the market. Without showing it to him, like. I'll pretend I'm selling mine. See what he says for dull old mouse.'

Money of my own, however small an amount, would confer on me some power I only dimly understood, but the thought was a spark of hope.

'You must tell no-one, Becky. Do you understand? No-one at all. I do not want anyone to know even that I have cut it. You must give me one of your mob-caps and in return I will help you with some of your jobs. You can teach me. My mother thinks I should go into service.'

It was my first transaction, and I found it intoxicating. For the first time, my thoughts were not always shared with others. I would bide my time and see which way the wind blew.

I will never forget my mother's face when she passed me one day in the hall, holding out a key in silent wonderment. 'He says I have to open the door! I have never unlocked a door. Not once in my life.'

It was Dr Foot, and he too was astonished to see my mother on the threshold. 'Why Miss Sutton! This is indeed a pleasure, but I fear it does not bode well for our friend.'

'Yes, doctor, I am afraid Mr Bowes is too weak to raise himself from the pillow. I am so frightened, doctor.' And to my horror, she started to weep silent tears.

I never liked Dr Foot, but to see him pat my mother's hand and promise her that she should not be afraid was something I chose to believe gave us hope.

Father shrank into the mattress like the carcass of a bird.

Dr Foot came and went in those last days. I once saw my mother in his arms, sobbing on his shoulder while he murmured, 'There there, my dear. Hush now. Never fear. I have promised, and I will keep my promise.'

Afterwards, he took me on one side and told me. Mama had not the courage, for she feared my blazing eyes, which I had to hide by looking at the floorboards in a semblance of demure.

'My dear, your mother has agreed to assist my daughter's governess. She will have a room in the attic of my daughter's house in Kensington. Nathaniel will work in the stables, and the girls will be found work in the kitchens.'

I continued to stare at the floor but I felt him watching. I did not want to look up into his leering face for fear that my eyes would show my revulsion. 'You, however, are something of a conundrum. I suggested that you might like to learn to be a ladies' maid, and a position could be found for you in my house, but your mother seems to think you have other ideas.'

'My mother is correct, Dr Foot. I have plans of my own.'

'My dear, you are barely, what, fourteen? You have no-one in the world outside these four walls. What plans can you possibly have?'

'I am going to work for Mr Palmer of Grey's Inn.'

'Indeed?' He made no effort to hide his amusement. 'I think you might find Mr Palmer rather less receptive to employing the bastard daughter of the notorious Stoney Bowes than you evidently expect. Relations between them have deteriorated somewhat.'

I looked up at him sharply, my eyes wide with shock. I struggled for some moments with the riot of indignation though I hope I kept my face neutral. So, here we have it. My father's protection, such as it was, clearly counted for nothing any longer. I must not show this man my strength until the time was right. When I look back now, I marvel at the self-possession I showed in these days, when my very life hung in the balance. Though I understood it only dimly, I knew I stood at the edge of a precipice. I must hold my nerve: I would not fall.

'Then I will go to my family in Ireland. I have the address and my father's sister said that I would be welcome.'

'How do you plan to get yourself to Ireland, pray tell?'

'I know not…perhaps you could help me, sir.'

'You have no money.'

I bowed my head meekly, acquiescent and apparently defeated.

'There, there, my dear. All is not lost. Fear not, your uncle Jesse has found a situation for you.'

My uncle Jesse had clearly observed my fear of my father and mistaken it for a lack of spirit. I must not disabuse him of his mistake. I composed a compliant face and injected gratitude and hope into its eyes. Then I turned it up to my saviour.

'An established friend of mine is willing to offer you a home. He is a gentleman and between us, we will take care of you.'

Here was no surprise. I had seen the way Dr Foot looked at me and having heard the nature of his loose talk when he was drinking with Father, I could well imagine the terms in which he had offered my services. This friend of his might well have a locked room already prepared. No: better the devil you know. I would strike out on my own while I still had a chance.

'Thank-you Dr Foot, that is very kind. May I refresh your tea?'

'Yes, my dear. Thank-you.'

As I busied myself about the tea things, my back to him, I quickly considered my safest course. He must not suspect that I still wanted to get away, so I continued pleasantly, 'Perhaps one day your friend, my new master, will allow me to visit my family in Ireland. Is he acquainted with my father?'

I heard the smirk in his voice, though I did not turn round.

'Oh yes indeed, he is acquainted with your father: your father owes him a considerable amount of money. I am sure if he finds you agreeable, it will go some way towards paying your father's debt.'

I turned to him now and brought tears to my eyes with ease. 'Oh but sir, I should so love to see my aunt again one day. Perhaps I will be able to save from my wages and beg my master to allow me a visit. Can you find it in your heart to give me hope that that might happen one day? It surely would not cost too much?'

I was setting his cup on the side table as I spoke, and allowed my hand to linger. Sure enough, he reached out and stroked the back of my hand with a fingertip, thoughtfully. I held still, willing myself to submit to the light scratch of that one curved nail.

He looked up into my tremulous eyes and smiled a dreamy smile, the smile of a crocodile, and spoke gently, 'Yes, my dear, I'm sure that he will allow that one day, if you please him.'

My temper clamped my throat, I lowered myself to my knees and bowed my head, taking a moment to suck in one deep precious breath. I felt his hand descend heavily on my head and it was trembling. That gave me strength: momentarily, I felt I had the power in this transaction.

My head still bowed, I pretended a sob and then, wiping away an invisible tear, raised my face to him. 'I have never had money of my own, sir. I hope I shall please your friend. Will it take me an awful long time to earn enough to pay a visit to my family?'

Seemingly transfixed by my eyes, which were apparently on the brink of tears, he spoke as if in a dream, 'No, no my dear, very little. A few pence it costs to travel the mail route to Dublin. I will give it to you myself if you are kind to me.'

He took both my hands in his and raised me to my feet. 'Now now, don't upset yourself, little one. Come here and let me comfort you,' and his arm slipped round my waist, drawing me close, the reek of tobacco and porter invading my nostrils. Enough. I had convinced him of my acquiescence. I stepped sharply back, unbalancing him, and made a show of wiping my tears and straightening my cap whilst muttering, 'Thank-you, sir. Now I must see to my mother,' and bobbing a swift curtsy, I left the room.

I went straight to Father's desk and set about searching his correspondence. It took me no more than five minutes to find Mr Palmer's address.

Becky was sitting in the kitchen, disconsolate. I sat down next to her and put an arm around her shoulder. Startled, she looked askance and then leaned her head against me. 'Oh, Miss, what's to become of me?'

'There, there, Becky. You said you had a new position to go to? Is that not the case?'

'Oh, I suppose so. It's just ... I get tired of moving on. Never belonging anywhere.'

'Have you no family at all?'

'No, none. Not that I know of, like.'

'You'll find a nice young man one day and make a family of your own.'

Somewhat comforted, she turned anxious eyes to me. 'Do you really think so?'

'Of course. You'll know him when you see him, and then you use your feminine powers to make him yours.'

Her smile was doubtful. 'If you say so, Miss. And what of you? What will become of you? You've not said. No-one's said. What are your plans?'

I looked at her for long moments. 'Can I trust you, Becky?'

Indignant, she straightened up and her bovine face was animated by indignation. 'You know you can! For didn't I sell your hair for you? And get you a fine price an' all?'

'Yes, you did, of course you did. I'm going to ask you to do something, Becky, and if you don't want to be involved, just say so and I'll find someone else. And when I ask you the question, you'll know my plans, but you must never tell anyone, for there are some that mean me harm.'

'You mean Dr Foot, don't you? I've seen the way he looks at you. Have no fear, if I can help to preserve you from that man and ones like him, I will do anything.'

'Dear, sweet Becky, I believe you. Thank-you. I believe I can find a safe haven, for I have a powerful friend whom I trust. But I do not know how to find him: I know so little of the world outside the prison bounds. If I can find him, I feel sure he will offer me a position.'

Her face lit up. 'I might be able to get you a position with me! There's always work for scullery maids. I know the housekeeper: she's kind. Come with me! We can be friends and work together, proper friends.'

How to tell poor Becky that I wanted more? More than her friendship, more than a life of servitude, more than the dirty streets of London? It was all she knew or would ever know.

'Bless you, Becky, but I made a promise a long time ago.'

'Really, miss? Who to?'

'My father's sister came to visit us once when I was a little girl, and she looked very like me. She has no children of her own, and it would break your heart to see how this dear sweet lady who had travelled so far yearned to make me her own child. I promised her then that when my father died I would go and live with her as a companion in her fine house. My own mother is so happy for me, that I should be safe and loved and in the bosom of a fine Irish family, and perhaps make a good match one day. Mr Palmer will help me stay safe until she should come for me. Will you help me, Becky?'

Sweet soft-hearted Becky's eyes swam with tears and she whispered her assent.

In the deep darkness of that January evening, two figures slipped out of the house by the cellar steps and walked rapidly away down Lambeth Road, arm-in-arm, for all the world like a lad and his lass. The guard up ahead was leaning against a railing, smoking a pipe in the dim light from a candle-lit window. To my alarm he straightened up as we approached, but I need not have worried, for Becky swept us past with a playful, 'See, Alfie Douglas, you can stop your teasing for I've got my own beau now!'

The woman who opened the door of Mr Palmer's neat terrace in Grey's Inn was clearly expecting someone very different from the gangly youth she found on the doorstep. Her eager expression gave way to annoyance and irritation and she swept her hand at me as if to push me off the step. 'Be off! Be off with you! We're expecting a very important visitor! No hawkers! Go on, shoo!' and she made as if to shut the door.

Just as I put out a hand to try to stop the door closing, I glimpsed a figure crossing the hall behind her ample frame. 'Mr Palmer! Mr Palmer, it's me!' I whipped off my cap to let my halo of cropped curls spring out. 'Molly Bowes!'

His face appeared at the woman's shoulder, an expression of benign puzzlement spread across his features. 'Bowes?'

'Yes, Molly Bowes! You acted for my father. We talked about Bewick.' Though the woman stood her ground, I stepped up and the light from the hall illuminated my features.

'Molly Bowes? Ah! I have it! Stoney's child! My, you have shot up. Whatever are you doing dressed as a boy?'

'Husband, really, whoever this child is, for Heavens' sake, get her out of the way before our visitor arrives.'

'What is it you want Molly? I really am very busy and I no longer act for your father. In fact...' and he straightened up, his face clouding as he clearly recollected some reason why the mention of my father was antagonistic to him. 'Go, child, go back to the King's Bench: your presence outside is illegal as long as your father is alive.'

'That's just it, sir! He will shortly die!' Suddenly, the enormity of what I had undertaken overwhelmed me, tears sprang to my eyes and I clutched the buttons at my breast. 'Please, Mr Palmer, please help me or I shall surely be taken by the wicked men. I'll do anything sir! Please find me a position where I shall be safe!'

Startled by the passion of my entreaty, his face registered conflicting emotions, but before he could respond, Mrs Palmer burst out, 'Lady Hamilton's carriage!' grabbed me by the arm and yanking me into the hallway, marched me down a corridor, opened a door and pushed me through it, hissing, 'Wait in the kitchen.'

I had to feel my way down the narrow stairs, which opened out into a dark room that smelled of roast meat. My mouth watered as I felt my way to the window, fumbled for the door and whistled for Becky. She descended the steps with frightened eyes and I pulled her quickly into the room. I leaned on the door, rubbing my shoulder and whispered, 'Well, I'm in!'

'Lady Hamilton!' She was all agog. 'I saw Lady Hamilton!'

'Who is Lady Hamilton?'

'You know! Admiral Nelson!'

'Becky, I don't know. I've heard of Admiral Nelson, but I thought he was dead, and who's Lady Hamilton?'

'His ... well, his wife in all but name. You must have heard of her. The scandal! The paintings! The clothes!' Seemingly at a loss how to communicate the wondrousness of this personage, Becky was reduced to shaking her head and clearly going over the vision in her own mind without imparting any more information to me.

'If she's so important, why is she visiting a lawyer in the night and why are there no staff here to serve her drinks or take her cloak or anything?'

'I have no idea. Perhaps it's a secret visit!'

It was certainly a short one, for it seemed no time at all before we heard the front door open and rushed to the window in time to see nothing but the hem of a skirt brush past the railings and mount the carriage steps. Horses snorted, the carriage door slammed, the wheels creaked and then it was gone and the street was silent.

We heard heavy footsteps overhead, then Mr Palmer's wife opened the servants' door and called sharply, 'Molly Bowes, come up here this minute!'

Becky cowered in the corner. Signifying that she should stay there until I appeared outside, I said, 'Yes, Mrs Palmer. Just coming.'

Still clearly irritated with my presence, she bustled me back down the corridor and pushed me into a fire-lit study, where Mr Palmer stood by the mantelpiece looking preoccupied.

'Ah Molly, do come in. I suppose I must apologise for your reception, but you will understand that the circumstances of your appearance are ... unexpected and unconventional. Martha, you had better stay while I talk to the child.' Mrs Palmer sat in one of the leather armchairs and fixed me with a hostile gaze.

Continuing unperturbed but clearly thinking he should attempt to mollify his wife, he indicated a chair placed by the desk. 'Molly, I will give you five minutes. Sit down over there and tell me why you have come.'

Grateful to be addressing the back of Mrs Palmer's head, I summoned my best speaking-voice. 'Thank-you, sir. It is I who should apologise. In truth, I am afraid for my life. My father is not long for this world and I do not know what is to become of me. You once indicated that I should come to you if ever I was in need.'

'Really?' Casting an anxious glance towards his wife, he said, 'I cannot for the life of me imagine why I would have said a thing like that. You were a little girl, Molly. I think perhaps you misunderstood me. What are you hoping I can do for you?'

'Forgive me, Mr Palmer, for as you say I was but nine or ten when I last talked with you. You were so kind. You talked to me about my precious book, Bewick's Birds. You told me how the pictures were made and you explained to me about the tailpieces. We both preferred them to the bird pictures. Do you remember?'

'Why, yes I do, now you mention it.' He chuckled warmly. 'I remember you had a quickness of mind and an unusual sensitivity. You pointed out details to me that I had never noticed. Exquisite work. Did you ever get to see Water Birds, by the way? I have a copy here...' He made a move towards the bookshelves, but his wife barked the one word, 'John!' and he arrested his movement, seeming to recollect himself.

'Thank-you, I would love to see Water Birds one day, but for now my need is pressing and your time is short. My mother and my siblings have been offered a home and I have no fears for them, but the same person on whom they will depend has another future in mind for me. And I fear it, Mr Palmer.'

He considered me in the firelight and seemed to come to some conclusion. 'Yes, I see.'

Mrs Palmer had bent round the chair to look at me more closely and I felt I was gaining an advantage.

'What do you think, wife? Can we think of a place for Molly?'

'How old are you, child?'

'Fourteen.'

'What has happened to your hair?'

'I cut it myself.'

'Whatever for?'

'To be safe. To try to make myself less noticeable. I do not like to be noticed.'

'And you have your letters? You can read and write?'

Mr Palmer answered for me. 'Yes, a clever girl, I would say, Martha. Quite precocious, in fact.'

'And she must live within the bounds of the King's Bench?'

'Yes, until her father dies.' He looked at me. 'I'm sorry, my dear, for your imminent loss. Your father…well, perhaps I should say no more.'

I returned him a steady gaze. 'As you once said to me, I think we understand each other.'

He laughed, 'Did I say that? You really are a clever girl, Molly.' He considered me, his head on one side like a blackbird listening. 'You know, Mrs Palmer, I think I have a capital idea.'

'I was just thinking the same thing.' She pulled herself to her feet and stood beside her husband, entirely blocking out the heat from the fire.

'My dear, perhaps you could put our idea to Molly.'

This was a step too far and thankfully Mrs Palmer demurred: 'No, no husband, it is your client.'

'A client of mine, whose name I do not give, is shortly to take a house within the bounds of the King's Bench Prison. She is doing this voluntarily, I may add. As a precaution.'

The gossip burst out of Mrs Palmer, 'Before they can arrest her, for that would be scandal indeed!'

He patted her hand, 'Yes, yes, just as you say, but we really should keep that to ourselves for now, Mrs Palmer.' Seeing that she had subsided once again now that that juicy nugget was out of her, he continued thus: 'This lady is very troubled, for she is very well-known and is being treated with much injustice. She has until now managed to keep up a façade. Her stay within the prison bounds is, we hope, temporary. She has a daughter of your age. This child is also troubled, and as you can perhaps appreciate, she will become even more so when the move takes place. As yet, she is unaware of it. It will be a terrible shock to her and, more so than the mother, she will certainly lose all her friends, for girls of that age must always be chaperoned and no respectable mother will want her daughter to visit the environs of a debtors' prison. Her father is dead and they have no male protector at present.'

He considered me once more, his head still cocked.

'Mrs Palmer and I have a mind to put you forward as a companion for the daughter of my client. If this is agreeable to them, how will you approach the matter with your parents?'

'My father has not communicated for some days. He is largely insensible and Dr Foot expects the end to come any day now.'

'Dr Foot – ah yes.' His tone told me everything I needed to know about Mr Palmer's opinion of Dr Foot.

'My mother will be happy that I have found myself a situation. She will not concern herself where it is. I will send her messages to assure her of my continued safety.'

'You do understand that your presence here is against the law, Molly? I must bring our interview to a close now and ask you to leave by the cellar steps. If you were to be discovered here would compromise my reputation. Do you understand?'

'Yes, I do, Mr Palmer, and I apologise. I believed you would help me and you did not let me down. Thank-you so much.'

'You are not alone, I take it?'

'No, our maid, Becky, is with me. She guided me here.'

'Go home now, Molly. Within forty-eight hours I expect to have an answer for you. If it is agreeable to the lady in question, I will write the address of the property I have rented for her on a piece of paper. I assume you will want to make your departure without leaving a forwarding address? Yes, quite so. You are still at 12, Lambeth Road, I take it? Very well then. Can you think of a place near your home where a small piece of paper can be folded and left without fear of discovery?'

'There is a small stone falcon at the top of the steps of number 14, next door. Just one.'

'Capital, just the thing for two bird enthusiasts. There will be an address on the paper, no other words. As soon as you are ready, go to that address and present yourself as having been sent by me. They will be expecting you.'

When Becky brought me that piece of paper two days later, my heart lifted and I felt I should cry with relief and excitement. I could hardly wait for nightfall: she and I once again assumed our roles as a courting couple and slipped through the streets to a house that proved to be just two streets away but considerably grander than our own. The conversation I had with the housekeeper in the shadows of the kitchen yard was short and conducted mostly in whispers: I had to tell her that my father was unlikely to live more than a day or two. I would come as soon as I could. 'Don't worry, her Ladyship has not yet moved in: we are expecting them next week, which is just as well as the place is a midden and not fit for her. Poor lady.' Her soft, doughy face crumpled and she dabbed her eyes. 'To be brought to this!'

I was wild to know Lady Hamilton's story, but Becky was no use and I could not dare to ask anyone else for fear of laying a trail. I would have to wait until I was part of the household. Part of a household: the words were like an incantation to me.

My father was by that time at death's door: every morning brought the expectation that we should find him dead in his bed. Expectation? Nay, I'll be honest. Hope. It was hope.

He died on 16th January 1810 and was buried in the vault of St George's Church, still within the rules of the prison.

We came back to the house to find our few meagre possessions in the hallway. My mother was horrified to find that the trunk and all the plate, anything of value all gone. Creditors had been circling all week, and Becky, bless her, had passed on a warning that not even Dr Foot had seen fit to give us. She had heard from a neighbouring property that we should hide any items we could, for when a debtor died the crows were swift in their descent.

My mother, complacent as ever, had selected only a cravat of my father's. I had to force her to put the silver mirror in her bundle and some small items of jewellery. I begged her to send some larger items to the house of Dr Foot's daughter, but she could not think how to go about it, only passively waiting for Dr Foot to send a carriage.

My two most precious possessions were my book and the embroidered handkerchief. The exquisite embroidery seemed to me a symbol of hope, of a life in clean sheets.

Chapter 7

Oh, but the sheets were clean in the house of Lady Hamilton and the crystal sparkled and the plate shone: it was as though I had entered fairyland! Great people came and went and all was a flurry of gaiety and laughter. Or so it seemed to me at first. It was a great wonder to me how such a house could exist, let alone with in the bounds of the prison. I simply did as I was told and kept my head down, neatly dressed in my maid's uniform. (For the housekeeper had decided I had the height and bearing to be seen in public and should not be wasted cleaning fires.) 'For Lord knows I have few enough staff as it is, let alone how I should manage to entertain kings and princes!'

Kings and princes! I swallowed the exclamation that leapt to my throat for my concern was to blend in, deflect attention, watch and learn.

I had glimpsed Lady Hamilton's daughter but her demeanour did not inspire confidence that I could ever be her companion: from what I had seen she was sulky and haughty and on my third day I heard her shouting at her Mama, careless of who could hear her. 'How could you bring us to this?' she shrieked, and then there was a thump, as if an object had been thrown, then the low murmurs of Lady Hamilton's beautiful voice, then sobs, I know not whose.

Lady Hamilton was simply the most beautiful woman I had ever seen in my life, though well into middle age and somewhat ample. Her wide eyes were astonishing, like those of a much younger woman: they were like deep peaty pools, large, brown, thick-lashed, full of good humour, mischief and kindness. Her hair was luxuriant, dark and wavy, and reached the small of her back when once I saw it let down after her bath. She was swathed in a towel, and playfully raised her arm and peeped over her shoulder at the reflection of herself in the mirror.

From what I gathered, and I was somewhat hampered in my investigations by my resolution not to ask questions, this was a woman I could learn from, for though she was famous as the mistress of Lord Nelson and the widow of an important man, from what I could gather, her birth had been lowly and her past somewhat shady. Meaningful glances and raised eyebrows often accompanied the snippets I heard, but it was clear to me that everyone loved her.

Very quickly, I fell in love with her too. The dazzle of those first weeks soon deepened into complete admiration and a lasting love that I still feel to this day. Though I never got close enough to have a conversation with her, I watched her with increasing fascination. To her, I was largely invisible, but to me she was the sun and the moon. I saw her dance and sparkle for her high-born visitors; I saw her act, declaim and strike her classical poses for their entertainment; I saw her uncanny ability to spot an empty glass, a thoughtful expression, a lost thread - and provide what was needed: a hug, a diversion, a question, an anecdote, another drink. Never on her high horse, always with a kind word which felt like a warm caress. No matter what the weather or the circumstances – and as well as her dazzling public face, I saw her exhausted, in pain, despairing, pleading, weeping – she never lost that warm and genuine …I didn't know what to call it then, but I do now: charisma. When I think of her now it is always in celestial terms – sun, moon, heaven, star. Light and warmth seemed to emanate from her and she drew all eyes.

I never did become Horatia's companion, but I gained so much from my time with their household that I find it hard to enumerate the ways in which I benefited. My eyes and ears were wide open every minute of every day. It formed the foundation of what I was to become: I learned polite manners and conversation; I got a taste for art and literature; I learned that princes could be boors and footmen could be gentlemen; I learned that I wasn't the only one who hid their thoughts and feelings, for I saw Lady Hamilton go from deepest despair to the heights of gaiety at the opening of a door. I even learned to swim, for in one of the reprieves from her imprisonment, when her hopes were at their highest, we went to Brighton to join the Prince's party and two of us accompanied the ladies for a swim in the sea!

I had only the faintest comprehension of her circumstances and saw my taciturn acceptance of everything as an unquestioning loyalty to my goddess, but when the whole edifice came crashing around our ears, I learned the truth.

With the understanding that time and experience have given me, I look back and experience a terrible pity, for the truth was painful in the extreme, and though it hurts me to account for it, I never forgot the lesson.

The magnificent strutting peacocks she entertained on Sundays were the brothers of the Prince of Wales: a portly pair, booming and guffawing like much older men. They were William, Duke of Clarence – whose lecherous eye fell on me once and sent me scuttling back to the kitchen in a panic – and his wheezy younger brother the Duke of Sussex, who had apparently been a regular guest of Lord and Lady Hamilton when they lived in Naples. It turned out that Lady Hamilton continued to entertain them, regardless of the expense to her depleted purse and to her health, in the hopes that they would influence their brother, then the Prince Regent but soon to be King George IV. Her hope was that he in turn would press her plea to the Prime Minister, Lord Liverpool.

All these loathsome men held my Lady's fate in their sweaty hands. I imagine how they laughed as they rode home in their fancy carriages, replete with Lady Hamilton's port. To this day, I cannot bear the smell of port. The one who came into my room one night when I was sleeping, put his hand over my mouth and raped me – he reeked of it. Stale port and acrid sweat. A great fat body pinned me down and hurt me, though I struggled and scratched and fought for every single second of it. But I must not dwell on bitterness. What's done is done.

But Emma's suffering was not in vain, for I will never forget, nor will any woman who witnessed it. Men too, for there were good and loyal and kind men whose admiration and love for Emma Hamilton led them to try to save her. Men like Joshua Smith, leader of Southwark Borough Council, who it turned out had been propping up the whole hollow edifice of Lady Hamilton's glittering soirees, believing that justice would prevail, that Lord Liverpool would grant the pension that Lord Nelson had trusted would be hers, that his brother would honour the will and ensure the safety of his beloved Emma and their daughter.

But ironically, it was the very depth of that passion that brought her downfall, or more accurately the perfidy of another man, one she had trusted with her papers.

It was an April morning, a morning of tender leaves, young blossom, welcome sunshine. The night had been full of light from the fireworks celebrating Napoleon's abdication. Everyone seemed happy, full of hope. When the news came, the sky fell down. The Herald had a scoop: Lord Nelson's letters to Lady Hamilton were to be published, with all their intimacies, endearments, confessions and salacious details. I have never read them myself: I could not bear it.

She was ruined, all her hopes of respectability and acceptance dashed. It all happened so quickly that it was barely credible. Within days, she and Horatia were smuggled out of the country under cover of night and I was on my way to Ireland.

In truth, I did not know where else to go. In the two years I had spent with Lady Hamilton, I had seen my mother only once for a hasty exchange of news in the darkness of the garden of her lodging. The next time I went, the house was empty and they had left no forwarding address. My aunt's letter was by then some six years old, still safely folded into my book.

My favourite of the Bewick tailpieces was a tiny depiction of a farmyard. As is the way of these things, in the mind of the child that I still was, the image was inextricably linked with the words. One day, I would ride in an open cart through the fresh green air of Ireland, marveling at the rolling hills, the water running clear, and everywhere birds in a clear blue sky (for they burn peat in Ireland, I had learned, and rarely coal). A friendly old Irishman would pull up the cart at those gates, I would step down with my small valise, pick my way through the farmyard, delighting in the smells (I knew only horse manure, for the smell of which I still have an abiding fondness) and the door would be opened by a motherly housekeeper, whose physical appearance in my mind's eye was based closely on how I imagined Lady Hamilton's mother to have looked. She would be a fine, statuesque woman with a direct gaze and an immaculate pinny. Her eyes would widen and then soften in a smile, for my resemblance to her mistress would be clear to all, in fact the rest of the servants would gather in silent wonder. There would be much wide-eyed hushing, and then I would straighten my back and open the door of the room they indicated in excited whispers.

Ideally, the room would be a library, filled floor to ceiling with books. My aunt would look up from her page, preoccupied, her distracted expression immediately being replaced by a look of wonder, for would she not be looking into the face of the daughter she never had?

It would be a homecoming. And I would have a home.

It didn't quite work out like that, for is not my tale a one of unexpected twists and turns?

I would travel as a boy, I decided, much safer. In snatched evenings in Lady Hamilton's small library, I had by then read the Shakespeare plays recommended by Mr Palmer. 'Notice especially the independent young women, Molly. Learn from them. Make them your models. Be like strong and resourceful Viola; clever, wise Portia; and of course Perdita, the lost girl who survives.' In the hubbub of servants hastily packing and moving on, I quietly availed myself of my means of disguise.

Thus it was that a tall young man in voluminous scarf and oversized hat climbed aboard the mail coach at Euston that evening with only a tendril of curled red hair on his collar to give him away.

And give him away it did.

My companions were a rowdy bunch of Irishmen, laughing and singing until they all subsided into sleep. I hunched myself in the corner by the window and kept my counsel, fearful that my voice would betray me.

One was going home for a funeral, but the most talkative amongst them was going home for good. 'I cannot stand it any more – I'd rather starve in the green fields of Derry than choke to death on this London smog. I knew it when I first saw this godforsaken land – from Chester onwards – nothing but slag heaps, sickly fields, nothing like our emerald green! I cannot wait! My eyes are greedy for the green, so they are! And hills! What I would give to see the fields!'

All of this fed my fantasies of Ireland, and as the crowded coach rocked and creaked its way through the darkened streets of the capital, I pressed the side of my face against the glass, hungrily watching the houses fade to hovels, the gaslight recede and the red sky fade to black. I would not sleep, for fear of murmuring in my dreams.

Despite my efforts, my head dropped once or twice, but I summoned my will and pinched my palms inside my mittens. We stopped only once for a change of horses and drivers, and I pretended to be asleep whilst the others availed themselves of whatever comforts were on offer, and soon we were on our way again.

'I can smell the sea!' called out one of my company – his cry awoke me from a dribbling dream and my head snapped up, hurting my neck and briefly threatening to dislodge my cap. Whether they noticed that, or a stray tendril, or whether my voice gave me away in my sleep, I know not, but what was clear by the time we reached Holyhead was that the two men in the opposite corner knew or at least suspected my sex.

I had no idea what would happen when we reached the boat, nor did I have much concept of a paddle-steamer. What I did apprehend quickly was that I would be vulnerable at sea, for if they were hatching evil intentions, they needed only a dark corner aboard ship and I would be lost overboard, and no-one any the wiser. I don't think I had ever understood with such utter clarity how alone I was.

I would forgo my passage: wait for the next sailing. I would get down from the coach at the first opportunity and place myself in the care of some kindly woman or elderly couple. I could even offer myself for work, stay a few days, wait until the coast was clear and be on my way. The more I thought about it, the more appealing it seemed to spend some of my precious savings on a meal or maybe even a room for the night.

As soon as the coach rocked to a halt, I opened my door, dropped to the ground and hastened into the inn. Rapidly scanning the room, I saw a table in a corner where a lady in a demure bonnet sat with a boy of about ten. They were drinking soup and the child was making appreciative slurps which had the woman whispering and looking around the room as if expecting to be reprimanded for his ill manners. As I watched, a gentleman emerged from the back of the room and sat down opposite them.

Behind me, I sensed that the other passengers were entering the room. I didn't look round, but immediately went over to the family and spoke quickly to the gentleman. 'Sir, I apologise for the intrusion but may I sit with you and act as if I know you? I am travelling alone and fear for my safety.'

Bless him, the man did not change his expression one bit, but merely patted the seat beside him and I sat down and started chatting animatedly, I hoped in low enough tones to prevent anyone overhearing the banality of my observations. When the serving maid passed by, the gentleman asked for another bowl of soup.

I ate my soup in grateful silence, my back to the room. 'Have they gone?' He nodded. 'Would you mind watching my bag whilst I speak to the landlady?'

The serving-maid told me that the landlady was preparing a room and would be ten minutes, so I slipped out of the back of the inn towards the water-closet. I was feeling terribly nauseous again, so I stood in the cool night air and tried to breathe freshness into my lungs. Saliva filled my mouth and I swallowed and swallowed to try to avoid the inevitable. When I knew I would have to vomit, so I stumbled into the long grass and hoped not to be seen.

I jumped when I heard a voice, but it was female. 'Oh dear, pregnant are we?'

I couldn't see where it came from, so I put my head down and walked on towards the privy, hoping she was talking to someone other than me. It was a vain hope, I know, but it's hard to describe the effort of will it was taking for me to keep on believing that I was just travel sick, just suffering from a bug, had just eaten a bad piece of bread. I felt a deep conviction that if I could just get to Ireland, all would be well.

'Hello? You deaf as well as preggers?'

A girl about my own age was leaning against a wall at the back of the inn, smoking. Her long lank black hair hung in straggles about her pale face. I thought of ignoring her, as if that would make the truth go away: it seems mad when I think of it, but the mind does strange things when you're scared.

I stopped, straightened up and turned. 'Hello. No, I'm not deaf.'

'But you are pregnant?' She came forward, stubbing out the cigarette with the toe of her boot.

'It looks like I might be.'

'How far gone?'

'I don't know.'

'On the game, are you?'

'No.'

She shrugged. 'Well, I hope you've got another idea.'

Now that she was close to me, I saw how very pale her skin was and how marked with red blotches. Her shoulders were narrow and she shivered in the cold night air.

'What do you mean?'

'What ya gonna do? You got a plan?'

'I'm going to Ireland.'

Her immediate scorn shocked me. 'What? Yer barmy! Why would anyone want to go there? Yer mad.'

'Why?'

She grinned a sickly grin and stuck her grubby index finger up near my face. 'One, no-one'll help you cos they're all Catholic. Two, everyone's starving. And three, they're all coming over here.'

'I...I've got an aunt.'

'Catholic, is she?'

'Yes, I ... yes, she is.'

She turned away, dismissive. 'I think you must be a bit simple. Good luck.' And she disappeared.

When I came back into the inn, the couple with the little boy were just getting up to retire for the night. I was desperate to know what to do, so I did the only thing I could.

'Excuse me, madam. Could I have a word with you in private?'

She looked faintly alarmed, but after nodding at her husband, who then left with the boy, she walked with me back towards the table and we sat down.

'I'm sorry to have to ask you this, but I urgently need some advice.'

Her eyes softened, although I sensed a wariness. 'Are you entirely alone?'

'Yes, I am. I have an aunt in Ireland, and I was intending to travel to her, although...I do not know her.'

'Where does she live?'

'Tipperary.'

'Does she know you are coming?'

'No, she doesn't. The thing is, and I hope you will not judge me, but...' I suppose I hoped she would guess or say the words for me, but she didn't, although I saw something dawn in her eyes. She got up, and so did I. I would not be judged by this woman: I had done nothing wrong. My expression must have shown my indignation, because she looked startled and stayed where she was.

'If I were you,' she began carefully. 'I would reconsider. Do you have any other family in England?'

'No.' I was beginning to feel tearful, through I wrestled to control it. I hate to be pitied and I was still too angry at my first taste of what it is to be looked at as a 'fallen woman.' I put up my chin. 'I have money. I'm not begging. I'm looking for advice. If I do not go to Ireland, where shall I go?'

She seemed to settle then. 'Look,' she said. 'We are here to meet family from Ireland and take them back with us to Lancashire. There is plenty of work in the cotton industry. You may travel with us, I will offer that much. You must pay your own way, and when we get to Middleton, what you do is your own business.' She took a step away, looking ready to go before I had answered.

I didn't hesitate. 'What time do we leave?'

And Fate laughed.

Chapter 8

Every day I went out, often on errands for the family: on the outside, I was still the wild-eyed questioner of strangers. But as the weeks passed, I slowly became aware of a growing sense of calm. When I first confronted this, I had slept the whole way through a long November night. When I awoke in the cold grey morning, my first thought was guilt, as though by not having woken several times in the night to think of her, I had somehow let her down. As I often did at that time, I brought before my mind's eye the face of the woman: examined it, saw its kindness, thought of the firm cheer with which she had spoken, the glow of her health, her neat basket with its modest provisions. I found reassurance in this exercise. I could choose to believe that Charlotte was somewhere safe on this cold winter's morning, warmly wrapped in a woollen blanket and nestled in a wooden crib. A carved crib. A crib made with care, perhaps on rockers. That she would be woken with a kiss and gathered into loving arms.

As I lay on my back under the warm blankets and through brimming tears watched my breath billow and dissipate in the chill air, I thought back to my own mother, to the ease with which she had said goodbye. Did she think of me from time to time, and wonder where I was? If I heard that she was deeply distressed by my absence, would I go back? No, I knew I would not.

Suddenly, I understood. My mother had turned her back not through lack of love: it had been acceptance, perhaps even hope. She had done as much as she could to keep me safe until I was grown, and in the circumstances, that was a real achievement. (What had become of Jack?) At the time I had had only a vague idea of the dangers that surrounded us, which of course was down to her. I smiled when I remembered how at the age of twelve, I had watched her fluttering about, trying to protect the little ones from one of Father's rages: instead of being frightened or irritated, I had whispered to my sister some wise words from Bewick: "If a cat or other voracious animal should happen to come near the nest, the mother endeavours to divert it from the spot by a stratagem similar to that by which the partridge misleads the dog; she springs up, flutters from spot to spot, and by such means allures her enemy to a safe distance."

She had done all she could and I had grown into a strong and resourceful young woman who towered over her: I sensed she was a little in awe of me. I had been hurt when she had said such a blithe goodbye, but now I was a mother myself I found I understood. Charlotte might never be found, in fact, for the first time, I felt that as a real possibility. And what then? How would I live? Would I search for her for the rest of my days? I had no doubt that I would, but I had come to a new acceptance that there was a limit to my resources. All we can do is keep our children safe for as long as we can. I would never give up the search, but for the first time, I felt ready to look around me, take hold of the tiller of my boat and move forward, but in which direction?

The answer presented itself as soon as I asked myself the question.

I suppose I had always known that I would go to Gibside: the oft-overheard word was freighted with promise and danger: it intrigued me. My ideas were vague and unformed, my impressions confused: rights, entitlement, guilt...

And there was another place: Streatlam Castle. I was, after all, part of the Bowes family and so was Charlotte. They could help me: they had wealth, connections and power. Theirs was a great ship to which I could tie my small boat.

I had held onto the faint possibility that the woman could have heard Hannah call my name. The monogrammed handkerchief was tied around my baby's head: she would remove it, see the initials...I had told myself that she might show the handkerchief to someone who would recognize them. Mary Eleanor Bowes had been famous, notorious: I had learnt that in Emma Hamilton's house.

In that direction lay new hope. It seems absurd now, but when you have little, you cling on to what you have.

These people had been so kind. They had sheltered me and fed me and asked nothing in return. They had patted my hand and sat quietly beside me, night after night. They were the source of my new sense of calm: their way of being had seeped into mine. On that morning, I let it rise to the surface of my being and become part of me.

Quakers speak of an 'inner light' that cannot be extinguished: it might become dim; it might be reduced to a pinprick, but it could never die. The family's present guests, Ezra and Rebecca, had been visiting a relative who was being treated at the York Retreat, a Quaker hospital for the mentally ill - they would never use the word asylum – and I had been moved to hear the way in which they spoke of his affliction. Patients were given what Quakers believe they needed: not manacles and purges but peace, security, privacy, therapy, productive activity.

The family had given me what I needed. I felt an inner calm and the light within me was strong once again.

It was time to move on. I would go to Streatlam Castle.

Chapter 9

By the time we arrived in Barnard Castle, Ezra and Rebecca were my firm friends: it took us seven hours to travel the sixty miles – all the hours of daylight a grey November day had to offer, and I spoke more in that journey than I had spoken for months. I had learned enough of the ways of the Society to blend in, although I remained silent and contemplative when they spoke of the scriptures, which they often did. I told them about what had happened in Manchester, that I had no immediate family but was hoping that my distant relatives would be able to provide me with help and support in my distress.

'And what is the name of your relatives, Molly?'

'Bowes.'

Rebecca's serene face registered not a ripple of surprise, which was somewhat disappointing as I was eager to learn what I could of the family's reputation. 'And they live in Barnard Castle?'

'I believe so, yes.'

'If you are unsure, someone there will know. Ezra's mother will be able to help, I am sure, for she has lived there all her life.'

'There is a great family of that name, I believe?'

'Yes, at Streatlam Castle, just outside the town. And of course there is the town of Bowes, three miles in the other direction, where others of that name no doubt reside. You will find your people, Molly, be assured.'

'I should like to be independent, though. I would like to find work, if that were possible.'

'Ezra's mother will no doubt be able to help you there: her husband's ironmongery business is now run by Ezra's brother. There is plenty of work to be had for those who are sober, industrious and honest. But fear not, whilst you find your feet, you will be given shelter and food without having to earn it. It is our way.'

Just as she had promised, I was accepted without question, given a small plain room under the eaves and left to my own devices. I maintained my quiet, downcast ways and moved through the house, the shop and the offices like a ghost. Watching, always watching and learning.

Free to roam about in the handsome market town, on the second day I set out for Bowes, three miles to the west, intrigued to see the ruined castle of that name. The road was straight and flat, bordered by trees in autumnal reds and golds. Beyond them, I glimpsed gently rolling hills to north and south, and as I walked, I felt uplifted. I stopped a while at the side of the road and listened to the birdsong: a new energy and hope came to me. This was a very beautiful place. I breathed the clean sweet air into my lungs and held it there.

Bowes was a small town with a sloping main street above which the small ruined castle was visible. I don't know what I expected to see or feel: I suppose that it was a way of learning about the area, building my confidence before I actually presented myself to the Bowes family at Streatlam. I knew nothing whatsoever about them: they might not even be in residence. All I knew was that I had to try.

Returning quickly to Barnard Castle, I went straight to the carter and asked about deliveries to Streatlam Castle. He agreed to take me the following day.

In my dark clothes and demure bonnet, I must have looked a curious sight beside the broad-shouldered carter in his rough fustian breeches and braces. As we rode along, he plied me with questions to which he received minimal answers. My heart was fluttering with nerves and I struggled to breathe in the cold November air. Several times I thought of leaping down and running back to the safety of my monastic cell.

We turned off the road into a wide sweep of cultivated park sloping downwards. No house was visible and the track wound downhill for over half a mile. Single oaks stood in isolation in the still air, their leaves pale gold in the clear light.

When the house came into view, it took my breath, for I had never seen such a large and splendid isolated building. Three storeys high, with three domed towers looming above and a columned portico for an entrance. There were at least a dozen windows on each floor – how many rooms must it have? For one family? My mind spun. And this had belonged to my father? I could barely comprehend that he could once have lived here and been brought so low as to die in prison. What had he done?

On a stone bench under the shade of a curiously limbed evergreen tree sat two figures in close conversation. It was too dark to see them, but I watched as the cart rocked past and neither of them turned a head to look at us.

The carter drove round to the side of the house, leapt down and knocked on a door, which was opened by a small round woman the shape of a cottage loaf. 'Rory! Come on in and take a bite. Who's yer friend, like?'

'Quaker lass from the town, wanted a look at the place. Yer comin in Molly?'

'No thank-you, I'll stretch my legs. How long will you be?'

'Well I've to gan up to the stables after I've had a drink and a bite, so an hour should do it?'

'I'll be back here in an hour. Thank-you.'

I walked back round the corner to the front of the house and stood in the darkness watching the two figures: they had left the bench and were walking slowly towards the portico of the house. I saw that though they were of a similar height, they were perhaps mother and young son. The woman was petite with an ample bosom. The boy no more than ten, tall and loose-limbed but stooped in sorrow. Both were in mourning clothes.

I could not intrude. But I must. In an agony of indecision, I forced my feet forward and emerged from the cold shade, only to stop, frozen with what? The enormity of my situation took a grip on my senses and immobilized me.

I had not seen a gardener approach but a soft male voice came from behind me. 'Go on, introduce yourself. Miss Bowes will not stand on ceremony.'

'Miss Bowes? Is that not Lord Strathmore's widow?'

'No, it is his sister, Mary Bowes. She is often here, though she lives in Bath. Go on, she is kind and friendly.'

I did as he said, walked quickly across the gravel and stood with my head bowed before the steps. They were still some yards away but could not fail to notice me. I stood holding my breath with my heart and mind racing. I felt I should faint.

The gravel crunched and I looked up. 'Miss Bowes, forgive my presumption, but if you would allow me to introduce myself.'

Something in her expression became alert and her focus sharpened. Sliding her arm from that of her nephew, she stepped forward and squinted up into my face. Her expression was curious but kind.

'Forgive me, young lady, but for a moment there I was reminded of someone I once knew, and it was not a happy recognition. But it is gone now.' She stepped back and linked her nephew's arm again. He continued to stand still, looking at the ground.

'I...' her response had disarmed me, and for a moment my spirit failed, for though I knew not what the reaction would be when I revealed my identity, I feared rejection and anger most of all.

I looked again at the bowed head of the boy, and Miss Bowes followed my gaze. 'You go on inside, John, and I'll follow you momentarily.'

He lifted his head slowly and I saw his large grey eyes were red and raw from crying. He looked at me without interest, and then with a flicker of impatience, said, 'What is it? Who is this?' with what seemed to me like an attempt to sound like a man.

Miss Bowes patted his arm. 'Now, John, courtesy please. This young lady clearly has something she wishes to say to me.'

'To both of you, really. If I'm not intruding.'

'Well I have to say that this is not the best time, but you are clearly a bold young woman with something pressing to say, so out with it, come come.'

I took a deep breath. 'My name is Molly Bowes.'

I saw her register what I had said with no evidence of surprise, merely a nod, as if it was what she had suspected. But how could she?

'Ah. That accounts for it. I have no wish to be cruel, Molly Bowes, but whatever you expect by coming here, you will be disappointed, I'm afraid. You are not the first.'

'Not the first?'

She looked over my shoulder, where the gardener was probably listening whilst appearing to go about his business.

'I have no wish to humiliate you, my dear. I suggest you return to assist the carter and then leave as you arrived. There is nothing for you here.'

'But you don't understand, I have not come in hope of gain. I have come because we share a name.' And suddenly, the threat of tears blocked my throat.

She had not noticed my distress and made as if to move past me.

'Wait! Please! My baby!'

She stopped now, and the boy too, both arrested by my desperate outburst.

'Your baby?'

'Charlotte. She was taken from me this summer, in Manchester. The woman who took her lives in this area, I am sure of it. She may think that I am dead, but…'

'Dead? Why my dear, calm yourself.' She put her small hand on my wrist, and it was a warm and surprisingly strong grip. I took a deep, shuddering breath.

'John, if you would like to wait inside, I shan't be long.' The boy seemed unwilling to respond but stood and watched me, his face impassive. 'No? Very well then. Now Molly, start again please. Explain yourself.'

'I was in Manchester, at a rally in St Peter's Field.' I saw her hand go to her face, and the boy stood up straighter too. 'I see you have heard of it.'

'The Peterloo Massacre. Horrific. An abomination. I am sorry to hear it, Molly. And your baby?'

'I was with friends, other weavers from Middleton. We sat on a high wall overlooking the field, the wall of the Friends' Meeting House. A woman offered to hold my baby. When it happened, I was pulled off the wall and trampled and I never saw my baby again. I followed the woman to York, and searched there for weeks. Charlotte has distinctive red curly hair. There was a possible sighting but the trail has gone cold. I don't know what to do. My only hope is that the woman knows Charlotte's name is Bowes. Perhaps she will contact your family…'

'A desperate story indeed. I am very sorry to hear it, Molly. I trust you have posted bills in York and Manchester? Well then, I can think of nothing more you can do.'

Seeing my expression, she took both my hands in hers. 'But you have done the right thing, dear. Leave us your address and I will ensure that all the staff are aware of it.'

I did not know how to respond. This was not enough. I was angry.

'But we are related, you and I! Charlotte is your relative! There must be more you can do!'

Her expression became stern and she started a sentence she did not complete: 'How dare…' and then collected herself. 'Molly, you must understand two things. The first is that there are many young people like yourself who claim a connection to this family. The second is that this is a house in deep mourning, and as sorry as I am for your distress, I must tell you that you are in fact intruding. Now good day.'

And before I could think how to respond, they were gone. From the darkness of the hall, I saw the boy's white face give me one last rueful look before the door closed behind them.

I swiftly returned to the kitchen door, where the carter was sitting outside on a barrel, his face turned to the weak sun. When he saw me, he creaked to his feet. 'We off then?'

'Well you are. I've been offered a job.'

He turned an incredulous face to me. 'A job? What – here? What as, pray tell?'

'Miss Bowes said they'll find me work in the kitchens. I've to see the cook now. You go on up to the stables. If I'm not here when you come back, go home without me. I can walk.'

Complaining under his breath, he grunted up into his seat and flicked the reins. I waited until he had gone before I knocked.

'Miss Bowes said I could ask whether you have any work.'

The loaf-shaped woman squinted up at me. 'Oh she did, did she? I very much doubt that.'

Impatient and frustrated, I pulled off my bonnet. I wanted to shake out my hair. I wanted to shout. I felt I should run mad. But I must keep control if I was to ingratiate myself into this house. I had been impulsive. I must make amends.

'I'm sorry, I lied. But I am desperate.' The break in my voice was not forced: suddenly, the whole situation had become too much for me and the tears began.

'Oh my dear, come on inside. Sit you down and tell me all about yourself while I make you a cup of tea.'

I sat down at the large oak table and held my handkerchief against my face whilst I covertly gaped at the enormous kitchen, the rows of gleaming pans, the shelves groaning with preserves, the doors leading who knew where? Such a house I could never have imagined. And my father...

The kindly housekeeper listened to my story then patted my hand and left the room. Five minutes later, she returned, touched my hand and said, 'Come along, Molly. Miss Bowes has agreed to talk to you.'

I followed Alice through carpeted corridors whose walls were adorned with paintings large and small, many in ornate gilded frames. Pausing outside a gleaming oak door, she knocked and then opened the door on a room in which Miss Bowes was sitting and writing at a large desk. She did not look up. Alice motioned for me to go in and she closed the door. I listened for her footsteps but heard none: she was listening outside the door.

Miss Bowes finished her writing, placed the pen on a golden cradle, looked up and her face lit with a smile. 'Ah, I see you are a beauty, Molly Bowes! You hide yourself away in your Quaker garb.' She stood up. 'A wise decision, I imagine you would attract unwanted attention otherwise.'

'Yes. I am alone in the world and must be careful.'

'You are not a Quaker then?'

'In all but name. No, I am not a member of the Society of Friends but I am of their mind about how to live.'

'Entirely?'

Flustered, I managed to answer: 'Well, perhaps not entirely. I do miss decorative beauty. My eyes thirst for colour and invention.'

'I hear you have succeeded in getting your feet under the kitchen table. You are a determined young woman. You wish to be a maid, Alice tells me. Alas, it is not in my gift for this is my sister-in-law's house now.' As she stood up, I heard her mutter, 'For the time being anyway.' She came round the desk to look at me more closely. 'But I will mention you to ... the Dowager Countess. I trust you have the proper references?'

'Yes, I worked as a maid in London. I have a reference from Lady Hamilton.'

She looked up at me then with real interest.

'London? Lady Hamilton? I thought you said you were from Manchester?'

'I travelled to Manchester after father died.'

'Forgive me for asking, Molly, but do you mean your real father? You knew him, then?'

'Why yes, of course!'

'Who was your father, Molly?'

'His name was Andrew Robinson Stoney Bowes.'

She nodded. 'It is as I thought. But you actually knew him?'

'Yes, of course. We all lived together. Why do you ask?'

She was clearly digesting this news.

'How old are you, Molly?'

'Twenty-two.'

'Then you were born while he was in prison.' Her tone was sorrowful. She sat on the edge of a flowery sofa and patted the seat beside her. 'Sit down here, child. Tell me all about yourself.'

When I'd finished, and I told her everything, she sighed and lay back on the chair.

'...and so I know full well that my Father was a scoundrel of some sort. But he was my father and the only one I've known, and although I know nothing of the story, I understand it was divorce that brought him low.'

'Yes, quite so.' Having fallen into a reverie, she seemed to recollect herself. She sat up straighter, looked at me intently, then got up and walked to the window to stare out at the park.

'What do you know about your father?'

'Only that he was born in Ireland and came to Newcastle as a soldier. That he married Lady Strathmore but they divorced. He said many things about her, but I know enough not to repeat them.'

She turned from the window to cast me a sharp look. 'Nor indeed to believe them.' It wasn't a question.

There was a silence that lasted some minutes. Finally, I said softly, 'Miss Bowes, I have no conception of what relation he was to you. I am sorry ... I merely hoped that if the woman was to try to find my baby's family, this is where she might come.'

She didn't answer immediately, but then slowly turned and came back to sit beside me.

'I want you to understand that I do not need to tell you anything, Molly, but I am mindful of your situation and I pity it.'

I bridled and sat up straighter, snapping before I could stop myself, 'I do not ask for pity.'

She smiled, but her smile was haunted. 'I see you have a temper.'

I subsided. 'Yes, I'm afraid I do. I cannot help it sometimes. Like my father.'

Her eyes flashed. 'Oh, he could help it. Never lose sight of that. And you can too. You must learn to master that temper and not let it master you.'

She looked at me again and her eyes softened. 'Tell me about your mother.'

'She was called Mary Sutton but she got Polly. She was from Essex. She was seventeen when she had me. I am the eldest of five.'

'And she met your father in London?'

'Yes, in the King's Bench Prison. Her father was in debt.'

'And she was still with your father when he died?'

'Yes.'

She looked at me wonderingly and then said. 'She must have been very special, your mother.'

'Yes, she was. She was quiet and gentle but strong. And resourceful.'

She smiled a sad smile. When I think of this conversation, of all that she could have said, my respect for Mary Bowes knows no bounds.

We sat in what felt like companionable silence for some time, side by side on the sofa, lost in our own thoughts.

Finally, seeming to come to some decision, she stood up and looked down at me, though when I sat up straighter to hear what she had to say, we were almost eye-to-eye.

'I am touched by your story and I am struck by your pragmatism. What I am going to tell you might surprise you. I have more understanding of your past that you might suspect. We have much in common, you and I. My mother was Mary Eleanor Bowes, the Countess of Strathmore. When she conceived me, she was a young widow with five children. She never married my father. His name was George Grey. Instead, for reasons you may learn one day, she married an Irish soldier.'

My face must have registered my shock.

'Yes, one and the same. Andrew Robinson Stoney married my mother whilst she was carrying me. I see your eyes soften. You think he did it through kindness. I will say no more on that point, Molly, but suffice it to say that he did not know she was pregnant.'

She paused, watching me absorb this information. 'I was born only a few months after they married, and the date of my actual birth they attempted to disguise for the sake of my reputation. Do not be embarrassed, Molly, for you know, as the scholar Robert Burton put it "Almost in every kingdom the most ancient families have been at first princes' bastards."

I barked a shocked laugh, so astonishing was it to hear such a word come out of such a lady's mouth. 'Ha! Forgive me, Miss Bowes, but I have been spending time amongst religious folk, and I am mindful of what the Bible has to say on the matter.' A slight nod gave me leave to go on: "A bastard shall not enter into the congregation of the Lord; even to his tenth generation shall he not enter into the congregation of the Lord." Deuteronomy 23, verse 2.'

'Ah yes, the Bible. "Visit not the sins of the father upon their children." I much prefer a rousing Shakespearean quotation: 'I grow, I prosper! Now gods, stand up for bastards!" And comically she shook her fist towards the chandelier.

The tension between us dissolved in that moment, and we laughed together at the ridiculousness of the world.

'You see, my dear? We have more in common than you dreamed! We have bonded over bastardy!'

Suddenly serious, she said, 'And alas, we have another innocent member of our select coterie, for young John's parents were not married at the time of his birth. I fear that the boy will suffer for it.'

She turned away, clearly minded to bring the conversation to an end.

I stood up and spoke to her back: 'Thank-you, Miss Bowes. I am honoured that you trusted me with this information.'

Her laugh was sad and cynical, 'Oh, fear not for the whole world knows the circumstances of my birth. They learnt it when I was sixteen years old and about to make my entrance to London society, thanks to…' but she stopped herself and shook her head. 'And so, my dear, I must go now, but is there anything more you would wish to know before I take my leave?'

Oh so much! I did not want to be parted from her at all, but if I must, then I should learn all I could about the family's current situation. 'So, as I understand it, the gentleman who has recently died, Lord Strathmore, John's father, was your half-brother?'

'Yes. Eleanor had five children to the 9th Earl, and John was the eldest. Then she married Stoney and I was born. Later she had one other child to him, William, who has since drowned at sea. They divorced and…'

'…and I know the rest.'

'Oh my dear, I'm afraid you don't know the half of it, but you know all you need to know.'

Chapter 10

I returned to Barnard Castle on foot, somewhat deflated but also nursing the pleasure of having such a connection to such a wonderful woman, and to have it acknowledged. I regretted that she lived so far away and was soon to return to her home in Bath, but I had promised to write to her when I found a situation and perhaps she would reply.

It seemed a vague hope that I would be offered work in the castle. I imagined myself living there, albeit in the servants' quarters: such a quiet house, the very air breathing sadness, people coming and going, having hushed conversations about inheritance. I had thought that I could make my life there; that I could stay in the heart of the Bowes family and wait for Charlotte to be returned. But I was fooling myself: I knew that now.

Entering the town, I passed an ironmonger's cart pulled up at the side of the road; a strapping young man with fair hair was leaning against it while he chatted to another. They both stood up straighter as I approached and I realized I'd been striding out unaware. I must have left my bonnet at Streatlam. I dropped my gaze and altered my walk but it was too late. One of them called out, 'You look like your head's on fire!'

The other nudged him so hard that he staggered. I ignored them both and walked on briskly towards my destination.

Moments later, I became conscious of someone walking by my side. 'Sorry about that. My friend there is very rude. You have beautiful hair. Haven't noticed you before. Are you staying at the inn?'

I stopped and squinted up at him, startled to see how handsome he was, his own hair a blond halo lit from behind by November sunshine.

He smiled, clearly aware of his impression on me, and then bowed low. 'Joseph Raine at your service. And you are?'

'Molly Bowes.'

'Bowes eh?' We were standing outside the inn's archway and he patted the mounting block, which was in full sun. 'Come, sit beside me and tell me all about yourself, Molly Bowes.'

I hesitated only briefly and sat down beside him, turning my face to the sun. I was conscious of him looking, but I said nothing, just enjoying the rest and the warmth on my face.

'Are you the one that Rory took to Streatlam Castle then?'

'Yes, why?'

'He was moaning about it, but he said you were a Quaker. You don't look like a Quaker.'

'I do when I wear a bonnet. I left it at Streatlam.'

He jumped up. 'I can take you back if you like.'

'No need, I don't think I'll wear it anymore.'

'He said you'd got a job there?'

'Yes, if I want it. Not sure I do.'

He sat back down and was quiet for a few moments before he tried a new tack: 'Did you see the arch?'

'Yes, I noticed an arch. Why?'

'They say it was built for love.'

'Really? Who built it?'

'George Bowes, the late Lord's grandfather. He had married a young heiress from down south and he had it built to welcome her the first time she came here.'

'How romantic. That's a lovely story.'

'Not so lovely. She died. She was only fourteen. He never got over it, they say. Took against Streatlam. Never really lived here again, though he kept his racehorses here. Preferred his other house up Newcastle way. Sad really.' When I didn't answer, he tried again: 'They're not very lucky in love, these Boweses. Pots of money like, but not much luck.' I still didn't answer. 'How about you? You lucky in love?'

I couldn't help but smile though I kept my lips tight shut: I didn't want to be too encouraging. In truth, I was enjoying this: it had been a long time since I had had a frivolous conversation with anyone, let alone a handsome young man of my own age. But he saw what he wanted to see, as they do.

'I love your hair. Not seen any like that, ever.'

I turned to him, meeting his eyes for the first time. They were dark blue with long blond lashes. I don't know whether he was more startled by the eye contact or the sudden seriousness with which I spoke: 'If you ever do see hair like mine on a baby, you must tell me.'

'I don't understand. How do you mean?'

'A little girl, under a year old, with hair like mine. If you ever see a child like that, you must tell me.'

'What if I told you I have seen just such a one?'

I leapt up and gripped his arms. 'You have? When? Where?'

Taken aback by my agitation, he stuttered, 'I-I'm not sure. A couple of weeks ago maybe. Market day in Middleton. Just noticed it because the bairn was crying.'

Instantly my heart contracted. The thought of Charlotte in distress without me to comfort her was agony.

I took a deep breath and sat down beside him. I must extract the full story, not scare him off. Any detail at all. "Middleton? Where is that?'

'Middleton-in-Teesdale, up the valley. It's where I live.'

'Think back, please, it's very important. Tell me what you saw.'

'Well let's think, it was a rainy day, towards the end of the market, people taking stalls down and counting up. Everything grey and a bit subdued like. Heavy rain all day, not good for the market. Sun never came out. I was stood outside our shop talking to my dad. Suddenly a shrieking set up, fit to crack the windows, and a woman walked past carrying a little lass wiggling and screaming, you know, like they do, temper tantrum, and she's pulled off her bonnet and the woman stopped and put her down and fastened her bonnet and the little lass is screaming and waving her little fists. Anyway, such a grey day and this pop of colour all of a sudden, bright orange, even brighter than yours. I'd never seen the like before. No-one round here's got hair that colour.'

'How small, the child, when she put her down?'

'Oh just tiny, you know, not standing yet. Maybe she could…Oh, I don't know!'

'And the woman? Can you tell me anything about her?'

'Not really, didn't look at her, just caught a glimpse of this flash of hair. Dark dress, that's all I remember. Didn't see her face. Why?'

I thought quickly. I didn't want to leave Streatlam, but it was not in my nature to sit and wait for something that might never happen, and I had to face it, if the woman was going to give Charlotte back, she'd have done it by now.

'Is there work to be had in Middleton, Joseph? For such as me?'

His face brightened. 'Well now, funny you should ask - my dad was only saying this morning we're short-handed in the shop. We've an ironmongery. Me mam's not too good and now my sister's got married, he's just got me and a daft lass from the village who's only fit to clean the shelves. He's a soft touch, my dad. He's always on at me to get back quick from my rounds, but I like to take my time and sit and have a bit craic. Like this. Though not often with anyone as pretty as you.'

'Are you going back now?'

'I'm away up to the stables, then yes, all done and I'll be going back.'

'How long until you leave?'

'Fifteen minutes if I'm quick, an hour if I get chatting.'

'I'll be back here in an hour and I'd like to come to Middleton with you please. If your dad likes me and offers me the job, will I be able to stay with your family?'

'Well I don't like to say. It's all a bit sudden but I can't imagine it'll be a problem. Even if they don't want to give you my sister's room, there's a little one in the attic you could share with the skivvy. That's if you don't mind, like. And there's boarding houses.'

Joseph was a gentle giant, powerfully built and softly spoken. If I hadn't been so determined to remain independent, I had no doubt that a future as an ironmonger's wife would be mine for the taking. His shy sideways glances told me that his running commentary on the attractions of life in Middleton-in-Teesdale was not just an expression of civic pride. 'It's a fine place to live. We have everything needful here in our sheltered valley, and now the London Lead Company have made us their northern headquarters...well, the town's on the up. Look at that, for instance.' It was clearly a fine new building with a hipped roof and a clock tower. 'That's the company yard. That's where the offices and stables are. That big house over there? That's just finished, that is. Fine isn't it? That's Middleton House, where the company superintendent lives. There's plans to build what they're calling a model village for the workers. They'll all have allotments attached. Every house with a long garden to grow their own veg. It's a big thing with the company, horticulture. Good for the soul, they say. They really look after the workers, you know. They provide doctors, wash houses, evening classes, there's a brass band...'

He noticed me looking at the swiftly flowing stream as we crossed a bridge. 'That's Hudeshope Beck: it powers our corn mills on its way to join the River Tees.' Behind the handsome sandstone houses, ploughing terraces patterned the steep valley sides and above the terraces, the moors filled the horizon.

We drove through Horsemarket and pulled up outside a handsome shop frontage above which were painted the words, 'J.Raine and Son, Ironmonger.'

Mr Raine was very much like his son, broad-shouldered, blond and soft-spoken. Deliberately to increase my power and to signal to myself that I was moving on to a new stage of fresh hope, I had done my hair in two thick plaits and coiled and fastened them into a loose arrangement on the top of my head. As we came into the shop, Mr Raine's reaction to seeing me come in with Joseph was a picture. His mouth actually dropped open, and when he heard that I'd come to enquire about a job, he hastened to pull up a chair in front of the counter and sit down in front of me, scrutinising my face with an air of wonder that was partly gratifying but eventually uncomfortable.

'Mr Raine, I hate to say this, but is there something about my face that disturbs you? A smut perhaps?'

He was instantly abashed and I felt sorry to have been the cause. "No, no, far from it, sorry to stare. We get used to seeing the same old faces around here, and you'll notice a lot of us all look alike, big-boned, fair-haired. You're a sight for sore eyes, if you don't mind me saying, Miss ...?'

'Bowes.'

He blinked once and then got up, and it seemed to me that he was avoiding my eyes, whether through embarrassment at my challenge to his gaze or because of the revelation of my name, I knew not.

The job was mine, as was the sister's room.

As soon as I had put my bag on the bed, I asked Joseph to show me around the town and point out where he had seen the child. Mr Raine raised no objection, although he had clearly been waiting for Joseph to come back from Barnard Castle to man the shop. As we walked briskly about, I cautioned myself that I must not take advantage of these good people. I would work hard and earn my keep.

My short time with the Raine family passed pleasantly: they were kind and humorous people and they took me to their hearts, teasing me gently for jumping and whirling round every time the bell rang, forever sure that the next person through the door would be carrying my baby daughter. Whenever I wasn't behind the counter, I walked the streets asking the same question.

It was in the third week when my new handbills had just been printed that I had my breakthrough. I rushed back to the shop, my face aflame with excitement. I rushed straight to my room to pack, brushing past Daisy the skivvy on the narrow staircase. I shut my door behind me and sat on the bed to gather my wits and steady my breath.

At supper, I broke the news to them. Immediately, Joseph burst out, 'Why would you want to go to Stanhope?'

'Because a woman and a red-haired baby were aboard a cart that went that way two days ago.'

'It's a wild goose chase. Stay here where you're safe. You're needed here.'

Mr Raine chomped loudly on his chop bone, took a swig of ale and announced, 'Stanhope's a wicked place: Wesley said so.'

'Aye, like dad says, they're wild there.'

'Well I think if the London Lead Company hadn't come, we'd a bin wild ere.'

I couldn't help but be curious. 'How do you mean?'

'The price of lead. That's what I mean. Since the end of the wars and that, lead prices…miners in Stanhope are starving.'

'I'm sorry Mr Raine, I don't understand. How did the end of the wars affect the price of lead?'

'All them musket balls? Where do you think they came from? Weardale, that's where! The price of lead went up and up. But then... well, we know what happened then. And they've no common land, you know, not any more. There's men starving. Good men an' all. That's how the battle kem about.'

'See what I mean?' Joseph said to his father. 'She knows nowt. She's an innocent.'

Turning to me, his face a picture of earnestness, he said, ' Stay here, Molly. Don't go to Stanhope.' His voice was openly imploring now, and I saw his father look at him with pity in his eyes.

'I think the lass has made her mind up, Joseph. We'll have to let her go, though we'll have you back, Molly, don't you worry about that. Like a shot, won't we Joseph? Don't look so stricken, lad.'

The doorbell rang then, so I made myself scarce. The following morning, when I came back into the shop, Joseph had gone and his father was climbing up and down a stepladder loading heavy items onto shelves.

'I'll help you, Mr Raine. It's the least I can do. Thank-you for being so understanding. I have to follow it up. It might indeed be a wild goose chase, but I cannot....' Suddenly upset, for I was genuinely fond of these people, I hastened to change the subject.

Conversationally, as I handed him a densely packed box, I asked, 'So you were saying about the Battle of Stanhope, Mr Raine? I was quite alarmed to hear they are such warlike people over in the next valley?'

'Not to worry, lass, they had cause. A band of starving lads went up the dale to get what they could to eat, moorhens mostly. But it's the Bishop's hunting ground up there, allus has been. "The fat man of Auckland and Durham the same / Laid claim to the moors and likewise the game." Deer everywhere. All for sport. Imagine how that plays when you're a good man, working hard, who can't afford to feed yer family. Moorhens is all they were after, as you'd call red grouse.'

He heaved a great box out from under the counter. 'But oh no, they weren't to be allowed even that, sent word he did. And laws too: the dogs to have claws taken out of their front feet to protect his fekkin deer. Fekker. But the Weardale men told him to go whistle his orders to the wind. So the Bishop's army's dispatched to deal with em.'

'The Bishop has an army?'

'Aye, these Prince Bishops have always had an army. They're like the kings of Durham. They've a Castle next to their cathedral for to keep their army in. So the army comes trooping along and sets about rounding up poachers. Locks 'em up in the cellar of the inn overnight. But no no no, Stanhope's having none of that. Word spread, men gathered round the inn. Pitched battle. Bloodshed. Lots of it. Soldiers mostly. Miners freed, off up the dale and away. And you've to understand, this is rebellion to the Bishop. He can hang 'em for it.'

'People actually died? Attacked by soldiers?' I sighed, 'I was in a battle too, where unarmed people were killed by soldiers.'

'Peterloo? Aye, we heard about that. Bad business. No, make no mistake, these lads weren't unarmed. Sent the troops back to Durham a few men less, and with their tails between their legs. Hahaha! He's not been back since.'

He started to fold the stepladder. 'What date are we? It's the fair next week. There'll be plenty going over to Stanhope for that: there's a lot of to-ing and fro-ing nowadays, especially for the fairs. Never used to be like that: my granddad used to say they were savages over there, spoke a different language.'

'Really? How far away is it?'

'Only ten miles or so, but it might as well have been a hundred in them days. Goes back to the olden times, different breeds. Different language, different looks apparently. I never thought about it much, but I've been going to classes. Vikings settled in this valley. Them over in Weardale were Anglo-Saxons, always fighting among themselves. Called becks and burns 'hopes'. Makes no sense. Stanhope means stony valley. And it is. So think on what you're leaving behind, Molly.'

But leave I did, sitting on the back of a cart on bumpy tracks that zig-zagged up the steep valley sides, green at first with a scattering of small farms at lower levels, but when we reached the high moorland, the grass was overtaken by gorse and bushes and low-lying trees that swept to one side like Bewick's windy landscapes.

My companion was a kindly old chap who spoke at length about every natural feature we saw. He asked nothing of me but an attentive ear, just turning occasionally to check that I was still listening, giving me a toothless smile and carrying on. He described rocks and landscapes, spoke of moving continents, tropical seas, molten rock and ice sheets, minerals and mining. 'These uplands are no good for farming, just sheep,' he said. 'It's hard dolerite rock, part of the whin sill. These upland grasslands – there's lovely flowers, ones as love the lime. You'll have to come back in the spring. There's wild thyme, common rock rose, fairy flax, spring gentian, Teesdale violet....Lovely. So delicate but tough. Like a good woman, eh Molly?'

We crested a rise and there below us lay Stanhope, hidden in a fold, deep in the green ribbon of the River Wear. With a flutter in my chest, I thought of Charlotte, also hidden but possibly close, possibly even just down there in that lush valley.

Soon we had descended the green terraces and reached the valley bottom, the embrace of trees meeting over our heads as we passed a large farm by the river that he said was called 'Unthank', swooshed across the icy water of the ford, along the river bank and up into the market-place.

As we clopped into the market square, I looked around me and saw the Parish church of St Thomas and opposite, a large turreted building that looked like a newly-built medieval castle. Two public houses faced each other: one called the Black Bull which was the site of the battle of the Bonny Moorhen, and the other well-named the Packhorse: a line of pannier-laden animals stood tied to a rail outside, their breath billowing into the darkening afternoon. Handsome sandstone houses glowed pale in the winter light.

When the cart rocked to a halt, I dismounted, lifted down my bag and before I bade farewell to my companion, I asked him, 'Is this where carts always drop off their passengers?'

'The market-cross, yes. It's a general meeting place.'

I looked around and had the strongest feeling that I was getting close, that here in the air that surrounded me was air breathed out by my own sweet Charlotte, that on the ground near me I might find a curl of russet hair.

On a stone bench a wizened old woman watched me through the smoke of her clay pipe. I sat down beside her, as if to pass the time of day.

'It's a fine town.'

'Was.'

'Have you always lived here?'

'Yup.'

'This your favourite spot?'

'Aye.'

'Do you always watch the comings and goings here?'

'What you after?'

To my own surprise, tears sprang to my eyes. I was almost afraid of asking the question. 'Two days ago, did you happen to notice a woman arrive with a baby?' I turned so that I could watch her reaction when I said the crucial words. She was watching me, impassive. 'Not yet a year old. A girl. With red hair.' I saw it. I saw the flicker in her eyes, though not a muscle of her face moved. She looked away and took a drag on her pipe.

After a silence that lasted an age, she muttered, 'Might've.'

'If you did, what would it take for you to tell me which way they went?'

'Shillin.'

'That's a lot. How do I know you're telling the truth?'

'Curly.'

'That's a guess. You can see I've got curly hair and you've put two and two together.'

She snorted and carried on puffing her pipe.

I got up and made to go, although I had no intention of it. She let me walk a few steps before she croaked, 'Shillin.'

Quickly I went back to the bench and crouched before her. 'Please. I have very little money and I am desperate. My baby was stolen four months ago. If you have seen her, please tell me.'

The walnut skin of her forehead crumpled and I thought I saw a flicker of something like pity in her eyes. There was a rustling under her shawl and she extended a bony claw, palm up. 'Shillin.'

I took out my purse and placed a shiny coin on her palm, but held it there, ready to withdraw. She held my eyes, and then with one nod of her head, indicated the castellated building across the road.

For a moment, my courage faltered. 'Whose is that house?'

'Cuthbert Rippon.'

'Cuthbert Rippon?'

'Aye. He's a one. Does as he likes. Has his trollop in there while his wife lives not far away in another great house. Does just as he likes. I like to watch the comins and goins. Masons, all of em. Jack Lambton, I saw once.'

'Who's Jack Lambton?'

'Who's Jack Lambton?' Scornful, then curious. 'Where you from then?'

'Manchester.'

'Oh aye? What's that like then?'

'Smoky. Grey. Wet. Dirty. Wretched.'

'Fekkin hell.'

'Yes, it was.'

'And your little lass?'

'Someone took her. Have you heard of the massacre?'

'Yes.'

'We were there. A woman held my baby. I was trampled. She was gone.'

There was a long silence. We watched a long line of pack-horses trail towards the pub.

'Knock at the kitchen door and ask for Colleen.'

Chapter 11

My hands shook as I tied my scarf at the nape of my neck so that no stray hairs should give me away and alert her to my mission. The door was opened by a tall footman: his stiff livery jacket hung open, his collar was unfastened and in his hand was a large glass of something black. When I asked for Colleen, he turned without a word and led me through to the back of the dark house. Our footsteps echoed on the bare boards.

He opened the door on a nondescript room lit by a solitary candle. When I stepped through, he shut it and I listened to his footsteps creak away. I stood still in the semi-darkness, waiting.

A few minutes later, I heard his footsteps return accompanied by another, lighter step. The door opened and a woman came into the room. She was wearing a pinafore over a dark dress but until she moved forward I could not see her face.

When she did, I froze. It was her.

I held my face still, not wanting to betray my cause. She could vanish with one slam of a door and my Charlotte could be here in this very building.

'Hello? Do I know you?'

I shyly indicated that I'd be more comfortable talking if the door was closed.

'Thank-you, James, you can leave us.'

After the briefest pause, an unseen hand closed the door and heavy footsteps moved away.

She sat down opposite me and her eyes were as blue and as kind as I remembered. The tumult of emotions in my breast prevented me from speaking, and as I looked into her face, so many different ways of beginning the conversation offered themselves that I choked. In the end, there was only one way. I loosened my scarf and let my hair fall about my face and shoulders, all the while watching her eyes. I saw shock, understanding, then fear. She jumped up, but I was quicker to the door. I stood with my back against it and could utter only one word: 'Please.'

She slumped back into her chair and covered her face with her hands.

'I don't know what to say.'

'Tell me. Where is she? Is she here, in this house?'

'No.' The sorrow in her voice told me it was the truth.

'She is gone from here, but she is safe.'

Now I was angry. "How can you say that? How can you know? How can she be safe without me? I'm her mother!'

She was sobbing now, we both were. 'If it is any comfort to you, I have felt myself to be her mother these past months. I am bereft.'

'You? How can you say that? How can you be bereft? She's not your baby! You have no right to be bereft!' I shook her shoulders. 'Tell me! Where is she gone?'

'To Newcastle. To a rich family. She will be taken care of. She will be loved, I am sure. They have gone to such trouble to get her.'

'I don't understand. Why would you steal her, put me through all this, and then give her away? Tell me.'

'I don't know how to begin. Please sit down, be calm, please. I know what you must think of me, but I had a reason, a good reason, and she is well, she is well, I promise. And gone in safe arms to a new life. A life of comfort and happiness, I promise.'

'Who has her?'

'A kind woman whose name I do not know. I had met her only once before. She and her husband arrived yesterday in a private carriage and took her. It was all arranged. I know no more.'

'You stole my baby to give to someone else?'

'Yes, yes I did.' She was sobbing now, seemingly engulfed in guilt. 'It seemed as though God had given her to me.'

'God had nothing to do with it. You stole her. Why? Tell me! Tell me everything!'

'I don't know where to start. I don't know what to say! I am all adrift! I don't know right from wrong any more!'

'I care not one jot for your distress. I want to know why you took a baby from Manchester and brought her here, and I want to know where they have taken her.'

'I ... I was on my way to Liverpool and home to Ireland. My parents... they rely on me. Someone, a man I barely know, he heard that I was going to be travelling home and he made a threat, a very frightening threat. That he would harm someone I love if I did not return with a baby girl. And she had to have bright red wavy hair. There was money, he said. To find such a baby, a healthy baby, for a rich couple.'

She turned a blotched and tear-stained face up to me, beseechingly, 'I could not believe how it happened, it seemed fated. I followed you, you and your friend. I thought if I could get a baby and return quickly, the danger would be over quicker. I had no hope or expectation that you would just hand her to me: it seemed an act of God. I told myself it was meant to be, that the child was destined. I stood there with her in my arms, and you and your friend laughing together on that wall with your backs to me, and I told myself she would be better off... that you too you would be better off without a baby, you having no wedding ring and all. Several times I thought to flee but my courage failed me, and then when you fell... Well, I just didn't think, I ran. Everyone was running. It was chaos, and the screaming! I ran and ran, the child in my arms, and I was saving her, you must understand. I saved her!'

I felt numb. My silence calmed her and she talked on, reassuring herself that she was acting in the baby's best interests and in accordance with the wishes of her God.

'I didn't go back to my relatives. I walked where no-one knew me and I hid in a barn. I had food and water in my basket. I got milk for Charlotte. I was ready. I was calm. She was always in good hands. I convinced myself you were dead or injured and if I didn't take her, it would be the orphanage or the workhouse ... she was best off with me. To be honest, I just didn't let myself think of any alternative. I was happy. Charlotte was happy, too. She did not cry, only little whimpers when she was hungry. Such a good baby, so special and beautiful, with a kind of golden glow. It was meant to be. I left Manchester for York the next morning. I sent word from York. I needed money if I was to cover my trail. Each place I stopped, I was told to wait a few days or weeks to make sure I wasn't followed. It wasn't until I got back here that I wrote again. The people came for her the very next day.'

I was still silent. Her voice implored me for understanding, forgiveness, even gratitude. 'I miss her. I do really. People here think she was my little orphaned niece from Ireland. My own children died and I am a widow. There were times when I thought of vanishing with her, keeping her for myself, but I could not. I loved her.'

I stared into her eyes the whole time she talked, and I saw that it was all true. When the tears came, I froze, for they seemed to invite pity, but I was angry. So angry. I could envisage no threat that would make me steal another woman's baby and deliver her into the hands of strangers. My heart was racing and I could hear my pulse in my ears. For a moment, I felt I would faint, and she saw it and got up to put a hand on my shoulder. I had not the presence of mind to bat it away. I wanted to run from here, I wanted to think of nothing. I had come so close, so close! If only I had acted as soon as I heard of the sighting. If only I hadn't been weak and considered the feelings of the Raines. Feelings for others weakened you. I already knew that. How had I let it happen again? Charlotte had slipped through my fingers and now I might never find her. I felt my heart contract and harden into a stone in my chest.

The woman, Colleen, was still holding my shoulder. I reached up and flicked her fingers off me. Far away in the house I heard loud laughter. Men. The kind of laughter that powerful men do. I had heard a good deal of that laughter in Lady Hamilton's house.

A glass of water appeared on the table and Colleen's skirts softly rustled as she sat down opposite me. Her face was blotched and her eyes swollen and wet. Mine, I knew, was as dry and hard as stone.

When my voice came, it sounded different in my own ears and I saw fear come into her eyes again.

'Tell me about Cuthbert Rippon.'

She was taken aback by my question. 'Why? It has nothing to do with him.' She leaned forward, suddenly having a new cause for anxiety: 'You would not tell?'

'The man who told you to bring back a baby, who was he?'

'From Newcastle. I only know because of his accent, though he disguised it at first.'

'How did he find you?'

'I don't know, but I guess from talk in the public house.'

'He came here?'

'Yes, the night before I was leaving for Ireland. It was hot. The door was open. There was a few of us sat on chairs outside the door there. I had made ginger beer. It was a kind of farewell party for me. We were all a bit…giddy. He appeared, all smiles and greeted me as if he knew me. "Colleen!" he goes. "Off to the Old Country, I hear?" Sounded Irish. A big man, broad shouldered, smartly dressed. The others were giggling at me, as if he was my secret beau. And then he takes my hand, all courtly-like, and pulls me to my feet. "Walk about with me, won't you, Colleen," he says, "for I have a thing I want to say to you." There was beer on his breath but he was not drunk. So there seemed no harm, and I was giddy and excited for going home, so I walked with him, just about the garden here, and the others were watching and laughing. I could hear them.'

'What manner of man?'

'Not rough, not a toff. In between.'

'And not Irish?'

'No, definitely not. Geordie. I know that accent. Unless he's a fine mimic.'

'And his hands, soft or rough?'

She looked at me as though I was a great genius or something.

'Why, soft. Very soft. I would say he hadn't done a tap of work in his life.'

'Go on. What did he say?'

Her eyes changed then. 'I have never been so frightened in my life. He'd been linking my arms as we strolled and just chatting on about the fine garden and the peacocks. He did a mimic of the peacock's call. Jaysus, I hate to hear it now. And we reached the apple tree boughs, so the others could see our feet but not our faces, and he stopped and turned and clamped his arms round my waist and bent down and whispered into my ear. "You're going to do a thing for me, Colleen, and if you don't, your little old mammy and daddy at home in their cottage in Clonmel will find one day that their fire has thrown a cinder on the rug and they'll have burnt to death before they know it."

And I was so shocked, I was stunned. And he goes, "Crackle crackle go the flames, licking at their ankles where they sit, and oh dear they can't get up, because you know what, they're tied to the chairs! And their flesh starts to melt. It smells like pork, you know." He said it like he was talking about the weather. And then he says, "You're going to come back from Ireland with a little red-haired baby girl. A healthy one mind, make sure it's healthy and you've a story ready. And when you've got it and you're back in England, you'll send a letter to an address I'll give you and you'll wait to hear what's next. It's to be curly-haired, mind, and less than a year, the younger the better." My face and neck were ice cold from his words. And he straightened up, still holding me tight, for all the world like we were lovers, and he smiled down at me and said, "All clear?" And I just nodded, for I was terrified.'

She had raised her hands to cover her mouth and I saw that they were shaking.

'Go on.'

'So he says, 'And who am I?' And I didn't know what to say, and then I saw that he wanted me to make something up, to tell the others like. And so I tried to speak, but I couldn't, I'm just going I...I...I... So he says, I'll tell you who I am, I'm your future. If you're not very careful. Do as I say and all will be well, you will be well and your folks will be well. Better, in fact, for you will be better off. Think of it!" And he smiles, and he has a big smile, a nice smile. It's hard to believe what he's so wicked. "In fact," he says, and here he lets go of me with one hand, and he draws out of his pocket a folded piece of paper, and when I take it, I feel that there's a coin in it, a large one.'

'And then?'

'And then he takes the paper from me, and he tucks it in my bodice. And... I...oh there was threat there too.' Her voice rose and she reached out to grasp my fists, clenched there on the table. I wanted to punch someone but it wasn't her.

'I was so frightened...' she reached for my name but found that she didn't have it, so I told her.

When she said it, it was as though she was trying it out for the first time: 'Molly. I never knew your name. You told me your baby's name, but not yours. I was glad in a way. It made it easier not to think of you and what you must be going through.' Her voice softened, 'I am so sorry, Molly.' When I didn't answer, she said, 'What will you do?' and her voice was small, like a child's.

'Do you still have the address?'

'It was a coaching inn, in York. I went there with the letter. It was addressed to Charlie. I gave it to the barman. I didn't want to, but he insisted. He said he didn't know which Charlie but he would give it to the innkeeper. It was a rough place, packed and loud. I didn't stay. Don't think of going there, Molly. You'd get nowhere.'

'No, I'm going to Newcastle.'

'How will you get there?'

'I've no idea but I'll find out. Now tell me about the people who came to collect her.'

'I can only tell you it was a private coach and pair. It was black, with no livery that I could see. It pulled up in front of the house and I was to come out of the back door and walk straight to it with the baby and hand her in.'

'Had you seen the coach before?'

'There are many coaches like that: our master has so many visitors.'

'The horses?'

'Black. Gleaming, beautiful horses. Well cared-for.'

'Nothing distinctive? Nothing at all?'

There was something about the way she said no that reminded me I could not trust her. I could not trust anyone.

'And the people?'

'I only saw the woman, though there was also a man in the coach. She opened the door herself, stood on the step and I handed Charlotte over, wrapped in a shawl, fast asleep.' She started to cry silently.

'And what did she say?'

'She…she lifted the shawl and looked at her face and her hair and she smiled. A happy and tender smile. And she kissed her forehead. And then she covered her up again and she said, 'Thank-you. Thank-you so much.'

'And what manner of woman was she?'

'Older. Maybe my age, forty. White skin, brown eyes, brown hair, a bonnet. A nanny, I would say. That was my impression. And she seemed genuinely happy. I would say she was on the verge of tears. Happy tears.' She swallowed. 'And then they left.'

'You say the coach pulled up at the front. Was it expected? Did anyone come out of the front door? A footman?'

'No.'

'Is that normal?'

'I don't know. What do you mean?'

I took a breath, impatient with this woman's slow wittedness. 'I am trying to find out whether the coach was expected. From inside the house. Whether anyone else knew that it was coming and that it would not be staying. Do you see?'

'I don't know.' Now there was a sullenness to her tone.

'Are you sure? What would normally happen when a coach pulled up? The drive is gravel. It would be heard, surely? A footman would greet it?'

Her voice was sorrowful now, not shifty, and I saw that I would get no further. 'There is nothing more I can tell you.'

'There is one more thing. When I handed Charlotte to you, she had a handkerchief tied around her head.'

'With initials embroidered upon it. Yes, I have it here.' And she drew from her bodice a crumpled piece of cloth. 'It is somewhat crusted with her milk. I wiped her mouth. It still smells of her. I could not bear to wash it.'

She gave me the handkerchief and I looked at it wonderingly. It was then that I cried. And once I started to cry, I found I could not stop.

'There, there Molly, please don't cry. She is safe, I know she is. Oh there now, you cry. Let it all out. Shall I find you some food? A drink of tea? What can I get you? Anything. Oh please. My heart will break.'

Through my sobs, I cried, 'Do you have anything else? A lock of her hair perhaps?'

'No, I do not. I am sorry.' She patted my shoulder. 'I will go to the larder and find you some bread and cheese. There is a chicken I think. From last night. I won't be long.'

Alone in the room, I calmed myself and straightened out the handkerchief. It smelt only of stale milk, not my baby. When she returned, I had rinsed it and had it spread on the table.

'Oh, you have washed it. I....' She placed a plate of cold cuts and a piece of bread before me, but I could not eat and sat staring at the handkerchief. In it lay my hope and I felt my courage returning.

'It is very fine, the embroidery. Did your mother do it?'

'My mother? No, no. They are not my initials. I see you would think that. No, I have no middle name.'

'Then whose?'

I did not answer at first. I was still thinking.

When I finally replied, I must have sounded distracted. 'They are the initials of the late Lady Strathmore, Mary Eleanor Bowes.'

'And how came you by this? Did your mother work for her ladyship?'

I thought for a while before I answered. 'No, I am related to Lady Strathmore.'

This clearly astonished her and she gave no answer at first.

We sat like statues, each with our own thoughts.

And then she whispered, 'Then you will go to Gibside?'

'Yes,' I said. 'I will go to Gibside.'

Chapter 12

When I woke the next morning, Colleen had already gone out. She had given me her bed - "It's the least I can do" – and I neither knew nor cared where she had slept. Her frightened eyes and constant apologies meant nothing to me: when I looked at her white face, all I felt was anger and jealousy that she had held my baby. Held her and given her away.

Her room was plain, the bed large and comfortable. I wondered briefly whether she had shared this room with her husband or whether she had come here after he had died. When I opened the curtain and saw the glint of gold from the crucifix over the bed I thought of her justifications for what she had done and I wanted to slap her.

The dress she had offered to me was still hanging on the outside of the wardrobe. It had been my instinct to refuse but now that I saw it in daylight and thought how useful it would be to have such a dress, I took it down and folded it into my bag.

As I dried my face and hands, I saw that on the dressing table she had left a sheet of paper, an envelope and a pen as I had requested, so I sat down to write to Mary Bowes in Bath:

Stanhope-in-Weardale
21st November 1819

Dear Miss Bowes
        Thank-you for your kindness whilst I was at Streatlam and for your request that I should write to you: you provided more comfort than I was able to express.

        My stay in Middleton-in-Teesdale bore fruit: I was told of a possible sighting which has led me over the moor to Stanhope, in the valley of the River Wear. Here I have found firm news that Charlotte was deliberately stolen from me. I can say no more on that matter for fear of incriminating a person who was coerced.

        I am informed that my child has been taken to Newcastle, there to be handed over to a family of status, though I know no more than that. Whether they reside in Newcastle or will take her away from there, I know not: I only know I must follow.

I realise the delicacy of what I am about to say, and you are not likely to be able to help me more than you already have, but I have been told on good authority that Charlotte's distinctive hair was the reason for her abduction. If this gives you any kind of clue, I beg you to impart it to me.

I am leaving this day for Gibside. I know not what I will do or say when I arrive, but I will make myself known to the house and if you have any news for me, or any clue whatsoever, I beg you to send it there.

Kindest Regards to you and to your nephew,
Molly Bowes

When I stepped out onto the gravel drive in the darkness of that November morning, I saw the sun was already lighting the moors high above the town and I yearned to be on my way. A figure wrapped in a black shawl was coming towards the gate as I emerged into the square: it was Colleen. I stood still and waited for her to look up as she hastened towards me, her eyes downcast. She was almost past when I spoke her name in a voice like a command.

'Oh! Molly!' The tip of her nose was red and her eyes watery, through cold or crying, it mattered not a jot. My heart was in an icy grip when I looked at her ingratiating face. 'I have found him – the carter I mentioned who lives in the Derwent Valley. He is leaving at midday. He wants money, though, and I have none, I'm sorry. His horse and cart are tied up outside the Packhorse Inn.'

'I am taking my letter to the mail office.'

'Yes, of course. I will prepare you some eggs and bread for breakfast. It will be ready by the time you get back.'

I nodded my assent and left her to her conscience.

The carter was a tiny bird-like man with a wizened face and an accent I found impenetrable: at first I doubted that he was speaking English. By the time we reached the tops, I had become used to it and realised that he had been exaggerating it for my benefit. Its sing-song intonations sounded cheery even when he was grumbling, and brought to mind the coal-merchant Mr Peacock who had been imprisoned with us for a time and whose shouted threats to my father I had mimicked to entertain and reassure the little ones.

107

The horse laboured up steep Crawleyside Bank towards the sunshine. When the blade light hit my eyes I squinted to see light glinting on frosted pastures, and beyond, a line in the field where the frost had melted and the sun-warmed grass began. Here was hope. I was getting closer. It was only fifteen miles to Gibside, I had been told; and just three miles beyond that the Tyne; and on the Tyne the walled medieval town of Newcastle, wherein my baby lay like a changeling in a fairytale.

We reached the crest of a hill and the carter pulled up to relieve himself. I climbed down from the cart to move around, warm myself and stretch my legs, fizzing with impatience. At that moment the sun came out from behind a white cloud and lit the scene spread out before me into a haze of gleaming fields, greys and blues and the palest greens, lilacs, yellows…every colour rendered pale in the early winter light. Such beauty of landscape I had never beheld.

We had reached the highest point and beyond the long levels I could see for miles – further than I had ever seen before. It felt like the very top of the world, a frosted wonderland of glints and promise.

We soon came to a fork in the road, and my companion declared with jubilance in his voice, 'Left to Blanchland, right to Edmundbyers.'.

'How green it is still, down there in the shelter of that valley!'

'Aye, it's a fine river, the Derwent, and a rich land.'

'Rich?'

'Natural riches - the Land of Oak and Iron. Finest oaks make the finest ships, and there's the iron ore and the coal near the surface and the river full of salmon and fast-flowing waters for the mills.'

'It sounds like paradise.'

'Folk come from all over.'

'How do you mean?'

'Well, there's Belgian ironworkers in Winlaton; the Germans of course, in Shotley Bridge.'

'I'm sorry, I really don't understand. There are Germans living in the Derwent Valley?'

'Aye. Finest sword-makers in the world.'

'But why? Why are they here, so far from home?'

'Ah divvn't knaa, pet. Ye can ask when we get there.'

It was early afternoon when we arrived in the handsome village of Shotley Bridge and turned into the yard of an inn called The Crown and Crossed Swords. Daylight was fading fast and I was beginning to be concerned about reaching Gibside before darkness fell, but I did not protest at the delay as my hands and face were so numb with cold that I doubt I could have spoken. The carter had jumped down before the horse had come to a standstill: it clearly knew where the water trough was and didn't need tying up, because he had vanished inside before I managed to climb down. Although he had left his load unattended, I did not want to risk my precious few possessions, so with painful fingers I took the handles of my bag and pulled it down.

The air inside was smoky and warm when I emerged into the bar room. While the carter stared into a pewter pot before lifting it to his lips and glugging the beer down like nectar, I accepted a glass of water and went to stand before the fire. An old man was sitting by the fireside smoking a clay pipe and staring into the flames. He nodded without looking at me and continued to puff complacently on his pipe. I felt the knots loosening in my shoulders as the heat worked its burning magic on my outstretched hands.

Finally he spoke: 'Pull up a cracket, pet.'

I looked round to see that he meant, saw a small wooden stool, and obediently placed it to one side of the fire and sat down on it, staring rapt into the flames. Perhaps I could just stay here. Outside, the winter light was fading fast, and I was suddenly very tired. I don't know whether I had nodded, but I heard the old man chuckle, 'Wakey wakey sleeping beauty. Yer man's finishing his pint. Ye'd better not get too comfy. Oh no, yer alright, he's ordered another. Hehe, hope you haven't far to go?'

'I was hoping to get to Gibside today, but it's getting dark.'

'That feller lives at Derwentcote, doesn't he?'

'I don't know. He said he'd take me to Lintzford and I could walk to Gibside from there.'

'Well, it's another four miles from here to Derwentcote and a mile further on to Lintzford, then a two-mile walk to Gibside, so if I were you I'd get comfy and stop here the night.'

I couldn't hide my disappointment and I didn't want to have to pay for a room. He saw my face and said kindly, 'If he offers you a bed for the night - and he should, the bastard - don't worry, his wife's a lovely woman. She puts up with a lot. He's a lazy sod and a drinker, but there's no harm in him. I see him pass through here a lot. Well, when I say pass through, I mean call in.'

I tried to muster my spirits and show some interest in the conversation. 'He told me there are people here from Germany?'

'Aye, the Oleys own this pub.'

'Oh, I thought they were sword-makers?'

'Yes, that too. They've been here generations. The Germans have been the making of this town. The finest blades anywhere. Anywhere in the world. Though things are changing now, mind. You must have heard of Shotley Bridge swords?'

'No, no, sorry I haven't. Swords are not a thing I've ever heard about, nor given a thought to, if I'm honest.'

'Well give them a thought now,' he said, suddenly belligerent, 'because if it weren't for them, things might have turned out very different in the wars with the French.'

'I'm sorry, I … there must be a great deal of skill in making a blade. I have just never thought about it.'

'There is,' he said, subsiding again and taking a draw on his pipe. I could see he was settling down for a lecture and I struggled to reconcile myself to listening to this old man instead of getting to where I wanted to be. I slid a sideways glance at the carter and saw that the barman pass him his pint pot. Surely not the third?

'There's an art to sword-making. See that blade there?' I looked round to look at the gleaming thing mounted on the wall. 'That one was engraved by Bewick himself.'

Suddenly I was awake. 'Thomas Bewick?'

'None other.'

'He worked here?'

'No, he worked at Amen Corner in the Toon. Apprenticed to Beilby at the time. Learned his craft on Shotley swords. Came here once, that I know of. Walked. He always was a great walker. Walked to Scotland once, and all about! Course, he was a young man then. Ah don't suppose he covers many miles nowadays.'

'He's still alive?'

'Far as I know, aye. Nigh on seventy, I think, bit younger than me. I knew him as a lad. Why so surprised?'

I must have had my mouth open. I could not think it, that Thomas Bewick was a real man, who lived nearby, and was once young and learning his craft. I tried to gather my wits and make some sense in responding to this old man. I could not hope to convey what his work had meant to me, so I simply said, 'I have long admired Mr Bewick's work. I have read his History of Land Birds. His prints are a thing of wonder.'

'Aren't they just? The man's a genius, and well-loved too. You know the one of the Cathouse Plantation Tidestone?'

'No.'

'It shows a carved stone leaning over, like a gravestone only with the three Newcastle castles. It's on the Tyne at Wylam, marks the limit of the Port Authority. The Tyne's tidal up to that spot. Well Mr Bewick found out the mason hadn't been paid. And he made sure he was. You don't argue with Bewick.'

As I absorbed this information, my airy idea of this godlike being called Thomas Bewick floated down from the clouds and took flesh. 'Where does he live? Is it far?'

'Well Cherryburn's not far, just follow the Derwent down to the Tyne, turn left and walk towards Wylam. His brother still lives there and Bewick's often there, from what I've heard. Nice spot. He himself has a fine house in Gateshead.'

'And is he well? Still working?'

'Aye, that feller'll nivver stop working, not 'im. He's just done Aesop's Fables. Not seen it yet but I bet it's a corker.'

Just then the carter came over, burped loudly and announced it was time to go. 'Come on pet, I want to get home before dark.'

'Where are you dropping her? The lassie cannot walk to Gibside from where you live, not in the dark and with a bag to carry.'

Somewhat shamefaced, he mumbled, 'Why, I'm only going as far as Derwentcote, she knew that.'

'Aye, but you know damn well she didn't expect it to take this long! It's only fifteen miles from Stanhope to Gibside. If you've taken money off this lass, give it her back.'

'I've spent it.'

'Then you owe her, so either get her a room here and put it on yer slate, or take her to your missis and give her a bed for the night.'

The barman piped up: 'Robert's right, Lem. You owe the lass.'

Begrudgingly, he muttered, 'Oh all right then, come on. But don't tell my missus how much you paid me.'

I stood up and bent to shake the old man's hand. 'Thank-you. I'm in your debt. I hope to see you again when my circumstances are better and I'll buy you a drink.'

'Naah, yer all reet pet, divvn't worry. It's only right. I've a granddaughter same age as you and I like to think folks would look after her if she goes off on an adventure, God forbid.'

The carter had turned sullen, so as I climbed up beside him I tried to elicit some conversation as we climbed the hill out of Shotley Bridge in the darkening afternoon.

'Will your wife mind? I don't need feeding, just somewhere to lay my head and in the morning I'll be on my way.'

He clearly sensed his advantage and tried to press it home, grumbling, 'Hmm, well she'll not be best pleased.'

'Well the only alternative I can think of is for you to take me to Gibside.'

'Not a chance. Not even if you paid me.'

'I did pay you, you remember.'

'Aye. Well.'

We rocked on in silence as the mist rose over the river and spread across the shadowed fields.

At one point, his head lolled forward and I nudged him hard.

'Nyurr! Oy, what you doing?'

'Trying to keep you on the road. It's awfully bumpy – I don't know how you can fall asleep.'

'Awfully? Oo, get Miss La-di-da!' He pulled up, jumped down and openly peed copiously onto the verge. I looked away, discomfited and wishing I had never agreed to this man's terms.

When he climbed back, he said teasingly, 'You posh then?' and my heart recoiled to think he might have flirtatious intent. The three pints of ale had changed his demeanour entirely and I felt myself to be in a dangerous position: my mind skittered about. 'If that's what you want to call it, then yes. I am related to the Bowes family.'

112

'That why you're going to Gibside? There's no Boweses there. He's died, the Earl. But you know that, being related an all.' And he chortled to himself in an unpleasant way.

It made me angry. I sat up straight and said with an affectation that makes me blush to think of it. 'Show some respect.'

To my shock and chagrin, he spat voluminously over the footboard. 'Respect? For that fella? No better than me, worse some'd say. At least I don't consort with whores and I know where my loyalties lie.'

Ignoring the first assertion, I was too curious to let the second one go by. I needed to stay safe, mollify this man, charm his wife and learn all I could from them.

I spoke more meekly, with what I hoped sounded like a rueful chuckle. 'I didn't know him, to be honest. I'm only distantly related.'

I didn't hear the first part of his answer: I was trying to work out what my relationship to the dead earl was. If his mother had been married to my father, I suppose we were step-siblings in a way, but I felt no confidence in claiming any such relationship.

Lem was rumbling a monologue into his scarf. The temperature was dropping rapidly and I huddled deeper into my cloak, trying to hear what he was muttering. 'Bloody toffs, they should be shot, the lot of 'em. We should do what the French did, chop their 'eads off.'

'I've heard that idea before. It'll never happen.'

He turned his head and suddenly his eyes were sharp and focused. 'Don't you be so sure. Come the revolution, you'll all be done fer, the lot of you.'

I was genuinely startled. 'Oh, I haven't done anything. And the Bowes family seem perfectly charming. Young John...'

'The bastard, aye. And his scheming trollop of a mother. All of em.' And he made a sharp chopping motion to the side of my neck. 'Ha ha ha!'

'I'm sorry, Lem, but you are frightening me. You surely don't mean that you would put innocent young lives to the sword?'

'The guillotine, aye! And why not? They do the like to us.'

'Us?'

'The workers!'

113

'But you know, I have heard that in France the populace ran wild. Law and order demolished. Bloodshed, factions, vengeance. I can't imagine it happening in England.'

'Oh we'd make a better job of it, and that's for sure.'

'So, tell me, have you a particular reason for saying Lord Strathmore didn't know where his loyalties lay?'

'Yes I bloody have.'

'Will you tell me?'

'No I bloody won't.'

'Oh, please, I beg you. I won't repeat it, I promise.' I widened my eyes and settled on a display of girlish ignorance. I had seen Emma Hamilton hide her wilful intelligence in this way and this man was no London sophisticate. It worked.

'There was this thing called Peterloo.' I kept my silence and clenched my fractured heart. 'Hundreds and hundreds of workers were killed by toffs.' He spat again. 'All over the country, there wus riots. On the Toon Moor, thoosands gathered. Our lads, Crowley's Crew led the way...' I thought of interrupting to ask questions but decided to let him flow on without hindrance. I could find out more from someone else. 'It built up'n'up, more an more workers gettin' involved with the demos, miners and metalworkers and brickmakers and labourers... Well finally there's this huge gathering on the banks of the Tyne and the Wear. Massive it was, some say 20,000 men.'

I couldn't help myself. 'And women?'

He ignored my question and was clearly working himself up to the climax of his story. 'So who do you think sends word to the parliament?'

'Lord Strathmore?'

'Yep. His very self. His bloody lordship. Frightened we'd trample his bowling green, I'll wager.'

'So what happened?'

'Nothing happened.'

'So no-one was hurt? No soldiers came?'

'No.'

We travelled the rest of the way in silence.

His wife was a bustling little body whose rosy face cancelled all my fears: her face lit up the moment she saw me. Not one trace of suspicion crossed her features, just warm curiosity and welcome.

'And who have we here? Come in, pet, come in, you must be frozen!'

I stepped into the dazzling furnace of a hot red kitchen. The small range was pushing out more heat than one would have expected it was capable of and the other three walls were decorated with hanging dried herbs. A rack hung from the ceiling with a few items of clothing dangling and floor was covered with spotless red quarry tiles.

'Here, let me take your cloak, pet. I'll hang it up to dry off. That your bag? Let me just put it up here out of the way.' And she took down a wooden chair from a hook on the wall, gestured me to sit on it and hung my bag in its place. 'So. Who have we here?'

'My name is Molly.'

From over my shoulder, I heard Lem mutter, 'Says she's a Bowes.' She looked up and I guess he winked, because she smiled kindly at me.

'Well, hello, Molly Bowes. I'm Lizzie, and I'm saddled with this one for life.' She didn't look too unhappy about it, though, and I felt myself relax.

'I'm sorry to impose on you, Mrs Lem, but your husband had hoped to be able to get me to Lintzford before nightfall…'

'But he had to stop for a pint at the Crossed Swords, don't tell me.' She rolled her eyes and her smile never waivered but there was something about the set of it that suggested he might hear more of this when I was gone.

'Don't you worry your pretty head, Molly. And my, it is a pretty head! You are a real beauty, that's for sure. And you're a Bowes, you say?'

'Distantly related, yes. I'm on my way to Gibside.'

She shook her head. 'Sad business. Poor Lord Strathmore, fifty is no age. And him with a young son. I never saw a man who loved so well. Poor Mary Milner.' And she dabbed her eyes.

'Give over, you soft tart. He was a traitor to his kind.'

'He was no traitor, and don't you go saying that. His kind? Are Crowley's Crew his kind? No they are not.' She patted my hand. 'Don't listen to him, Molly. He doesn't mean it. Lord Strathmore was well-loved around here. He was a lovely man. Got Gibside back on its feet, he did. Yes, well-loved. When I think of that little lad…' She dabbed at her eyes with the hem of her apron.

'Give over with yer, woman! He'll be all reet. The bairn's at boarding school anyway. Won't know no different.'

'Haway with you, man! You only had to see them together to see he was loved, poor pet.' She dabbed her eyes again and then brightened suddenly, 'Are you hungry, Molly? We'll just wait for his nibs to see to the horse and then we'll eat. There's plenty and I've baked today, so you're in luck.'

Over supper, I learnt all about their family, which was interesting, and the cementation process, which wasn't.

Eventually, I tried to steer the conversation to the Strathmores: 'You said earlier that the Earl had got Gibside back on its feet. What did you mean? Has the estate had troubles?'

'Oh, my, has it indeed! It fell into the hands of the very devil. Devastation, wickedness. Such suffering and destruction, I can hardly bear to tell you!'

Something, some premonition, some suspicion that I had never confronted closed its icy hands around my heart. 'The devil? What can you mean?'

It was her husband who said the words I somehow knew I would hear. 'Stoney Bowes.' He spat into the fire and wiped his mouth with the back of his hand.

His wife didn't even blink. 'Nay, never give him their name, he doesn't deserve it. He deserves to rot in hell.'

I lay that night on my cloak in front of the glowing range and I don't know whether I slept, dreamed or lay awake. I only know my mind was a whirl of images and emotions. By the time I heard them stirring behind the curtain, I felt exhausted and ached in my bones.

Whatever whispered conversation they'd had in the night had led to a change of manner from Lem, and when we were breakfasting on a thick porridge, he offered to drive me all the way to Gibside. He said he had a pie and some laundry to take to his brother-in-law, a childless widower who worked in the paper mill on the Gibside estate.

His wife returned and ushered him out of the cottage so that I could wash and change. I had confided in her that I wished to make an impression when I first arrived at Gibside and that I had a fine muslin dress in my bag. I have fond memories of that short time we spent together in that warm red kitchen, she clucking round me, fastening buttons, stitching a small tear and then sitting me down so that she could brush my hair. When she finally stood back to look at me, she blinked back tears. 'Ee Molly, you're a stunner! What a transformation! I hardly know what to say!'

Lem's face was a picture: his mouth actually dropped open and his manners improved tenfold on the instant.

As we followed our billowing breath out of the cottage, greens and golds were emerging from the mists that crept across the fields from the river. Voices drifted across the mill-pond and a donkey brayed once. The world was hushed and the pair of us stayed silent all the way to Gibside.

Chapter 13

Entering the estate, we followed a track along the river, serene in the hushed misty morning and I saw a heron rise ghostly into the air to drift along the river, as if to lead us.

When we came to a small hamlet of cottages clustered along the banks, I straightened my posture and looked around me for the great hall of which I had heard so much. To our right, the bright reeds and grasses of water-meadows stretched away to where the hill rose into woodland. No great house was in sight.

Lem's brother-in-law was a powerfully built man though no taller than Lem: he looked disconcertingly like a threatening dwarf. On that cold winter's morning, he stood in his shirtsleeves and showed no sign of feeling the cold as he looked up at me with frank astonishment.

Lem had climbed down and walked round the front of the horse like a strutting little cockerel. 'This is Molly,' and he too stood looking up at me as though he'd never seen me before. 'Ah've no idea what she's about, she's geet cagey. See if you can get more out of her than our Lizzie did. Says she's a Bowes.'

I gathered my skirts and accepting the proffered hand, descended from the cart in a more elegant manner than I had ever previously achieved. This dress and the reactions it elicited were improving my confidence, though inside butterflies fluttered and my breath came short. I could not believe I was finally standing on Gibside land.

I stood up to my full height and looked down at the two men, neither of whom reached my shoulder. 'No, I didn't say I was a Bowes. I said I was distantly related. I'm looking for work. My name is Molly Sutton.'

'What kind of work? I'm guessing not in the brick factory.' The two men nudged each other and laughed.

'If you could direct me to the house, please, I'll look after myself from here.'

'Follow that path across Ladyhaugh and enter the woods. Climb the steps and you'll soon see the service wing through the trees on your right. D'you want to leave your bag with us? They'll likely give you short shrift at the house. They were laying people off in the summer.'

'No, really, thank-you, it's fine. If I have no success I'll come back here, if you don't mind, and perhaps you can introduce me to someone who might be able to help me.'

This was greeted by silence, the two men clearly not knowing what to make of me, and in truth I hardly knew what to make of myself. To my own ears, my accent was wavering between my best imitation of Emma Hamilton and the local sing-song, which I found so pleasing to the ear that I could not help gently adopting.

As I walked away, I heard a guffaw and the muttered words, 'There'll always be work for such as that, eh?'

The ground was soft and damp and my soles were thin, so by the time I reached the drier earth under the trees, my feet were soaked through. I put down my bag, took off my worn cloak and folded it inside. Lizzie had plaited my hair into a thick braid and now I lifted it over one shoulder and laid it down the side, where it hung heavily down to my waist. The bodice of the muslin gown was a little tight, and I anxiously tugged at the neckline to ensure that I made a modest impression.

Taking a deep breath, I began to climb the stone steps. I soon saw a small water-reservoir and beyond, a sandstone wall. I looked up and saw that the wall rose three storeys high and a stone staircase led to an arched door on the first floor.

The door was answered by a tall young man of perhaps sixteen whose eyes lit up when he saw me. He didn't speak or move and a moment later he was roughly pushed to one side.

'Out of the way, Edward, stood there like a moonstruck calf!' A large woman with a huge frontage covered in a white apron took his place on the threshold and said, 'Good morning, miss, how can we help you?'

I had practised this. I took a deep breath and spoke slowly. In what I hoped was a modest but quietly confident tone, I said, 'Good morning. My name is Molly Sutton. I have travelled from Streatlam, where I met the young Lord Strathmore. His aunt, Miss Mary Bowes, suggested that I might find employment here at Gibside. I come from London, where I was employed by Lady Hamilton.' I paused: their reaction to her name was important to me. Both looked impressed and neither had the sneer that I'd sometimes seen it elicit.

'Oh I'm sorry, pet, there's no work here. We had to lay people off after Lord Strathmore died, may he rest in peace. But leave your reference and your address and when things have settled down, we might be hiring again.'

I was ready for this too: I knew I could bring tears to my eyes with ease and I used my eyes to their best advantage. Even if the woman could resist, I knew the young man would not be able to, and from the way he was leaning over her shoulder I could see that they were close. Sure enough, still gazing at me transfixed, he gave her a gentle nudge and said, 'Surely there's something Molly could do, Elsie? What about the library?'

'Oh no, no, no, we can't go taking on just anyone when there's folks of our own who need work.'

'The library?' My heart had started to beat very fast.

'Aye, the library, bane of my life. The dust! They want it done for Christmas, though heaven knows they've not decided whether there's going to be anyone here to notice. Oh, I don't know! I'm all at sixes and sevens! Poor Lord Strathmore!' And she disappeared into the darkness of the corridor.

The young man stepped forward and picked up my bag. 'Come on in Molly, she'll come round. Follow me.'

He opened a door into what I took to be a staff parlour and indicated a sofa. 'Sit you down here. Things are a bit strange around here at the moment.' He sat down on a chair opposite and leaned forward, his hands on his knees and his arms stiff, as though he was unconsciously imitating someone else, someone older with more authority.

'Aye, aye,' he shook his head sorrowfully. 'No-one knows what's to happen.'

'In what way?'

'Well, the young lord's only a bairn. We're calling him young Lord Strathmore but no-one knows whether he will be.'

I waited. 'Will be?'

'Well, he's his father's son all right, but the late Lord Strathmore didn't marry Mary Milner until he was on his deathbed. No forethought, you see. A romantic, Elsie says.'

'But why would that be a problem?'

'Cos he's not a Strathmore, is he really? And the Strathmores are powerful, you know. And the late Earl's brother Thomas is claiming the title. And if he gets the title, he gets Gibside.'

'Oh. I didn't know that. And does he have a chance of winning?'

'Oh aye, he knows the King. He petitioned the King as soon as the earl died. See, to them, young John's a ...'

'A bastard?'

'Why, yes. Only I didn't like to say.' Encouraged, he came to sit beside me and lean in to whisper conspiratorially. 'The late Lord's been living over the brush with Mary Milner. Young John...wrong side of the bedsheets, ye knaa.'

'But he did marry her. So she is ....'

'Lady Strathmore, well yes but it doesn't sit right with some. We've to call her the Dowager. Who knows, though? Is it legal? Will it stand? He could hardly have....'

'Consummated?'

'Why aye. That. He could hardly have done that. He had to be carried into church and then died that very night.'

Just then, there was a bustling of skirts behind us and an abrupt, 'Edward!' caused him to spring to his feet like a scalded cat.

'I'm sorry, Elsie, only Molly was cold so I thought there was no harm...'

But her face was rigid. 'Were you gossiping? What have I told you about gossip? If you weren't my grandson, you wouldn't have this job. And if you gossip, you will not keep it. Do you understand me?'

Shamefaced, he looked at the ground, having clearly had this threat before.

'I mean it. This is the second time. Things that you've heard me and your mother discussing are not to be repeated. Do you hear me? It is perfectly possible that you will lose not only your own job but mine too. Now go.'

Without another word, the boy left the room and closed the door softly behind him.

Sitting down beside me, Elsie sighed. 'Now Molly, tell me what the boy has been saying to you.'

'I...'

'I know I am putting you in a difficult position, but I need to know. There are ...certain circumstances that mean we are not as safe as we were in our employment. And if we lose our employment, we lose our home. The boy lacks discretion. He had a serious warning not two weeks ago and was all contrition, but now, I suspect he has offended again. I cannot risk it, Molly. I need to know the extent of his offence.'

'I understand. He was...somewhat indiscreet, but you can trust me.'

'That's not the issue. He doesn't know you from Adam. You could be from Glamis, for all he knows.'

'Glamis?'

'The seat of the Strathmore family, in Scotland. There is an inheritance matter that is still to be decided.'

I waited before I answered. 'He did indicate something along those lines, yes, but he said nothing that could incriminate you.'

'Are you sure? Nothing about the legal status of the young master?'

I was silent.

'He did, didn't he?'

'I'll tell you exactly what he said if you will consider giving him one more chance.'

'No, that's not how it works. The boy's a menace. He'll have to go. Don't worry, we'll find something for him, just not in the house. He'll be apprenticed in the brick factory. It's what his father wanted for him anyway. It's a pity, because he's a good worker and I had high hopes of attaching him to the young earl, perhaps as a valet. There's only a few years between them. But it's not to be.' And she started to heave herself up from the table.

'Elsie, wait. I have an idea.' She sat back down, heavily expelling a sigh.

'I have thought of a way of frightening the boy. I am a good mimic. I can do a Scottish accent. I will pretend that I am indeed from Glamis and dismiss you both. I can act. I will not let him see one sign that it is not the truth. He must learn the value of discretion and the consequences of indiscretion.'

She thought for a moment and then her face lit up, but soon clouded over. 'How do I know I can trust you?'

'I can tell you something that I had thought to keep secret. I feel I can trust you.'

'You can, Molly, discretion is my middle name, as the Earl always said. But please reconsider and do not tell me anything you will regret.'

'I will be telling no-one else, for I am ashamed, but I feel I should tell someone here.'

'And it is nothing that will put me in danger, or in a quandary about whether to call the constables?'

'No, nothing like that. It is a personal secret. About my origin.'

'Something you want to get off your chest, eh? You can tell me, Molly, I have girls of my own.'

'My father was Stoney Bowes.'

Her reaction shocked me: it was nothing but dismissive. 'Aye, you and an army of others. No offence, Molly, and it's not your fault, but Stoney Bowes had offspring all over the shop. Some reckon as there's upwards of forty of you. All over.'

I didn't know what to say, it was as though a great chasm had opened at my feet.

'Oh I'm sorry, love, I've shocked you. I'm sorry, there there. Here's me telling off young Edward for his lack of discretion and then I go blurting that out. Only none of the mothers was under any illusion about Stoney. He was... or he could be... a charmer.' She said this gently, but I was conscious she was watching closely for my reaction.

There was a gentle knock at the door and Edward stuck his head round, all contrition. 'I'm sorry Nan. No harm done, eh? I've finished the boots. What would you like me to do next?'

'Go and find Fred and the pair of you do the gun-room. Be careful, mind. Do as Fred tells you. And then you can come back here. I want to talk to you but I'm talking to Molly at the moment.'

He looked at me, but receiving no encouragement, backed out and shut the door.

Elsie had stood up, and now she turned to study me. Making her mind up about something, she sat down heavily in the chair opposite.

'So, you come from London, and you're what, twenty?'

'Yes.'

'I thought he was in prison twenty years ago?'

'He was.'

'So who was your mother?'

'Her name was Polly.'

'And she…?' Hardly knowing how to frame the question, I let her squirm for she had cut me to the quick and I couldn't yet find my feet.

'Was that true? What you said about my father? That he had so many children? With how many women?'

'Now Molly, you don't really need to know, do you? There's nothing to be gained from it. I only meant for you to learn that you were not … alone.'

'And are there any of his children here, at Gibside?'

She chose wilfully to ignore the true intent of my question. 'Miss Mary Bowes is at Streatlam at present, comforting the young earl. Her brother William drowned.'

'I have met Miss Bowes. She knows who I am. She spared me the shocking information that I have just learned from you. She also told me what she said is common knowledge – that she is not the child of Stoney Bowes but of Mary Eleanor's former love, George Grey.'

'Well yes, quite. But that is all in the past now.'

'Not for me, it isn't!' She was taken aback by my fierceness. 'If I have siblings here, I need to know!'

'No Molly, you don't. Put it out of your mind. Now tell me what brought you here. For you already know that you will not be welcomed. Your father brought a great deal of suffering to this estate. You do not need to know the extent of it, or the nature. If you want to stay here, it is better that you forget he was ever your father. And even more important that you tell no-one.'

I got up. 'I'm sorry Elsie, I need to assemble my thoughts. I feel quite distressed. Please excuse me. I should like to go for a walk to compose myself. Would that be acceptable to you?'

She stood up too, and surprised me by putting a hand to my face. She spoke tenderly and then I knew I could do it. If I played my cards right, I could find a home here, at least for the time being.

'Of course. Do forgive me, Molly, I spoke without thinking. I am upset by that lad betraying my confidence, truth be told, but that's no excuse for what I said to you. You go for a nice walk and when you come back, I shall lay out some lunch and we can have a good talk. And then we can see whether or not I can find work for you. Temporary mind. There's others that have a claim on jobs in the house. But what I do lack is a lover of books. Now if you fit that bill...'

I kept my face still in its expression of deep distress and heaved a shuddering sigh. The handkerchief was in my pocket: I withdrew it and dabbed my eyes, my shoulders slumping. She squeezed my arm reassuringly and opened the door.

'Where would I best be advised to walk?'

'Oh, the whole lovely place is full of walks, you'll be spoiled for choice!'

'I have a question before I go. When letters arrive, who receives them?'

'The butler, Albert.'

'And if a letter arrived for someone whose name he did not recognize, what would he do with it?'

'If the family were in residence, he would leave it on the tray for the master to decide. If they are not, he generally keeps all the letters in his office. He has a small office between the Hall and the service wing.'

'There is a possibility that a letter might arrive addressed to Molly Bowes. Would it be possible for you to keep an eye out for it? I will write to my friends to tell them to address me as Sutton in future. If I am to stay.'

'Oh, I think you will be staying, Molly Bowes, one way or another. Have no fear about the letter. Albert is my husband, and with your permission, I will tell him your secret.'

Chapter 14

The winter sun was at its zenith in a clear blue sky as I emerged from the woods at the side of the great hall. Having climbed the path amongst the trees, I had been unable to grasp the size or shape of the house, and now I was dazzled by both sunlight and structural beauty. Like a long, low turreted sandcastle, it hugged the hillside, sunlight glinting from its multitude of mullioned panes.

I carried on walking towards the sun in order to get a view of the house and mounted a steep bank onto a raised avenue. Turning to get a better look, my eyes were arrested by the sight of an exquisite chapel at the furthest end of the avenue.

I know not how long I stood in that spot, for never had I felt so awake to the beauties that were possible in a landscape. The sheep calling from the pastures which sloped away to my left, the sunlight on the exquisite jewel of architecture in the distance, the house spreading long, low, golden and turreted, and behind me a great column at the top of which a golden statue stood surveying all, just as I did.

Reflecting on what I had learnt, I now realized that my father's links to the Bowes family, far from being of potential benefit, were something I must hide. My feelings were so mixed. I was drawn to know more: such was the beauty of the place and the kindness of its people, that I felt I somehow needed to stay, if not to make amends, at least to understand what had happened and my place in the world. Here I felt safe, for what danger could lie in such beautiful surroundings? If I went into Newcastle, I knew no-one and would be in danger. In the twenty-four hours since I had left Stanhope, it had begun to seem increasingly unlikely that Charlotte would still be in Newcastle: having gone to so much trouble to ensure she could not be traced, they were unlikely to have her brought to them in the town in which they lived permanently.

If they had a substantial home in the town, the odds were that they would be known to the Bowes family and their circle, possibly even their staff. If I could achieve a position in the house, I could keep my ear to the ground. I had made a good start and must capitalise on what I knew. Elsie was tender-hearted and felt guilt for what she had told me: I must push home my advantage. She had said the library was the bane of her life, so I tried to think in what way that could be so. I had never seen a library, strange as that seems now. My own precious book had no doubt been destined for this very collection. The thought of row upon row of books, purchased with limitless money and placed on shelves made for that specific purpose, to be read at leisure... I could barely imagine such riches.

It must be more than dusting – if she needed a book-lover, perhaps there was some skill involved, something no-one else wanted to do, or could not do properly. And then it came to me. This was a family of clever, bookish people who had lived in the same house for over two hundred years. It was perfectly possible that the book collection was huge and disordered: perhaps it was difficult to find particular volumes. It was the only possibility I could think of – the books needed to be organized, listed or recorded in some way. At first I could only think alphabetical, by title or author, but in a large library, that would make it difficult, so perhaps it was by subject.

I had been walking slowly towards the chapel, and now I saw over to my right a columned building of great beauty, with a pitched slate roof edged by a row of decorative urns. In the centre of the paddock before it, a man was clearing leaves from a pond. I would go and talk to him to glean what I could before I returned to the house.

The grass in the paddock was long and damp: by the time I reached him, my skirts were wet and I shook them out as I greeted him.

'Hello young lady, not seen you before. Just visiting?'

'Yes, I'm hoping to apply for the position of librarian.'

'Oh aye? Didn't know there was one going. They won't be hiring at the moment, surely? Things being as they are, like.'

I reached out my hand, and startled, he took off his glove to offer me a hard and soily hand. 'Molly Sutton.'

'Cuthbert Stephenson, at your service.'

'Have you worked here long?'

'Oh aye, allus. And me da before me, and his da before him.'

'Are there many families like that at Gibside, who've always worked here?'

'Oh aye, all of us really. Yes, there's comings and goings. Some sons'll go to work in other places, mines an that, metalwork, but they allus come back.'

'And the girls?'

'Well, some go into service with other families, work on the land, mining jobs... There's a lot of work keeping a place like this going.'

'And the gardens, they are very fine?'

'Aye, well, to my mind they are. Nature, you see. Not poncified, if you know what I mean. Woods and grass and shrubs, all natural-looking like. Course the woods are not what they were, not since all the oaks got clear-felled.'

'Clear-felled?'

'Aye. Still makes me angry to this day, and I was just a bairn when it happened. That bloody bastard, shoulda bin hung drawn and quartered.'

I stayed silent. He needed no encouragement to expand.

'Needed money, didn't he? For his debts an that. Clear felled all the oaks. Nobody'd buy 'em like, just lay there like a slain army.'

At the mention of debts, I knew. 'This is Stoney Bowes, is it? I've heard of him.'

In answer, he spat onto the soil and then scuffed his boot over it. 'Beg pardon, miss, but the mention of that name round ere, even the women spit.'

'I'm sorry to hear that. He must have been a very bad man.'

'The worst. The devil incarnate.'

'Pardon me, but chopping down trees does not seem the work of the devil. Not a pleasant thing to do, destructive of course, but evil?'

'Oh that's not the half of it. He was vicious. Abuse, beatings, bullying, punishments, evictions, rapes ... no woman was safe... and as for what he did to our ladyship... Well, I hope he rots in hell. We all do. Now, see, you've got me all agitated.' He threw down his rake and took a wad of tobacco out of his pocket. It already looked well-used, but he put it in his mouth and chewed angrily.

'I'm sorry to have upset you: I am a stranger here. Perhaps you'd be kind enough to tell me this building? It is very fine!'

'Ah yes,' his face softened. 'Mary Eleanor's Orangery. Aye, bless her. It's beautiful, isn't it?'

'I never saw the like! Such elegant proportions. I have lived in London, and there are buildings there with fine columns, but none so beautiful as this. It seems to have risen out of the landscape.'

'Well it did in a way. The stone was mined here. The masons were from this estate, and Cuthbert Palliser's granddad made the windows and the staging. Mary Eleanor collected exotic plants, bless her. She put the gardeners through their paces, I can tell you! They never knew what they'd be given next! Raised all sorts, they did. Plants from America and Africa, Australia, all ower. All gone now, like. It's sad. Haunted, they say. Her little study all empty. Her daughter Mary took her little cabinet where she kept her specimens, to keep it safe, like.'

'I know Mary Bowes.'

His face lit up. 'Wonderful woman! Just like her mother, that one. George Bowes in female form. Wish she lived here, like. Instead, who knows who we're going to get now. And as for Mary Milner and that bairn…I don't know what'll become of them.' He turned away and went back to his raking.

When I got back to the house, I slipped in through the outer door, intending to knock at the parlour, but Elsie was just coming towards me along the corridor.

'There you are! Now let's sit you down and we'll get to know each other.'

'My bag! Where's my bag?'

'Ee pet, don't worry, I've asked Edward to take it up to your room.'

'My room?'

'Now don't get your hopes up. I can't offer you a job, but it strikes me you could do with a safe haven for now while you sort yourself out. You'll be fine – there's plenty of space in the servants' quarters, sadly. I can let you stay for a few days at least.'

'That's very kind of you, Elsie. This is such a beautiful estate, the little I've seen of it. I never saw such a beautiful place. It's … harmonious somehow.'

'Aye, soothes the soul. Many people say that.'

Something inside me had uncoiled and it made me wary. I could not think myself safe. Not yet.

'I would very much like to work here if possible. You mentioned the library. I have some experience of caring for a library.' I took care to keep my eyes on her face and not look away. My father in his cups had once told me that trick. I was a small child and he had sent away some fellow quite satisfied that he would get his owings the following day. Congratulating himself, he had spoken to me, though I had my head in my book and took no notice, "Watch and learn, little Molly. When you lie, keep a steady gaze. If you don't concentrate, your eyes will flick away. People see it: they don't know they do, but they do. They know you're lying. Always keep a steady gaze and people will believe you. Ha!"

'Really, Molly? If that is so, you could be the answer to my prayers!'

I kept my eyes steady, wide and bright. 'Lady Hamilton had a library at Nelson's house' - I had never heard her say this, but it seemed feasible, 'and it had outgrown its space. Lord Nelson had always complained that he could never find what he wanted, so when it was being moved into a larger room, I had the idea of organizing the books by topic. For you know, Lord Nelson was a very widely-read man.' I had absolutely no idea whether this was the truth, but it was clearly impressing Elsie. I had better not push it too far. 'He was dead by the time I went to work for Lady Hamilton of course, and she cried when I had the idea of cataloguing his library. She praised me to the heavens and wished I had been sent to them before he was taken from her. At the Battle of Trafalgar.' I saw that that was a step too far, for Elsie blinked.

Her tone was heavily sarcastic and I thought for a moment I had ruined the effect. 'Yes, thank-you Molly. I was aware how Lord Nelson died. News did reach us, even here in the far north.'

But then she brightened. 'Your words are music to my ears. The late Lord Strathmore's brother wants an inventory. Looking forward to the day it's all his, I suppose. There is a plan: it was done by George Bowes himself, and after he died, Mary Eleanor - such a bookish child by all accounts – she added to her father's ideas. When she married the 9th Earl he had no interest at all in the library, but then after he died and she married you-know-who... well, he stole books, he did. Sold them. Rare editions, too. She was desperate and hid some, I heard. They weren't found until after she was dead, when her son started the building work on the top storey. Bless her, such a little mite but the strength of two men, they say. Anyway, John was just like her, loved his books, and he wept when we showed him her plans for organizing it. He gave us some more notes and a diagram, because of course it's trebled in size since George Bowes's day. The work's been started several times, but always something went wrong and people gave up. He thought it was in progress and I had assured him it was. Thank heavens he was so often at Streatlam: he never knew we had let him down.'

'Did he prefer it at Streatlam?'

'No, I don't think he did. His heart was at Gibside, but after Lady Tyrconnel died here…'

'Lady Tyrconnel?'

Flustered, she got up. 'Oh, I shouldn't have mentioned her. That will do for another time, Molly. Lord Strathmore was often at Streatlam because that's where his horses are kept and trained. The Streatlam Stud is widely known and very successful. He was just like his grandfather in that love of horses.'

'And his grandfather was? Forgive me, I know so little.'

'Why George Bowes, of course! Mary Eleanor's father. The finest gentleman that ever lived! Glory Bowes. It is thanks to him that the estate is so beautiful: we are all proud of it. He wasn't one for spending on the house though, I have to say. Poor Lord Strathmore loved this house. I've to do my rounds now, you can come with me.'

We came to a great oak door and Elsie creaked it open, explaining, 'This is the door between the service block and the main house. It must always be kept closed.' We stepped through into a dark corridor that seemed to run along the centre of the ground floor, for it had no windows. The door at the other end was open, and dust-motes floated in a shaft of hazy light from the small square windowpanes. We were in a large hallway from which a wide oak staircase rose. I loved the place from that moment. I had expected to see columns and gilt, plush carpets and oriental cabinets, but Gibside Hall was quite different from the houses of the wealthy that I had heard about in London.

Like the Orangery, it seemed to be in and of the nature that surrounded it. The oak floors creaked, the carpets were threadbare, the tapestries smelt musty. The furniture was dark and intricately carved. There was little light in the rooms and the glass panes were ancient and mottled between the soft stone mullions. But best of all, the walls were adorned with paintings: tiny etchings, classical watercolours and large landscapes. As I lingered before yet another portrait, this time a luminous young woman, Elsie bustled on, 'This way, Molly, come come, we'll be all day at this rate.'

'Who is the young girl? Is that Mary Eleanor?'

'No, that's Eleanor Verney, the first wife of George Bowes. She died only ten weeks into their marriage. Poor Mr Bowes was heartbroken and didn't marry again for seventeen years. When he was finally blessed with his only child, he named her after Eleanor. Not sure how his second wife felt about it, like. That and having to look at portraits of her husband's lost love. There are six of them! One over the bed! Imagine!'

She turned the handle of another large oak door but then changed her mind, 'No, let's save the library until last. We'll just check the bedrooms then I'll send for some tea to the library and we can have a talk about it.'

We doubled back to the foot of the stairs and Elsie started to climb them, which she clearly found hard work as she held on to the bannister and her breath quickened. When she stopped on the landing, she ran a finger along the frame of a painting while she caught her breath. I went to stand at the bannister and look down into the hall, then turned to study a dark landscape of muted browns and greens until she was ready to carry on. It showed shepherds in the foreground and a three-storey mansion nestling in a wooded valley.

When Elsie came to stand beside me, I said, 'Where's this?'

'It's Gibside Hall before the alternations. Seen from Cut Thorn Farm.'

'It looks so different!'

'Yes, it used to have a third storey, but it was leaky and draughty and unused, so Lord Strathmore had the idea of making it more like a castle. More like Glamis, I suppose. He spent part of his childhood there.'

'Glamis is where the Strathmores come from?'

'Yes. After the 9th Earl died and Stoney Bowes came on the scene, they had Mary Eleanor's five children made wards of Chancery and they took over their upbringing.'

'Leaving Mary Eleanor to her fate?'

She gave me a long look before she answered. 'Yes. Leaving Mary Eleanor to her fate.' Then she was all bustle again and set off along the landing. 'See?' It was another portrait of the pale young woman, Eleanor Verney. 'And then of course poor Lord Strathmore lost his great love just as his grandfather did. And both of them dealt with their grief by pouring their energies into Gibside.'

Just then man's voice calling, 'Elsie!' could be heard from downstairs.

She called, 'Albert, we're up here! Be down in a mo. Put the kettle on, love.'

My face must have fallen because she said, 'Don't worry, Molly, we'll have a look at the library this afternoon. Time for some lunch, I think. You can have it with me and Albert. There's rabbit pie, how does that sound?'

Albert was as tall and lean as Elsie was small and fat: they made a comical pair and I smiled to see them together, he leaning over like a fishing heron to place a kiss on the top of her mob cap.

He had clearly heard all about me and accepted my presence at the table as though it was the most natural thing in the world, chatting about poachers and guns and then telling a funny story about a goat in the walled garden. I listened and laughed and struggled not to cry. These people could have been my parents for all the warmth I felt and the pleasure they seemed to derive from my presence. I wanted to stay here. I would do anything to stay here. I kept my smile wide and my eyes bright but tears were coming unbidden and unwished-for. I got up and took my plate to the sideboard, staying with my back to them whilst I struggled to maintain my composure. They had fallen silent. They must not suspect. They must not show me any solicitude or all my defences would melt and I would be washed away on a tide of grief for all that I wished and all I had lost.

I straightened my back, turned to the back to the table, and said brightly, 'You mentioned an armoury?'

134

Albert answered. 'Yes, there's the gun-room and the armoury. Both kept locked, of course. We've always had an armoury at Gibside: there's always been a lot of action in these parts, what with border reivers, Scots, Cromwell's army and all that. And of course the late Lord Strathmore raised a troop of cavalry.' Musingly, he flicked out a bright white napkin and wiped his impressive moustache. 'Who knows what will happen to the Derwent and Gibside Yeomany now? The lads have stood down, it's very sad. Of course if the Scots take this estate…'

'Now now Albert don't upset yourself.'

I asked, 'Have they seen any active service?'

'No, though there was an occasion recently when they were in readiness and fully expected to be deployed. The whole situation was diffused by Lord Strathmore himself'

'How so?'

'In the wake of Peterloo – you know about Peterloo? – parliament was debating bills to prevent trouble brewing in any other industrial areas. They were trying to make it illegal for large numbers of people to gather, and illegal for any citizen to receive arms training. It angered people. This is meant to be a free country. Our own Earl Grey spoke up in defence of civil liberty. He was our saviour, really. Anyway, people were angry and a great mob gathered on the banks of the river.'

'This river? The Derwent?'

'No, the great river three miles hence. The Tyne. Some said there were fifty thousand. Lord Strathmore let it be known that it was his duty to inform parliament. He sits in the House of Lords, he has a duty. Had. Anyway, it was a gamble really but it worked. The crowd dispersed and there was no harm done.'

'And the bills? Were they passed?'

'Greatly modified, thanks to Earl Grey. Crowley's Crew better watch out if anyone gets wind of their activities, that's all I'll say.'

It was the second time I'd heard of Crowley's Crew, and although I had no idea what it meant, I understood they were feared and respected. I wanted to ask so many questions but Elsie spoke for me. 'How do you mean Arthur?'

'The Unlawful Drilling Act. Penalty transportation. That's all I'll say.'

Chapter 15

That night, snug in my tiny room, I realised that for the first time in three months, I had had moments that day when Charlotte had not been in my mind. Guilt immediately flooded me and I could think of only one thing to do. I took a sheet of Colleen's writing paper from my bag and sat down at the dressing-table to write to Mary Bowes.

Gibside Hall
24th November 1819

Dear Miss Bowes

I hope this finds you well. I have arrived safely at Gibside and Elsie has very kindly allowed me to stay for the time being. As you can imagine, I am anxious to make myself useful so it was a great relief to be offered employment in the library here. I imagine you are aware of the great undertaking: I hope to make progress in the momentous task of cataloguing and organizing the collection. It is a great honour and I will engage myself to the very best of my ability.

Having learnt more about my father, I have kept my identity a secret known only to Elsie and Albert, who have been exceptionally kind to me. My illusions are entirely shattered and I retain no loyalty to him, so pray tell me what you will without fear of resentment. Now that I have an inkling of the truth, I would wish to know more of it, for I do believe that it is only by knowledge that I may arm myself.

I try to believe that my Charlotte is being cherished, wherever she is. I must believe this to be true or else I would run mad. But I have by no means given up hope of finding her. I trust you to tell me of any little rumour that may come to your ears.

I hope to work here through the winter. When the spring comes, I plan to look for an opportunity to go to Newcastle, though I know not how I should proceed or where I should go.

I would very much appreciate your thoughts, suggestions or reassurances. If you are kind enough to reply to me, please address the letter to Molly Sutton.

Kindly pass on my regards to the young Lord Strathmore and assure him that I will work hard on his library, for it is to be his, as we all devoutly hope.

With fondest regards,
Molly

I will never forget my first sight of Gibside's library. Never in my life had I seen so many books in one place and if I had known nothing of the story of its evolution, I do believe I could have deduced it for myself.

The notes were on a series of sheets of thick paper held in a leather folder. I could see that the earliest sheets were of fine quality and immaculately kept, being held in place by leather corner-pieces. The topmost sheets were of poorer quality and a practical hand had covered them with writing, at first neatly and then with increasing signs of frustration and despair. The sheets at the bottom were thickest and most elegantly presented: clearly produced as a fine copy rather than a working document.

The writing was large, old-fashioned, and generously looped, but the categories as defined by George Bowes were as clear as the day he had written them seventy years previously, probably in this very room. In a fine, large hand and centred on the page both horizontally and vertically, he had listed his major categories: Agriculture and Gardens; Architecture; Biography; Classics and works in translation; Dictionaries and Grammars; Fine Arts; History, Ancient and Modern; Learned Societies - publications thereof; Literature – Classical and Modern, to include works in translation; Natural History; Philosophy; Poetry; Politics - general and British; Science and Technology; Travel, maps and plates.

The ensuing pages were each headed by one of the categories: beneath, he had listed subdivisions for each, and the writing here was similarly large and authoritative. On each of these sheets, however, another hand, smaller, sloping and more feminine, had appended notes by means of an intricate series of symbols, the key to which was provided in an appendix.

It appeared that the writer, whom I assumed to be his daughter, had discerned weaknesses in her father's plan, a need for refinement, perhaps in view of her own interests or recent acquisitions. Several

categories were untouched, but it was immediately clear where her passion lay: where her father's interest in gardens appeared to be structural and aesthetic, including as he did a section on parterres and vistas, hers was botanic: to his broad category 'plants' she had appended a large and forceful asterisk and inserted a sheet headed by another large and ornate asterisk as large as a thumb-print which had been ornamented by doodles as the intricate sub-divisions poured out of her: "native and exotic, hot-house, evergreen, flowering, self-seeding, propagation methods, heating of greenhouses – working buildings, improvements in propagation of exotic fruits – NB treatment of tanners' bark for pineapples / where to situate the orchid house – nurserymen in the locality and further afield – categorization – Linneaus and learned volumes – TRAVEL – Captain Cook!" At length abandoning all attempt at order, she had simply allowed her pen to follow her thoughts.   *Bath*
1ˢᵗ December 1819

Dear Molly,

Thank-you for your letter and I am happy to hear that you have found productive work at Gibside. Elsie and Albert are very kind and if you consider it necessary to keep your identity secret, it will be safe with them.

I must tell you that I was astonished to hear of the circumstances of your birth and upbringing, and the more I reflect upon your achievements thus far in life, the more impressed I am by your resilience. Having surmounted the obstacles of your childhood, you must be an exceptional young woman to have come so far, and be assured that I will assist you in any way I can.

I am in an unusually sentimental mood today: forgive me if you find what I am about to say presumptuous. As you know, I have no children of my own and I find great pleasure in my role as an aunt. There is particular value to be found in offering support to the young people of my acquaintance who have need of an extra parental figure, especially one who is allowed a fallibility not always extended to parents. You and I barely know each other, but we perhaps have more affinity that you might suspect. I will explain.

138

Andrew Robinson Stoney was not my father, although I believed him to be so. He announced my illegitimacy to the world when I was sixteen: just as I was being introduced to society. I tell you these bare facts. There are many more facts I could tell you about the Stoney that I knew but I am conscious you may have a different perspective. Perhaps one day we will share our thoughts and memories. I am not a person who harbours ill-feeling, Molly. I do not wish to dredge up memories which will distress me and perhaps you. I do not wish to give them light and warmth: they will stay buried.

I can barely imagine the ways in which you and your family may have suffered: forgive me, but I do not wish to envisage it.

I picture you bridling when you read these words: your father's temper might yet dictate your feelings. Perhaps you even dashed my letter to the ground, angry at my unwillingness to attempt to share in your suffering in some way. But now you read on: you are perhaps wishing to stoke the fires of a newly-ignited bitterness towards me; but I will choose to believe you are intrigued by such complacency from me, of all people.

You will notice I said that I choose to believe. This is a concept that is very dear to me, and one on which my contentment depends. (Indeed, when I was a child, it was one on which I often felt my sanity depended.) I offer you this remark without further elaboration: if you wish to know more about the circumstances which at times threatened the balance of my mind, I will tell you another time.

You do not know me and I do not know you. We have something in common in that we have both suffered at the hands of a madman. What else shall we call him? Once, when I was perhaps ten or eleven, in a burst of anger and frustration, fear and loneliness, I wrote down all the names I could think of to describe the man who was the cause of my suffering and that of my mother. I cannot recall them all now, but I know that among them were such terms as liar, bully, sadist, abuser, despot, devil, bastard. The irony being, of course, that I myself could lay claim to that last word, though I knew it not at the time.

Have I shocked you? I think not. I think you and I can speak plainly to one another, Molly. I repeat that I do not wish to dwell on his wrongdoings: I offer you this confidence in order to show you that there are likely to be aspects of your past that I will understand.

I shall see young John at Eton this weekend: I shall pass on your good wishes. If you wish to reply, and I hope that you will, I shall be at home in Bath until Easter.

I read this letter several times and I find it difficult to express how much it moved me. Before I could think how to reply, a second letter followed and when Albert gave it to me, he smiled and said, 'You clearly have a friend in Miss Mary Bowes, Molly. Such a kind lady, a friend to cherish. Does she send you puzzles?'

'Puzzles?'

'Oh, she loves her puzzles and conundrums! She used to send them to Lord Strathmore all the time! Stumped him often, she did – he used to show me. Couldn't make head nor tail of them myself. He loved getting her letters. Always used to open them first and always smiled and laughed when he read them.'

Dear Molly

I had only just dispatched my last letter when I found that I must think more and more upon your baby. Not having had any of my own, I find it hard to appreciate how much the loss of her must mean to you, and once I reached out my imagination to how you must feel, I found I could not stop. From what I have seen of you, you have not let grief overwhelm your faculties, and from what you tell me, I have been doing some deductions.

The facts as I understand them are these: you know that the Irishwoman was told that what was wanted was a girl-child with curly red hair, young enough not to be talking. This of course suggests that one or both parents have that colouring and the couple wish the baby to pass as their own. You were told that they were affluent and that that they lived in Newcastle. Many wealthy families have a home in Newcastle but another in London or Scotland: some have homes abroad. If we assume that it was true that they have a home in Newcastle and that Charlotte was taken to them there, she would surely not be immediately produced in public. The sudden addition of a child almost one year old could be explained away, of course: a bereavement, a relative... but the specification of red hair is a real clue. They would not care what colour the baby's hair was if she was to be explained away. No, they are passing her off as their own. In order to do that, they must have been away from their main households for at least a year and my guess is that they have been on the Grand Tour of Europe. I would say perhaps their honeymoon but for the fact that they specify a girl. This to me suggests that they already have a boy, although I am not wedded to that idea. For a wealthy family, a male heir is often of primary importance, but that is not necessarily so for the existence of a sole female heir is not insurmountable, as evidenced by my own mother. (Although perhaps we should not revisit the circumstances brought about by that state of affairs!)

These deductions lead me to suggest that there is a narrow field of suspects and that some very specific enquiries will produce an answer.

But here I stop. A course of action suggests itself but before you proceed down that line, there are two possible consequences that I want you to consider, Molly. The first one is the danger of drawing attention to yourself. Remember that to these people, you are entirely expendable. The family who wanted a child so badly that they would put themselves in the way of such people are either naïve, wicked or very clever. They certainly have resources, and having successfully achieved their desire, they will not easily relinquish it.

The other aspect to consider is Charlotte's wellbeing. I think we can safely assume that she will be well cared for, but perhaps that is wishful thinking. I stopped myself here from issuing banal reassurances about her future but I realize that my imagination cannot reach so far as to imagine how you would feel if you did ascertain her whereabouts. Is it too much to suggest that you might reassure yourself of her welfare without revealing your identity? Forgive me, I know nothing about the circumstances of her conception or your hopes for her future. I only ask you to think very hard before proceeding. Do not act on emotion: be pragmatic, always.

Here we are much preoccupied with the court case. The judgment is in April. After that, everything might change. Who could ever have imagined that Gibside and Streatlam would pass out of the hands of the Bowes family? None of us. The thought cannot be endured. And how Thomas Lyon-Bowes can put his own nephew through this, I cannot understand, nor can I forgive.

Chapter 16

That winter seems like a dream to me now. I became so immersed in the library and its contents that I do believe I could happily have been sealed up in there, away from the world. I took my meals with Elsie and Albert, and though I met several other members of staff, I had no interest in anything other than the books. It was as though I had discovered a great deep parched empty well inside me: every day I was pouring a vast quantity of water to saturate its hollow spaces and seep into the very soil of my being. I was filling out, my mind expanding, my bruised soul gaining redemption and stimulation. The treasures the library held, the vast worlds of knowledge and erudition, ideas and existences, the skills and the care which had gone into the creation of each artifact in it… I felt alive in a way I never had before.

The task of cataloguing came naturally to me: I discovered that I had an aptitude for organization and my mind was alive with its challenges. I had been a blank slate: no preconceptions distorted the way I saw each book and I found I could anticipate the ways in which different people might seek these treasures.

I had to force myself to go outside, but every day I did, if only to walk up and down the front of the house where the deep snow had been cleared. When the ground was not covered in snow or ice, I trudged the estate in borrowed galoshes, through fog and wind and sudden surprising days of crisp sunshine. Even on the bleakest days, there was delight: I remember one foggy day I walked across the avenue, jumped down from the ha-ha and set off uphill, hoping that I would come up into sunshine; I was just about to turn back defeated when a friendly farmer emerged from the cloudy air with a ewe trotting at his heel and a newborn lamb in his arms.

Mary Bowes and I corresponded regularly: she would tell me which plays she had seen, what books she had read, sometimes snippets of news from the outside world, occasionally an acrostic she had composed for her own entertainment. She would always enquire about my progress and I would always be sure to tell her anything I had found that I knew would interest her. Once, I found a poem in

Mary Eleanor's hand, folded into a book of John Donne's Songs and Sonnets. She was delighted to receive it and begged me to send her anything I found of her mother's.

Every day, Albert made sure to give me an account of the post, whether there had been anything for me or not. Apart from Elsie and Albert, I barely spoke to anyone, though housemaids and grooms and gamekeepers passed through the kitchens. It seemed I was accepted, barely noticed, and that made me so happy: I felt I belonged. Solitude suited me: when I thought of the crowded rooms of the prison, the shared servants' beds, the pressing masses at Peterloo, my heart recoiled.

One of my favourite walks was along the riverbank: there was always something to see. The picturesque shallows, overhanging branches, hidden hollows, waving reeds, shining pebbles and industrious wildlife fascinated me: Bewick's tailpieces come alive.

One morning, I passed a young man fishing on the shingle beach below where the twin oaks grew together. He was tall and broad-shouldered with long wavy dark hair. Although I saw him notice me, I gave no indication that I had seen him but walked on, turning away and striding quickly across Ladyhaugh meadows and back towards the house. It was early spring and Albert had told me the snowdrops would be out in Ice House Woods: unusually, I wanted to prolong my walk before I went back into the dark library.

The following day, I saw the same young man walking towards me in West Wood, two pheasants slung over his shoulder. He had evidently seen me before I saw him: he was standing in the middle of the path and watching me with a languid smile. I considered stepping off the path to go round him but feared a playful advance: his look was mischievous.

'Are you going to report me?'

I stopped. 'I don't know you, how would I report you? And why would I?'

'There's plenty of food in these woods, and there are them as needs it.'

'It seems a land of plenty to me.'

'You're not from round here.'

Something about the certainty of his tone irritated me so I said the first thing that came into my head. 'Shotley Bridge.'

'Liar.'

'I beg your pardon?'

'I said liar. You're no more from Shotley Bridge than I am.'

'What's it to you? Kindly leave me be. I'll be on my way.'

But he fell into step beside me, the brace of pheasant still slung over his shoulder.

'Work here, do you?'

'Yes, in the house.'

'What as?'

'Mind your own business.'

'It is my business. My sister worked in the house and they let her go.'

'I'm only there temporarily. I'm a librarian. Lord Strathmore engaged me to catalogue his library.'

'Not much use to him now, though eh?'

'No, but the family want the work completed.'

'Then what?'

'Then I'll move on. To some other gentleman's library.'

'We could use you in Winlaton mebbes.'

'Pardon?'

'In Winlaton, we have a library.'

'You have a library in Winlaton? I thought it was a village of metalworkers.'

'You're really not from round here, are you? Where you from?'

'I'm from London.'

'Where else?'

'I'm sorry, but I find your questions intrusive.' We had come to a fork in the path, and I indicated the one that ran downhill towards the house. 'I'm going this way, and I suggest that if you don't want to be seen with your loot, you take the other route.'

'No, I'll walk with you.'

'But you'll be seen.'

'Aye, no doubt. There's some rough people in these woods, poachers and that. I'll look after you, don't worry.'

'I don't need looking after, thank-you.' I hastened my pace.

'By, you can walk fast for a lass. Bide a while. You're missing the snowdrops. Look.'

I stopped and saw two large clumps of pristine snowdrops, their delicate stems bent to the rich soil. Rapt, I spoke more to myself than to him: 'I do love snowdrops.'

He was smiling down at me, and I saw that his eyes were a startling blue, his lashes thick and dark. I felt an unaccustomed stirring. He sensed his advantage and smiled. 'Gabe Thornton, at your service.'

'My name is Molly.'

'Molly what?'

'Sutton. Molly Sutton.'

'So how do you come to be here, Molly Sutton?'

'I told you. Lord Strathmore engaged me to catalogue his library.'

'And where did you meet Lord Strathmore?' He asked the question pleasantly enough, but I was irritated again.

'I didn't meet Lord Strathmore. I was appointed through a third party. I have a reference from London.'

'And where else have you lived, besides London?'

I stopped. 'You ask too many questions, Gabe Thornton.'

'Well you could ask me some. It's called making conversation.'

'But you see I don't want to know anything about you.'

'Now that's just hurtful. And rude. It's quite rude.'

'Nevertheless, it's true. I'll bid you good day.'

I varied my walking routine after that. I wanted nothing to intrude on the smooth surface of my life and I had a feeling that Gabe Thornton had every intention of intruding, so I stuck to the open areas, circling Green Close, patrolling the avenue and delving into Snipe's Dene. I couldn't stay away from the river for long though, and sure enough, one May morning, there he was on the opposite bank.

'Good morning, Molly Sutton. Fine day, isn't it?'

'Helping yourself to the fish stock now, are you?'

'Aye well, all the carp are gone from the Octagon Pond. Divvn't knaa what happened to them like.' Even from a distance, I could see his eyes twinkling in a way I found disturbing, so I set off to walk on, but a female voice came from behind me. I turned to see a statuesque dark-haired young woman carrying a large wicker basket and walking leisurely towards us across the meadow. Behind her, the yellows and blues of spring flowers waved in the long grass. Her hair glinted conker-bright in the sun.

Her voice low and teasing, she said, 'I think you know fine well what happened to those carp, Gabe Thornton!'

She smiled and waved at him and then fell into pace beside me. 'Mind if I walk with you? I'm just going to the mill.'

I smiled assent but was suddenly shy and I did not speak.

'My name is Belle and you are Molly.'

Startled, I simply said, 'Yes.'

'I was glad to hear they'd found someone to finish that library job. A few of us had a go at it, but ... God, it was thankless. And dusty. And boring.'

'Not to me.'

'No, quite. Each to his own, eh? Me, I like sewing. I'm good at it and I make enough to live on.'

When I didn't answer, she fell quiet and we walked along in silence for a few minutes. I was just thinking of turning back when she touched my arm and stopped, facing me.

'May I ask you something, Molly?'

'If you must.'

'Would you rather walk alone?'

'Yes.'

'May I ask why?'

'Because I like my own company.'

'I thought as much. You are quite content. Then I will leave you.'

Her face was so serene, so understanding, that something in me began to unfurl. 'I'm sorry if I seem rude. I am just...quite self-contained. I will not be here long. My work is almost done.'

'And then where will you go?'

'I don't know. I...'

'Do you have a family?'

I don't know whether it was the warm day, the spring, the interaction with two teasing young people, but suddenly tears were in my eyes. Seeing them, she took my arm and walked me with her to the mill, where she sat me down on a sunny step while she went in. I could hear voices inside but not what they were saying. I considered just getting up and disappearing, but suddenly I had lost all motivation. I turned my face up to the sun and let it warm me through.

When she rejoined me, I got up, she linked my arm and we set off back the way we had come. She chatted amiably about the weather, bread prices and somebody having delivered a baby, and then she said, 'Would you like to come home with me for a cup of tea? I live in a cottage on Cut Thorn Farm, just there on the hill.'

As we climbed the steps at the side of the hall, I considered cutting into her cheerful monologue to bid her good day, but in truth it was so nice to be with her that I was loath to leave. She sometimes lapsed into silence but required nothing of me, so it was easier to go along.

'I know I am lucky to have such an extended family. We have always lived here, on the Gibside estate. My mother and her siblings are the fourth generation of tenants of Cut Thorn.'

'And your father?'

'My father's dead. There's three families living on the farm now. We all muck in.'

'Do you have any brothers and sisters?'

'Just me and Gabe.'

'Gabe's your brother?'

She smiled sideways at me as though we shared a secret. 'Yes, he is.'

'And does he work on the farm?'

'Gabe? No, he has no interest in farming. He's a metalworker. He learned his trade on the estate but now he works in Winlaton. We see plenty of him, though, as you know. He likes to come here to do his...shopping.'

'Ah, I see.'

I somehow sensed she was waiting for a question, but I resolved not to ask any. Eventually, she carried on talking about her brother regardless of my apparent lack of interest: 'Gabe's a good man but he's not afraid of getting in trouble. He's angry about a lot of things.'

I could not help it. 'What kind of things?'

'Injustice, mainly. Injustice in all its forms. And there's a lot of it about. He's been worse since he went to work in Winlaton.'

'I'm fairly new to the area, and I don't know anything about Winlaton. I keep hearing about it. What's special about it?'

'Ah, that's a good question. It's always been a special place, well, for the past hundred years, since an iron-master called Ambrose Crowley set up his works there.'

'But isn't it on a hill?'

'Yes, but the mills are just below on the river at Winlaton Mill and Swalwell. The hill's defensible, you see.'

'Why did he need to defend an ironworks?'

'I don't know. I've never thought about it. Mam'll know.' She opened the door to a low stone cottage and stepped aside to let me go in first. A tall woman in her sixties was sitting at the long table and she looked up as we came in. She had the same serene expression as her daughter and the same thick dark hair swept up in a generous bun. I could see she had once been a great beauty.

Belle put down her basket. 'Molly, this is my mother, Dorothy. Molly's new to the area - she's the one who's doing the library - and she was just asking about Winlaton, why Crowley's set up on a hill. It's never occurred to me.'

Dorothy's voice was low and gentle, like her daughter's. 'Hello Molly, nice to meet you at last.' A kindly look passed between mother and daughter. 'You must ask Gabe to tell you all about Crowley's. They say it was because the workers he brought were Catholic, from Belgium. It was a bad time to be a Catholic in England. Crowley had had a factory in Sunderland but they'd been persecuted there. We have Sir William Bowes to thank for the suggestion that he move to the Derwent Valley: this area had plentiful iron ore just waiting to be exploited. Plenty of accessible coal for the works, a fast-flowing river for the mills. Gibside supplied the charcoal: it suited everybody. And besides, this was a safe place to be Catholic. Other local landowners shared the faith, the Widdringtons and Tempests.'

149

Belle brought cups to the table. 'And the Tyne right on the doorstep for transport of the finished goods?'

Dorothy spoke with pride, 'The anchor chains they made were the finest in the world. Admiral Hood himself praised their quality after a storm at sea. The ships with Crowley's chains and anchors were the only ones not to break.'

Belle said in a subdued tone, 'There's other sorts of chains that are best not thought about.'

'So what's Crowley's Crew? I've heard them mentioned as though they're to be feared.'

'Why aye, they are to be feared if you're on the wrong side. Like the press gangs!' She and her mother laughed.

'No, they're fine men for the most part, though there's troublemakers amongst them, especially nowadays. Business has dropped off since the end of the French wars, and the company's failing. Thing is, in Crowley's time they were well looked after – strict rules, curfews, Crowley's even had their own courts. But in return they got medical treatment, pensions, schools, a library. Big believer in workers' education was Mr Crowley. It was like nowhere else that I know of.'

'And now?'

'Well, things aren't what they were in the iron business. Nor across the country, there's trouble all over, for all sorts of reasons.'

'Yes, I was telling Molly about the corn prices.'

'Aye. If there's trouble from Durham to Berwick, you'll find Crowley's Crew.'

'What kind of trouble?'

'Demonstrations. Our Gabe was arrested after the Peterloo one.'

My mouth must have dropped open. 'In Manchester?'

'No, in Newcastle. After what happened in Manchester there was a huge demonstration on the Town Moor. You must have heard about it? They reckon it was the biggest political demonstration anywhere in the world.'

'I… yes, I…'

'Are you alright, Molly? You've gone quite pale.'

'I… I was at Peterloo.'

150

Both their faces registered shock and without hesitation, without knowing me, Dorothy put her arms around my shoulders.

'Oh Molly, it's unthinkable. Poor bairn. Were you injured?'

It was as though a great torrent burst in my chest and out it all poured.

I was unaware that someone else had entered the room. Weeping, sometimes uncontrollably, I told them the whole story. Gabe heard it all.

Chapter 17

I suppose it was Peterloo that brought us together. I had had every intention of maintaining my protective shell: I would never have shown any man all my pain and vulnerability, but he heard it all. And when I heard his story, a bond was forged. When I look back, I am reminded of Othello and Desdemona: 'She loved me for the dangers I had passed and I loved her that she did pity them.'

When Gabe told me the story of the demonstration, he intoned the words from the newspaper report as though they were from scripture, his head held high: 'When the ancient rights of public meeting and petition exercised by the Radicals of Manchester were violated in the name of law and order, the people of Tyneside assembled on the Town Moor of Newcastle and spoke with courage and self-reliance against the outrage. We assembled near the Castle Garth on 11th October 1819 and marched in procession, tens of thousands strong, along Collingwood, Pilgrim and Northumberland Streets to the Town Moor. Hustings were draped in mourning, leaders carried white wands decorated with crepe and white ribbon; the national emblem was carried at half-mast.'

There was no courtship, no flirtation: our relationship bypassed all the usual stages and went straight to serious matters of the heart. Throughout that spring and summer, we walked the estate together, talking, talking. There was laughter, there were kisses, but in my heart, I always had misgivings. Gabe had no interest in my work and I was neglecting it in favour of sunshine, companionship, laughter and kisses. Elsie and Albert smiled indulgently when Gabe came to the door and never asked when I would be back, though they did once tease him about neglecting his work. In truth, it was easy for me to forget that he was meant to be a blacksmith: he was so often in the woods, so adept at stalking and hunting that I thought of him as one of the estate workers. Some of my happiest memories of that summer were of watching deer and badgers, learning to bait a hook, paddling in the river and collecting flowers in the walled garden.

I was still reading avidly in the mornings and evenings: sometimes I snatched a day in the library. I tried to explain what drew me back, the pleasure I found in it, how close I was to achieving order and completing the catalogue, but Gabe would yawn and roll his eyes and pull me outside, laughing.

I was happy for a time, throughout that spring and early summer, but soon I began to have misgivings: he could be so serious about the things that mattered to him, but when I tried to talk about the ideas that animated me, he would turn the conversation or try to kiss me or make me laugh. His dismissiveness began to irritate me, and when I was alone, I had to confront the fact that I should be in Newcastle searching for Charlotte.

In a weak moment, I opened my heart in a letter to Mary Bowes. The reply came swiftly but it was disappointingly short as she was on her way to London for the decision about the Strathmore Peerage case. She ended, 'If, as we believe, Charlotte is being cared for by a wealthy family with homes in other cities, they will at least be able to keep her safe from the cholera epidemic which has taken so many young lives in Newcastle this summer.'

In my stronger moments, when I was alone, I knew that I could not bring myself to trust, to open my heart permanently to the possibility of love. If I am honest, nor did I want to settle to the life of a blacksmith's wife. Once I was married, there would be children as naturally as autumn follows summer. Once there were children, my life would no longer be my own. My freedom would be gone, my time devoted to children and keeping house: there would be no time for anything else. Gabe was not an earner, I knew that: unless he changed, our existence would always be hand-to-mouth. Once, when I was afraid he was leading up to a proposal, he had spoken earnestly of the good wages that were to be earned in mining. A friend of his, Richard Robson, who was courting Belle, apparently wanted Gabe to join him in a mine with the romantic name of Stargate.

But even if he did find regular employment and stick to it, I doubted that he would be happy either. I could certainly not imagine that he was serious about going down a mine, but also his freedom, which I knew he took for granted, would be forfeit if he was to provide for a dependent wife and the inevitable children. And if anything happened to the wage-earner, what would become of me and my children? I thought again of my mother's circumscribed life. No, I would not relinquish my independence.

News of Lord Eldon's decision reached Gibside the day after the judgement: to general jubilation we were told that the Strathmore Peerage Case was finally settled. To our great relief, the English estates of Gibside, Streatlam and St Paul's Waldenbury were settled on the trustees for fourteen-year-old John Bowes. The title and the Scottish properties were confirmed as belonging to his uncle, Thomas Bowes-Lyon, now confirmed as the 11th Earl of Strathmore.

In the wake of the decision, Mary's reaction was typically optimistic: '*I am so relieved that it is settled and my nephew no longer has the spotlight upon him. He can look forward to a life free of Scottish encumbrance and independent of interference from them.*

And now I am free to turn my thoughts to you, my dear Molly, and matters of the heart. Forgive me for the delay in responding to your soul-searching letter and I must beg further forgiveness if events have moved on. You have perhaps by now been in receipt of a formal proposal: I am in ignorance of your current situation, but nevertheless, I want to talk to you about love, the love that is possible between a man and a woman. Now you might think, what can she know, old spinster that she is? I am not talking about marriage, Molly, indeed the couple I wish to tell you about never married. (There! I have already told you the end – what need you read on? I am teasing.)

It strikes me as strange that we say 'falling' in love: the word has connotations of loss of power, prostration, diminished strength...perhaps that's how it feels for some, but for my brother and his first true love it had the opposite effect.

It is a good story, and a long one. I shall entertain myself in the writing of it. Perhaps you are not in the mood just now to read it. If that's the case, put this letter aside for now and go about your business. Then later, find a time and a place where you can be safe and undisturbed and comfortable: prepare to transport yourself and open your mind to the possibilities of love.

To an onlooker, John Bowes had everything: he was wealthy, handsome, aristocratic, well-educated. In company, he was reserved, dignified, perhaps a little shy. His public pastimes were typical of a young man of his class: theatre, horse-racing, gambling.

In private, he liked to read and was interested in the arts, particularly architecture. At twenty-one, he had just come into his inheritance and taken up residence at Gibside, the rural estate designed by his maternal grandfather, George Bowes.

But anyone with an eye for such things would see that there was more to the 10th Lord Strathmore: those clear grey eyes were clouded, the brow contracted, even in repose. A stiffness to the way he held his neck, an unconscious tension in the way he repeatedly clasped and unclasped his right hand. Inside every stuffed suit is a beating heart, and the heart of the young lord was a bruised thing.

His mother was my mother, and I loved her dearly. There is no blame in what I am about to say, and no betrayal of confidence. As you are no doubt aware, childbirth affects women's minds, as well as their bodies, and after John was born, Eleanor could not love him. The reasons for this were manifold and complex and now is not the time to go into them. He did not want for love, for he was the pride of the family and the darling of the nursery, and in time he had brothers and sisters, but he was always treated as special, being the heir.

No doubt his father loved him, though it was not in his nature or upbringing to show it: John was to follow in his footsteps and in time would inherit great responsibilities. Even in childhood, he must be trained: he was sent away to boarding school. What none of them were prepared for was for his father to die when John was only seven years old.

What followed is another story. Andrew Robinson Stoney was evil incarnate: you and I experienced his cruelties at first hand, you for longer than anyone. As we all know, Eleanor suffered terribly. Young John, however, was protected from witnessing such depravity because he was taken firmly into the care of his father's family and ultimately he and his siblings were made wards of court.

We cannot know his thoughts on his mother's suffering, what worry and shame he endured, how his classmates teased him, what he thought of the salacious cartoons that portrayed her preferring to suckle her cats than to nurture him. What we do know is that when Stoney abducted Eleanor from a London street and took her out on to the wild moors of the northern Pennines in winter, young John left Cambridge without permission or protection and set off on horseback to save his mother.

And so, when the drama was over, Stoney captured, Eleanor rescued, the whole litany of vile abuse aired in the courts; while she recuperated and fought for justice and Stoney lied and plotted and escaped from prison; when the frenzy of hearings and testimonies, scandal and gossip had subsided, she was reunited with her five Strathmore children, thanks in no small part to the efforts of her eldest son. And it was he who helped Eleanor to insist that Stoney should be forced to reveal my whereabouts and release me and little William into the care of our mother.

Here, of course, is where our stories intersect, Molly, for at the point where I was released from captivity and reunited with my mother, your suffering was set in train.

His father's English estates having been violently exploited by Stoney, the tenants and miners unpaid, abused, even evicted, John inherited a devastated Gibside and Streatlam. He set to work repairing the damage, gathering round him the dejected workforce, thanking them for their loyalty to the Bowes family and for the part they played in supporting Eleanor through the years. He set about rebuilding lives, providing work and fair wages; he opened up the estate to the local populace, as it had been in his grandfather's day; and he fulfilled his mother's dying wish that the chapel should be completed at last and her father's remains should be brought home to Gibside.

What has this to do with love, you ask? Well here is the point of the tale: when he was just twenty-one and freshly settled at Gibside, he was invited to a theatrical evening at Seaton Delaval Hall. And what could be more entrancing to a young man from such a blighted family than to step into the fairytale world of the Gay Delavals? At first sight, she glowing at the centre of the stage and he awestruck in the audience, John and Sarah fell in love.

Sarah Hussey Delaval was no young ingénue: in her way she had as fraught a past as John Bowes-Lyon. The beautiful, vivacious, daring star of the Delaval firmament, Sarah had been married at sixteen to a thirty-year-old divorcee, Lord Tyrconnell, who was a friend of her father's. Imagine it. Then go on to imagine how her husband and father could encourage young Sarah to accept the advances of Frederick, Duke of York, son of George III. Thereby hangs another tale.

Suffice it to say that the two of them together were reborn.
Together, they could endure any opposition, notoriety and public
ridicule: they adored each other. Despite her father's opposition,
Sarah lived at Gibside with John. They had eight blissful years
together and then she tragically died, in the same year as John's
mother and of the same disease as his father. He was devastated.

If you have found true love, Molly, you need not marry. You
need not have children. Carve out your own path. Read A
Vindication of the Rights of Women. Be brave and get what you want,
as so few women do, but I know you can.

With all good wishes, Mary

I was haunted by this story: it was so romantic, so tragic, so
close. I looked out of the window, lost in imagining of these two lost
lives.

In the light of such a story, Mary's advice to me seemed
persuasive. There was no reason why I should not stay in this
beautiful place. Perhaps I could persuade Gabe to come back to work
on the farm. And I could continue to work in the house, perhaps in
some kind of administrative role after the library cataloguing was
completed. And if I was careful, there would be no need for babies.
Not yet.

'Belle, may I talk to you about something very personal?'

'You know you can.'

'Gabe wants to marry me. I don't know what to do. I am very
fond of him, but restless. Were you happily married?' Belle's first
husband, a farm labourer, had died only a year after their wedding.

'Yes, I would say so, happier than most, perhaps because I never
had to leave here. I couldn't imagine any other life. My mother's
family has always belonged here. It must be in my blood.'

'Your father's too?'

Her face closed. 'No.'

'Where was he from?' I was thinking she would say Winlaton or
Streatlam: in truth, I was barely listening, so preoccupied was I with
the momentousness of the decision before me. But she didn't answer
so I looked at her properly and my heart froze.

'Ireland,' she said. 'My father was Stoney Bowes.'

I left without saying a word. When I look back, what must they have thought of me? The shock was so great that I knew nothing until I reached the house. I slipped inside, packed my bag and left. I saw no-one, I spoke to no-one. I covered my hair, bent my neck, shouldered my bag and left.

Now I had my answer: Gabe could not be my husband because he was my brother.

Chapter 18

It was early autumn when I left Gibside, and the melancholy fall of leaves suited my mood. By the time I reached the turnpike road, my heart had calmed and I was filled with new resolution. I had tarried too long. I reprimanded myself for the loss of time, though I reasoned that enough time had passed for the family who had taken Charlotte to have become complacent. She would surely by now have been shown in public. Once accepted, she would be paraded with increasing confidence and when I reached Newcastle, I might well see her. I made myself believe: it made the pain of leaving more bearable.

In my mind's eye, Newcastle was a walled town surrounded by orchards and to the north a great park they called the Town Moor, where sheep and cattle grazed. As I walked rapidly along the turnpike, I thought back to Bewick's engravings and realised that they had shown me more than a rural paradise along the banks of a wide shallow river. In the background there had been chimneys and windmills. In the foreground wide shallow boats that I knew were called keels. There must be great houses in the town, perhaps in elegant squares like the ones I'd seen in London. I imagined Charlotte's nursery, the high windows, the comfortable cot in which she slept, the fine linens, her hair upon the pillow. She was eighteen months old now: would she know me? Would we recognize each other the instant our eyes met?

I did not have to wait long before a carter pulled up and offered me a lift. 'I can take you as far as Derwenthaugh. From there you can travel by boat into Newcastle. There's a good deal of traffic today. Today's a holiday – there's royalty coming and those as can afford it'll be dressed in their best and attending the festivities.'

'Is it the king?'

'No, one of his good-for-nothing brothers. The Duke of Sussex or somesuch.'

Immediately, a port-red face exploded into my mind, a barking laugh, wheezy breath on my cheek, a whinnying laugh, small hands out of all proportion to the size of his head and his belly. And always a glass in that hand, the little finger crooked.

'I have seen him before. I'll not be wanting to see him again.'

'He's never been here before, except as guest of Radical Jack, I'll wager.'

'Radical Jack?'

'Jack Lambton. Fine fellow. They're both freemasons, so I'll wager they're pals. Look after their own, those types do. How did you meet him, lass?'

'In London. I worked for Lady Hamilton.'

He looked at me then, his open mouth displaying a complete absence of teeth. 'Nivver!'

'I did. Is it so hard to believe?'

'Whore, was she? After Lord Nelson? Go back to her whoring ways, did she? Was it a brothel?'

My temper choked me but I answered him with a shaking voice. 'No. She was far from being a whore. She was devoted to the memory of Lord Nelson and only wanted her dues as his widow. She was left with no means to provide for his child.'

'Aye,' he muttered darkly, 'if it was his child. Mebbes that was it. Mebbes he knew.'

Once again the injustice of man's view of woman clenched my fists, but I held to the Quaker way: be still and cool in thine own mind. And the voice of Mary Bowes whispered in my ear: 'Be pragmatic always.' This man could not help his ignorance. I stayed silent and looked around me. Such a beautiful, fertile valley, so many trees tinged with the golden hues of early autumn.

After a time, he spoke again: 'I miss the war, I do.'

'That seems like a strange thing to say. Surely we are all glad it has ended?'

'Not all of us. I'm from Winlaton, though I live in Swalwell now. Orders have dried up. Aye, things have not been the same since the defeat of Boney.'

This was the opportunity I had been waiting for to hear some other view on the village: listening to Gabe, I had gained the impression that the place was a powder-keg, awaiting only a spark. I said, 'I've only been in the Derwent Valley for a few months and I know very little about Winlaton.'

'Everyone knaas Winlaton!'

'I can promise you everyone doesn't. What is it about the place that makes it so different?'

'Well, Crowley's of course.'

'Tell me about Crowley's.'

His tone was scornful, as though I was pretending ignorance. 'Ironworker. Been dead years now.'

'And he set up a factory?'

'Aye. Cem here from Sunderland on account of his Belgian lads, like.'

'Belgians?'

'Aye. Experts. Brought 'em 'ere on account of the trouble in Sunderland. They were Catholics.' As though that explained it.

'So he set up a factory on the hill there?'

'Aye. Converted the mills on the river, set up in Swalwell. Aall awer. Best employer anywhere. Ever.'

'In what way?'

'In every way! Skills, prices, wages, houses, pensions. Even a court! They had to obey, like. Curfews, temperance and that. But do right and it was a fine life.'

'Making metal objects? For farms and the like?'

'Pah! That wasn't the half of it! You could get anything made! Quality products. Known all over the world.'

'Really?' I was sceptical. 'All over the world?'

'Why aye! Like ah said. Quality! Top quality! Winlaton anchor chains the best in the world.'

'So now?'

'Well, the French wars was the best time – business boomed! But since Waterloo, well, it's all ower. Back to the nails and wheels.'

'So people are unhappy?'

'Well of course they are, ye daft lass! Ye get used to the good times. Not enough work for them all now. Some have set up on their own, they're the lucky ones, but the rest are stuck with poor pickings. All the admiralty orders dried up, see?'

I looked up at the village on the hill.

'There'll be trouble, you mark my words.'

'What kind of trouble?'

'Well, they're hard as nails, them lot. Even the press gangs were afeard to go there. And if they're not happy, folks are going to hear about it.'

'Idle hands and all that, I suppose?'

'Well it's more than that isn't it? Clannish, they are. Folks are fine as long as they've food in their bellies, but people are going hungry now and they're asking why. It was all King and Country while the sun was shining, but now there's bother. Dark mutterings. Insurrection.'

Now I understood. Like the Lancashire weavers, these people were suffering and feeling powerless. No wonder they had demonstrated in the wake of what happened in Manchester: it could just as easily have happened here.

We travelled in silence past the hamlet of Winlaton Mill and into busy Swalwell, where chimneys loomed and the air was smoky. We were getting near to the convergence of the rivers at a place called Derwenthaugh when he stirred himself to say, 'I'll drop you at the Skiff and you can find someone who's going into the Toon. Mind yersel with them keelmen, like.'

My first sight of the great River Tyne was a surprise: it was far busier than I had ever imagined, intersected by great staithes loaded with sacks and crates. Black keelboats were tied up against the jetties while men shouldered heavy burdens and hoisted or slung them into the waiting craft. In the middle of the river, multitudes of laden keels sitting low in the water were sailing past on their way from Newburn, Stella and Blaydon. An older woman took me under her wing and the two of us sat in the stern as a powerfully built man rowed us rapidly with the outgoing tide towards Newcastle and the sea.

He too had his complaints and voiced them loudly in an accent I found incomprehensible. My companion translated for me: 'He's moaning about the plans to deepen and straighten the river so that the big ships can get all the way to the tidal reach. Says it'll do them all out of their jobs.'

We rounded a bend in the river and a great stone bridge with several low arches came into view. Ships and boats of all sizes and shapes were packed against the riversides and jostling for position in midstream. The quayside was a seething mass of people, and behind I

162

could see half-timbered houses: the land that rose steeply from the river was covered with close-packed buildings and narrow alleyways teeming with people. The air was black with smoke and I could taste coal dust on my tongue.

The place where we disembarked was called Sandhill. Having ascertained that I was alone and had no knowledge of the town, the woman said, 'Well I've just come in to see the great event. There's royalty coming to lay the foundation stone for a posh new building. They're going to transform Newcastle, they say. See over there on the Gateshead side? That's Bottle Bank and the carriages will be coming down there, crossing the bridge and then going up towards the cathedral. We'll set off up here but it'll be packed and steep until we get to the top of the burn: try and stick with me. If we get separated, ask for the cathedral: there's more space up the top.' Swept along in the good-natured crowds swirling around the curious lantern-spired cathedral, I only saw the tops of the carriages, which were apparently being pulled along by over-excited citizens who had uncoupled the horses in order to lead the great personages to the site of the new 'Lit and Phil.'.

I spent the night in the dormitory next to The Old George Yard. It wasn't until I was lying under a thin blanket on a horsehair mattress that my isolation hit me. In this city, I knew not one person. As I slipped into a fretful doze, I wept.

It takes me a long time to surface from sleep and often feels as though I am drifting up from a great depth, drifting hither and thither on the currents and eddies on the edge of sleep. My night had been deep and dreamless and as my mind's eye began to catch the glimmers of wakefulness, an idea came to me. Is it ever the way with you? Sometimes, the mind throws upon the beach of consciousness a piece of driftwood in the shape of something real. That morning, surfacing in the women's communal room of the Olde George Inn, long before the horses woke or the grooms called to each other across the cobbled yard, an idea came to me that was so simple and so obvious that I blinked in the brightness of it. Thomas Bewick.

I took my precious book from its muslin binding and turned to the print of the Eagle-owl. As a child, I had formed the impression for some reason that the face of this bird most closely approximated that of Thomas Bewick. Something about its large round eyes suggested humour as well as uncanny sight. As I grew older and more worshipful of the man who had created these marvels and written so kindly and knowledgably about the world, I began to imagine him as a godlike being who had a snowy beard and lived on a cloud. The reality of the man with the rough hands who had carved the blocks from boxwood had struck me with the force of a revelation in Shotley Bridge, when I learned that he was still alive.

I would go to him: I believed in my innocence that he would surely know me as I felt I knew him. At least the idea gave me an impetus that propelled me out of the bed.

I marshalled my thoughts over breakfast. I had a fine hand, an understanding of order and a logical mind. The deficiencies in my education had been at least partially remedied by my time in Gibside's fine library. I knew enough to convince people that I knew more. I was willing to learn. Everyone in this town knew Mr Bewick: it surely followed that he would know everyone in his turn. Someone here could surely use my skills.

The landlord's wife was a whip of a woman with an intimidating manner, but I braved her. 'I wonder could you direct me to Mr Bewick's workshop?'

'You're nobbut a few steps away, lass.'

A male voice spoke: 'I pass by Mr Bewick's workshop and can escort you if you wish.' I turned to see a tall older gentleman sitting at a table on which a large newspaper was spread out. He looked up as he closed the paper and folded it. 'I'm ready to leave on the instant.'

'That would be very kind. Thank-you.'

He stood up, the top of his head almost brushing the beam. 'Although if you're hoping to meet Mr Bewick, you won't find him there, I'm afraid. He does call in occasionally but he's an elderly gentleman now and lives across the river in a fine house in Gateshead. If you don't find it an intrusion, what is the purpose of your visit?'

'I am looking for work.'

'Of what nature?'

'I... my great interest is in books and libraries.'

'Well, you are certainly in the right place. Newcastle's reputation is what I imagine has drawn you here.'

He was looking at me in a way I began to find uncomfortable.

'I wonder... please don't take offence, young lady, but the singularity of your appearance prompts me to ask whether you would consider working as an artist's model?'

I bridled. 'No, I would like to use my brain. I have experience of working in two gentlemen's libraries. I thought perhaps I would be able to find work cataloguing, recording, organizing paperwork, something of that nature.'

'Well. I can certainly introduce you to someone who will be able to help you to find a suitable source of employment, although I cannot promise that you won't be lured into the profession which your eyes so expressively indicate is repellent to you.'

'I'm sorry?'

'When I suggested you might model for an artist, your glance could have sliced my cheek.'

'I apologise. Someone I cared about very much indeed was ill-used as a result of surrendering to the male gaze. It is something I promised myself I would never do.'

'That would be a pity. You might find that once you accept the respectable nature of portraiture, you are willing to sacrifice your scruples. It is a matter of trust. Your arrival is timely: there are exciting developments afoot in the art world of this town as well as in its literary life.'

'I am new to the city. I have been working in the country. In County Durham, in the library of a gentleman's country estate.'

'Might I ask the name of the gentleman?'

'I... Forgive me, sir, but if am to be interviewed for a position, I will answer any questions necessary. At present, I do not know your name.'

'My name is Henry Ketchin...and yours?'

'Molly ... Molly Bowes.'

'Then I think I can guess the name of the gentleman. I take it you are a relative?'

'A distant relative, yes.'

'And will you be able to provide a reference?'

'Yes.'

'Come, I will explain as we walk. Mrs Kyle, I shall escort Molly to Brunswick Place and there introduce her to Mr Richardson. It is possible that a position could be found for her at the Institute.'

I had been concerned about the true intentions of the gentleman, plausible and courteous as he was, but now I felt a flare of hope. 'The Institute?'

'I shall explain as we walk. One moment, please Molly. Is this your bag?'

'Yes. May I leave it here, Mrs Kyle?'

'Aye. I'll put it in the storeroom. There's nothing of value in it, is there?'

'Just one thing. A book. I shall take it with me.'

I put the book on the table and bent to fasten my bag and hand it to the landlady. When I turned back, Mr Ketchin had unwrapped the muslin. 'Ah, Bewick's Land Birds! You are a devotee, I take it? Who is not who knows his work? The man is a genius and a fine fellow to boot. Perhaps you will meet him today, for he too is on the committee of the Institute.'

We walked out onto a cobbled square called the Bigg Market, and Mr Ketchin seemed to know everybody we passed. 'These are exciting times for Newcastle, Molly. No doubt you witnessed all the excitement yesterday? The Literary and Philosophical Society, of which I am a founder member, shall shortly have a permanent home. Our existence so far has been nomadic, to say the least.'

'Yes, I had heard a little about it, and of course I saw the crowds for the laying of the foundation stone. Exciting times indeed. And there is a community of artists?'

'Newcastle has a fine reputation for printing, engraving and illustration, thanks in no small part to Thomas Bewick. Those of us concerned with the artistic life of the city would like to increase our status in the eyes of the country and so we have banded together under the auspices of the gentleman you will meet shortly and formed The Northumberland Institution for the Promotion of the Fine Arts.'

'That sounds very grand. Do you have premises?'

'We are on our way to the home of Thomas Miles Richardson, who has built a gallery onto his house in Brunswick Place. The first exhibition opens in two weeks. But that is only the beginning. Mr Grainger and Mr Dobson's plans for the city are supremely elegant: Newcastle is to be transformed into a 'city of palaces'! We hope as part of that transformation to have a home of our own: a purpose-built gallery, and perhaps an Academy to bring on the young artists of the future.'

'Are there any notable painters of portraits in Newcastle? For the wealthy families?'

'Not so much. Landscapes are quite the thing. This northern light, you know: the drama and the sea, the perspectives of the hills. Northumberland lends itself more than any other county to large canvases: such light and distance. Mr Richardson's earliest masterpiece, 'Newcastle from Gateshead Fell' was inspired by William Turner, of whom you will no doubt have heard.'

'But no portraitists?'

'I see you are disappointed. Do you have a particular interest in portraiture?'

I thought quickly. 'I am interested in art collections and libraries. My dream is to be employed by a wealthy family and assist in curating their collection of art and literature.'

'A laudable ambition. May I ask something of your origins, Molly? You strike me as a most unusual young lady.'

'As I mentioned, I am distantly related to the Bowes family of Streatlam and Gibside. I was brought up in London and my first position was in a household with a modest but interesting collection.'

'And your personal circumstances?'

I lifted my chin. 'Forgive me, Mr Ketchin, but there are particular circumstances which I would find it too upsetting to speak about. I am... determinedly independent.'

'And you have independent means? A private income, perhaps?'

'No. I do not.'

His tone was avuncular. 'It would be far more usual for a young woman like yourself to become a governess.'

'I am aware of that, but I have an active desire to work with books and paintings.'

I caught a sideways glance that looked faintly alarmed, and reflected that my tone might have been unnecessarily fierce. To reassure him of my good nature, I added with a rueful smile, 'Besides, I do not enjoy the company of children.'

'Ha! I likewise! I am a grandfather and expected to dote upon the moppets, but I have no interest until they are fit to converse.'

'Yes, I am perhaps unusual among my sex. Some of these wealthy families, they dress up their offspring like miniature adults for the artist.'

'I must confess, I share your bemusement.'

It was tempting to lead the conversation to portraits of children but I could think of no natural way of asking whether he had seen any recent ones of red-haired baby girls without alerting him to the cause of my curious intensity.

When we reached Brunswick Place, there was no mistaking which building belonged to Mr Richardson, for a procession of workmen were piling packing cases on the pavement in haphazard manner. The front door was open and I could see large canvasses precariously propped up against the wall in the hallway.

A ruddy-faced gentleman with prematurely white hair and whiskers was standing at the foot of the staircase, his fists on his hips and his eyes popping with anxiety.

'Ah Thomas! How goes it?' My companion hailed the man with a breeziness that I expected would send the other into apoplectic rage. Instead, he ran forward and practically fell into his arms with evident relief.

'Henry! Thank God you've come! Oh, pardon me, young lady. I had not seen you there. Excuse me, I must speak with you in private, Henry.' Taking my companion by the arm, he made as if to guide him away to talk in private.

But Mr Ketchin stopped him with a smile, patting his arm reassuringly. 'Fear not, Thomas. I have brought you just what you need. May I present Miss Molly Bowes. Our assistant.'

Chapter 19

Those first few frenzied weeks at Brunswick Place are a blur in my memory: in addition to all the secretarial work - and it seemed to me that these important men were unable to put down a piece of paper without losing sight of it - I found myself involved in the physical labour of mounting the exhibits, carrying pamphlets and catalogues and tickets to and from the printers, even taking down curtains to improve the lighting. The idea that I would contribute some household duties in exchange for my bed and board was soon forgotten: I would fall into bed at the end of another fourteen-hour day, sleep like a dead thing without moving a muscle and wake stiff and cold to do it all again. I was told I was an angel and a godsend so often that the other staff teasingly used both words as though they were my name.

I was happy and useful and stimulated and I had no time to dwell on Charlotte or Gabe. On my first visit to the mail office, I had sent a brief note to Belle explaining my sudden departure, but it was still a surprise when amongst the profusion of post and invoices, I found a letter addressed to me and postmarked Rowlands Gill.

Dear Molly

What a relief it was to hear from you. We had become close, you and I, and it seems that neither of us had any suspicion of our closer connection, for as you say, we are sisters! I must immediately reassure you that Gabe is not your brother and beg you to return, for he is pining for you terribly.

You will wonder at this news. Have no doubt of my mother's morality: Miss Mary Bowes will vouch for her: when she was a little girl, my mother was her nursemaid for a time. Indeed (and I know this will shock you, but you and I need have no secrets now) such was the nature of our loathsome father that when he forcibly took my mother's virginity, little Mary was asleep in that very room.

We harbour no bitterness – it is all a long time ago now and bitterness harms the sufferer, my mother always taught me.

Her name then was Dorothy Stephenson and she was known for her beauty. It seems it had always been Stoney's intention to despoil her and to that end, she had been lured from the family farm to London, where she was promised a respectable job as nanny to baby Mary. When her parents heard the truth and that she had given birth to me, they went to London to try to find her, and can you believe that Stoney hid us away in a brothel? A young mother and her newborn babe?

I don't know how much you have heard about his conduct towards Lady Strathmore. Perhaps one day my mother and I will sit with you by our fireside and tell you what we know. When Mary Eleanor finally escaped into hiding and began court proceedings, Stoney did worse to my mother. In order to make her testify in his favour, he separated her from her baby. I am sorry if it shocks you to hear more of our father's devilment, but there it is.

When we were finally reunited through the intervention of Lord Mansfield, the Stephensons brought their daughter and baby granddaughter home to Gibside, whereupon the man I prefer to call my father, Gabriel Thornton, married her and raised me as his own flesh and blood. Gabe was their only child. So you see, nothing stands in the way of your love for Gabe and his for you! Come home, sweetness, and make your family happy!'

Your sister,
Belle

Is it wrong of me? Not once did I consider this offer, even though Belle's letter was followed by one from Gabe. He must have dictated it to someone, perhaps his mother, and began by offering me forgiveness that I had not realised I needed. He told me about his job down the mine, steady income and his wish to make me his wife. I felt nothing. Gabe was a ghost to me now. I never once felt tempted to succumb to the life of a labouring man and I didn't reply to either of them.

My life was here now, among the cultivated literary and artistic people of Newcastle. The opening day was drawing near and still I had not glimpsed my hero: his name was mentioned often but he didn't appear. Once, I heard, 'Ah, Bewick!' and looked up sharply from my work, the blush rising swiftly to my face, but the diffident young man who had come into the room I took to be his son, Robert, who was also on the committee.

The day before the exhibition opened, I was as nervous as a kitten for I knew that the whole committee would assemble for the preview. Dressed in a russet gown that Mrs Richardson had kindly pressed upon me, I hung at the back of the room, overcome with shyness. Thomas Miles Richardson led the large group into the exhibition hall, and though I knew exactly who was there, for had not I written all the letters and invitations, I could no more easily pick out individuals than discern one rook in a whole parliament. Committee members Joseph Crawhall, John Dobson, Henry Perlee Parker, James Ramsay, Thomas and Robert Bewick and their families, important dealers and from London and Edinburgh, journalists from national and local newspapers - they trooped in, milled about, exclaimed over exhibits, bent to speak to their wives and daughters, but no one figure stood out until into the room came a tall, well-built, rustic-complexioned gentleman and there was no mistaking who it was, for didn't the whole room seem to turn and greet him by name? The mood of polite self-conscious conversation evaporated on the instant and the whole room erupted into convivial chat and laughter. I almost wept for happiness that I was there. I could no more have spoken to him than taken wing and flown around the room.

On the day of the opening, dressed in the same russet gown, I avidly watched the wealthy and aristocratic families arrive, but none of them had the merest hint of red hair.

I was aware that the watcher herself was being watched: I had been introduced to that young artist before but couldn't for the life of me think of his name, but he was looking me with an open admiration that was frankly uncomfortable. By the time he had plucked up courage to speak to me, I suspected what he was going to say.

'Pardon me, miss, but have you a moment?'

'I'm afraid I am busy. I may not look it, but I am.'

'My apologies. I have no wish to distract you from your work. Nevertheless, in the absence of anyone else in our immediate vicinity, I shall.' He bowed. 'My name is Thomas Sword Good. Perhaps you have heard of me.'

'I hate to disappoint you, but I have not.'

Crestfallen, he went on. 'We have been introduced, but perhaps you do not remember. I am an artist, a successful artist. Although I must confess my success so far has been modest, I feel I am on the cusp! All I lack, so to speak, is a muse. And unless I am very much mistaken, I have found one!'

'Really?' I looked round ostentatiously. 'Where?'

'Oh. I see you jest with me. I think you know that I have been watching you. For, you know, it is you! Yes, you are my muse!'

'Forgive me, Mr Good, but I think you will find that I am no-one's muse. I am Mr Richardson's assistant.'

'Ahem. Yes, I deduced as much. Nevertheless, in the face of your disdain, I persist. For, like a courtly lover, I thrive on rejection! Yes! Pain drives me! See how your eye falls on me with indifference! It thrills me! For I must win you! And win you I shall!' And to my utter horror, he fell to his knees, gazing up at me and wringing his hands.

'Get up, Mr Good, I beg you! You are causing a disturbance. People are looking!'

'Let them look! For most assuredly, look they shall when I have immortalized you in paint, you extravagantly lovely creature! Skin of porcelain, eyes of ice and hair of flame! You shall ignite my talent and my fame! What is your name?'

'I will not answer until you get up. Stand up, sir, for heaven's sake!'

His friend urged him, 'Good, for God's sake, get up, you fool!'

'I must prostrate myself at the feet of this divine creature! Tell her she must sit for me!'

'Young lady, you must sit for him.'

'Let me take you to Richardson's studio now!'

'No. Go away. I'm busy.'

'Seriously. I'm serious. I really would like to paint you. I will make you famous! As Emma Hamilton was to Romsey, you shall be to me.'

My smile froze. I looked away.

His companion spoke: 'It seems that was entirely the wrong thing to say, Thomas. Make amends.'

'Oh, I'm sorry. I can be civilized and restrained. And serious. I beg you. Agree to sit for me in Richardson's studio. I ... I...'

172

Beginning to enjoy the pair of them, I said light-heartedly, 'Oh dear dear, you are a successful artist and yet you have no studio of your own?'

'I have, but it is in my home town of Berwick upon Tweed, some miles north of here. I also rent a studio in London.'

'I'll be honest with you, Mr Good. I have no intention of being an artist's model. I have my reasons. Your reference to Emma Hamilton was unwise and unlucky because she was my friend.'

Understanding dawned.

'I am sorry. I hardly know what I am apologizing for, but I am sorry. Can we start again?'

'That won't be necessary. The answer is no.'

I bent my head and pretended to be reading my ledger. I saw his feet retreat, shuffle and stop. Then the whispered words, 'I am a fool. See how her hair catches the light. Such beauty of colour.'

Any mention of my hair brought me to Charlotte. I looked up. 'What nature of pose had you in mind?'

'Oh! I would be so grateful. It's the light, you see. You can sit here, in the light from the window. I am very much interested in shafts of light. Your hair is of such rare colour and texture, a portrait cannot fail to be striking.'

'How long would it take?'

He was all seriousness now, though I saw he was finding it difficult to hide his excitement.

'I... well I would need you to sit for head and hands. I can always use a local sitter for the body, though I have to say...'

'Don't.'

'Come to Berwick. I live with my mother. You'd be quite safe.'

'How far is it?'

'Sixty miles. It's on the Scottish border.'

'No, of course I am not going to come to Berwick.'

A thought came to me then. 'Mr Good?'

He looked hopeful.

'My hair is, as you say, a rarity. Did you ever see the like?'

'No, I must confess, I have not.'

'Never? Not even on a child?'

'No, I'm afraid not.'

The droll voice of his companion drifted over his shoulder.

173

'The Blairs have hair like that.'

'The Blairs?'

'You know, Thomas, the Blair family of Pitlochry.'

'Oh aye?' he said distractedly. 'No, I don't know them.'

I could not help myself. I got up and trying to affect a languid curiosity, I said to his companion, 'This Blair family, are they wealthy?'

'As Croesus.'

'I beg your pardon?'

'Wealthy as Croesus. Great pile up in the highlands, chateau in France, town apartment in George Square Edinburgh.'

'And they all have hair like mine?'

'The menfolk do. All of 'em, like a race apart. No eyelashes though, or at least that's how it strikes you. Uncanny-looking.'

'I should like to see them. I have never come across anyone with hair like mine in all my life.'

'They come to Newcastle sometimes, for the horse-racing mainly. They have a house in Eldon Square.'

I tied my headscarf tight and put a bonnet on top then went straight to the house and watched carefully for any signs of life. Eventually a skinny girl of fourteen or so came out with a slop bucket and threw the contents fiercely across the yard below.

'Hello, is this the Blair family residence?'

'Aye. What of it?'

'I've been sent.'

'Well you've wasted your journey, they've gone, dunno where.'

I actually felt my heart sink. Still, I must find out what I could.

'What are they like to work for?'

'Not saying. What's it to you?'

'I'm a nanny. Is there any work for a nanny?'

'No, they bring their own. Snooty Scot like the rest of 'em.'

Emboldened, I leaned with my back against the railings and said conversationally, 'Aye, I've met a few of them in my time.'

'Not here much nowadays. Plenty to do, like. I'm just a skivvy. Go in and ask.'

'It's nice out here. Have a sit. Take the weight off for a minute.'

I sat down on the low wall, my back against the railings and my face upturned to the sun, for all the world as though I hadn't a care in the world. 'I was a skivvy once,' I said musingly. 'Not much fun.'

'No, I'm sick of it.'

'What d'you want to be?'

'Ladies' maid. Nice and clean. Or a nanny.' She stole a sly sideways look at me and I pretended not to notice.

'Play your cards right and I'll get you a job.'

'You got a job?'

'Yes but I fancy a change. Bit of travel. Maybe a nice little girl to look after instead of two lads. Bloody handful they are, I can tell you.'

'They have a little lassie, the Blairs.'

'Just the one?'

'Aye.'

My heart was beating very fast.

'How old?'

'Just a tiny toddler. Proper little sweetheart.'

I swallowed hard.

'What are you like with babies?'

'Don't know. Never get near. Never get a chance.'

'Well if you come and work with me, I'll teach you. How long have you worked here?'

'Three years now. Used to just do the fires.'

'So you'll have known her all her life, the little lassie? She born here?'

'How d'you mean?'

'The bairn. Born here? In this house?'

'Dunno. No. Don't know where she was born. They've got lots of houses.'

I stood up, dusting down my clothes as though making idle talk. 'Is the mam nice?'

'She's alright, kind. Quiet. Meek. Nicely-spoken. Not a Scot, like.'

'I think I might have seen them actually. I think they've visited where I work. He's tall with red hair, isn't he?'

'Tall, yes, and I think he had red hair but it's pretty grey now. No lashes though, gives me the willies.'

'It's to be hoped the little lassie doesn't take after him?'
'No, she's got lashes, lovely lush lashes.'
'Red head though, like her dad?'
'Aye, bless her. Lots of curly red hair.'

Chapter 20

That autumn and winter flew by: in addition to the invoices and administrative activities connected with the first exhibition and the one that was to follow, I began to be asked to draft descriptive pamphlets. The first time this happened, Mr Richardson had clearly assumed that I was better read than I actually was. His large canvas, of which he was inordinately proud, was an illustration from Sir Walter Scott's Marmion. I accepted the writing task without hesitation and availed myself of his copy of the book, which I consumed swiftly. So overjoyed was he with my resulting pamphlet that he lost no opportunity to show off about my skills, referring to me as his protégée. As a result, I was called upon to assist several of his acquaintances with various acquisitions and correspondence. It seemed that my style of expression was agreeable, apparently due to my female viewpoint. Less prickly than I had ever been, I took it all in good part and blossomed under the praise of such cultured gentlemen.

One of my tasks was to assemble newspaper cuttings about our Institute, as well as comparable ones in the provinces and the capital cities of England and Scotland. From hearing the gentlemen discussing these articles I was enlightened, if somewhat baffled, to learn that we were not merely engaged in celebrating life, beauty and artistic endeavour: in the eyes of some, we had a much more elevated purpose. 'Listen to this!' Mr Richardson called out in exasperation, 'Tyne Mercury 1st October 1822: "The religious and scientific institutions, the theatre and exhibitions of the fine arts we conceive to be united in their object, which is the moral and intellectual improvement of the human mind." Have you ever heard such utter twaddle? What's wrong with these people that they cannot simply enjoy the aesthetics but have to attribute some great moral purpose? Bah!'

Such was the success of the Institute that it wasn't long before Mr Richardson and Mr Parker commissioned John Dobson to design a purpose-built home for the Academy. When it became apparent that they were in negotiation with Richard Grainger to buy a plot of land at the corner of Eldon Square and Blackett Street, I was pleased: it meant that I could keep an eye on the comings and goings at the Blair house without drawing attention to myself. In no time at all, a beautiful frontage of ornamental polished stone with two large Corinthian columns arose as if by magic amongst the mundane but handsome brick buildings around it.

Thomas Sword Good was one of our earliest visitors to the new premises and upon seeing me in a green silk gown at the reception he caused me great embarrassment by dramatically sinking to his knees, imploring me to sit for him until he had gathered a crowd of delighted onlookers in the midst of which I stood, mortified.

I continued to watch number 28: I had seen no movement at all during the winter and early part of spring. Then one bright day in May, I noticed that the front door stood open and items were being loaded into a row of carts lined up along the front of the houses. Rashly, I went straight across and spoke to the dark-clad man who was standing on the steps smoking a cigar.

'Is there to be a change of occupancy?'

He looked down at me and did not answer, instead regarding me in sullen silence, his face inscrutable beneath the rim of his hat. Then he said, 'What's it to you?'

Accustomed as I was to politeness, I was somewhat taken aback and didn't know how to respond. I decided to brazen it out, though I was already regretting having been so impulsive. 'I'm friendly with one of the maids.'

'Then you'll know she doesn't work here anymore.'

'Well clearly not or I wouldn't be asking.'

I was shocked when he turned on his heel and vanished into the house. I went to the top of the kitchen steps and saw that the windows were shuttered. Disconsolate and somewhat unnerved by the rudeness of the encounter, I walked back to the Academy and climbed the stairs.

By mid-morning, all the activity had ceased, the carts were gone and the front door was closed once more. I went quickly across to see whether there was anyone in the gardens of any of the neighbouring properties from whom I could glean any information, but there was no-one about. Assuming the house was empty, I felt bereft. I had to

178

confront the fact that I had quietly believed that the summer would bring the family back to Newcastle for the races.

I was staring up at the windows cursing myself for my complacency when suddenly I realised that there was a face at the window. It was the same man. I saw him stiffen and turn into the room. There were heavy footsteps and then the door opened. 'You again. What do you want?'

'Have the Blairs moved out then?'

'Yes. Now be off with you.'

'Have they taken another house in Newcastle?'

'Look.' He came swiftly down the steps and loomed over me. 'I don't know who you are or what your interest is, but if you were known to the Blair family or any of their employees you would know that they have given up the lease on this house. They no longer keep a house in Newcastle. If you wish to contact them, I suggest you write to one of their other properties. I assume you have the addresses?'

I turned without a word and walked away. I could feel his eyes on me all the way to Blackett Street and I cursed myself for not covering my hair.

In truth, I cursed myself for more than that. So sure had I been that Charlotte was with the Blair family and that they would return to Newcastle with her that I had sat back and waited. I now saw that that had been a great mistake, for there was no guarantee that the child they called their daughter was Charlotte. I had wasted time, indulging myself again, just as I had at Gibside.

When I got back to my room, I re-read Mary Bowes's letter to convince myself of the truth of her reasoning. In all the months I had spent at the Art Institute I had not once caught a glimpse of a family with red hair, nor had there been a mention or a sighting of a portrait of a red-haired child. The Blairs had a child of the right age and with no explanation they had vacated their Newcastle house, despite their habit of attending the races. They were a Scottish family and I must find them. The only person I could think of with links to Scotland was Thomas Sword Good, who had never ceased importuning me to sit for him, latterly by letter, in which he was no less florid and entertaining than he was in person. It seemed that the more I spurned him, the more his ardour intensified: it was a convention of courtly love, apparently.

Mr Richardson had frequently asked whether I would like to take some time off, but having nowhere to go, I had politely refused. It was time to take advantage of his offer. I found him in his office and without preamble, so agitated did I feel, I asked for two weeks leave of absence.

Bless him, he didn't blink an eye. 'I should be glad for you to take a vacation, Molly. Where will you go?'

'To Scotland. I should like to see Edinburgh.'

'I can give you an introduction to the Academy there, if you wish. Do you have somewhere to stay when you get there?'

'No. I should be grateful for your recommendation.'

It crossed my mind to ask whether he knew anything of the Blair family, but I stopped myself. Mindful of Miss Bowes's warnings, I resolved to save my questions until Scotland, and then ensure I asked them of people who would be unable to describe me or provide any other information about my provenance.

'And shall you stay in Berwick on the way?' I caught a sly glance as he said this.

'Would you recommend it?'

'Well of course you could call on Thomas Sword Good, for you know he is extremely smitten with you. You would be quite safe, you know. He's a fine chap and he lives with his mother, so it would be entirely proper. I'm sure he would be very happy to see you and perhaps you would relent and sit for him.'

I thought of Thomas and my heart softened, but then I smothered any temptation to tender feelings and stiffened my resolve: he had knowledge of Scots families and could be of use to me. 'Perhaps.'

'Capital! Then I suggest you take the Royal William Coach. It leaves The Queen's Head at eleven-thirty every morning. You'll dine in Alnwick, leave there at four o'clock and arrive in Berwick at eight. You could send a letter with today's mail and no doubt Thomas would meet you from the coach.'

'I would prefer that he did not meet me. I shall stay in the coaching inn and perhaps surprise him in the morning. In fact, if I make haste I could leave today if that wouldn't inconvenience you.'

He looked at me with scepticism and a degree of fatherly alarm, but then shook his head, smiling.

'You are a remarkably independent young woman, Molly Bowes.'

Independent or foolhardy? You be the judge. Whether I was followed from Eldon Square, I know not. When we arrived in Berwick and dined in the King's Arms on Hide Hill, perhaps it was my questioning that drew attention. I'll never know.

Chapter 21

The journey was smooth, the company convivial. I proved myself adept at deflecting questions and subtle at asking them. Or so I thought. In fact, I was so complacent at my own cleverness, so far from being in fear for my safety, so thoughtless of the warnings impressed upon me by Mary Bowes, that after spending the evening by the fireside of the King's Arms, I walked out alone to admire the moonlight before retiring to bed.

A man approached me, I know that. He spoke and I turned to answer.

I know nothing of what happened next: I can only surmise.

It is a blessing, I think.

I know the moon was full, or almost full, so they must have found a dark place to do their dark deed. I don't think about that, no.

My upbringing prepared me well for extremes of fear and distress and I learnt early that if I can control the direction of my mind, I can calm my heart. And if I can calm my heart, it calms my head. And if my head is calm, I can force it to seek and create a reality that makes the calmness endure.

So what happened to me in that time of deepest darkness, when I was as alone and as close to the abyss as I have ever been, has in my head become something that happened to another. A story told by a fireside. The story is fearful and savage but now it is as if it happened to some other girl. I would pity her but I choose to admire her instead: she was strong and she survived.

The stage is set thus: the moon, painted on a backdrop, lends an unearthly glow to two figures high on the cliff-top. The features of the unconscious young woman lying at their feet will have looked serene, cast into marble by the moonlight.

I have given them names and features: it lessens the fear. It helps me believe that if I saw them again, I would know them. One was tall and in command: in my imagination, he was the one who spoke to me outside the inn. The other – I don't know, but I have made him small and squat, thick-set and thuggish. When they had done what they did - and I know they did it – they might have gazed for a moment on the face of the unconscious young woman, then bent and tenderly lifted a tendril of hair away from her face.

For whatever reason, possibly even without realizing he had done it, one of them pushed me into the crevasse not with his foot but with his hands, quite gently: when a conscience is ravaged, small and unexpected things matter. The pair of them then walked away briskly and disappeared into the sea-mist.

Darkness was all I knew.

And then there was pain - vivid slashes on the edges of the blackness like advancing lightening: consciousness growing like a red dawn.

Every part of my body hurt. My senses were sluggish, disorientated, trying hard to decipher signals. And then it came to me, and a nauseous chill of fear crept up my throat. I was lying on hard, cold rock and water was lapping at my feet. And I was either completely blind or immersed in the blackest darkness imaginable.

Slowly, my skin and bones protesting, I gathered myself until I sat on the gravelly floor of what must be a sea-cave. I carefully raised my knees, claggy in their damp skirts. I was chilled to the bone and my head ached dully. With freezing tentative fingers, I dabbed at the back of my head through the thick clumps of wet hair and drew a breath sharply. My teeth chattered and the muscles of my back and neck were rigid with cold, pain and a creeping sense of deep, primal fear.

I strained my eyes into the darkness, yearning to discern something, anything I could recognize as a possibility for hope. There was none.

Be still and cool in thine own mind. I made a determined effort to gather my wits and speak firmly to my quaking spirit. All my parts were working, painful but working. The head injury I had sustained could have been so much worse. If there was some light coming in from somewhere, there was air too. It was difficult to guess how high the roof of the cave was, how far I had fallen, but when I got slowly to my feet, I clasped one hand over my head and stretched the other up above as I rose carefully to my full height. Nothing.

I stood still and listened. There was a faint rushing sound - I couldn't identify what it was or perceive how near it was. I strained my ears: it sounded more and more like the surge of the waves.

Reaching down to the water near my feet, I immersed one hand and held it up above my head, listening intently to my skin. It was hard to tell with my hands being so cold, but I became convinced that it felt a little warmer on the back, so I turned round slowly and took a deep breath. Fresher, warmer air was coming in from somewhere above, and it seemed that as I forced my eyes to penetrate the darkness, shapes began to loom out of the corners.

Whilst I stood still, examining the forms as they emerged from the shadows, the water suddenly surged forward in one smooth determined movement, sending an icy lasso around my ankles. It withdrew as quickly as it had come, and then, to my horror, surged forward almost immediately with much more strength, soaking my skirts up to my knees.

Horrified, I froze: the realisation of what was happening hit me in the chest and took my breath away. The tide was coming in and it was rising fast. Panic rose like bile.

Although I already knew the answer, I reached out until I found a wall of rock, and slid my fingers across the wall at shoulder height. They came away covered in slime. I reached higher and was horrified to have it confirmed. The water would soon rise to a level far above my head. I had to move quickly, but where?

Instinctively turning my back on the water, I dropped to all fours and started to feel my way forward, my knees flinching at the pain from sharp rocks and pebbles and limpets.

I came to a boulder and reached round as if to embrace it. It was wider than my outstretched fingertips could reach, and I got quickly to my feet, feeling for crannies where I could gain purchase with my fingers and toes. The swoosh of pebbles and surging water behind me seemed to gain pace: each surge sounded larger and more determined than the last. I scrambled up the rock, heedless of my injuries, and crouched on the top of it, panting.

I had to think clearly, but my brain was sluggish and the pain in my temple had sharpened with the exertion. I struggled to focus on my predicament. There was no point in staying atop this boulder if it was isolated. I had to move quickly to find out whether others adjoined it, hopefully taking me higher and higher towards the back of the cave.

My fingertips closed on yet more damp sea-weedy growth, and I scrambled to my feet with careless haste, suddenly aware that the sounds of the encroaching water were now on both sides as well as behind me. Grasping the weed for support, I slid my left foot sideways and it found an obstacle. Shuffling in that direction, I slid my foot up until it found a flat enough surface. Pulling myself upwards and sideways, I gained a couple of feet in height and crouched in my new position to draw breath.

The sounds below told me that the water had covered the floor of the cave and was no longer expending energy on its ebb and flow: it was simply rising inexorably towards me. I had rarely swum and then always in safety, the rounded pebbles of the Derwent or the wooden steps of the Brighton bathing hut within easy reach: could I keep myself afloat in icy water, in the darkness? My spirit quailed at the impossibility of the task and I sank to my knees, sobbing.

I lost myself then for a time, curled into a ball, my head bowed low, my face pressed against my knees, my fingers interlocked around my head, as though I could protect myself like a snail or a hedgehog. Then a curious thing happened: the white sheet of fear that had enveloped my mind snagged on the thought of the hedgehog and a memory awoke and poked its nose out, warm and twitching.

Was this how it happened? You know you are going to die and suddenly your brain brings up all the beauty of life to flash before your inner eye? Is it torture or a farewell? My mind was a chaos of colours and memories: the bright blue sky, the embrace of the sun-warmed grass, flowers, flickers of faces, drifts of music – it was all so precious and now it was gone. Fear and self-pity overwhelmed me and as the water crept up my body I cried the gulping, convulsive grief for all I had lost and all I would never know.

The storm eventually abated, leaving me exhausted but calmer, breathing deeply the lungsful of air that I knew would be my last. And death, when it came, what would I feel and see? Would I hold my breath until the last possible moment or just let myself go as the sea closed over my head, and take the deep draughts of water into my lungs as though they were welcome? I would become a thing of water, floating in the senseless sea, ebbing and flowing with the ceaseless tides over all the centuries to come, until one day someone would find a part of me, a small piece of thigh-bone perhaps, or a skull, or a tooth, washed clean and softening and eroded, no longer a part of me but returning to dust...

Grief exhausted me and I drifted, awaiting death with a cold stoicism. I felt almost languorous, even imagining myself to be warm. When the water reached my neck, I made myself relax and float, woozily wondering what would happen next. I looked down on myself from a great height and wondered if this was how it felt to take laudanum.

I felt my feet lift from the rock and I lay back lazily, my face turned towards the roof of the cave and almost certain suffocation. Which would be preferable? I wondered idly.

I wasn't aware of time passing as I lay there in a dream-state, suspended between rock and sea, air and water, life and death. I may or may not have lost consciousness, I may even have fallen asleep, but the warm, floating sensation drifted on until a dawning realisation began to lap at the shores of my consciousness, just as the water had begun to lap at my feet, oh...aeons ago...It had stopped rising.

Lazily, languidly, as though I had all the time in the world, I raised a heavy arm above myself like a dead thing - and touched rock, just a few inches above my head. My sluggish heart began to beat just a little bit faster and my lungs drew more deeply on the pocket of air. Suddenly, the idea that this was not the end became a real possibility and I felt the stirrings of hope, like a distant memory. Unable to move much beyond a fingertip examination of the area of the roof of the cave against which I was trapped, I tried to turn my flickering mind to thoughts of escape.

I had no idea how much time had elapsed, but the idea that I might survive was drifting past my consciousness and I summoned the ghost of my willpower to reach out and grasp it. Tides turned. They reached their peak and then they receded. The water would withdraw. I only had to survive until it began, and then there would be real hope. I might see the sky again, and colours, and leaves…and Charlotte.

The tiny spark of hope was glowing brighter.

I must concentrate. There had been daylight when I woke to find myself in here, so it had probably been morning, and the tide was coming in. I had no idea how many tides there were in a day, but surely it must go out on the same day…even if it came in again, it must go out…

The water was obviously coming in from the open sea, so there was a possibility that there could be an opening big enough to get through, even if it was below water level at low tide. I knew I would have to use every available bit of light to find the opening. I made myself think of it as the exit to the cave.

Sleepiness lapped at the shores of my consciousness again, and I fought against it. I relaxed into the warmth and my senses drifted. Suddenly a spark of understanding lit in the corner of my huddled brain. As a child, I had once been shut in a cupboard for hours: I had become so cold that I began to feel warm. Clasping me to her and holding my frozen painful feet in her warm hands, my mother had told me that extreme coldness could trick the brain. If that ever happened to me again, that I felt so cold that I began to believe I was warm, I must not believe it. I must move about and hug myself to keep warm. The devil had been trying to get my soul, she said, and he used all his tricks to get the good ones.

I spoke to myself now in my mother's voice: Molly dear, you are not warm and sleepy: you are in danger. The cold has addled your brain and fooled your body. You are freezing to death and suffering from delirium.

I dragged my consciousness towards the light:

Think…think…you must… how will you find the way out?

I made a supreme effort to waken my scattered sleepy mind.

I examined my memory of the tide's rise. There had been no sound of gushing or sloshing into the cave, so the opening had to be below water level.

My shift must still have been damp, but it trapped the warmth of my exertions: stiff and painful though it was, I stretched and rotated my arms, lifted my knees, flinching. A few more minutes then I would rest. My heart was a thumping fist and the pain in my head had found its sharpness.

I looked down at my hands: where once there had been a corpse-blue, I could begin to discern a more natural colour. It took a moment to realise that I could actually see past my hands to my feet, and I looked up in hope and expectation.

Six feet away, the cave's roof curved smoothly down and slipped under the still water. Beyond that wall of rock, I had to believe there was daylight, sunshine, warmth. Somewhere out there, seagulls were wheeling in a bright blue sky, and fishing boats would be pulling in their first catch of the day.

The thought spurred me on and hope infused every part of me. You can do this, I told myself. I knew that I needed to be as warm as possible before I attempted it, so I found a patch of sandy ground and began to run on the spot, lifting my knees higher and pumping my arms, feeling my life and youth and energy and hope suffuse my body like sap rising in the spring.

Finally, when I judged myself to be ready, I saw that the light was as good as it was going to get. I started by examining the edges of the water to see whether I could detect any brightness flickering below the surface. Nothing. The wall seemed to be smooth and sheer below as well as above the water. If there was a gap or an opening deeper down, I might be able to see it underwater.

If I waded in, I might be able to detect a difference in temperature to indicate where it was. If I left it too long, the tide would start to come in again, and getting through would be more difficult.

Now or never, I told myself, and took a few careful steps down the sloping beach. The seawater grasped my feet like icy hands: I recoiled and felt my muscles clench with fear.

Soon I was up to my waist, walking forward with tiny steps. Suddenly the floor dropped away from beneath me, plunging me in over my head and knocking the breath from my body. I surfaced, coughing, but made myself breathe slowly whilst I stood on tip-toe, holding my ground. When I was ready, I moved slowly forward, my calf muscles stretched to keep my toes on the floor and my face above water. I began searching the length of the wall with my feet and hands. Nothing.

It must be there, I told myself. It's deeper than I'd hoped, but it has to be there. I had to go closer, I had to be brave. Taking a very deep breath, I raised my arms, took a step forward and dropped underwater, reaching out blindly to feel my way along the wall in the deep darkness.

Suddenly, where there had been unremitting rock against my foot, there was nothing. Could it be my imagination, or was that really the distant teasing tickle of sun-warmed water?

Careful to remain directly above the spot, I rose quickly and took a few deep breaths, then descended again. When I found that both my feet felt no rock, only a sensation of warmth, my heart began to race. I reached down and found I could trace a jagged opening about two feet wide and a foot deep. I rose to the surface again, steadied my breathing, filled my lungs and this time went down with my eyes wide open, hungry for hope.

There was light.

It was a tunnel, certainly two or three yards long, but at the end of it was a rectangle of dancing water lit by sunlight.

You can do this, Molly. If you can survive the things you've survived, you can do this small thing.

There was no space for any movement of the arms, but if I could fill my lungs with air and let it out only when I really had to and then very slowly, I could do it. I needed to keep calm, keep effort to a minimum, avoid knocks and gasps, perhaps use my hands to pull myself along.

The Devil whispered, you will wedge in there and you will drown.

Dismissing the thought before it could take on any kind of vivid reality, I started to fill my lungs with more and more precious air.

Finally, I felt I was calm enough and ready. Careful not to rush, I slowly sank to the mouth of the tunnel and confronted it directly, my eyes stinging, wavering and blinking in the salty water. It did seem to be much narrower at the far end, and lack of perspective made it hard to judge how far away the end was.

Still, there was no alternative. It was risk this or die.

Rising gently for the final time, I filled my lungs once more, darted to the entrance, and went in head first.

My hands on the floor of the tunnel, I kicked my feet to propel myself forward, but the sudden sharp crack of the back of my head against rock lost me breath and equanimity. I must edge forward more carefully, my lungs still full to bursting.

My toes had just scraped the entrance and the end seemed no nearer when my shoulders suddenly jammed. Panic. Heart beating too fast. A jet of air escaped and I struggled not to breathe in water through my nose. I wriggled as gently as I could in my rising panic, and found that by tilting my shoulders to the diagonal, I could edge forward, praying over and over again please please please…

The veins in my temples pulsed and banged, and my eyeballs felt as though they were bulging out of my head. My heart was hammering against my chest-bone. A sudden jet of the warmer seawater from outside knocked me up against the ceiling of the tunnel, and again I lost air unwillingly, spurting it out in a bloody jet before pursing my mouth and consciously sealing my nose while my throat gagged on the blood.

Blood banged and my heart pounded and my eardrums bulged, ready to implode, and suddenly, with a whoosh I was out like a newborn babe and up, up, up to burst into the sunlight gasping and coughing and choking and crying and finally, when with shaking hands I had cleared the tears and blood and mucus from my mouth and nose and filled my lungs with sweet warm air, I turned my face to the sun and I cried like a baby.

Chapter 22

'Molly! Whatever has happened to you?'

When I opened my eyes, the evening sun was slanting in thorough a small window and for a moment I could not gather my thoughts at all. My head was aching and the light hurt my eyes.

The voice came closer and I felt my hand enfolded in a large soft one. 'Molly. It's me, Thomas. I cannot believe you're here.'

I felt his breath on my cheek and his hand in my hair. His earnest face was beside me but I did not turn to meet his eyes; instead, I struggled to be upright, pulling my hand out of his.

'Water. Please bring her some water.'

I saw that I was in a small cottage with whitewashed walls. A man and woman with weather-beaten faces were standing behind Thomas.

'These good people sent for me. You murmured my name.'

That focused my mind. I sat up properly, though it pained me to do so, and I gathered the blankets around me. The full force of what I had endured came crashing in on my consciousness and I found I was shaking.

'What has happened to you, Molly? How did you come to be at the foot of the cliffs? These people say they found you at the foot of the cliffs! How came you there? Had you fallen?'

'Please, let me gather my senses. I am...somewhat bruised.'

I must think before I answered. Thomas was all solicitude and would accept whatever I told him. In truth I was terrified. Those men had meant me to die. It was a miracle I had survived. They must not know. They must not hear of this rescue. I needed to hide and be safe. I had to exploit Thomas's kindness – I had no alternative. And if I needed him to court me, he must not know what my body was telling me it had endured. But first I must find out what these people knew.

'She's full of cuts and bruises,' volunteered the man. The woman was watching me with a steady unnerving eye.

191

'Thank-you so much for rescuing me. I…I don't know what happened.'

'Looked to me like you'd fallen down the cliff. It's a miracle you survived.'

'She couldn't have fallen to where you found her, you daft article. She'd have been shattered into a thousand pieces. She's no broken bones that I could see. No, she's gone in the water somewhere else and been washed up.'

'And you…picked me up?'

'Aye. Just back from a morning's fishing. The missis undressed you. Your clothes are drying on the hedge.'

I caught her eye and could see that she knew. I prayed that she would stay silent, for Thomas's muse would surely topple from her pedestal if he found out she had been raped.

'I…oh, I don't know what happened. I can remember arriving at the King's Arms.'

'Were you coming to see me? Why didn't you write?'

'No,' I flashed him a look that deliberately said the opposite. 'I am on my way to Edinburgh. I decided to stay overnight in Berwick, have a look around and then leave on tomorrow's mail. I…I went out for a stroll after dinner. I came to the cliffs, and I can remember no more.'

'Dearest. You fell. By some miracle you were saved. Come, let me take you home.'

'No, really thank-you. I have taken a room at the King's Arms. It would not be proper.'

'Then I shall take you there. Do you feel well enough to walk? Shall I call a surgeon?'

'I do not know. I need to stand. I need my clothes.'

'I'll get them, though they are still wet,' said the woman, who clearly wanted me gone. She opened the door and a sweet sea-breeze wafted into the room. When she bustled back in with my dress draped over her arm, she muttered, 'Out, out!' to the menfolk.

The door closed, she offered me an arm to steady myself. 'There's your shift. No breeches, like.' She cast me a look I could not read: it was freighted with suspicion, blame and understanding all in one. A complicit look, from woman to woman.

I reached for her hand and held it tight, though she tried to draw back. I considered saying, 'I did not court it. I did not deserve it. I am innocent.' Instead, I said simply, 'I am in your debt.'

I held my breath. At length, she patted my hand in acquiescence, though her eyes were cold and she turned her head away immediately.

When I emerged into the soft light, the view took my breath away. Thomas was staring entranced at the pinks and blues of the sky and the water. I took my place at his side.

'I can see what draws you back to Berwick.'

He turned and smiled down at me. 'Aye, that and my mother.'

Mrs Good was a dear, sweet old lady in a lacy cap who welcomed me at once, all concern and bustle. Their house was small and cosy and at first I thought I could not stay. But it transpired there were three narrow storeys and she helped me up to a tiny bedroom on the top floor. From the window, I could see the bend in the river and the bridge and the green fields beyond. She washed my wounds with salt water and sat by my bedside until I fell into a troubled sleep.

I struggled down to breakfast early the following morning, my legs and side painful and stiff. Thomas was all attention and offered to take me for a gentle walk down to the river, 'If you can bear it, dear heart.'

'Thomas, please!' His mother reprimanded him sharply and threw me a rueful look that said, *'the boy is quite besotted. Forgive him for his inability to hide it.'*

'Thank-you, I should like that. I saw large white birds upon the water. They wouldn't be swans, would they?'

'Yes, Berwick has many pairs of swans. They feast upon the brewery's leavings.'

When we reached the water's edge, I could scarcely believe what I was seeing. Thomas watched me with pleasure, 'You seem entranced.'

'I am. I…I cannot believe I am seeing angel-birds at last.'

'Angel-birds?'

'I have never seen a swan. I knew they existed, but I don't believe I have ever seen one except perhaps flying overhead, far up, too far to see.'

'Pardon me, Molly, but for me that is difficult to imagine. Berwick swans are much-loved but as common as house-sparrows. They are beauties, though. Here. Sit down beside me and tell me all about yourself.'

I looked at him, guarded. 'Thomas. I am happy just to sit here and watch the swans. Do you mind?

'Then let me sit here and watch you. I will be quiet and respectful.'

'No, please don't look at me like that.' My tone was gentle, regretful. 'It makes me uneasy.'

'I mean no harm, Molly. You know I want to paint you. Will you let me paint you?'

'And you have no other intention?'

He blushed, suddenly bashful. I kept my gaze steady. 'You are very beautiful.'

'I am very independent.'

'I am in love with you.'

'That's nonsense. You do not know me. What you are feeling has another name.'

'Ha! You make me laugh. I know of no other woman like you. Do you tease me?'

I regarded him steadily. 'Look me in the eye, Thomas, and understand this. I mean what I say. I am not looking for love. I do not need a man to complete me.' His crestfallen face moved me but it stiffened my resolve, though I softened my voice. 'I thank you for your kindness. You are a gentleman and I am grateful for your attention but I do not encourage it. I wish only to converse with you as if we were friends.'

'Ah, but if you stay here love may come. Tell me it may come.'

I turned away. It was so difficult. My impulse was to rebuff his advances and leave. But again, I had to be pragmatic. He was a good man and if what had happened on the cliffs resulted in pregnancy, without a husband I would be lost, barred forever from respectable society. And it was so hard to go back. I had climbed onto a life-raft once and now, through my own impulsive carelessness, I had fallen again. I was caught, trapped, at least until my monthlies came. I had thought I had escaped from the spectre of the brothel or the workhouse, but if I was pregnant and alone, there was nowhere I could go. Do not hate me. I know I used Thomas. I hardened my heart and I used him just as my father used my mother and many men used Emma.

'I do like you Thomas, you make me laugh. You are kind and handsome. But you need to understand. The things I want to do with my life are many. Marriage is not part of my plan.'

'But I can help you with your plans! Let me love you. I ask nothing in return.'

'Nothing? Truly?'

He cast me a mischievous glance. 'Well, only that you let me paint you.'

'I will. For now, let me sit and watch the swans.'

We sat in companionable silence.

'The purity of the whiteness of their feathers, the expressive elegance of those long necks. They drift so serenely...'

'Yes, we cannot see their means of locomotion.'

After a silence, I said, 'My mother was like a swan.'

'How so?'

'She always seemed to be calm on the surface.'

'But beneath?'

'Sometimes her eyes showed she was frightened; often she was sad.'

'Tell me about her.'

'Her name was Polly.'

'Did she look like you?'

'No, she was small and fair. I take after my father's side.'

'And who was he, your father?'

'Difficult to answer that.'

'Try.'

'Tall, striking, Irish. Commanding.'

'That tells me very little.'

Fiercely then: 'Why do you need to know?'

Thomas was taken aback, but then he smiled. 'I love that about you, that flash, that transformation. And then it's gone and you are all mystery and serenity. Perhaps you too are like the swan. You have hidden depths, don't you Molly? Secrets. Tell me one of your secrets.'

So many secrets. What should I tell him? And then I knew what I must say. 'Are you ready to hear this?'

'Don't be coy, Molly. I want to know you. Tell me something I don't already know.'

'Even if I risk changing the way you see me?'

'Nothing could do that.'

'I am a widow.'

Out of the corner of my eye, I saw him draw in a breath and hold it. A moment later, he exhaled and said, 'That does not surprise me. There is sadness in your eyes. And knowledge.'

He touched me when he said that.

'There is more.'

'You have a child?'

I looked away, my eyes suddenly burning. 'Yes, and she is lost!' My voice caught on a sob.

'Tell me.'

I took a deep breath. I was ever to find Charlotte, the experience of the last twenty-four hours had taught me that I could not do it alone. 'I have information, reliable information, that she was taken to a wealthy family. They are pretending she is their own.'

'Do you know who they are?'

'Not for certain, but I think I may have been followed from Newcastle. I had a suspicion of who they might be. I was unwise. I asked questions. I drew attention to myself.'

'And then you travelled alone in pursuit? That was more than unwise, Molly: that was foolish. So you think that was why you were attacked?'

'Perhaps. Yes, I fear it is.'

'You were foolhardy. You do know that now, don't you? You wouldn't do anything like it again?' When I didn't answer, he said, 'Who are they?'

'Their name is Blair.' He did not react and his continuing silence unnerved me. 'Do you know them?'

'I know of them. Everyone in society between Newcastle and Edinburgh knows of them. They are very wealthy and they have friends in high places. They have a proud reputation. Why do you suspect them?'

'Charlotte was only six months old when she was taken. She has distinctive curly red hair. I was told the Blairs have just such a child.'

'That's not enough, surely? But how could people not suspect? Ah, you need not answer. They are often abroad. I believe they have a house in France.'

'I don't know what to do.'

'Now here it is, Molly. Listen to what I am about to say. If your daughter is indeed being brought up by the Blair family as their own, there are far worse fates. No, hear me out.

'In these days, when so many children have dreadful lives and many never live to become adults, your child is as safe as she can be. The Blairs have a good reputation: they are philanthropic. They are patrons of the arts. If their daughter is indeed your Charlotte, then I have to say you would be wise to accept it.'

'No, no I can never...'

'But don't you see? How long is it since you saw her?'

'Almost two years.'

'I think you must accept things. You need to be realistic, Molly.' The heart of me burned with indignation but my head told me he was right. 'And the other important thing is your own peace of mind. If you believe their daughter to be Charlotte, think of the life she is having! Think what they must have gone through to want a daughter so badly. Think how she must be loved.'

'I know the truth of what you say, Thomas. Enough now. I will come to a decision in my own time.'

'Good. I will leave you now. It is time for mother's constitutional. But before I go, tell me about the angel-bird.'

I sighed. 'My childhood was...unusual. Difficult. Perhaps I will tell you about it another time. I had one book, Bewick's Land Birds: I have it still. As a child, it meant everything to me. I cannot describe how it helped me, what it gave me. But the swan, above all other birds, seemed impossible. My mother told me how they carry their chicks upon their backs, in amongst the feathers, where they nestle and are safe. I used to think of it when I was allowed to sleep in my mother's bed, where I could nestle. And be safe.'

I stayed still, watching, and at first I thought he had gone. Then a hand touched my head. 'Molly, you break my heart.'

197

That summer I spent in Berwick was recuperative and undemanding. Once I had bled, I knew I could relax. My body healed swiftly: I was still young. I spent my days helping Mrs Good; posing for Thomas and sometimes his students; and learning the properties of paint and various artistic terms from him and his brother, who kept a shop selling artists' materials. Thomas was well-known and Berwick being such a picturesque place, there were often artists visiting. I widened my circle of acquaintance and broadened and deepened my knowledge of the art world.

There were times when I thought I should succumb to Thomas's allure, times when my attachment to his mother tempted me to regard the little house on smelly Windmillhole as my home. I once began a letter to Mary Bowes with the news that I was contemplating accepting Thomas's proposal. I wrote the words. I stared at them. I saw stretching ahead of me care of children and my aging mother-in-law and my heart grew cold and I tore the letter up.

By the time the autumn came, the restlessness outweighed the comfort. Boredom and ill-temper became more difficult to disguise and Thomas could not fail to be aware of it. When he announced one day that he had to go to Newcastle, it was no surprise to him that I decided I would go with him.

Those were such exciting times in the blossoming town and despite my guilt and grief, my heart soared to be back. The whole

centre was being redeveloped, medieval dark and twisted streets being replaced by wide curving avenues of pale golden ashlar sandstone. The new home of the Literary and Philosophical Society had risen from the ground during my absence and stood like a tall elegant temple of civilized thought.

I hadn't had time to write to Mr and Mrs Richardson, so their welcome was very genuine and touching: 'Molly! You have been greatly missed, my dear! Your room is just as you left it, although you will barely be able to open the door for letters!' He smiled indulgently at my embarrassment. 'There is certainly someone in the Derwent Valley who is missing you! Oh, I apologise – I see I embarrass you. There has been a letter a week since you left. I would have forwarded them but Mrs Richardson assured me that while you were staying with Thomas Sword Good, you would not want them. I deduce that they are from a spurned lover. Oh, I am sorry Molly. I see your discomfort. I am a meddling old man.'

The two letters from Belle I did open. The first begged me to come home for her wedding day. In the second, she told me how it had passed and regretted my continuing silence. She told me that Gabe and her husband went off to Stargate Pit like brothers and that she wanted her sister to come home. Stargate. I was singularly struck by that name: since I had first heard it, it had conjured a romantic notion of lying on my back in a forest looking up at the stars like diamonds scattered on black velvet. It could not have been further from the reality.

When I came back downstairs to the office, Mr Richardson was sitting at my desk. Though I had no right to consider it mine, kind as he had been about my prolonged absence.

'Well, Molly, glad as I am that you are back, I have to say the systems you put in place are remarkably efficient and we have been able to maintain order effortlessly. You are a marvel. It is time that I shared my angel and godsend with another. I have had a capital idea. Wait here please.'

When at length he returned, he was accompanied by a pale, sandy-haired gentleman who did not look at me. Always uncomfortably aware of men's eyes, I was instantly at ease with Thomas Hodgson: he was an ascetic-looking, shy man who wore his glasses perched on the end of his nose.

'Thomas, I'd like to introduce you to Molly Bowes. Molly, this is Mr Hodgson, editor of the Newcastle Chronicle.'

'Pleased to meet you, Mr Hodgson.'

199

When he still didn't speak or look at me, Mr Richardson winked reassuringly and said, 'I was just telling Mr Hodgson about your organisational skills, Molly, and that you have been so efficient as to be invaluable, and yet now we find there is little for you to do. Amongst all his other activities, for you must know that he has made the Chronicle the leading political organ between York and Edinburgh – now, now, Thomas, don't look so bashful - Mr Hodgson is working with the Literary and Philosophical Society on their library. I will leave you two bibliophiles to talk.' He patted my hand kindly. 'Don't let him take you away from us completely, Molly.'

Mr Hodgson looked uncomfortable at being left alone with me, so I opened the door that Mr Richardson had closed. Still the silence lasted. 'Would you like a drink of tea, Mr Hodgson?'

'No, no thank-you Molly. In fact, I must go.'

'Oh!' I found myself suddenly profoundly disappointed. 'Please do tell me about the Society's collection. Mr Richardson may have told you that I catalogued the library at Gibside.'

He looked up, clearly startled. 'You? And you alone?'

'Why yes.' I adopted a teasing tone. 'I shall choose not to be offended by your evident astonishment.'

'But I know that library: I supplied many of the volumes myself.'

'Oh? I thought you were a newspaperman.'

He smiled. 'It seems we have much to learn about each other, Molly. Let us sit down and talk.'

I stayed behind the desk and he settled himself in the chair opposite: it must have looked as though I was interviewing him instead of the reverse. Now he did look at me, though he quickly looked away and addressed a ledger that was lying on a shelf behind my head.

'I am a printer by trade and I partly own the Chronicle. At heart I am an antiquarian, however. The Strathmores must have over a thousand books by now, a fine collection. I last visited the year before John died. I assume you worked with him?'

'No, sadly I never knew him. I arrived at Gibside just after his passing.'

'Sad business, and now young John Bowes…alas.'

'Yes, I met John very briefly soon after his father died. I regularly exchange correspondence with his aunt, Miss Mary Bowes. We are distantly related.'

'Well then, let me tell you what I am about. The Lit and Phil has a collection of eight thousand volumes. Like the Strathmore collection, they were organized by size until only a few years ago. They are in the process of being moved into their new accommodation.'

'Such an elegant building!'

'Yes, we are all very pleased with it. Initially, we will have to accommodate an extensive collection of natural history specimens, but we hope in time to transfer those items to a dedicated Natural History Museum. My main concern is of course the books. William Turner's catalogue is useful, but I have begun work on a more detailed version which I hope will enable people to search the contents of books without having to locate them and bring them down from the shelves. For you know, many of these books are very fine and very old.'

I decided to risk it. 'Like many of the gentlemen who read them?'

'Ha! Molly, you make me laugh. I do not often laugh.'

It was the beginning of a beautiful friendship, and I made many more in the weeks I worked at the Lit and Phil.

One day, I heard the town crier on my way to work, as I did every day. I was chatting to my companion, a young woman who had started work as a cleaner in the building, and at first I did not perceive what the man was shouting.

The bell rang again as he passed us, and I put my hand on Lily's arm to silence her. A cold wind had brushed my neck. His voice ricocheted off the buildings but the words rang clear: 'Explosion at Stargate: scores feared dead.'

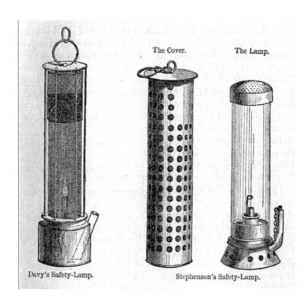

Davy's Safety-Lamp.   The Cover.   The Lamp.   Stephenson's Safety-Lamp.

Chapter 23

We all have moments in our lives that change us forever: for me, this was one of them. No matter who the casualties were, whether Gabe was one of them, or Belle's husband and his brothers, my view of the world would never be the same. I stared at the impossible beauty of the façade of the Lit and Phil and suddenly I understood. The beautiful pale gold sandstone from which it was built was hewn out of the earth. The coal by which it was heated was hewn out of the earth. The wood from which its shelves were made was cut and transported and planed and shaped by working men. The paper on which its treasures were printed was made in the mills. The leather for the bindings was stripped from carcasses. Everything that went into making an artifact of such great beauty was the product of toil and dirt and danger.

Being so intoxicated by the books, I had barely paid attention to the lectures and experiments that went on in the Lit and Phil but now I saw that the engineering and scientific advances on which the committee placed such emphasis had one common purpose: human advancement, and that included the safety of those who laboured in the earth.

I was in a trance, my sensibilities shifting: it felt like the opening up of the ground beneath my feet. I knew I must go to Gibside.

When I arrived at Dorothy's cottage, there was a group of people clustered around the door speaking in subdued voices. I knew none of them. Reluctant to push my way through, for I had no claim, I spoke to a bent old woman standing alone.

'Can you tell me anything of who is hurt and who is lost?'

In answer the woman shook her head, gathered her shawl to her mouth and shook with silent tears.

A man nearby put his arm around her and spoke over her head. 'The Robson brothers are all gone.'

'Belle's husband?'

'Aye. Deed.'

'And her own brother?'

'Hanging on so far. Burnt. Face an' that. Crushed too. Not looking good, like.'

'Is he in there?'

'Aye.'

The people parted to let me through. In the cottage, the air was thick with smoke and a sharp smell like burnt meat. I discerned that the figure sitting bent over the bed was Gabe's mother. A gentleman who had been washing his hands in the basin touched her shoulder briefly and then left. The room was silent.

'Dorothy?'

She didn't react. Unsure whether to leave or stay, I hesitated in the doorway. And then her voice came, a whisper. 'Leave.'

I did not know whether she was sending me away because she knew my voice or because she didn't. I had to try.

'Dorothy. It's me, Molly.'

I saw her back stiffen. Then she took a deep sigh. I went towards her and put my hand lightly on her shoulder.

Now I could see the figure on the bed. Gabe, though I would not have known it, for there were no dark curls on the pillow and the flesh was melted from one side of his face. No breath disturbed the blankets.

I held my own breath and watched for what seemed like interminable minutes. One hand lay across his chest and though it was dark with coal dust, it was otherwise unmarked as far as I could see. I focused on that hand, willing myself to discern a movement, a gentle rise to show me he was still alive. Nothing.

I do not know how long we stayed like that in the still room where dust motes hung in the spring light. Time suspended.

At length, I could bear it no more. Though it seemed clear to me that Gabe was dead, I could not bring myself to say the words to his mother.

'Dorothy, please tell me what the doctor said.'

I thought at first she would not answer. But then she rose in silence and I looked into the serenity of her face.

'They have brought him home to die.'

'Is it certain there is no hope?'

'It seems so, yes. Sit with him a while. I will send those people away.'

'And Belle?'
'She is in Winlaton. Her husband is dead and his brothers too.'
'I…Dorothy…I don't know what to say.'
'Say nothing. Sit with him. Hold his hand. Perhaps he will be aware. We cannot know.'
I sat. I held his hand. And I stayed with him.

There were thirty-eight dead. Thirty-eight men and boys, the youngest just ten years old. I could barely believe it: I had never given a thought to the realities of mining. But now it was all I could think about. The Stargate pit, far from being the romantic hollow I had envisaged, was the deepest pit in the area: five hundred feet down into the ground. Unimaginable. While I sat beside Gabe's shattered body and over in Winlaton, Belle washed the corpse of her husband, others waited at the pit-head for the bodies of their loved ones to be retrieved. By other miners who had to go down into the mine to get them. And bring them up a ladder made of knotted ropes. Perhaps they carried them in the baskets meant for the coal. Perhaps they were not whole men. My mind shrank from the thought.

How could such a thing have happened in these times? I asked the question with the indignation and incredulity of the young and naïve. Because of the Lit and Phil's role in their development, I had been proud to know about safety lamps: surely they were used? It was ten whole years since George Stephenson and Humphrey Davy had invented similar lamps at the same time. Lamps invented for the purpose by clever men, lamps with a flame enclosed by mesh to keep out the firedamp, to stop the flame igniting. Lord Strathmore himself had presided over the committee that supported their development and examined their relative benefits. It had seemed to me such a fine example of the role of the Society, the encouragement of such research, the weighing of advantages, the recognition. How naive I was to believe that therefore all mines were safe from explosion.

It seemed that the Stargate pit had been known for its good ventilation. The miners had taken candles into the pit. Candles they bought themselves. There were no lamps provided.

The explosion happened at three o'clock in the morning. Even that I found difficult to comprehend. How had I lived for twenty-six years in rooms heated by coal and not known that men went down into the earth to dig in the depths of the darkness while we all slept safe in our beds?

No-one knew what had caused it to ignite: an accumulation of gas, perhaps caused by a fall of rocks or a collapse of earth and wooden shuttering. It was the start of the shift: everyone was in either the main tunnels or the shaft, and no-one had had any shelter to deflect the blast. The explosion swept back effortlessly through the workings, tossing aside and burning men, boys, ponies and all else that lay in its way. Tossing them aside and leaving them burning in its wake, it exploded up the shaft and bellowed to the world the news of what it had done.

Imagine it. Your man has gone to work, perhaps taking your eldest son with him, a boy of ten. Proud to be a man and go to work like his da. You had their bait ready, you saw them off; you shut the door and sat down by the fireside or maybe went back to bed for an hour our two before the bairns awoke. Life's hard, but it is what it is. All's well with the world.

Except it isn't, though you don't know it yet. Beneath your feet, five hundred feet down, a monster coils in wait. Perhaps there was a rumble. Perhaps the pots on your dresser rattled.

Perhaps you stood up then, a premonition. Perhaps you were on your feet when you heard it, when the mouth of the pit erupted with a mighty roar and rained down on the earth flames and death and destruction: destruction of lives and families and hopes and incomes and homes: destruction of innocence.

And what did it leave behind? Unimaginable pain and grief and loss and poverty. An annex of Hell, open to the skies. And we all fall in, all of us. The innocent - the widows and orphans and mothers and fathers and sisters and brothers; and the guilty - the mine-owners and managers who don't ensure safety; and all the people sleeping safe in their warm houses who have never given it a thought. For if we have a conscience, we should all of us be in hell that we let this happen.

They died together and they are together for all eternity, for most of them were buried beneath a rockery mound in the graveyard at Ryton Church. But Gabe was not among them.

He was the ghost of the man he had been. In every way, he was diminished. We thought at first that his brain was profoundly damaged, for he was mute. The face on the pillow grew cavernous beneath the melted skin. No expression animated his eyes. He took soup and water and when he swallowed, we only knew he had pain because his eyes closed until it passed.

When at last, after days of silence, he murmured an answer, his voice creaked, we thought with disuse but as time went on, we realised the damage was permanent. Perhaps his throat was scorched with air that burnt.

When finally he rose from his bed, his eyes closed against the pain, he could not straighten and the exertion hurt his ribs. His broken hip was healing crooked, but no-one cared, for he was alive.

When we helped him to his seat by the fire, he stared into it unblinking. Who knows what he saw in the flames? He never spoke about it.

I rarely left his side. He seemed to me the embodiment of all the suffering and strength of working men everywhere. He asked nothing of me and I asked nothing of him. I was as peaceful in those months as I have ever been in my life: my very existence had a centre and a purpose.

But God I was angry.

Chapter 24

When I answered a knock on the door the following April and found Thomas Sword Good standing on the threshold, it was like a vision from a dream, a previous life of colour and ease. I stood blinking into the spring sunshine like an emerging mole.

'Molly! As beautiful as ever!'

'Thomas. What a surprise.' But my voice, I knew, lacked welcome.

Somewhat discomfited, he went on, 'I asked at the Hall. They told me what had happened. I was so very sorry to hear it. How is your friend?'

'A little better each day. He can walk a few steps now.'

'He? I understood you had come to tend to your widowed sister?'

'My half-sister, yes. Belle lost her husband in the disaster, but her brother was severely injured too. Come in and meet him.' I stepped to one side to let him pass but he did not move and to my eyes he looked afraid. In that moment I hated him.

'Come in,' I said more firmly.

'I ...I cannot stay. I have something to show you, Molly. It's at the Hall.'

'Come in.' I said it in a voice that brooked no opposition. He looked me in the eye and then stepped past me into the parlour.

'How do you do, Mr....'

Gabe had stood up, though I knew it pained him, and he answered in a stronger voice than I had yet heard: 'Thornton.'

'Mr Thornton. I cannot express how very distressed I am to think of what you must have endured.'

When he answered, and I will never forget it, I saw for the first time that he was still Gabe. His good eye glinted and he said, 'I am sorry to cause you distress.'

Then he looked at me and winked.

Thomas entirely missed his ironic tone and turned to me. 'Molly. I don't have much time. Will you walk to the Hall with me? There is something I must show you.'

I had dismissed it the first time he said it, thinking he wanted to show me his latest painting, or even offer me his mother's ring again, but suddenly something in his voice broke upon me. Flustered, I said, 'I'm sorry, Gabe. Do you mind?'

'Of course not, I'll be fine.' He held on to the back of the chair to steady himself as he sat. 'Don't worry about me. I'm not going anywhere.'

As soon as the door was closed, I pulled Thomas's coat sleeve. 'Tell me! Is it something to do with Charlotte?'

'It might be. I don't want to raise your hopes but you did beg me to tell you of anything I heard or saw. I am travelling to London with some canvasses from Scotland for an exhibition at the Royal Academy. Four of them are from private collections. One in particular will be of interest to you: a portrait of the son and daughter of the Blair family. It's in the library.'

When we entered the room, I didn't even look around but went straight to the object lying on the table.

The painting showed a little girl sitting on a low stool and a slightly older boy offering her a bunch of flowers. Both children had curly red hair but nothing about the little girl's face spoke to me. I blinked and searched her face for anything, any flicker of recognition. I felt nothing.

Eventually, I said, 'It is her.'

'How can you be sure?'

My watery eyes rebuked him. 'I cannot. Of course I cannot. But I can choose to believe.' I looked back at the portrait and my eyes drank it in. I would remember this, I would hold it to me in dark moments.

'You are quite different Molly. I see it.'

'I am. I am older and more resigned. More accepting. It is as you say. She is well, she is happy, she is cared-for. What more can I ask?'

'Don't you want to see her?'

'This is enough. I know. I wonder at myself.'

'What has changed in you? I hesitated to show you, lest you set off for Edinburgh on the instant you saw it.'

'I have learnt acceptance. It's hard to explain. People go through so much with such forbearance. Mary Bowes, Dorothy – Gabe's mother – I cannot begin to tell you what she endured as a young woman. And now Belle, such dignity. And Gabe.'

'Tell me about Gabe, Molly. Here, sit down beside me.'

'But you are short of time.'

'I have time enough for you. In truth, I only said that because I was jealous. I wanted you to myself. And now I have you to myself and don't want to part from you. Let me hold your hand.'

'I will hold your hand, Thomas, but only as a friend. Nothing has changed in that regard.'

'And yet Gabe…? Do you love him, Molly?'

'In all honestly, I don't know how to answer that question. I have no idea what love is. If it means I care deeply and want to do everything I can to care for him, then yes, I love him. If it means I feel incomplete when I am not with him, then no, I don't love him. I look around this room now and this is what I love. I love the worlds contained within this one room. I love the dedication that went into the making of every one of these books. I love the thoughts and histories and worlds of interest contained within them. I love the smell of them and the feel of them. I love the skill that went into the making of them. I love books and libraries and art and ideas.' I looked around the shelves with a sense of having awoken. 'It is a curious thing, I know.'

'Do you think you will ever love a man?'

'I love plenty of men. I love Thomas Bewick; I love Mr Richardson…'

'You know what I mean, Molly. I am asking you whether you will ever love a man enough to share your life with him. Enough to marry him. Marry me, Molly. I beg you.'

'I'm sorry Thomas, I don't think I will ever marry. It would not be fair.'

'Fair? How would it not be fair? You would make me the happiest man alive!'

'But don't you see? You love me now because you cannot have me, but that would fade. And what would my life be? Having babies,

210

caring for them, tending house for you...my own life subjugated to the needs of others. I am free, Thomas. And I want to stay free.'

He looked at me for a long time. I held his gaze and watched emotions flicker across his face.

Finally, accepting, he stood and offered me his hand. 'You are a remarkable young woman, Molly Bowes, and I salute you. When I first saw you, I offered to serve you as a courtly knight. I shall wear your favour. Give me a coil of your hair. You are and shall always remain my first true love.'

He took a small pair of scissors from the desk and held them out to me. I reached up, untangled a coil of hair, snipped it off and handed it to him.

Gravely looking down at the curls in his hand, he said, 'I must ask you one thing. If you ever change your mind, please tell me.' He looked up then and there was the twinkle back in his eye. 'Though I must warn you that there are others who might beat you to it. A daughter of Thomas Bewick has taken quite a shine to me.'

'Write to me.'

'I shall, you can count on it. And if ever there is any news about this little one, I will tell you.'

'Let me look once more before you cover it.'

In need of some solitude, I went for a walk before I returned to the cottage. It was a beautiful spring day and the sun was dazzling, so I didn't see the seated figure on the drive until she spoke.

'Good morning.'

'Oh!'

'I'm sorry I made you jump. You were walking so slowly that I sketched you into my picture. Look.'

She showed me a sketch of the house and indeed there I was.

'You looked deep in thought.'

'I was. I … I need to think things over.'

'Then don't let me disturb you.'

'I'm sorry, I'm being rude. How do you do? My name is Molly. Molly Bowes.'

'I'm Martha Helen Davidson. I had not been aware that there were any members of the family in residence.'

'I'm not a member of the Bowes family. Distantly related.'

'I too. Susan is married to my cousin Peter Davidson.'

'Susan?'

'Sorry, I assumed you would know. Susan is the daughter of Anna Maria Bowes.'

'Ah, I know of Anna Maria, though I have never met her. She is a daughter of Mary Eleanor.'

'Yes indeed, the youngest. She is widowed and lives in Bird Hill House.'

'Is she the one who…?'

She smiled conspiratorially. 'Eloped? Yes, imagine the scandal! And on a ladder too!' She giggled, her face hidden behind her hand.

'A ladder?'

'Seventeen years old only! She and the young man, Henry Jessup, had been consorting in secret across the street and he obtained a ladder by which she escaped! They went off to Gretna Green! Imagine!'

Although I must admit I was entertained by this story, I found myself concerned for the reputation of the family. 'And how was the news received? By the family, I mean? In view of their…recent history.'

'You mean the scandal of her mother? Oh well it brought fresh shame, as you can imagine. Her brother, the 10th Earl, made sure she was married.'

'It's like Pride and Prejudice! Strathmore Darcy!'

'Quite! You are a fan of Jane Austen?'

'Oh yes, I'm an avid reader.'

'I too!'

'All those clever girls reduced to catching husbands.'

'Gruesome, isn't it? I once thought I would marry, but it seems the time has passed.'

'You are Elizabeth's friend Charlotte then. Perhaps your Mr Collins will come.'

'Oh no, not now. If ever I have doubts, I read Mary Wolstonecraft. I am quite content. I travel about all over and I love my art and my poetry.'

212

'I do not wish to marry either. It seems it is incomprehensible to some.'

'Well it's a necessity for young women such as we. To have a profession is the only alternative and I could never condone being a governess.'

'I do have a profession.'

'Really? I am all astonishment. And what is it?'

Suddenly abashed, I found it hard to put into words. 'Well, I have worked in gentlemen's libraries.' I straightened my back, realising for the first time the impressive nature of my experience. 'First in London and then here at Gibside. After that I assisted the Art institute, cataloguing and correspondence and so forth. And then I worked for a short time in the new library of the Literary and Philosophical Society.'

'I was recently there! I just live on Westgate Street, a stone's throw from the Lit and Phil! Do you work there still?'

'No, not at the moment. I am helping to care for a friend who is injured. But I hope to go back there one day.'

'And are you living in the Hall?' I detected a note of jealousy and smiled.

'No, in a cottage on Cut Thorn Farm over yonder, with the Stephenson family. I am...somewhat related to them too.'

'I was in the Hall on the day of my cousin's wedding here in the Chapel. This place is so special, so picturesque, so melancholy. Such beautiful grounds! Though the Bath House is in a state of disrepair. It is a pity that no-one lives here properly, although there are rumours...'

'Rumours?'

'There may be residents quite soon. You know young John is at Cambridge? Well it seems that his mother, the Dowager Countess, is quite enamoured of his tutor, William Hutt, and there are rumours of marriage.'

When I got back to the cottage, Gabe was sitting on the stone horse-trough with his face turned to the sun. I thought he hadn't heard me approach so I paused for a while by the gate and watched him. His hair was growing back, and although it was patchy, it improved his appearance a great deal. The corner of his mouth was turned up and it made me happy to see his pleasure in the sunshine. His hands were spread on his knees and I marvelled again at the length of his fingers.

Impulsively, I said what I was thinking: 'You should learn to play the piano.'

His smile grew a tiny bit wider and I knew he'd been aware of my presence. 'Bit late now.'

'No it's not! Why not? There's an instrument in the hall – I'm sure Elsie would let us sneak in.'

'Nah, no interest.'

'Would you like to learn to read then? You enjoyed me reading to you and it would be good to be able to read for yourself, surely? It would help pass the time.'

He opened his eyes then, narrowly looking at me. 'Your friend gone then?'

'Yes.'

'Going to tell me about it?'

'No.'

I sat down beside him. There was little space on the step but I told myself we were like brother and sister. 'What about reading, then?'

Silence.

'Gabe?'

'What?'

'Let me teach you to read.'

'I'll let you teach me after you've told me about that feller.'

'What do you want to know?'

'Everything.'

'Well, he's an artist. I met him when I worked at the Institute. I sat for him.'

'Oh aye?'

'Aye! Just sat for him. In a studio.'

'And what exactly does sitting involve?'

'Well, surprisingly, it involves sitting. Still. In the light. And not moving.'

'Wearing?'

214

'What do you mean wearing? What does that matter? He just wanted to paint me. He didn't do it very well, as it happens, which frustrates him, so he wants to do it again.'

'I'll bet he does.'

'I shall ignore that. Now, I've answered your question. I shall now commence your lessons.'

'What did he want to show you?'

My heart flipped. Charlotte. He wanted to show me a portrait of a child who might be my daughter. 'Just a painting.'

'And?'

'And what?' I jumped up, suddenly irritated. 'Mind your own business!' I paced about in front of him, suddenly yearning to be away. I had had enough of this farm. This morning had awoken all sorts of things in me and I impulsively decided it was time to leave.

I stood in front of him, hands on my hips. His eyes were shut.

'You're in my sun.'

It was on the tip of my tongue to answer him sharply *well I won't be for long* but I stopped myself and sat back down beside him. 'Gabe?'

'What?'

'I think I'll move on now.'

'How do you mean?'

'Well, I have a job you know. The Lit and Phil said I could go back when I'm ready. I think I'm ready.'

I felt a flex of tension in his thigh but he gave no other sign that he'd heard. Eventually he said, 'It's him, isn't it? Thomas Sword Good.'

'What? Oh no! No.' I stood up again. 'I'm restless. I'm not needed here now you're so much better. I'm ready to go.'

'Does he want to marry you?'

'Oh for goodness' sake! Stop talking about him and listen to me! I'm trying to tell you that I'm leaving. It's nothing to do with him. I admit, talking to him and being in the library... well, it brought it all back. I enjoy my work and I want to go back to it. You'll be fine now.'

'Oh aye, fine. I'm just dandy.'

'Stop it. You're fine and you've much to be thankful for.'

215

He stood up then and loomed over me. 'Oh aye, I'm thankful every day!' but his tone was sarcastic. 'Thankful!' he spat and limped quickly away across the yard where he stood gripping the gate and staring out across the fields. When he came back to stand before me, his tone was quieter. 'I can't be thankful, Molly. I'm bitter. I'm angry. I'm other things besides but that'll do for now.'

'I understand, no, honestly, I do. I try to imagine how you must feel. But do not pity yourself, Gabe. Try to remember how lucky you are.'

'Lucky?' He stood up straighter and looked over my head at the sky. 'You have no idea.' And he went back inside.

I stared at the empty doorway. He had been so resilient, rarely showing the pain he must have been in, but of course the pain was deeper than skin and bones. I sat back down on the step and tried to imagine how he must be feeling. A man of action and activity, he had been trapped in female company for too long.

I had to accept that I could not walk away. Not just yet. 'Gabe?' I called. The acknowledgement, when it finally came, was more of a grunt than a word: an injured bear in its cave.

'It's a lovely afternoon. The pony and trap are free. How do you fancy a jaunt?'

Chapter 25

When we set out, I left it to him to decide where we'd go, for of course he had to drive, though it took him some time to prepare and mount the trap. I stayed inside and left him to it, though several times as I watched him struggle I almost offered to help. But I must not. If I was to leave, as I intended, I must be sure that he would be fine without me.

I thought perhaps we ought to avoid the places where they knew him and would look at him with pity, but really there was one obvious place. If he was to re-enter the world, he needed to go to Winlaton. When I suggested it, I saw him hesitate, but then he flicked the reins and turned the pony's head to the north.

He was quiet on the journey: I think the jolting of the cart hurt his hip, though he would not say so. As we climbed Mill Lane, he began to sit up straighter and I sensed his excitement.

I said, 'I've never been to Winlaton before. Do you know many people here?'

'Used to.'

'Not now?'

'The lads I knew have probably all left by now. Them as haven't been killed.'

'Were there many at Stargate who were from Winlaton?'

'Aye, a few.'

'So they were metal-workers but they went to be miners?'

'Aye, and to the brickworks, bottle manufacturing, that sort of thing.'

'There are still foundries here though?'

'Oh aye, people will always need metal. Some set up on their own, but it's just small stuff now, nails and the like.'

A man walking beside a mounted horse coming the other way caught his eye. 'Howay Geordie!'

'Gabe? Why man, how are ye?'

He came over, squinting up at Gabe in the low afternoon sun. 'How ye doin man? Why, we were just talkin about ye!'

'Nivver! Am doing fine. First time out like.'

'Who's the lassie?'

'That's Molly. She's just a friend.'

'Come for a drink. Ye picked a good time to come up here. There's a meeting.'

'Meeting?'

'The Blacksmiths' Friendly Society. At the New Inn. 6 o'clock.'

'Ah knaa nothing aboot it, man.'

'Come on. The lassie can wait, can't ye pet?'

I was uncertain how to respond, being torn between irritation at being dismissed and relief that Gabe had someone to talk to.

'Where can Molly gan, like? She knaas no-one.'

'Tell you what, wor lass'll look after her. I'll hop on and we'll gan hyem. The wife'll be surprised, she won't be expectin to see me again the neet.'

At the top of Sandhill, two pubs faced each other and Geordie hopped down to tether our horse to the rail outside the Crown and Cannon on the east side.

'The meetin's in the New Inn, like, but it'll get busy soon. We'll just have an hour, eh Gabe? Put the world to rights. You gan on an' get 'em in. I'll introduce Molly to the missis.'

Introductions have rarely been as brisk as the one he gave me. Opening a door in a tiny house, he pushed me in and shouted, 'Ivy, this is Molly,' then shut the door behind me.

The woman was breastfeeding by the fire with another child on the proggy-mat at her feet. She rolled her eyes at me, completely nonplussed.

'I'm sorry, I'm intruding. Your husband is having a drink with my friend Gabe. Don't worry, I'll leave you in peace.'

'No, yer all right pet, sit down.'

'Really, they said they're just having one drink. I can go for a walk.'

Scornful, 'Oh aye, just the one. We all know what that means.'

'He's a meeting to go to at six, he said.'

'Oh he did, did he? He's not going to the meeting, just likes to be in on it. He's not even a blacksmith.'

'What does he do?'

'Pack-horse. Him and his horse gan all ower. I've no idea where he is half the time. Earns good money, like, so I can't complain. Even though he drinks most of it.'

'Is it true there's a library here in Winlaton?'

'Aye. House opposite. Up the stone steps.'

'I should like to go and have a look at it.'

'It's closed now but Mrs Hudspith next door has the key.'

I spent a happy hour in the library, which was modest but well-stocked and immaculately organised. Thanking Mrs Hudspith, I crossed the narrow street in the darkening afternoon and knocked on Ivy's door. She opened it, her arms free of babies, and whispered a welcome. We sat down for a fireside chat and it was dark by the time we heard men's loud laughter in the street. She leapt up and hushed the pair of them as they came lumbering into the tiny room, instantly filling it with beery breath.

Gabe's face was transformed by the drink and the company, so I hadn't the heart to complain, but ushered him out, helped him onto the trap – he was feeling no pain this time - took the reins and turned the pony homeward in the darkness.

I'd thought he'd go to sleep and wondered how I'd keep him from falling off the trap, but he was in talkative mood and it did my heart good to hear him.

'There's hope yet, young Molly.'

'Hope?'

'The lads. Pulling together like. Thing is, Crowley's used to look after everyone: six generations have grown up under Crowley's, they reckon, and since the firm's gone, they've all been a bit lost. Some people are doing all right, like, but others aren't. Well some of them got talking and got together the landlord of the New Inn, John Cowen, he called a meeting last year in his long room.'

'Long room?'

'Upstairs, in the pub.' It was even good to be answered impatiently, so keen was he to get on with his tale.

'There was twelve of them at first but it's getting bigger and bigger.'

'What is?'

'The society! It's called a Friendly Society. They're going to build a fund "For the mutual relief of each other when in distress and for other good works." It was mainly blacksmiths to start off with but they reckon they're going to extend it to other trades.'

'And what do they do?'

'They're hammering it out now.' And he actually laughed. 'Hammering it out! Get it? Blacksmiths!'

'Ha, yes, thanks Gabe, I got it. What exactly are they hammering out?'

'Well they're talking about other trades to allow membership. They know they want no miners or any other kind of pitmen. Or seamen.'

'Whyever not?'

'Well, you can understand it, like. It's the risks those men take. They're only taking people on if they're a good bet. Ye've to be of sound mind and body, "of good character" – that means no boozers or scrappers.'

'But they hold the meetings in a pub?'

'It's upstairs, man! Where the business is conducted. We saw them all gannin' up. Prosperous types. I knew nearly all of them! Douglas, Humble, Robson, Robert Parker – he used to be known as the turnip thief but you should see him now! Then there's the Renwick brothers, known them years, and my old mate Joe Cowen. He's the youngest by a long shot, but he's the secretary. His dad's the landlord. They're doin' all right for themselves. They've picked themselves up and done well. And now they want to organise so they can look out for each other when times are hard. How good is that?'

'That's good. That's really good.'

'Cos it doesn't do to just wallow and be hopeless, does it? Not when you can band together. There's strength in numbers. If the company's gone and the government doesn't care… They'll always know they have someone lookin' out for them, and for their widows and families if anything happens.' His voice changed. 'They have to limit to those in perfect health, so I've no chance. That and not having a trade.'

'Well, not at the moment, but you can learn a new trade.'

'Aye, perhaps I can.'

'You sound as though you have an idea.'

'Well I have. Um, Molly,' he took a deep breath, 'I need to learn to read. And quick.'

'Really? I wonder who could help you do that?'

'Thing is, I told Joe Cowen I could. He knew I couldn't before, like, but I told him I'd learnt since … while I've been bad. He said if I'm looking for work, I've to come to the brickworks and see him.'

'And you said?'

'I said I'd be there on Monday.'

'You mean the day after tomorrow?'

'Yep.'

'Well we'd better get to it then!'

He was a quick learner, as I knew he would be, though when asked to read aloud he was too anxious to grab at the sense of the words and often made mistakes. I wasn't confident he could pass muster by Monday, but I did my best to bolster his confidence and never presented him with words of more than two syllables to read. When I saw his face light up the first time he read out a sentence from the paper, teaching Gabe to read felt like the most worthwhile thing I had ever done in my life.

That sense redoubled when Dorothy, Belle and I listened to him over dinner that night. As he talked, they both kept smiling their thanks towards me. I think that if he had left the room, we'd all have dissolved into tears of relief and happiness.

'Joe's new to the brick business but he's full of ideas: they're going to start making gas retorts, sanitary pipes, all sorts. He's working on a new invention that he thinks could make his fortune and he wants me in on it! It's a process to make clay fit to take the place of cast-iron in certain types of pipe. There's work I can do sitting down. I know he's doing me a favour, like. There'd be plenty able-bodied types queuing up if they knew his plans for expansion, but like I say, we're old mates. Me and Belle used to play with the Cowen kids, didn't we Belle? Witches Circle and all that. Happy days. His sister Mary married Anthony Forster, who has the brick-works, and he asked Joe to leave the forge and join him. They've gone into partnership and they'll be taking more on if this clay pipe invention comes good.'

221

Dorothy said, 'Eat your dinner, man, it's going cold.' She laughed and it did my heart good to hear it. 'Look, we've all finished!'

He put a big hunk of pie in his mouth and carried on talking, 'He's special, Joe is. Always was. Always a leader, always full of ideas even when we were kids.'

He suddenly thought of something and looked at me. 'He's the one who lead the lads to the march after Peterloo!'

'Never! On the Town Moor? But that was eight years ago! He can only have been…'

'Nineteen. Same as me. Only he's done stuff. Stuff to be proud of, not like me, messing about poaching and having a laugh. Well that's all behind me now. Like I say, he's special, and he wants me to join him. And not just in the brick factory.'

'What do you mean?' I said, suddenly alert.

'There's a lot going on, but if I tell you, you must keep it quiet.'

'What kind of thing?'

'Political things. Since Peterloo. You know what Chartists are?'

'Gabe, don't patronise me. Yes, I know what Chartists are. I was _at_ Peterloo, don't forget. Did you know what Chartists were before today? I think that's more to the point!'

Chastened, he glanced at me sideways and refilled my mug. 'No, to be fair, I didn't really. I'd heard the word but just thought they were troublemakers.'

'Like the people who were murdered at Peterloo?'

'Aye. Joe Cowen made sure that couldn't happen on the Town Moor.' He looked at me meaningfully.

I was scornful. 'How could that possibly have been prevented? Innocent people trampled and slashed by mounted soldiers?'

'Ay, but they made sure that if a cavalry charge happened, them soldiers wouldn't stay mounted for long.'

'Oh, you think it's so easy to pull a soldier down from a stampeding horse? You think those people could have stopped themselves being trampled and slashed?'

'No, no they couldn't, but Crowley's Crew made sure it couldn't happen in Newcastle, for they went prepared. Joe Cowen made sure of that.'

'Prepared? With weapons, you mean?'

222

'Aye, they had weapons alright, all made here in Winlaton, pikes.'

'I hate violence, Gabe. You know that. There's always a better way.'

He looked at me for a long moment, then said almost apologetically, 'Just little pikes, for self-defence.'

'How could they conceal pikes?'

'Not pikes like a pike staff, not to hurt men, just to stop horses, cut bridles, that sort of thing. A light pointed head with an axe on one face and a knife-edged spur on the other. Self-defence.

'A man may carry a Winlaton pike and not be noticed, not be arrested for going armed. Other things too, invented in Winlaton. Special weapons, specially to stop horses. Called a craa-foot, little thing, metal, four prongs, whichever way it lands there's a prong sticking up. Easy to conceal, quick to throw. Caltrop, you'd call it, not being from round here.'

I didn't answer. I had been feeling conflicted all day. Now that Gabe was mended, what did I want to do? Where did my future lie? Part of me yearned for the calm beauties of the Lit and Phil, but a greater part of me knew that I belonged with these people. Proud hard-working people who only wanted to live without fear. I could find a sense of purpose amongst them. They had established their own library. They valued and yearned for education. I could surely find a way of helping. I wanted to do what I could to improve lives.

Gabe had grown tired all of a sudden, and as he wiped his mouth, he spoke more to himself than to anyone else. 'I never really thought about politics. Nothing to do with me – that's what I thought. But Joe Cowen, he's explained things to me today. I feel like a different man.'

People came in then and there were general celebrations about Gabe getting a job, so we spoke no more about the Chartists, but that night I thought long and hard. If there was Chartist activity in Winlaton, I wanted to be in on it.

Chapter 26

In the morning, Gabe gathered his few belongings together, wrapped a pie in a cloth and helped Belle up onto the trap. He no longer needed help himself, and I was glad to see it. Staring resolutely ahead, he made ready to flick the reins.

'Come with us, Molly,' Belle asked one last time, bewilderment in her eyes.

'No, really. I have things I want to do.'

She knew that he and I had had a long conversation after the others had gone to bed. Although she knew nothing of the content of it, Gabe's demeanour told her enough.

As I watched them diminish down the track, I stood for a long time looking around me, and it seemed that the world was fresh and full of possibilities. The green valley shimmered in the sunlight and the long low hall hugged the hillside. My heart lifted.

In my pocket I fingered a letter from Mary Bowes. I would choose my place to read it.

The Orangery steps.

I walked directly down the field and climbed the ha-ha, crossing the avenue in full sunshine and descending the slope to cross the paddock. The grass was long and spring flowers bobbed and waved in a light breeze. Could I bear to leave this place?

The windows of the Orangery were all closed and a few dead plants were trapped inside on the wooden staging. It was so sad to see a place once so loved and alive with vibrant exotics now so bereft of life. A dead butterfly, desiccated and brittle, lay on the inside of the sill.

Sitting on the steps and stretching out my legs, I leant back and lifted my face to the sun, revelling in the simple bliss of being alive and healthy and free.

I was free.

A red kite wheeled above me, languidly sailing in easeful circles, glinting russet and gold.

Taking the letter out of my pocket, I laid it on the sun-warmed stone.

Dear Molly

I do hope this finds you well. I have received no reply to my last letter, sent after I received your dreadful news about Stargate. I was concerned, but have since heard from Elsie that you are still living in the cottage with the Stephenson family.

I was so very sorry to hear of the dreadful event that has befallen the area. As you say, it is incomprehensible that in these days of scientific advance, men would be accustomed to descend into the earth lit only by a tallow candle. I infer from the brevity and tone of your letter that this dreadful event has understandably had a profound effect on you.

I agree with you entirely: it should be a matter of regulation that such practices should be stamped out, and as you say, the responsibility lies in the hands of those with the power to ensure the safety of those in their employ. It has always been a great motto in our family that with wealth comes responsibility. You may think I am being over-sensitive, but did I detect some antipathy to all mine-owners in the wake of this catastrophe? It is perfectly understandable that anyone affected by such a tragedy should look for someone to blame. I have made some enquiries of my own, and it seems the circumstances of responsibility and ownership at Stargate are in confusion due to an inheritance matter. It is no excuse for what happened but it does in part explain it.

Lest you should tar all mine-owners with the same brush, I would like to offer a defence of the Bowes family's record. From the date of the first Gibside mine-workings, Lady Elizabeth ensured that anyone who leased one of her mines had to maintain safety standards. George Bowes did much to improve the wages and living standards, and more recently my late brother was closely involved in the progress of the development of the safety lamp.

I was glad to hear that you have found yourself able to devote your energies to tending to your friend's injuries and I am glad to hear he has made such a remarkable recovery. Do not take it amiss when I urge caution upon you. Gabe has extensive family. Your

225

connection to them is tenuous. You have told me that you see him as a brother. Unless your feelings for him extend beyond your professed sisterly concern, I caution you to remember how your attentions might appear to him. In my experience, men too often misinterpret the ministrations of a gentle heart.

It was clear from your last letter that your political conscience is greatly stirred by the plight of your friends in the labouring classes. Although you were of necessity discreet, I am left afraid that you will be drawn into dangerous undertakings. Please be assured that among the parliamentary representatives, sympathies extend further than you might expect. I urge you to maintain civility in the demonstrations: those with a tendency to demonise the working classes are quick to point at actions, call it savagery and hold it up as proof of the inferiority of the workers. The Whig party is in talks with the leading lights of the Radical movement. This may surprise you, Molly, and I urge you not to talk about this amongst the activists of Winlaton, for there are many Radicals who would despise such initiatives, but if we are not to see the horrors of the French Revolution, there must be a civilised way forward. The cap of liberty has long been a symbol for the Whigs and if you are reading this at Gibside, you need only look up and see the eminence which George Bowes himself gave to it.

I looked towards where the monument watched over the estate, noticing for the first time that patches of the figure of Liberty no longer glittered: the gilt had been chipped away by desperate men.

And now, on much a lighter note, I have some gossip for you. It seems that the Dowager Countess, on her frequent visits to Cambridge to see her son, has developed a close relationship with his tutor, a Mr William Hutt. I have a secret to impart! They are to be married! In March next year, they shall become man and wife and it has already been agreed that they will live at Gibside! Is that not exciting? I beg you not to pass on this gossip: it is between us.

Furthermore, young Molly Bowes, I have an idea and it pertains to you. Mr Hutt is considerably younger than his intended: he has political ambitions and in order to pursue them, an estate, a titled wife and a country estate can do no harm at all, as you will imagine! (Forgive me, I am in a mischievous frame of mind.) And what could be finer for a young man, newly married and unfamiliar with the area

226

than that he should be assisted with the secretarial devotion of a relative, however distant? Someone literate, articulate, well-organised; someone familiar with the area and its people: and in addition, someone in possession of an intimate knowledge of the contents of the extensive library of which he will shortly be custodian?

I have taken the liberty of mentioning your name to the Dowager Countess. You will like her, Molly, I promise. I urge you to consider this idea and do everything within your power to make it come to pass.

It was so tempting. Of course nothing might come of it, but for news of this possibility to arrive at this time: it seemed like a sign. If I believed in such things, which I didn't.

The choice seemed so stark: I had spent the night envisaging myself taking a small room in Winlaton, sustaining myself by teaching people to read. Perhaps I could help in the library. There was such a thing as Mechanics' Institutes: perhaps we could set one up in the village. I was drawn to the Chartist activities but afraid of the possibility of violence. More violence.

I stood up. There was no imminent need to commit either way. I would investigate Winlaton first and see whether I could envisage myself making a life there.

When Belle returned to the cottage, having deposited Gabe in his new home, I was sitting on the stone trough waiting.

'How did it go?'

'Oh, you know. Painful. Mr and Mrs Robson are so happy to have a young man in the house again, but it brings it home to them all that they've lost.'

'Three sons. It's unthinkable.'

'Gabe's happy, though I'm sure he'd rather you'd gone with him.'

'It needed to be you. They're your in-laws.'

'That's not what I meant, Molly, and you know it. What's going on?'

I stood up. 'In all honesty, I don't know myself.'

'Will you go to see him?'

I didn't answer at first. 'I'll see him, I've no doubt. I want to go to the next meeting of the Reform Society. Will you come with me?'

It was clear from the moment we entered the room that people knew who I was. Gabe and Joe Cowen met us at the door, as promised, and when we entered the room, a ripple went around and eyes turned to look at this exotic creature, a survivor of the Peterloo Massacre.

A group of women sitting round a large table beckoned us over and I saw that the table was spread with banners, needles and thread.

'Sit down here beside me, Molly Bowes. Hello Belle. Your first time, too? Here, pick up a needle and some thread – we sew and talk while we listen to the speakers. You'll find it's a rowdy meeting. No-one stands on ceremony or holds back if they want to say anything.'

We sat down on the long benches. I'm no seamstress, but I took up needle and thread as I was bid.

'I'm Martha, the wife of Thomas Hodgson.' She said this with some pride, as though I should know who Thomas Hodgson was.

Luckily, an older woman across the table explained. 'Thomas was a weaver. He was at the Great Meeting on the Town Moor and had a letter published in the paper afterwards.'

'Aye, he did. Ye'll have heard all about it, Molly?'

'Some. But I'd like to hear more.'

Mrs Hodgson needed no prompting. 'After what happened to you and your kin in Manchester, the mood was solemn and behaviour calm. We let our banners speak for us. We made fine banners, didn't we girls?'

A heartfelt murmur of assent went round the table and Mrs Hodgson went on: '"We mourn the massacred at Manchester", "When the wicked beareth rule, the people mourn" – that's Solomon. Many of them had scriptural authority. "Evil to him who evil thinks." Only a few were about reform - annual parliaments, universal suffrage, vote by ballot and all that. This was about what's right. It was about the right to peaceful assembly.' She slammed her hand down on the table.

The older woman spoke across the table. 'You don't have to tell Molly what it was about, does she pet? And you lost your bairn, they say?'

'Yes. Yes I did.'

'And you were injured?'

'Yes.' I think they were avid to hear detail from me, but suddenly shy, I could not heave my heart into my mouth.

The old woman sighed and shook her head. 'Aye, aye, poor pet. "These are the times to try men's souls." That's from Thomas Paine's *Common Sense*.'

'And what happened after the meeting?'

Another woman spoke up. 'Dignity. Solidarity, that's what. It didn't happen in vain, don't you worry. Peterloo brought people together. Pitmen and keelmen joined the radicals. Radical leaflets were much easier to come by after that. *The Black Dwarf* and *The Black Book*: pitmen carried them in their hats.'

Mrs Hodgson took up the story. 'Put the wind up them, it did. Loyalists wrote to parliament to say 'nothing to do with me.' Reverend Charles Thorp of Ryton probably feared for his life. Radical Jack Lambton tried to organise a petition but then he muckied his ticket by slagging Winlaton off. There were seven hundred of us there, you know, and word soon spread that we were armed.'

'What did he say?'

'He called us 'wild elements'! Bah! He was soon put in his place.' Her voice rose: this was her moment: 'My husband had his letter published in the Chronicle: I have it here.' She pulled a yellowed newspaper out of her sewing bag and unfolded it reverentially on the table. 'Here, Molly, read it to us in your ladylike voice.'

I smoothed it out on the table before me and did as I was told: *"23rd October 1819. Dear Mr Lambton. A person in your exalted station in life cannot be supposed to have much intelligence of what is going on amongst the lower orders of plebeians and on that account must be generally abundantly ignorant of what is known to every person but themselves. In short, the Reformers wish for such a reform in the House of Commons as will realise that favourite Whig toast, the Sovereignty of the People."*

229

The room had fallen silent and the elegance of those final words with all their great dignity and import lingered on the air. I saw Gabe smiling at me with pride.

One of the men said, 'The authorities were afraid, as they have been ever since the French Revolution. Loyalists hereabouts, and there's plenty in Ryton, demanded military support and got it. They say the mouth of the Tyne filled with the whole naval force of the North Sea! Yeomanry troops were even sent down from Alnwick, the Coquetdale Rangers. The local part-time regiments were built up, and patrolled the streets of Gateshead. There was trouble in Newcastle: soldiers were attacked, they said by drunks, while a mob gathered round chanting 'Liberty or Death! Death or Glory! Hunt Forever!'

Another spoke up, 'The rumour went round that thousands of men were gathering on the banks of the Tyne. This side of the river, your Lord Strathmore's Durham and Gibside Yeomanry was reinforced but things stayed quiet over here.'

'Aye, it's been quiet since but they're building up again now, and they know it.'

After the meeting, Belle went to see the Robsons, leaving me standing with Gabe. There was something about his demeanour that troubled me, a nervousness, almost a shyness, and I suddenly understood that he had asked her to give us time alone.

'I was proud of you tonight, lass.'

'I should hope you are always proud of me, as I am of you. We are brother and sister, you and I.'

He looked at me then, his eyes dark and serious. 'Aye, but we are not, are we Molly?'

'No, I suppose not.' I was troubled by this turn of events and turned towards the Robsons' door, but Gabe reached for my hand.

'Come for a walk with me. Come, we'll just walk to Scotland Head and look out over the valley.'

'It's dark, Gabe. I want to go home now.'

'I've something to ask you Molly.'

'No, Gabe, don't. Please. Don't change the way we are. We are easy with each other, are we not?'

'Aye, we are. But I would like more than that Molly. I want you to be my wife.'

230

I was silent.

'Before you answer, and I don't want you to answer tonight, think on it. There's more I must say, and this is very difficult for me. I mean it as a partnership. I know you, Molly. I know you want more than children and to keep house. I know that in the ordinary way of things, you would not consider a marriage offer.'

'How can you know that? We have never spoken of these things.' But I knew. 'Belle. Of course.'

'I made her tell me. After that artist fellow came to Gibside. I had to know.'

'How did you make her tell you?'

'Why, in the old way I always used. I gave her a Chinese burn.'

I had to laugh.

'See? I make you laugh. I can keep you safe. Safe from suspicion, safe from other men. Safe from loneliness.'

'Gabe. Please. I'm sorry. Find yourself a lovely girl. You have many admirers, you know. I am … complicated. I am … somewhat undomesticated. I would be trouble to you.'

'But I love that about you. I do not want you to keep house for me. We'll be a partnership, you and me.'

'You should have a devoted wife and a brood of little children like your friend Joe.'

He suddenly turned away and I cursed myself. As he walked a few paces with his awkward gait, I watched him against the sunset and felt a stirring in my heart. And yet I could not give myself to a man. No man had ever owned me nor ever would.

At length, his back still turned to me, he spoke softly: 'There is something I must tell you and I beg you never to disclose it to anyone. Not even Belle.'

I stayed silent.

'My mother knows. I am too ashamed. Perhaps you should ask her. But in private, be sure of it.'

I went to him, I held his hand, looked up into his eyes, spoke as gently as I could. 'I know there can be no children for you, Gabe. I tended you, remember?' When he didn't reply, I turned away, suddenly tearful though I tried to hide it. 'We are alike in this, you and I. There can be no more children for me either. I could not bear it.'

He wrapped his arms around me from behind and I felt his face in my hair. 'If that's what you feel, then there is no obstacle between us. Marry me. Please.'

Chapter 27

The Dowager Lady Strathmore: such a grand title, conjuring an elegant elderly personage of haughty bearing. I don't know what I had expected, but it wasn't this small, middle-aged, dark-haired woman with a heart-shaped face and smiling eyes. She stood up as I entered the room, something else I hadn't expected. Mary Bowes had told me I would like her, and I did, on sight.

'Do sit down, Molly. I feel I know you already, I have heard so much about you from Mary. I have to say, she didn't quite convey your appearance to me. Why, you are head and shoulders taller than me! I feel quite a dwarf!'

'I am very pleased to meet you, Lady Strathmore.'

She sat down and motioned me to do the same. 'I don't think I'll ever get used to people calling me that. Though in certain circles I insist upon it, I feel it fits me ill, like a hat that's too big and covers my face!' She smiled, but it was a sad smile, and I returned it, to show that I understood.

She settled back in her chair. 'All those years of being Mary Milner – in truth, I cannot change now, not in private. John never forced me to have a public face, bless him. It would have been too awkward if I had accompanied him on formal engagements or entertained important guests. England is so stuffy and class-conscious, you know.'

She poured tea into two porcelain cups, musing, 'Of course, if he had married me when John was born, none of this would have happened. But there it is. What's done cannot be undone.' She handed me my tea and her smile brightened. 'So yes, it gives me pleasure to see some people struggle to get the words out after all those years of casting me sidelong glances and muttering behind my back. My friends still call me Poll, which was my nickname from being a little girl.'

'My mother was also christened Mary but called Polly.'

'Do you ever hear from her?'

'No, I … it's a long time ago now.'

'I lost my mother when I was very small. My father remarried and my stepmother was cruel to me. Children endure such a lot, don't they? I am glad I have only the one to worry about! Oh! Forgive me, that was thoughtless!' She reached across and squeezed my hand. 'Forgive me, Molly.'

'It's fine, really. Is John here with you? I have not seen him since he was nine years old. I met him briefly at Streatlam soon after Lord Strathmore died.'

'Really? I did not know that. I was perhaps still in London dealing with the funeral arrangements and the endless lawyers. Mary was invaluable to us at that time, not only emotionally but also in dealing with John's family.' She gave me a meaningful look. 'Still, enough of that: water under the bridge. You asked about my son. He is on the continent, touring with the Reverend Arthur Pearson. He seems particularly smitten with Paris, where a university friend of his is living amongst the artistic community. I am hoping that the Reverend is supervising John closely, bearing in mind his age.'

'He is…?'

'Nineteen. In eighteen months, on 19th June 1832, he will attain his majority! I look forward to that day most fervently, I can tell you!'

'May I enquire why?'

'We will at last achieve independence from the supervision of the lawyers and the Strathmores. John will be recognised as master of the English estates and I imagine he will be a veritable new broom! There are some people on the staff at Streatlam who have not been kind to us, particularly since my husband passed away.'

Now we were getting to the matter closest to my heart. 'And … I hesitate to ask this question, for it seems impertinent, but you were so kind to invite me here... I can only speak for myself, but of course you must know that all of us here at Gibside will be wondering…'

Her eyes bright, she stopped me, 'Wonder no more, beautiful Molly! I have wonderful news – it is the purpose of my visit. You are among the first here to know that I am engaged to be married!' And she held forth her left hand, on which glittered a diamond of astonishing size and brilliance.

I had been prepared for this: Mary had asked me to tell no-one and I had received confirmation that I must act surprised. 'Why, Lady Strathmore, that is indeed wonderful news! And who is the gentleman?'

'His name is William Hutt. He is John's tutor at Cambridge. We have known each other for four years and grown increasingly close. We are planning to marry on 16th March next year and we will be coming to live at Gibside! Is it not wonderful news, Molly? A fresh start in this beautiful place. John always favoured Gibside, you know, although when we stayed here I always felt there was the shadow of his first love. I see from your expression that Mary has told you about Sarah Hussey. Tragic story. John was quite broken by her death, particularly as it came in the same year as his mother's.'

'And may I ask how your son has taken the news of your marriage to his tutor?'

'Well, you know boys. In public, he is cool and somewhat embarrassed, but in private he is quite beside himself with delight! William is like an older brother to him, he says, for I must tell you that he is considerably younger than me, being not yet thirty.'

'That is truly marvellous news. When shall Mr Hutt visit Gibside?'

'He is on his way, for the Cambridge term is just about to end and we will be spending Christmas here! Elsie and Albert and their staff are beside themselves with excitement and the preparations are already under way. In fact, forgive me, Molly, but I have just thought of something and must see Elsie as soon as possible. Would you like any more tea?'

I took this as a polite signal that our interview was at an end and rose to take my leave. I was disappointed that no mention had been made of the library or a role for me. Surely Mary would have prepared me if the possibility no longer existed? Casually, I said, 'Will Mr Hutt be travelling alone at Christmas?'

'Why yes, I should imagine so; unless John comes home, which I doubt. Why do you ask?'

'I thought perhaps he would be bringing a companion such as a secretary.'

I caught her sidelong glance. 'No, he will be appointing a secretary in this area. It is important for him to integrate rapidly, and the more local knowledge he can access the more quickly and confidently he will settle, I think.'

'So he will perhaps carry out interviews after Christmas?'
'Oh, I don't think that will be necessary. We already have someone in mind.'
Crestfallen, I could not hide my disappointment and answered distractedly, 'Oh, that's good.'
'All that remains is for him to meet the person, for the relationship will have to be mutually agreeable to both parties, of course.'
'Yes, of course.' I got up and gathered my things. I felt on the verge of tears. 'I'll take my leave of you, Lady Strathmore. I have taken up too much of your time.'
'Before you go, perhaps we could agree a suitable date. Mr Hutt will arrive on Saturday, so perhaps Monday? How does Monday at 10am sound?'

I look back fondly on those years I worked with William Hutt. From the start I was struck by the contradictions in the man. Though he was young and his face unlined, he had the air of an elderly undertaker. Though I rarely managed to make him laugh, I often heard the pair of them giggling away like teenagers. Though he was of slender build, he was strong and had a will of iron. Though he seemed like a creature of darkness and dust, he loved flowers with a passion. Though he projected confidence and stillness in company, I knew that in private he suffered agonies of nerves, particularly if he had to deal with working men. He once confessed that coming from a rarefied life of academic endeavour amidst the cloisters of Cambridge, his contact with the working classes had been hitherto limited to acknowledgement of the woman who had cleaned his rooms.

But he and I got along: though I found him charmless, it was enough for me that he made Poll so happy, and his fondness for Gibside greatly endeared him to me. He expressed his love for both through flowers: for Poll, he planted a rose-garden and built an orchid house in the walled garden.

His political ambitions grew slowly, which was lucky for me as I knew and understood so little about party politics. Like George Bowes, he was of the Whig persuasion: I would not have agreed to work with him if he had been a Tory. When they married, the Whigs had just swept to power under Earl Grey.

As Mary Bowes had indicated, there were movements afoot to bring the Radicals into the Whig fold, and three months after the wedding, he and I went to the Music Hall on 27th June 1831 to witness the two parties meet and establish the Northern Political Union. The Reform Bill was introduced in December of that year and there were celebrations the following spring when it finally passed through the House of Commons. Everyone was so disappointed when the Lords threw it out and Earl Grey resigned.

Those were febrile times and many radicals were not happy about what they saw as the castration of their cause. From Belle, I knew that there was deep unrest in Winlaton, although on the surface the town was remarkably peaceable; in fact Crowley's Crew rapidly gained a reputation as peacekeepers at demonstrations, of which there were many. After Charles Attwood asked the Crew to attend a meeting to stop others breaking it up, their reputation soared. The respect with which they were regarded was evident from the number of times they were sent for by the Northern Political Union to keep the peace at Chartist demonstrations. Wearing white tall-hats lined with green underneath the turned-up rims and armed with oak staffs from Gibside woods, Winlaton's clannish workforce of strapping blacksmiths formed the praetorian guard for the Chartist movement in the area.

The following year, The Duke of Wellington was unable to form a Tory Government and the triumphant Whig ministry under Earl Grey carried the Reform Bill on 4th June 1832. There were celebrations right across the country, but elation soon turned to despair when it became clear it had only achieved a partial extension of the franchise. The basic unfairness of taxation without representation led to more demonstrations. A gulf began to open up in the fragile alliance between the Whigs and the Radicals.

When Hutt was elected MP for Hull in the first general election under the new rules in December 1832, I had to explain to him the realities of how betrayed the workers felt and resentful of their former middle-class allies. When he made his speeches in the House of Commons in defence of the sailors of Hull and the Tolpuddle Martyrs, I like to think they showed far more understanding of the plight of the disenfranchised than he would have shown without my intervention.

I have to admit, I learnt a good deal from him, not only about the nature of party politics, but also methods of persuasion. While he was away in his constituency, I would often draft dramatic speeches in grandiloquent style. He would sit with me and patiently work through them, showing me how to turn a phrase, gloss over an uncomfortable truth, invite confidence, lead up to a crescendo. He taught me the classical skills of rhetoric, so that when I heard them in use, I would recognise how I was being worked upon. It made me a very critical observer of some of the speakers who came to Winlaton meetings and I did what I could to alert others to propaganda and manipulation.

When the Blacksmiths' Friendly Society finally agreed its rules in 1835, by which time they had over fifty members, I wrote out a fine copy of their constitution, which was to be placed in the Society's box with the monies and other documents kept by John Cowen in the long room of the New Inn. The Blacksmiths was a legitimate organisation but the government would happily have banned it if they could have linked it to Chartism, so the Chartists met in the Royal Oak in Back Street.

They were such tense times: the country was like a powder-keg. Rumours of civil war swirled about, and I'd heard that Gabe was becoming swept up in them. In a movement beset by differing demands, the Northern Political Union was one of the best-organised and most resilient of Chartist Associations, and a newspaper called The Northern Liberator had done much to consolidate the movement in Newcastle. When the People's Charter was published in May 1838, we were all relieved to see that six clear points had been hammered out: Every man over twenty-one to have a vote; the ballot to be secret; MPs need not be landowners; MPs should be paid;

constituencies should have the same number of voters; parliaments to be annual.

In the same month, Joe's father John Cowen died, and at his funeral in the grounds of the new church of St Paul's, I saw Gabe standing amongst a group of men with stony faces. His dark hair was streaked with silver and although I'm sure he felt my gaze upon him, he didn't meet my eyes.

I looked instead at Joe Cowen with his wife and four of his children. The eldest son, Joseph, was six at the time, the big boy holding on bravely to the hands of his little brothers, John and William. The two smaller ones were crying, but Joseph kept his chin up and as I looked at his brave little face, something strange happened. He turned his head and looked directly at me, holding my gaze for several moments. For the first time in my life, I felt a real premonition.

Chapter 28

That Christmas, the mood in Winlaton changed. Knowing that on Boxing Day Gabe would be in Newcastle to hear an eminent Chartist speaker called George Julian Harney, I agreed to accompany Belle on a visit to the Robsons. As we were leaving, I was dismayed to hear the rowdy voices of an enormous crowd coming up the hill from the direction of Blaydon. Belle and I stood in the doorway watching their approach, all clearly in high spirits, chanting and singing loudly and still holding aloft their banners. The Robsons had told us that Harney was in favour of violence, so it was no surprise to read the slogans: "Liberty! Or I shall make my arrows drunk with blood and my sword shall devour flesh!" "He that hath no sword, let him sell his shirt and buy one."

Doors and windows were opening onto the frosty afternoon air, people were coming onto the streets shouting greetings and questions, clapping each other on the back, hoisting banners from weary arms.

I turned to Belle, 'Come on, it's like a carnival! Let's join in!'

Belle pulled back, but I wanted to know what was happening, so I linked her arm and pulled her with me to join the crowd and walk along listening in on their conversations.

'There were sixty thousand there!'

'Nivver!'

'Rubbish man, more like eighty thousand!'

'It's true what he said, like: the moderates are too well-fed to threaten violence.'

'Aye, but let them labour for one week and go barefoot and hungry. They'd soon forget moral force - physical force is the only way.'

'Live free or die!'

'Harney's the man for us!'

'Harney? The man's a rabble-rouser!'

'He believes in direct action.'

'And with good reason.'

'He's been in prison.'

'Aye, and do you know for why?'

'No.'

'For selling newspapers and refusing to be bowed. Knowledge should be free.'

'How's selling newspapers an offence?'

'Because it was *The Poor Man's Guardian*, an unstamped paper. Printed without paying the newspaper tax. Them as want to read it can't afford the taxes. They don't want us to have a free press, do they? Don't want us to hear stuff, spread revolutionary thought an' that.'

'Harney stands for the liberty of the press, unlike them fekkin Whigs!'

Belle whispered, 'What does he mean?'

Because I worked with a parliamentarian, Belle looked to me to explain what was going on in the wider world beyond Gibside's protective borders. I explained to her in low tones, 'When the Whigs got in, we all thought they were representing the working man and they would repeal the fourpenny tax on newspapers. But they didn't.'

A red-faced man pulled my shoulder and shouted into our faces: 'Aye, they'd rather keep the working classes in ignorance so they can continue to dominate them, and that's the truth, like Harney said.'

'We can get newspapers for a penny, though?' said Belle.

'Pah! That's a mere sop. The penny weeklies like the *Penny Cyclopedia* are never prosecuted with their pictures of abbeys and birds, oh no. *The Poor Man's Guardian* tells about factory exploitation, the growth of trades unions. The Whigs with their 'mock reforms' – hang 'em all! They've ensured the death of the unstamped press by raising the tax on paper!'

'It's not knowledge Harney's peddling, it's revolution. He wears the tricolour sash. They say he idolises Marat.'

'Aye, and look how he ended up!'

'He wants a republic, for sure. Liberty, equality, fraternity. "Kings, aristocrats, and tyrants of every description…are slaves in rebellion against the sovereign of the earth, which is the people, and against the legislator of the universe, which is Nature."'

'Divide and rule. They'll do everything they can to stop the workers banding together. Trades Unions? Stamped on. And look at what they did to the Tolpuddle Martyrs! That was just outright savagery. Transportation for that?'

'Bring 'em down, the ruling classes, bring 'em all down!'

'Aye, let's chop off their heads like the Frenchies did!'
'Can't be doing with all that talk. It's not needed. Leave it to the negotiators.'
'Aye, but where's it got us so far?'

I had heard enough. I was determined to hear this Harney when he came to Winlaton. I didn't have to wait long: in two days, he was to be guest of honour at a meeting to be followed by a dance at the Highlander Inn. The impact he had had upon some of these people was frightening: I felt hostile towards him for his incendiary talk, so I was unprepared for the playful, slender twenty-one year old charmer who was welcomed into the village two days later. Wearing a red cap on his long brown hair, we watched him lead his partner in the dance, playfully placing his cap on her head and bowing to the assembled crowd. He sang, he danced, he laughed: he charmed one and all.

And as for his speeches, there was no arguing with anything I heard him say. No trace of the incitement to violence I had expected: 'England is a land of plenty where no person who works should want and yet thousands perish for want of the basic necessities through no fault of their own. The New Poor Law treats the unemployed as though they are criminals. Law should be used to improve society, instead of which it is being used to defend the propertied classes to protect themselves. They plunder the productive classes. The proletarian classes need to take their place in parliament and ensure the end of class legislation.'

He spoke in stirring terms about the need for a free press: 'Once it is established a new age will commence, the standard of truth and science will be erected among the nations of the world, and we may contemplate, with heartfelt satisfaction, the establishment of the dignified empire of reason and the improvement and happiness of the human race.'

Belle and I rode home that night in high spirits. With a man like Harney to represent us at the coming National Chartist Convention, we felt sure that sense would prevail.

But it was not to be. Despite the best efforts of the Chartists, the House of Commons refused by an overwhelming majority to consider their Petition.

242

Anger swept the country in a great tidal wave that threatened to wipe away all the good work that had been done around negotiating tables.

The Convention knew the time for decision had come and amidst considerable in-fighting, voted on 16th July in favour of a month of insurrection. It was to culminate in a General Strike to begin as soon as the crops were in. The date was fixed for 12th August.

Harney addressed forty meetings all over the North: in Cumberland, Northumberland, Yorkshire, Durham and Lancashire he whipped people to insurrection. He called upon the Chartist Convention to do its duty by raising the people in collision with their tyrants. It was his strong belief, based on the evidence of the French Revolution, that soldiers would be on the side of the people as they were in 1792. The more recent French Revolution of 1830 had clearly made him believe that civilians could defeat trained troops.

Newcastle magistrates warned the Home Office that they had no doubts about the Convention's power to cause a widespread cessation of labour and were well aware of the consequences that would follow. Inevitably, once that became known, there was civil unrest. In the heat of a July day, six thousand Chartists, many of them armed, entered into battle with two companies of infantry, a troop of dragoons and five hundred police and special constables. The magistrates panicked, warning the government that there were thousands more Chartists in the colliery and iron-working villages clustered around the town. Furthermore, the closest reinforcements in the battle to maintain order were a small contingent of troops sixty miles away at Carlisle. Sir Charles Napier, General Commander in the North, wrote to the Home Secretary, 'The people are ready to rise.'

Fires raged in the industrial centres of the midlands. Even the Convention began to be afraid of what they had unleashed, and on 3rd August recommended that no strike should take place. In an effort to keep control, it added that the 12th should be the first of two or three days of public demonstrations, and then it adjourned until 1st September, dissolving itself out of responsibility for what might happen. As Gabe put it, they chickened out.

On 10th August the Northern Political Union put up placards around Newcastle with notices of a national holiday to begin on 12th August. Everyone was apprehensive, not least the middle classes, who were rumoured to be arming themselves against 'the rabble.'

When the 12th August came, the strike was almost universal: no pitmen or iron-workers turned up for work. Accompanied by dragoons, the magistrates arrested bound pitmen and charged them with having violated their bond. Harney was imprisoned as a rabble-rouser. The strike quickly deteriorated and Tyneside was left bitter against the Chartist Convention who had abandoned their cause at the crucial moment. Although Napier reported a state of ferment across the north, the only violent outbreak was in Bolton, where Chartists with pikes and guns fought against troops for three days.

On Tuesday 16th August, when it seemed that the danger had passed, I went to Winlaton. The place was abuzz with the news that the cavalry were on their way. Two Chartists had arrived under cover of night to spread the word that Jacob Robinson had been arrested in Newcastle and charged with disorderly conduct. The police had found on him two pike-heads, and when he was asked where he got them, Robinson had apparently told the police that Winlaton was storing masses of them, made in the village to arm the populace ready for civil war.

I took refuge with the Robsons, unwilling to be involved but anxious to witness what happened and report it to Hutt. The thought of the Cavalry bearing down on innocent people again struck fear into my heart. I watched the streets anxiously from an upstairs window: Gabe was nowhere to be seen. In the distance, I could hear the fife and drum going round the town, alerting people to the danger. People poured onto the streets, but every one of them seemed to know where they were going. It was immediately clear to me that this had been rehearsed. The village had become a hilltop fortress. Men in small groups, each with a gun, were going to their places on all the approach roads. If any cavalry approached, the gun was to be fired into the air. At that signal, all out-lying sentries would fall back and take their places within the town. Every approach was sealed off; the sentries had views in every direction.

Inside the town, floorboards were being pulled up, pikes and spears and caltrops assembled. I heard Mr Robson whisper to his wife, 'Mind, the bulk of them are hidden in the tunnel so that we don't lose them all if the unthinkable happens.

'What are those men carrying?'

'You don't want to know, Molly. If it all kicks off, stay inside and away from the windows.'

'But what are they? They look like stoneware bottles.'

It was Mrs Robson who told me, and her voice trembled: 'They're hand-grenades, Molly. They're filled with metal.'

'But I don't understand. What are they for?'

Mr Robson explained: 'If they are attacked, they will throw them at the soldiers. They contain gunpowder and nail-rod cuttings. There's a fuse passing through the cork. They're wrapping them in stout canvas bags. They are fearsome weapons but fear not, they will only be used in last resort.'

An elderly fellow in the street below had heard our conversation, and now he laughed up at us, his few yellow teeth like tombstones. 'Divvn't worry pet, it'll not come to that. Ha! The last time the soldiers came up against Crowley's Crew, our lads made best friends of 'em!'

'What can you mean?' I was desperate for reassurance that this wasn't going to turn into a battle.

'Crowley's Crew had taken over the market stalls on the Sandhill in the Toon and started selling the meat at realistic prices! The soldiers sent to arrest them were turned into allies by a few choice words. We can defend ourselves with our tongues as well as our ironware, lassie!'

Suddenly, a deep boom shook the windows. I felt it in my chest and all of us fell silent. Then another: then another.

Wide-eyed with fear, I turned into the room to look at Mr Robson. He looked as though he had been expecting it. He held up a finger, listening, and sure enough, there came another boom. I saw that Mrs Robson had her shawl bunched in her hands and clamped over her ears, so I did the same. Her husband was now holding up all ten fingers, and as each ensuing boom rattled the glass, he folded one down.

As the last one faded, I let down my shawl from my numb ears and looked at Mr Robson.

'I'm sorry lass, I should have warned you. We knew to expect it. Them was fourteen ship's cannon being fired from the Sandhill.'

'How did they escape the inventory? They should be in Tynemouth Barracks with all the other confiscated armaments, surely?'

'Best not to know, pet.'

'But they were firing blanks?'

'Aye, the first round was blanks just to let them know we're armed. But they'll be reloading them now with grape-shot in case they don't heed our warning.'

The three of us sat up there all through the sweltering night and heard no more bangs, just hushed voices and barking dogs. None of us could sleep. At two o'clock, when I needed to visit the netty, I slipped across the silent street to where I knew the library key was hidden. Shelley's work was where I'd left it on the new acquisitions shelf, and though I was sad that no-one had borrowed it, I was glad to have it to read in these circumstances.

When I appeared carrying a book, Mrs Robson lit another candle and asked me to read to her. She didn't care what it was, she said. She only wanted to take her mind off what might happen.

'Have you heard of The Masque of Anarchy?'

'No. Poetry is it?'

'Yes, it was written in the wake of Peterloo. It urges non-violent resistance to tyranny.' I bent to the candle and found my place with ease.

Stand ye calm and resolute,
Like a forest close and mute,
With folded arms and looks which are
Weapons of unvanquished war.
And if then the tyrants dare,
Let them ride among you there;
Slash, and stab, and maim and hew;
What they like, that let them do.
With folded arms and steady eyes,
And little fear, and less surprise,

Look upon them as they slay,
Till their rage has died away:
Then they will return with shame,
To the place from which they came,
And the blood thus shed will speak
In hot blushes on their cheek:
Rise, like lions after slumber
In unvanquishable number!
Shake your chains to earth like dew
Which in sleep had fallen on you:
Ye are many—they are few!

Mrs Robson had tears in her eyes when I looked up and Mr Robson was staring at me, his mouth agape. He swallowed. 'Say that again lass, if you would.'

I read it again.

'That's marvellous, that is. That's right.'

Mrs Robson said, 'Have you read that to Gabe?'

'Yes, I have.'

'And what did he say about it?'

'Well,' I smiled. 'He was courting me at the time, so I think he said he liked it.'

'I'm not sure he would now though.'

'What do you mean?'

She shook her head. 'I'm saying nothing.'

When the first cockerel announced the coming dawn, we looked at each other with growing relief. I stood up and stretched to see the pink light creep up the clear sky.

Mrs Robson had just brought us tea when we heard the clatter of approaching boots and the deep rumble of men's voices. I saw Gabe separate from the group and open the front door below my vantage point.

I was just coming down the stairs, so he didn't know I was there. I heard him say, 'What an anti-climax. I was looking forward to getting stuck in.'

I stepped into the parlour and saw a flicker of surprise pass across his face, nothing more.

247

'You surely would not have hurt them?'

He didn't hesitate. 'Soldiers? Why aye! Class traitors, the lot of them.'

I looked him in the eye and saw that he meant it.

Chapter 29

Early in the summer of 1841, walking down Snipe's Dean on a breezy afternoon, I heard shrieks of high-pitched laughter over to my right, coming from the direction of the Column to Liberty. My first thought was children trespassing, and I decided to turn away and pretend I'd never heard them. There had been more and more instances of people coming into the estate without permission, and Mr Hutt was becoming increasingly agitated about it, but it sounded as though these were just children having fun, so I would leave them to it. I was just about to climb onto the Avenue when I saw two figures running round the base of the column, a full-grown man and woman. They came round again, the woman ahead this time, her full skirts held up so that her white-stockinged legs could be seen. It was the Dowager Lady Strathmore, and in hot pursuit came the Right Honourable William Hutt with his spindly legs and arms, his frock coat flying out behind him like a great black spider.

I laughed out loud then hastily ducked behind a tree in case they saw me. What a thing to witness! It must be as a consequence of the news that John's horse Mundig had won the Derby. It gave me no surprise to see the high-spirited Poll in such exuberant celebrations, but Mr Hutt rarely let his guard down in my presence, despite my having worked for him for ten years. He would be mortified if he saw me watching, so I doubled back and climbed up onto the Avenue out of view. As I walked towards the Chapel enjoying the soft breeze, I reflected how much happier he had been of late: after ten years representing Kingston-upon-Hull, where I knew he had felt no affinity at all, he had just been elected MP for Gateshead. His long-held interest in the colonies had settled upon New Zealand and he was to chair an important commission: his star was on the rise.

The greater his involvement in politics, the more often he was away from Gibside, which suited me, although I knew Poll missed him. She and I spent a good deal of time together, walking, reading, socializing, visiting the theatres and galleries of Newcastle. She often said, 'You are my dear companion, Molly, and I would not be without

249

you.' Occasionally I would accompany her down to London to visit her husband while parliament was in session. I continued to have a role in supporting Mr Hutt's constituency work, and I administered all the correspondence that came to Gibside, of which there was a great deal.

The most frequent letter-writer was always John, who by then had taken a house in Paris, a matter of great regret to his mother. She and I spoke often about the reasons for his preference for life in France: she was of the opinion that there he was free of the stigma of illegitimacy and she fretted that she had failed him somehow. I found it easier to believe that he simply liked the cosmopolitan life on the continent: he certainly spent a good deal of his time in galleries and theatres and I privately imagined the showgirls were a major factor in the appeal of his chosen lifestyle.

Most of his letters pertained to the administration of the estate, and although he always asked after his mother's health, she did pine for more details about his personal life. There was no doubting his commitment to Gibside, for the correspondence between him and Mr Hutt was frequent and detailed. There were plans afoot for a new coach road, and various estimates for alterations to the Orangery, although it continued to prove too expensive. A pet project of Mr Hutt's was to plant trees, preferably turkey oaks, along both sides of the Avenue. John repeatedly questioned the need for this and protested at the obstruction it would cause to the views, which I knew was precisely why Hutt wanted them.

An additional reason for Poll's high spirits was that John was on his way to Streatlam to prepare to stand in an election. He was bringing his friend William, who was apparently a gifted writer and would be producing his election pamphlets. Poll and I were to travel down that weekend and we were both excited about it.

When we assembled for pre-dinner drinks, John introduced me to his friend, a tall, jovial-looking fellow with a prematurely receding hairline. The two young men had known each other since university, and clearly shared a sense of humour.

'Molly, this is William Makepeace Thackeray.'

'Pleased to meet you, Mr Thackeray.'

'Entirely my pleasure, Miss Bowes. This is surely not the Miss Bowes who visited you at Cambridge, John? I wasn't introduced, but in my mind she was a much older lady, and far less...striking.'

'No, no, that was my aunt, Mary Bowes, my father's sister. Molly's relationship to me is far more complicated. Thereby hangs a tale.'

'A tale! You know how I love a tale Bowes! Out with it!'

The Dowager Countess looked aghast. 'John! Have a care!' She sat down and motioned me to sit beside her. 'Think of Molly, and I hardly think that is a fit story for the dinner table!'

I reassured her: 'Please don't concern yourself, Poll. I am forty years old: the child that I was seems to me like a different person. And besides, I have never heard the story in its entirety.'

John settled himself into a wing-back chair and took a swig of wine. 'Then we must begin at the beginning. Pin back your ears, Thackers. My grandmother was Mary Eleanor Bowes of Gibside. After my grandfather's untimely death, she was tricked into marriage by an unprincipled adventurer who subsequently ill-treated her to a scandalous degree. The case was a *cause celebre* during the reign of the last king.'

'Tricked? How so?'

'The cad was a soldier, an Irishman and a charmer. My grandmother was a young widow, extremely wealthy and well-known. He had polished off one minor Newcastle heiress, Hannah Newton of Burnopfield, who died in the same month as the Earl. Stoney set off to London in pursuit of a far richer prize.'

'Stoney? As in stony broke?'

'The very same. And for good reason.'

'And how did he achieve his prize?'

'Mary Eleanor was subjected to scandalous rumours in the gutter press. Stoney presented himself as her defender and called out the editor of the paper to a duel.'

'And they fought?'

'They pretended to have fought. Mary Eleanor was brought to his supposed deathbed and assured by the three doctors in attendance, one of them the King's own medic, Dr Caesar Hawkins, that Stoney's wounds were mortal.'

'And I take it they were not?'

'Far from it. The bounder extracted from her his dying wish, that she should marry him, he being about to die in defence of her honour.'

'My word! And she agreed?'

'Yes. She was a gentle-hearted creature brought up to believe the best in everybody. Two days later, he was borne into church on a stretcher, seemingly barely conscious and about to expire. The ceremony performed, Mary Eleanor returned to her home and thought it would be the last she would see of the swine. Pardon me, Molly. I forget.'

Thackeray looked from John to me and back again. 'Forget what?'

'I shall come to that.'

'Go on, pray. I shall not interrupt again.'

'A couple of days later, he's carried into the house accompanied by his uncles, two army majors, and the three of them proceed to take charge of her estates, dismiss her staff and abuse her person. As of course was his right, the husband being lord of all.'

'But she must have had friends? Family?'

'The Strathmores had already distanced themselves: they did not approve of her wilful independence. Quite soon they applied to the Court of Chancery and had the five children made wards of the Court of Chancery.'

'My word! Do go on, I pray you!'

'It seems the abuse escalated once he learned she was pregnant.'

'By another?'

'Yes, she had been planning to marry the father, a George Grey. She had seen lawyers and had a pre-nuptial agreement drawn up to protect her children's inheritance from any future husband. These two facts, once revealed to Stoney, escalated his violence rapidly. Molly, I am conscious that you may not wish to hear any more of this. Indeed, I perhaps should have saved the tale for another time.' He glanced at his mother, whose face was set. 'Yes, I should. I see that now. My apologies.'

'I don't understand. What has this to do with Molly?'

I let him off the hook: 'Tell him, John. It seems to me a tale of someone entirely distant from me. I would like to hear the clear unvarnished truth.'

'If you are sure, my dear Molly. Eleanor endured such treatment that after four years of marriage, she was a mere shadow of herself, rarely seen but by all accounts starved, beaten, dressed in rags. It doesn't bear thinking about.'

'The poor woman! But he did not kill her, surely?'

'No, for if she had died, the Strathmores would have ensured he was penniless once more. He craved money, more money for his gambling and his whores...'

'John, please!'

'... Mother, Molly wished to hear the full tale.'

'Nevertheless, there is no need for such language.'

I spoke up: 'I have to agree, John. The women you call whores deserve our pity. Indeed some of them were not whores at all. I am friends with one such: Dorothy Stephenson was a respectable farmer's daughter from the Gibside estate. Your Aunt Mary was a child being cared for by Dorothy when Stoney entered the nursery one night and raped her.'

'Molly!' She got up, her face flushed and her eyes watering. "I'm sorry, I can bear to hear no more of this. It is an entirely unsuitable topic for this company and should have been saved until after we retired. Come, Molly. Let us go and walk about the garden.'

I stayed where I was. 'Forgive me, Poll. This is important to me, for it goes to the heart of what I am and where I come from. I need no protection from the truth. I am sorry, but do please leave if it distresses you.'

She hesitated and then sat down. 'I'm sorry, you are quite right. We are all of us familiar with these words, I should not pretend otherwise. I have never said the 'w' word aloud. It distresses me greatly, for it has been directed at me in my time.'

Now it was John's turn to be scandalized and he half-rose from his chair. 'You, mother? Surely not? To your face?'

'Not as such, no, but whispered. Often it was whispered as I passed. Never in the company of your father, I might add. And I never told him.'

'You should have! Whoever addressed such a word to you should have paid the price!'

'One of them did.'

'Who? Your face tells me I should know. Ah, Dobson, of course! The fellow was a liar and a wastrel. His manner towards me from a child left a lot to be desired, but as I grew it became more obnoxious. He deserved to be dismissed. Indeed, it is a wonder he lasted as long as he did.'

Thackeray was clearly anxious to get back to the tale. 'Do go on, John. I am all agog. What happened to the poor woman in the end? Did the Strathmores come to her aid?'

'No. They took her children into their care and left her to her fate.'

'I can barely credit it. And the child she was carrying?'

'My aunt Mary Bowes.'

'And had she any other children to this bounder?'

'One. A boy. He grew to a man but died in the navy.'

'And so how did this sorry tale come to an end?'

'Things took an even darker turn. The swine turned his attentions to Mary Eleanor's daughter Anna Maria, then aged fourteen and as silly as any fourteen year-old is allowed to be. He hatched a plan to abduct the girl and take her to France.'

'But she was a ward of court?'

'Indeed. He blamed Eleanor, who was taken along of course, against her wishes, but crucially accompanied by her new maid, Mary Morgan. Morgan saved the day. The child was returned unharmed - as far as anyone could ascertain – and Morgan recruited others to enable Eleanor to be smuggled away into hiding. Whence she began divorce proceedings.'

'Phew! What a tale!'

'Aha, but that was not the end. It took years for her to extricate herself and in the midst of it all, he had her abducted from the street in broad daylight, carried north to this very castle and there began a chase all over the north Pennines. My poor grandmother was bound and gagged, carried on horseback about the hills. It is thought Stoney was attempting to carry her to Ireland, there to have her committed to an asylum.'

'But she was saved?'

254

'She was. There was a great deal of sympathy and loyalty to the Bowes family in the north country. The people of Gibside had suffered greatly, raised rents, evictions, beatings, rapes. They rallied to her aid. Miners encircled this very house and lit fires though the night to try to stop him escaping with his captive before the constables arrived from London.'

'And did they succeed?'

'Sadly not, and so began the chase. He was eventually knocked from his horse.'

'By a constable?'

'No, by an estate worker named Gabriel Thornton.'

I could not have been more surprised if he had said Queen Victoria.

'Gabriel Thornton?'

'Yes, I believe that's the chap's name.'

Gabe's father. It must be.

Thackeray sat back in his chair, his face rapt. 'Well Bowes, I truly believe you have gifted me with this tale.' He stood up. 'Excuse me ladies, I must relieve myself. Not only of this fine claret, but also of the idea that is buzzing in my brain.'

After dinner, when the others were sitting out on the verandah in the summer evening, I retired early, pleading a headache.

I lay down on my bed fully-clothed and my mind drifted, cut loose from its moorings by the evening's conversation and the wine. I had not seen Gabe since the siege of Winlaton, and nor had I wanted to. Whenever I visited Belle, who was by then nursing her mother, I made it clear I did not want to hear about him. I had never troubled myself to ask about Dorothy's husband, and now I felt ashamed. The mention of the role Gabe's father had played in the rescue of Mary Eleanor had made me thoughtful and melancholy and now I could not close the door in my head and lock his troubled face away.

In the morning, I ate my breakfast before the others had surfaced and then I went for a walk. I was standing under the shade of a standard oak tree when I heard a voice.

'Molly, excuse me. Am I disturbing you?'

'No, no, I'm just enjoying the view.'

'John has asked me to talk to you in private. Do you mind?'

'No, not at all. In what regard?'

255

'At dinner last night, the story of Stoney Bowes ... I am much affected by it. Indeed, I was awake half the night.'

I cast him a teasing glance. 'You must be very tender-hearted to be so distressed by the suffering of a woman who has been dead for nigh on forty years.'

Taken aback, he blustered, 'Oh, yes, indeed I am! Most affecting.'

'And you wish to hear the post-script?'

'No indeed, Bowes has furnished me with the ending. He has explained your relationship to the family. I wanted...'

'To offer me condolences for having such a man as my father?'

'Why, yes, of course. But also to...'

'Commiserate with me for having been brought up in prison? For the suffering of my own poor mother and all my siblings?'

'Yes, yes, I do. I do indeed.'

'And yet, I sense there is something else, Mr Thackeray? Perhaps you wish to discuss your ideas on how such a thing can be prevented from happening to other women? Some revision of the law, perhaps?'

'Well, yes.' Somewhat deflated, I watched him gather himself. 'No, in fact I must be honest with you, Miss Bowes. My motives in approaching you are rather more selfish.'

I fluttered my hand in front of my neck in the nearest approximation of flirtation I could muster. 'Why, Mr Thackeray! I am flattered! And you so much younger than I! And yet, as we have seen in the case of Mr Hutt and the Dowager, such a match can bring great happiness to both parties...'

'No! No indeed! You mistake my purpose, Molly!'

I affected to faint against the tree-trunk, my hand over my mouth to hide the smile. I had no such success.

'Ah! I see from your eyes that you are teasing me. Yes, very good. I will admit you had me there for a moment.'

'But alas, not for a lifetime. Alas and alack, it was not to be...'

'Molly, please be serious. I wish to obtain your permission for an endeavour that I have decided to undertake. In the dark watches of the night...' He began to pace about, and I watched him, highly amused for of course I had recognized the light of inspiration in him at the dinner table. 'I am possessed with an idea to which there is every chance you might object. John has no objection and he assures me that his Aunt Mary will be entertained by the idea.'

'I doubt that.'

'You do? But you cannot know what the idea is!'

'You propose to tell the tale of Stoney Bowes and dress it up as fiction.'

'I do. I do. But I can assure you it will be unrecognizable. It will bring no shame on the family. I propose to have my hero...'

'Anti-hero, surely?'

'Yes, yes of course, anti-hero. I shall call him Barry, I think, Barry Lyndon. He shall come from Ireland and he shall marry an heiress, but there the similarity ends. My Barry will be a charmer.'

'Like Stoney.'

'Well, yes, but far less wicked. Far, far less. He will be a gambler and a womanizer.'

'Like Stoney.'

'Well, yes, but there the similarity will end. He shall not come direct to England. I propose to give him adventures in Europe - Germany in particular. For you know, Bowes and I, we are Europeans and fascinated by the continent. He shall move freely about, for it will be during the Napoleonic Wars, you know. He shall live on his wits and work his way up through the ranks, which is far easier to do in Europe. This little island where everyone knows everyone's business - pah! Antecedents, which school you attended... it's all so...'

'Claustrophobic?'

'Yes! Exactly. No, Barry will be a self-made man, shedding his previous selves like a chrysalis. He shall arrive on these shores having learned to emulate a fully-fledged aristocrat. Then he shall snare himself a titled lady.'

'A widow?' I cast him a dark look.

'Not yet perhaps, a young and beautiful woman married to an ailing aristocrat.'

He came back under the shade of the tree and spoke gently, earnestly, the light glinting on his wire-framed glasses: 'Should you mind such a tale, do you think?'

I made him wait a few moments, my face serious, but then I smiled. 'No, Mr Thackeray. I should not.'

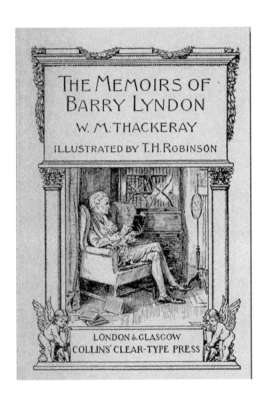

Chapter 30

'Belle, I have something delicate to ask you. It's about your father.'

'My father? Ah, I see you mean the man who caused us both to be here. I never think of him. He does not deserve to be remembered. I don't want to talk about him and I care nothing for his memory. I'm sorry, I know it's different for you having grown up with him, but to us he has been dead for almost fifty years. Since my birth, in fact.'

I was silent, chastened.

'I would much rather talk about my real father. Would you like to hear about him?'

'Yes, I should like that very much.'

'He was tall, like Gabe, and handsome, like Gabe. With dark curly hair, like Gabe, and it went silvery grey, exactly as Gabe's is doing now. He was strong and kind and steadfast and funny. He could do a trick with his thumbs. He could burp to order. He could lift that heavy oak chair with his little finger. You try! I cannot lift it with two hands! He was mild. He liked fishing. He taught us all the names of birds. He was always kind to me, though I was not his own, and when Gabe was born...'

'And he was the Gabriel Thornton who saved Mary Eleanor?'

'Yes, he was. It was a matter of quiet pride to him. He told me once that when they were young, they met by the river one morning, by accident, of course. She was sixteen and engaged to be married. He promised her that if ever she were to be in need of him, he would come to her. And he did.'

'You were blessed to have such a father. I wish I had known him.'

She slid her eyes sideways at me. 'Well, in a way you do. Gabe is very like him.'

I straightened, looked away.

'Molly?'

I didn't respond.

'He asks after you often.'

'That is kind. And he…he is well?'

'Very well, thank-you. Shall I tell him you asked?'
'No, I'd rather you didn't. Best left.'
'He is quite different now, you know. Much calmer. The brick factory is doing well. They are expanding, making a fortune, Gabe says. Joe Cowen is going to buy Stella Hall and it seems he will enter politics. To think…'
'And where is he living?'
'Gabe? He has taken a room with the family who live in the farmhouse by Path Head Water Mill. Shall we go for a walk tomorrow and see him?'
'No. Maybe another time.'
'Molly, what are you afraid of?'
'Nothing. I am afraid of nothing, Belle.'

But in truth I was. I was happy alone, in control of my life. But increasingly I felt living at Gibside to be far removed from reality. To be surrounded by such natural beauties was wonderful, a privilege, but it sometimes felt like being in a bubble. Real life went on outside, beyond the belt of trees and the rushing waters of the Derwent.

Boundaries preoccupied Hutt and Bowes very much indeed. There were always poachers, trespassers, thefts, sometimes vandalism. Notices were put up and rewards offered but the incursions from the outside world continued.

William Hutt had spent his life in the cloistered world of Cambridge and now the cloistered arcadia of Gibside. For ten years I had explained to him what I knew of real life, helped him understand the reality of life for what he still called, in unguarded moments, 'the lower orders.' I understood the issues and yet I could not vote? Winlaton, Blaydon, Whickham – all the surrounding villages were full of intelligent men and women, and yet none of them could vote? They could pay taxes but have no say in who should govern them unless they owned land?

And Gabe. His face before my mind's eye, I felt a softening in my heart. Was I lonely? Did I long to feel his arms around me? Was I a coward? Was I afraid of love? Was it true, as I sometimes thought, that I would not allow myself to love for fear of loss?

I was restless, unsettled. Instead of going back to the Hall, I walked up to the Octagon Pond to watch the swans, which always soothed me. I sat in the shade, my back against the rough bark of a tree and I heeded no discomfort. The reflections shimmered on the water. Pearly white, the swans drifted into view from amongst the reeds. Which was male and which female I could not tell, but whilst one fished in the bulrushes the other drifted about admiring its reflection in the water.

How long I sat there I cannot say. I watched them float and fish and preen, the timeless fascination of their elegant necks. Occasionally, they would meet, and once their beaks brushed against each other. Simple acknowledgement of their partner's continued existence, or an expression of affection, of belonging; or merely some prosaic function of mites and water?

I got up, brushed the grass off my skirts and walked quickly to the walled garden, where I knew Poll would be on a day like this. The scents of the full blooms were heady: some of the roses sent from Paris were truly exquisite. Poll was in raptures, excited to show me the first full flowering of a multi-petalled pink, but as I listened to her rhapsodies, my sense of dissociation grew into irritation.

Miners were on strike out there in the real world. It was a prolonged and bitter strike. People were suffering, families starving, and here was I admiring a flower.

'You haven't yet seen the orchids! William will be so pleased to see them. And John! I cannot wait to show him. Perhaps he will visit this summer.'

When I said nothing, she continued in a sadder tone. 'It seems unlikely, however. He has bought a theatre in Paris. I fear there is a woman at the root of it.'

I tried to master my feelings into a semblance of politeness. I should not take my feelings out on my friend. 'Now Polly, many's the time you have wished John would find someone.'

'Yes, but an actress!'

'You of all people would not judge another, surely?'

261

Chastened, she linked my arm as we walked towards the orchid house. 'No, you're right. If she is a good and faithful young woman with no shadow over her name...'

'And how does a good and faithful young woman acquire a shadow, pray tell?'

Startled by the harshness of my tone, she turned a face towards me.

'I'm sorry, I am out of sorts.'

'It's that book, isn't it? It's since you read Barry Lyndon. You have been quite different. I told you it was a bad idea to read it. It is not a happy tale, and the nearness to you.'

'I must go.'

'No, wait, Molly. Tell me what is wrong.'

'I... feel it hard Poll. I do not belong here. I...I'm sorry, it's hard to explain.'

'You do belong here, Molly, with me.'

'No, I want to be of use. I want to be involved.'

'Involved?'

'In struggle. I am too safe here. I feel I am half asleep, dreaming my life away. This is not the real world. There are injustices ... I want to help.'

'What is it you want to do?'

'I don't know, but I want to be involved. I don't want to live in this...bubble.'

She looked around the walled garden, its air potent with the heady scent of roses. 'It is a very beautiful bubble.'

'Yes, yes it is. I'm sorry Poll, but I find I can no longer be content.'

'I understand. No, I do. You have seen so much more than I. You cannot forget.'

'I cannot. Outside this great girdle of trees is a changed world. The rural idyll of England is no more.'

'I know. I choose not to think about it.'

'But I cannot. I cannot forget the suffering and poverty I saw in Manchester. The great industries are built on great suffering. Great wealth is built on cruel exploitation in this new industrial age.'

'But Molly, there is nothing you can do.'

'But there is, you see. There is.'

'What can you do? Alone?'

'Not alone. There are others, there are movements. You know I was involved with the Chartists. At that time, the status quo was re-established, but Poll, something must change! There are other ways of governing our country. Fairer ways. I read the newspapers. I have often urged you to do the same. Right across Europe, there is unrest. People

are rising up against tyranny and exploitation. Through no fault of their own, good people have terrible lives. It is my belief that education is the key.'

'And you want to help to educate?'

'Working people. Yes, I do. Everyone should be able to read. It should be a basic right in a civilized country. They should be able to read, to learn, to better themselves if they can: to understand and share ideas, to educate themselves, to learn about the world, to enjoy art and literature. To fulfill themselves.'

She stared at me, her face drained of colour. 'Please Molly, don't leave us. William and I rely on you, more than you know. And you do such valuable work here. Surely you can do both. You can live here with us and work nearby to help others who are not so fortunate.'

When I didn't answer, she took my arm and we walked back towards the house. She didn't speak again, but as the door closed behind us, she said, 'I have a gift for you, Molly. Will saw it at a sale in London and bought it for you. I think he finds it difficult to show his appreciation of all that you do for him.' My silence she took as assent. 'I was going to keep it until Christmas but in the circumstances, it seems a good time to give it to you. It is a print. I think you will like it.'

She led me to her sitting room and took it from the drawer in her little desk. It was folded between two sheets of tissue paper. It showed a man dressed as a peasant leaning disconsolately on a milepost and looking out over a stream. Something about his stance - the cap, the coat slung over one shoulder – suggested he was being portrayed as a hero. It resonated and moved me.

'He is contemplating a failed revolution.'

263

'Exactly so. It's called The Old Chartist. It was made by an artist called Frederick Sandys to illustrate a Meredith poem. The man has just returned from transportation.'

'It's lovely, Poll. Thank-you. There's someone I'd like to show it to.'

That Sunday, I set off in high spirits to walk to Path Head Water Mill. Passing through Winlaton, I saw old Mrs Robson hobbling towards me. Her face lit up. 'Molly! We haven't seen you for so long! Have you time for a cup of tea?'

We sat side by side on a pair of kitchen chairs outside her front door, passing the time of day and drinking tea out of tin mugs while we caught up on all our news. People out strolling in their Sunday best nodded or spoke their greetings and I reflected on the pleasures of this close-knit village. When I told Mrs Robson of my restlessness, she exclaimed, 'Heaven must have sent you!'

'Why?'

'Haven't you heard? We're getting a Mechanics' Institute! Young Joseph Cowen, all of nineteen and fresh from university – he's going to make it happen.'

Path Head Watermill nestles in a hollow on a hillside on the other side of Blaydon Burn. I had not seen Gabe for so long, and my heart began to flutter at the thought of his face. As I approached the mill, I saw him sitting by the mill-pond with a woman. Their heads were close together and as I watched, he put an arm around her shoulders and held her close. I turned and went back the way I had come.

Chapter 31

In the summer of 1851, I travelled with William Hutt to London to see the Great Exhibition in Hyde Park. He was intent upon the industrial exhibits, whereas I had arranged to tour the art works escorted by Thackeray. He and I had by then established an enjoyably jocular relationship which had been initially based on my dislike of Barry Lyndon.

Thackeray had been scornful of the art being exhibited in the astonishing 'Crystal Palace' but told me of a private gallery where I could see more work by Frederick Sandys. 'Prepare to be surprised, however.'

'In what way?'

'He somewhat extended his range since he has fallen in with the Pre-Raphaelite Brotherhood.'

'I have heard the expression, but forgive me, I know not what it denotes.'

'Scandal! Rebellion! Anarchy! Pornography!'

I was genuinely horrified for a moment.

'You mean he no longer makes designs for wood-cuts?'

'Haha! I doubt it very much! He lives surrounded by decadence, draped all about by luscious women in a state of undress. I doubt very much that he concerns himself with old chartists any longer.'

'Mr Thackeray, I see you are entertaining yourself at my expense. I ask you in all honesty for your explanation of the term 'Pre-Raphaelite'. I should appreciate an honest answer.'

'Forgive me, Molly. They are a loose collective of young artists and writers who share certain ideals which they consider revolutionary.'

'And you mock and despise their work?'

'Far from it. They have shaken up the art establishment. Their work has considerable merit. Many collectors have purchased paintings of young beauties, although…'

'And do they take as their subjects only young women?'

'No indeed. One of the first paintings to cause a stir is a portrayal of Christ as a boy at home with his family in the carpenter's workshop.'

'And why did it cause a stir?'

'Christ as a human child of working stock? There is insurrection right across Europe. The working classes are getting above themselves. We cannot have them claiming Christ as one of their own!'

'This interests me. If they can merge political thought with beauty and make works of commercial value, it can only be to the good. Sugaring the pill, so to speak. What does Frederick Sandys choose as his subject now that he is a member of this group? Is he successful as a painter?'

'In my humble opinion...'

'Come now, Mr Thackeray, when were you ever humble?'

He leaned in confidentially. 'The man's a draftsman: it's what he was born to do. Since he's been lodging with Rossetti, he's been aping his style, but he lacks the imagination. Commissioned portraits, that's what he should be doing. Painting from the life. Realistic representations of the great and the good, their properties and their possessions.'

'I should like to see his current work, nonetheless. Are there no pre-Raphaelite paintings at the exhibition?'

'No, but I will take you to see some. Rossetti's the man and he owes me money. He and Sandys shared a studio but they've fallen out. It's possible I'll see them tonight at the Arundel.'

'And will they allow us access? For you know you are very disparaging.'

His put his fingers to his lips, a broad smile across his features.

'Hush now. Tell them nothing of what I've said, for I am one of their 'Immortals', you know. It would hurt them terribly.'

'One of their immortals?'

He straightened up and struck a pose. 'Oh yes. I am aligned in their pantheon with the greats. Accorded two stars, I'll have you know. Along with Chaucer, Spenser, and whisper it ... Christ himself.'

'Ah, then I see they are playful and mocking of pretensions to greatness in the living. I look forward to meeting them.'

267

But there were no artists in attendance when we visited Rossetti's studio on Cheyne Walk: although he had been happy to allow Thackeray to show me, he would be on his way to Newcastle to stay at Wallington Hall as guest of Lady Pauline Trevelyan.

The housekeeper let us in and we followed her up a narrow flight of stairs. When she opened the door and let us pass into the light and airy attic studio, I was overwhelmed by what I saw. It seemed that every inch of wall space was crowded with images, a treasure trove of gold, far too much to take in on first sight. There were rails of ornate clothes, brocade and embroidered gowns; and boxes of exotic props covered all the floor space. Everywhere I looked, there were visual riches, luminous flesh tones, glorious hair. Whilst Thackeray stood back, smiling indulgently, I looked at each picture in turn, deciphering their subjects, many of which were evidently figures from Shakespeare and Arthurian legend. I was particularly struck by the unnatural poses and the curious passivity of the women.

Finding the large canvases gorgeous but somewhat gaudy for my taste, I was drawn to the quieter, more subdued studies, which were mostly on smaller canvases, often unframed, which leaned against the wall. There was a small sketch of a woman in tears, which perhaps represented Mary Magdalene. I lifted an intimate study of Danae, clad in a startlingly diaphanous robe with her abundant hair hanging down past her knees. It was a celebration of the female body more revealing than anything I had yet seen in modern art. I kept going back to the small pastel of Mary Magdalene.

Thackeray was rummaging through larger boards propped under the windows. 'Aha! See? This is what's brought it all to a head. See here, the model biting her hair? Rossetti's idea. Powerful isn't it. Rather suggestive.'

'I think that's in the eye of the beholder, Mr Thackeray. When I was a child, I used to bite my hair. It was a habit my mother tried hard to get me to stop. To me it denotes boredom, frustration, a feeling of being trapped.

'Seriously? I'm afraid I have to disagree. A beautiful young woman looking coquettishly over her shoulder at the viewer, her teeth clamped down on her own luscious tresses? If that isn't an invitation to carnal thoughts, I don't know what is.'

'The artist might have posed her like that. You cannot interpret the girl's mood from such a pose. And certainly not decide it's an invitation. If anyone had misread my girlish habit in such a way, I should have been mortified.'

'Still, these girls offer themselves to the male gaze.'

'Has it crossed your mind that their reasons for that may be entirely innocent?'

'Come come, no decent young woman would undress in such a way.'

'They may be artists themselves, or lacking education, they may be involving themselves in the world of art in the only way available to them. Women appreciate their own aesthetic value, and sometimes it is their only currency. You certainly should not make assumptions about their morality, Mr Thackeray. A young woman's reputation is a valuable thing, and once it is lost, she too may be lost.'

He looked as though I had slapped him, so accustomed was he to my benign playfulness. 'I mean it. I think you have little understanding of what it is to be a woman. I have never told you this, but your Lady Lyndon is a characterless cipher. She never comes alive on the page. You treat her like a chess-piece and put all your thoughts into the loathsome Barry. I ask you to reconsider your assumptions about the young women who model for artists. If you cannot bring yourself to do so, I will bid you good day.'

'No! Wait. I'm sorry. You are quite correct. I should not make assumptions. It is too easy.'

'And dangerous.'

'And dangerous to the young ladies.'

'And insidious. And easy. And reprehensible. For all their superficial beauty, I cannot like these paintings. The women in them are not themselves. They are a decorative object, artfully arranged. Like your portrayal of Lady Lyndon: she has no existence. These representations of women transmit no emotion to me. Only this one.' I lifted the small study of Mary Magdalene. 'See? She has expression. She transmits emotion. I believe in those tears. She possesses a complexity which engages the viewer. Mr Rossetti

269

clearly has a sensitivity that does not come across in these larger paintings.'

'That is not Rossetti's style. I would guess that is by Fred Sandys and has been overlooked. I see what you mean. It is very lovely. Better than I imagined Sandys capable of. I think he is best in miniature.'

'I am very taken with this. Do you think he would sell it?'

'I would imagine so. It is a study, merely. Unfinished, as you see here. I have seen the finished product, though it did not strike my eye at the time.'

'Being surrounded by gaudy beauties in diaphanous robes?'

'Exactly as you say. I blush to admit it. I will tell you a secret. Many of the patrons who buy those pictures keep it secret.'

He put the painting back where he had found it and opening the door, motioned me to walk before him. 'I will be lunching at the Arundel and Sandys may well be there. I shall make discreet enquiries as to price and so forth. Would you want it framed here in London?'

'No, I prefer it as it is. If I later decide to have it framed, I would do so in Newcastle.'

'Where will you go now?'

'I shall walk about the park and back to the Crystal Palace. I hear Charlotte Bronte is visiting today. I should so like to meet her. She knows how to represent women in all their complexity. Men too. It is a skill that cannot be taught, I think. A skill acquired through study of human nature. It requires imagination. An ability to enter the life of someone entirely alien.'

He looked affectionately bemused, an expression which I felt to be patronizing in the extreme.

'Your expression provokes me so I will go further. I have told you I found Lady Lyndon a mere puppet, and yet the woman on whom we both know she is based was a strong and fascinating multi-faceted woman worthy of respect. You should have talked to John's Aunt Mary, who of course is her daughter. Your Barry is wicked and loathsome, you said so yourself. Emily Bronte created a wicked hero in Heathcliff. Her portrayal far surpasses yours in its complexity, emotional range and ability to engage.'

He bowed, his face aflame. 'I accept your criticism unreservedly.'

Not having expected such a reaction, I deflated. Something about these paintings had disrupted my peace of mind.

'I'll allow you redeemed yourself entirely with Vanity Fair.'

'We live and we learn.' He bowed again deeply, his eyes full of his accustomed merriment. 'You are a remarkable woman, Molly Bowes.'

Walking alone in the park, I could not settle my thoughts. I found a bench and sat down to contemplate the still waters. Ducks came towards me, seething and clacking in their eagerness for bread. In the distance, a swan was serenely gliding, oblivious to the clamour. I watched the swan determinedly and felt the agitation in my chest calming.

I wanted to examine my thoughts, but they were churned up like mud on the bottom of a pond. Generalised feelings about the imbalance of power between the genders. All those girls and the easy assumptions about them made by even civilized intelligent men, simply based on their generosity. The appreciation of female beauty, so innocent in women who take simple pleasure in their bodies, faces, hair and clothes: without other artistic outlet, they became their own creations. The timeless beauty of the female form, the classical poses and adoration, but so often portrayed as passive or provocative. Emma Hamilton, who found genuine love and then when he died, was condemned to throw herself back on the mercies of the men who held the power, the purse strings.

As the mud settled and my breathing slowed, a face revealed itself, pale and lost, a drowned girl with luminous eyes and a determined chin. Biting her orange hair.

I found the Arundel Club without any trouble. I watched from across the street as gentlemen came and went, on foot and in carriages. Any one of them might be George Sandys – I had no idea what he looked like. Besides, if I left a message for Thackeray at reception as had been my original intention, I would need to explain my mood of repressed excitement. It was a fool's errand. There was no likelihood that the model was Charlotte. I dismissed the thought and walked away, forcing myself into my habitual mood of placidity.

I was a good enough actress to find out about the model without giving anything away. We had only one more day in London. I would be patient. If Thackeray succeeded in finding Mr Sandys and ascertaining a price for the Magdalene, I would do my best to ensure that I met him when the exchange took place.

But I found I could not settle, so hastily turning round I made my way back to the Arundel Club and wrote a brief note to Thackeray. I told him I would be in a coffee shop just along the street.

When he came in an hour later, he was accompanied by a tall, distinguished-looking young man of erect bearing.

'Mr Frederick Sandys, Miss Molly Bowes. Introductions made, forgive me for my swift departure: I have a report to write.'

'Mr Sandys, I am a great admirer of your work, the woodcuts in particular. I was presented with a print of The Old Chartist and would perhaps like another to give to…an old chartist.'

'Indeed? I am flattered, Miss Bowes. Thackeray tells me you are interested in buying an early draft of the Magdalene that I inadvertently left at Cheyne Walk.'

'Yes, although I haven't the faintest idea how much you would want for it.'

'You need not trouble yourself. Mr Thackeray has paid me. It is a gift for you. If you are free now, we can walk along and get it. While Rossetti is away I can make sure I haven't left any other works there.'

'You have secured a place in alternative lodgings?'

'Yes, for now, it's not far from the Arundel. In fact, shall we go there now so that you can see more of my work? I can slip into Rossetti's studio this evening.'

His lodgings were in a cramped basement crowded with canvasses. He looked around disconsolately. 'I cannot paint here. This is just temporary. If something doesn't turn up in the next few days, I think I shall return to Norfolk. I am somewhat torn.'

'In which direction would you like to take your art?'

'Thackeray and I were just talking about that. He is of the opinion that I should concentrate on portraits.'

'Yes, he said as much to me. Do you have commissions?'

272

'Yes, more and more actually: my fame is evidently spreading by world of mouth.'

'And yet you have enjoyed your time amongst the Brotherhood?'

'It has been great fun and I am sad that there is currently a rupture between myself and Rossetti. I have learnt a good deal about the use of colour and it is a stimulating environment in which to learn. You have seen only my woodcut and the Magdalene?'

'Yes.'

'Then I shall look forward to showing you more of my work.'

'Who is this dark beauty?'

'Keomi, a Norfolk gypsy. She and I are... close.' He looked at me, his head on one side. 'Would it shock you if I confide that she and I are lovers?'

'Not in the least. And this?'

'A former love.'

'And this?'

'An actress who sat for me for a time when I was in Norfolk. Miss Clive is her stage name.'

'You have captured her well, I think. She transmits emotion believably and you show an affinity in your portrayal.' I watched him carefully for a response. There was no mistaking the expression in his eyes. He did not reply.

'Her acting ability combined with her physical beauty must make her a popular model?'

'Yes.'

'Her hair is particularly spectacular. Though I imagine you heightened the colour to complement the tones of the brocade?'

'No. That is the actual colour of her hair. Like a cascade of gold coins.'

'She has quite a determined chin. Did you exaggerate that?'

'No, I paint what I see. I remember she was quite struck by the verisimilitude of her portrait.'

'You will paint her again, I imagine?'

'I hope so, yes.'

He was certainly beset by some memory or emotion but offered no elaboration. His face was sorrowful, and so I said, 'I suspect you were quite smitten by Miss Clive, Mr Sandys. Perhaps you will see

273

her again when you return to Norfolk.' I turned away from the painting, attempting to seem casual.

'No, she was with a group of travelling players. She was extraordinary. I should like to have executed more studies of her.'

'What did you manage to produce in the time available?'

'She sat for Danae in the Brazen Chamber, then Cassandra. Both sold immediately. And some studies for a greater work. They're here somewhere. I like to make the studies in coloured chalk. 'Fancy heads', I call them.'

'It was a study that caused the rupture with Rossetti, I believe?'

'Yes, he had complained before that my work was derivative, but when I produced this…'

I heard no more of what he said. Instead, I experienced a rushing sound in my ears and my heart dropped within me.

When I gathered my wits, I said, 'This is very striking, Mr Sandys. What do you call it?'

'Love's Shadow. Its official name is Love's Shadow. But in my heart I call it Proud Maisie.'

'Maisie? It is her name then? The model's name.'

'Her name is Mary Emma but she likes to be called Maisie.'

'I imagine she goes by several names, being an actress?' I held the study up to the light. 'I am interested in how you achieve such expression, how you pose your models. What did you say, for instance, to provoke such an expression in … Maisie, did you say?'

He barked an ironic laugh. 'Miss Clive chooses her own poses. She is a natural actress and remarkably expressive. The moods flicker across her face like quicksilver. I saw her biting her hair when reading a book. She was posing for Cassandra at the time, and I was attending to her feet. When I straightened up and saw her abstractedly chewing her tresses, I was taken.'

'The muse struck?'

'Indeed. Exactly so.'

'And Miss Clive, where is she now?'

'I know not. Touring with the company of players. Bath or Bristol perhaps.'

'And if she wanted to sit for you again, how would she find you?'

He looked embarrassed. 'My mother's house in Norfolk: Mother is under instructions to forward any mail.'

'She made you no promises, this Maisie?'

'No, although I must confess my feelings threatened to overwhelm me. I think she rather enjoyed her power. Her enjoyment of the itinerant life was waning, she said. London was where she wanted to be. For the theatre, you understand.'

'I understand. Mr Sandys, I am remarkably smitten by this sketch. Is it for sale?'

'No. I am too fond of it myself. It seems to me to capture her more than any other.'

'If you change your mind, or if Miss Clive should reappear to sit for you again, could I trouble you to write to me?'

'Why, of course. I must confess, she above all the models I have come across has lingered in my mind.'

'And your heart?'

'You divine correctly. Yes, in my heart.'

I wanted to know more and stopped myself from asking questions about her background. And I must remember, I could not know for certain. Only hope was such an unaccustomed feeling that I could not let it go. I had done enough. This was a man who kept his word, or so I believed.

In the foyer of the hotel, Mr Hutt was sitting at a table with papers and brochures spread out before him. As I took off my cloak and prepared to sit down opposite him, he looked up, his pale funeral-director's face lit with a new energy. 'Molly! And how have you enjoyed your day?' Without waiting for an answer, he prattled on, as was his wont. 'I have seen such marvels amongst the industrial exhibits! Your Mr Cowen is quite the star of the show with his gas retorts!' He looked back at his collection of brochures. 'I will write to John before we catch the train. He is disappointed to have missed this exhibition but he is much preoccupied with the theatre at the moment. I must convey to him what I have seen today: the advances in glass and iron technology that built the Crystal Palace make it possible at last to convert the Orangery into a conservatory and far more economically than Mr Dobson's estimate.'

I was not required to comment: as always, he was entirely heedless of my evident distraction.

'If, as he has indicated, he intends to marry Mademoiselle Josephine Coffin de Chevalier, perhaps he will consider the transformation of the Orangery as a gift to her.'

'I'm sorry, Mr Hutt, I am feeling a little tired. I may go to my room and have a lie down.'

'No no, come come, we will call for tea and cakes. Let's replenish our energy levels before we begin our correspondences.'

He rang the bell and thankfully sat silently scribbling notes in his incomprehensible hand, leaving me to my thoughts.

When the tea came, he ignored the waitress, as was also his wont, and she and I set out the tea things. I popped a tiny cupcake into my mouth and winked at her. She smiled and rolled her eyes at the oblivious Hutt.

By the time he looked up from his notes, I had drunk my tea, eaten another cake and was feeling much brighter.

'So, you were saying about the conservatory. You think Mr Bowes will embrace the idea? Does Josephine share his interest in horticulture?'

'I doubt that. They share a good deal of enthusiasm for art but I haven't heard him mention Josephine being interested in plants. But his mother would so love a conservatory! As would I, of course, to grow my auriculas.'

'May I ask you something, Mr Hutt?'

'Why of course, Molly.'

'It concerns Gibside.'

He put down his pen and took a sip of his cold tea. 'Proceed.'

'I understand that you and the Dowager Countess take care of Gibside in the absence of Mr Bowes, and it seems that this arrangement may continue indefinitely...'

Looking faintly alarmed and shuffling in his seat, Hutt spoke gruffly. He hated to be reminded of his real position as grace-and-favour tenant. 'Well, one would hope so. The arrangement works to our mutual satisfaction.'

'When Mr Bowes marries Miss Coffin de Chevalier, is there any likelihood of them coming to live in England?'

'Yes, I believe there is. The situation in France is combustible. And Mr Bowes so loves Gibside. And Streatlam of course, but I think his love for Gibside is less complicated.'

'And does that concern you? If they are to marry and decide to settle in England, that he might prefer to live at Gibside?'

He stood up, which he always did when he was about to dismiss me. 'I think there is very little likelihood of that, Molly. For you know, as I said, the arrangement works very well indeed. Personally, there is nothing I should like more than to have my friend and stepson here on English soil, where he belongs.

'Next year will be momentous, I think. Miss Coffin de Chevalier will be introduced to Lady Strathmore and myself: I imagine the marriage will be arranged for the summer and Mr Bowes seems likely to be elected Sheriff of Durham. I consider it a distinct possibility that we shall very soon have our family settled at Streatlam Castle. And who knows how it may grow?' And he winked a curious wink in which his eyelid descended from the socket as though it were made of porcelain.

Chapter 32

When we arrived back at Gibside, Poll handed me a letter: I saw it was from Mary Bowes. 'She has written to both of us, Molly. With her usual good humour, she is telling us that it seems she expects shortly to depart this world. I'm sorry to have to break this to you: I shall miss her and I know you will too.'

I went to straight to Mr Hutt and asked him to excuse me so that I could go to Bath.

'Really, Molly? I know my wife will be disappointed if you are absent throughout the Christmas festivities.'

It did briefly make me falter in my resolve: Poll had confided the sense of melancholy that swept over her at Christmas, but if the wedding did indeed go ahead, there was every possibility that this would be the last time she would not be with her son. 'She will understand. She knows how close I am to John's Aunt Mary.'

I left for Bath the following day.

She was in bed when I arrived and her maid asked me to wait in the morning room as the doctor was with her. It was a lovely light airy room with large windows looking out onto an elegant crescent. One wall was lined with books, and in an alcove was a beautiful ornate cabinet which I assumed must be the one belonging to Mary Eleanor.

I heard voices in the hall, the front door opened and closed and then the maid showed me up to Mary's bedroom.

She was sitting up in bed, tiny and sparrow-like, her eyes button-bright. It was a shock to see how much weight she had lost since I had last seen her but her voice was strong: 'What a wonderful surprise! If only I had known you were coming – I would have had two days of excitement.'

I sat down on the bed and kissed her downy cheek. 'I am so happy to see you, Mary. Your letter gave me to expect you were at death's door, though typically you made light of it.'

'Alas, I fear I've had more than my entitlement. I'm seventy-eight, you know. You see? I have turned into one of those old people who insist on telling their age: time to go.'

'Yes, but often people of that sort go on to complain about how much better life was in their day, whereas you, my lovely friend, take nothing but delight in every new invention.'

'We live in a time of constant delight if we are blessed with a roof over our heads and people who are kind to us. We two share an appreciation of this, having experienced prison!' She looked at me with real tenderness. 'And so, dearest Molly, what is your news? Still contented working for that dry old stick?'

Her refreshingly direct dislike of William Hutt always made me laugh. 'Oh, he's not so bad. His wife loves him. I may be deluding myself, but I feel that I have a moderating influence on some of his views.'

'You are still involved with your Chartists then?'

'Things are evolving in the working class movement. We have a new messiah in the North East. He is young yet but he is speaking in the temples. His name is Joseph Cowen.'

'He shares the Lord's initials! You must tell me more about this young man, but another time. I want family gossip. So tell me how you're getting on with Hutt.'

'He sees me as a safe conduit to the working classes.'

'He's still neurotically guarding his borders, I'll wager?'

'Yes, perimeters preoccupy him a good deal: I think he feels a great sense of responsibility to protect Gibside from outside incursions. Dear John seeks to reassure him in his letters, as does Dent. The three of them are very sweet, sharing their horticultural tips. Mr Hutt's orchids are a great sense of pride to him, and his every pineapple is greeted like a gift from the gods. To give him his due, under his tenure the estate is blossoming again. We have swans and exotic birds, an astonishing rose garden and even a canoe on the Octagon Pond. And have you heard about the plans for the Orangery?'

'No, do tell!'

'The slate roof is to be removed and a glass one put in its place! Is that not a marvel?'

'Astonishing! My mother would have loved to see that!' Her face clouded. 'Molly, make sure when I am gone that her little botanical cabinet goes to Streatlam. John has always loved that

279

cabinet and I am concerned that it will be forgotten: he has so much on his mind, poor dear.'

'Yes, he does so well in administering everything from so far away. We all have high hopes that he will marry Miss Coffin de Chevalier and come home to live in England. The theatre has become a burden to him I believe?'

'Yes, he has decided to close it.'

'All to the good. It's exciting, isn't it? There may yet be children to carry on the Bowes name. He seems to be quite besotted with his Josephine.'

'Indeed. I would have loved to have met her but it is not to be.' She sighed and lay her head back on the pillows, murmuring, 'Unjust as it is, it was not entirely fitting that his wife should still be acting. She must be a wilful young woman to have continued for so long in the face of gossip and poor reviews.'

I smiled. 'It is my impression that wilful women are predominant in the Bowes family.'

'Ha, you are right. My great-grandmother, Elizabeth Bowes was quite formidable, by all accounts. And of course Mary Eleanor's wilfulness was probably what saved her in the end.'

'And think of Anna with her daring elopement on a ladder!'

'And then of course we two are hardly shrinking violets.' She reached for my hand and suddenly her eyes were full of tears. I looked down so that she would not see my pain and her hand was like a pressed flower lying in my palm.

'I am not given to displays of emotion, Molly, but before I go, I want to tell you how much your friendship has meant to me. We are kindred spirits, you and I, and though we share no blood, I think of you as my … my much younger sister.'

'Or even your daughter?'

We needed no more words and just sat for a while holding hands. Mary dozed, her breath barely disturbing the sheets. Just as I was thinking of leaving the room, her eyes flickered open, and she said, 'And so, I imagine you still think of your own daughter from time to time. Do you nurture any hope of ever seeing her again?'

'No.'

'It's best, I imagine. Too distressing otherwise.'

I thought hard about giving breath to the hope I nurtured: it seemed so slight a thing that to bring it out into the daylight would make it shrivel and die. Mary had lapsed into fretful silence. It would give her pleasure to know this: I would give it utterance.

I took a deep breath. 'There is one glimmer, though I hesitate to speak it out loud. At heart I imagine I am being fanciful.'

'Tell me.'

'A portrait I saw in London. A sketch in coloured chalks, a study of a young woman. I felt a stab of recognition.'

'An intuition. Oh Molly, describe it for me.'

'Well the same artist made several studies of the young woman, and one in particular struck me forcibly.'

'So what did you do?'

'I ...asked him to contact me if she should reappear.'

'Molly! Is that really all you did? No attempt to find the model?'

'No. I really could not countenance the disappointment if it proved not to be her.'

'I struggle to understand but then I am not you. I only know that I would have moved heaven and earth on such an intuition.'

'If it had been straightforward I would not have hesitated, but the young woman is an actress with a travelling company. She has a stage name and may well have changed it or given Sandys a false one.'

'Sandys, you say? Frederick Sandys? Why he is well-known. He has made his name in London and Paris.'

'I did not realise. It is a long time since I spoke with artists. Mr Hutt has no interest.'

'John has always loved art, ever since he was a young man. I'll always remember how he came back from his grand tour carrying paintings! Since he has been with Josephine, he has become more and more serious about his collection. But back to this young woman. What was the stage name she gave?'

'Miss Clive.'

'I could tell you it was familiar but that would not be true. However, if you are staying in Bath, and I hope you will stay for a few days at least, you must visit the theatres and make enquiries! Nothing to lose!'

'Only my own peace of mind.'

Her look told me that that should not be my priority. Without another word, she drifted back to sleep.

The maid had prepared a room for me. When she showed me into it, she confided that the doctor had prepared the staff: Miss Bowes was not expected to last until Christmas. I had already decided that I would stay with her until the end, and I did.

In the following weeks, it became my habit to spend the mornings with her, have lunch together then leave her to sleep whilst I explored Bath. I visited several theatres but no-one had heard of Miss Clive.

One afternoon, it was raining and my spirits were low. I sat by Mary's bedside and watched her sleeping. Suddenly, she opened her bird-bright eyes and said, 'Boo!'

Startled, I laughed and she began to struggle to sit up.

'Heavens, this bedroom is stuffy. Open the windows please Molly. Let's have some lovely moist air in here.'

As I helped her to get comfortable, she said, 'I've had an idea. Let's compose a letter to Frederick Sandys. Don't look like that, Molly, we've got to try. Go and get some paper and I shall tell you what to write.'

I did as I was told.

6, Arden Crescent, Bath

Dear Mr Sandys

You may remember that we met in London during the Great Exhibition, when we were introduced by William Makepeace Thackeray. He purchased from you an unfinished chalk sketch of the weeping Magdalene, which he gave to me as a gift. You will perhaps remember that I was interested in buying a version of 'Love's Shadow': I believe you called it 'Proud Maisie'. You declined to sell it to me and were, I believe, awaiting the reappearance of the model in order to complete a more polished version of the design.

I am in Bath at the moment attending to my aged aunt at the above address and should be most grateful to receive a reply.'

With all good wishes
Molly Bowes.

Chapter 33

'I am feeling much brighter today, Molly. The prospect of seeing you has given me another pillow, you see? I am allowed to sit up. When they took away my second pillow, I felt I was doomed to lie flat on my back in preparation for being put in a box.' She chuckled. 'It reminded me of the first time I heard someone say I had *had a fall*. When one is young and bouncy, one may fall with impunity - *she fell over, she tripped* - but when it becomes A Fall, you know you are doomed.'

'You do make me laugh, Mary. You do look brighter today. Will you take coffee?'

'I will. Good and strong. The doctor says I may not have it for fear of my heart becoming over-excited, but I would rather die of laughter and excitement than lie flat listening to it fading away with every beat. Coffee, yes, and cake! And perhaps a nip of something in my coffee. The maid has hidden my rum, but I'll wager you can find it, resourceful Molly. Go! It is your quest!'

'I'll put a girdle round the earth.'

'And when you come back, you can tell me more about your Mr Cowen.'

The rum spread warmth in my chest and I watched Mary's pleasure as she drank her hot toddy. She settled back onto her pillows. 'Now, tell me.'

'Joseph Cowen? Gabe and I are friends of his father, who was a blacksmith, then a brick manufacturer. He made his fortune and bought Stella Hall in Blaydon five years ago. Now he is an MP and chair of the Tyne River Commission: they are beginning to straighten and dredge and deepen the Tyne. Lord Armstrong wants to expand and bring the island at King's Meadow into Elswick. Progress, I suppose, though it is sad to see Bewick's winding meanders going. I only hope the island at Blaydon can be preserved: apart from the furnaces at Wylam, the industries upriver are small and scattered. There's Cowen's bricks and pipes, and of course the coal, lead, glass-making...'

'I once went to a kind of festival on one of those islands, The Hoppings I believe they call it. It was packed! Such wonderful people, the Tynesiders. I remember the day so well, it's still so vivid to me: exciting horse-racing, a marvellous kind of dancing whilst manipulating swords of astonishing flexibility, and such singers, those people! There was a wonderful troubadour I particularly remember who sang and spoke such wonders of wild inventiveness that he was like a character from Shakespeare. They called him Pom – have you heard of him?'

I smiled. 'I have. He is well known and loved: his name is Neil Pomeroy.'

'Oh, I would love to hear him again,' she said wistfully. 'I think that day of the Blaydon Races was the most colourful and vivid day of my life. It would be a great pity to lose those islands. But people adapt. We cannot stop progress.'

I answered more sharply than I intended. 'Progress does not need to bring suffering. The conditions I saw in Manchester thirty-five years ago have worsened, they say. Engels and Marx have publicized the horrors to the world.'

Her face fell.

'I'm sorry, Mary. You do not need to hear this. Let's talk of flowers and music. Would you like to do a puzzle with me?'

'No, no, no. I have had enough of puzzles. I want to know how the world wags outside these four walls. I want to know that the people I care about are happy before I take my leave of them. I want to know about you and your hopes and dreams.'

'I do love you, Mary Bowes.'

'And I you, Molly. Now carry on. Tell me about what you think and feel. I sense you are agitated about more than the possibility that you might find your daughter.'

'You divine correctly, as always.'

'Tell me.'

'I feel... frustrated. I feel I can do more. I love Gibside but I feel increasingly... isolated there. It feels unreal. An Arcadia ringed by trees, while outside the real world is dark and troubled.'

'But as you said yourself, you do valuable work in representing ideas to the parliamentarian who employs you.'

'But it's all just words! There are real things I could do. To help people. Real people. With real troubles. Not just worrying about whether the frost will kill their auriculas or whether the pineapples will ripen in time for Gladstone's visit.' Her eyes clouded and I felt ashamed of my outburst. 'I'm sorry.'

'No need to apologise. I can't tell you how refreshing this is. I'm sick to death of people tiptoeing around me, whispering in corners then talking to me as though I'm simple. I'm dying, I know that, and I've come to terms with it. I'm ready, or I will be when I've understood what it is you need.'

'You have helped me already. You've made me write to Sandys, and … well, just that outburst has made me see what I must do.'

'And what is that, Molly?'

'I must involve myself in real life and do what I can to help people.'

'You are afraid that the conditions you saw in Manchester are coming to Newcastle? But what can you do about it if they are?'

'No, I had it explained to me that Newcastle has no one dominant industry as Manchester does cotton.'

'Then you need not be concerned.'

I almost 'leapt onto my hobby-horse' as Gabe used to put it, but her voice was listless and I saw that her attention was fading. I got up and kissed her brow, whereupon her eyes flicked open and she struggled to right herself.

'Hush now. You rest, we can speak later.'

'No, no. I am afraid to sleep for fear I will never wake. Call Martha for cakes and coffee. I want to know more about your Geordie Messiah.'

I laughed. 'That's marvelous! I shall tell Joe that his son has a title. The Geordie Messiah!'

'And he is speaking in temples, you say? Tell me what he says.'

'Joseph was only nineteen the first time I heard him speak publicly a few years ago. It was electrifying.'

'And what had he to say that struck you so hard?'

'He made the case for revolution across Europe.'

'You frighten me, Molly.'

'His hero is Cromwell, not Robespierre. The workers' movement is a very broad church, which of course is their problem.

He is trying to bring the strands together under one umbrella, the Northern Reform Union. They are fighting for the one thing they can all agree on, which is universal suffrage.'

'Even women? That sounds very laudable. As you know, I am not a political creature but I do like to hear you talk. Having said that, this war against the Russians is enjoying more popular support than one would have imagined possible. I read stirring words in the newspaper with regard to the brave Turks and their righteous crusade against Russian aggression. But it all seems so far away and unrelated to England.'

'That is what's exhilarating. Across Europe, workers are uniting against despots. The Poles and others have welcomed this war as a long-awaited opportunity for an uprising of suppressed people everywhere. "What now glitters in the desperate grasp of Turkey is the brilliant lightning of revolution." '

'Who said that?'

'Victor Hugo. He lives in exile in Jersey. Those words were printed in the Northern Tribune in Newcastle.'

'It is a paper I haven't come across.'

'It is Joseph Cowen's newspaper. He owns it and Harney writes for him. You remember I used to talk about Harney when I first became involved with the Chartists in Winlaton?'

'No, I confess I didn't listen very hard. You were so clearly in love with Gabe that I dismissed your political talk as mere girlish prattle.'

Indignation flared in me, but I wouldn't let her see. 'Harney is an idealist and his views are far too extreme for many.'

'What does he believe? I do fear anarchy.'

'His words are burned on my memory: when I heard them, I understood for the first time how hard it would be to reconcile the extremes of the working-class movement. Wait, I have them: "It is not the mere improvement of the social life of our class that we seek; but the abolition of classes and the destruction of these wicked distinctions which have divided the human race into princes and paupers, landlords and labourers, masters and slaves. It is not any patching and cobbling of the present system we aspire to accomplish but the annihilation of that system."'

'Annihilation? The word makes me shudder.'

'Ah but you see, this is where young Joseph Cowen comes in. Harney's experience of poverty makes him too radical. Cowen is a moralist: to him, a republic is a latter-day Athens of duties and virtues. "Capital has its duties as well as its rights."'

I watched her face, fearful of tiring her, but she said, 'Go on, my dear, you stimulate me more than I have felt for years.'

'Are you sure? Please do stop me when you've heard enough.' I took a deep breath. 'There are radicals in the middle classes too but such as Harney would not countenance dealing with them, and because of that the radical working classes could be defeated: apart from withholding their labour and breaking machines, they were powerless. Joseph Cowen sees that. He has harnessed Harney's fire and idealism and forged an alliance with middle-class radicalism: he will wrest power from the Whigs. He is a great believer in working-class organisations to aid self-help, friendly societies, trades unions, mechanics' institutes and co-operatives. Progressive forces made for self-improvement. And their strongest bond is shared sympathy for European movements: for the overthrow of Napoleon, for Hungarian and Polish independence and the unification of Italy. Through his work helping Hungarian and Polish refugees to settle on Tyneside, he has gained the friendship of Mazzini and Kossuth. Garibaldi himself came to Newcastle last year.'

'Giuseppe Garibaldi went to Newcastle?'

'Yes, to Blaydon too. He stayed at Stella Hall with the Cowens. He was in command of a great thousand-ton vessel, the Commonwealth, loaded with coal for Genoa. Joseph Cowen organised a collection amongst the working men and they presented Garibaldi with a telescope and a sword. Newcastle has become the focal point of the English agitation for European freedom.'

'And you really think there will be revolution in England?'

'Another revolution,' I corrected her. 'Yes, I really think that Joseph Cowen has the charisma and idealism to make it happen with his brand of democratic radicalism. He has already created the Republican Brotherhood.'

'Republican? You cannot mean he would behead the Queen?'

'No, no, please be assured of that. Victoria is quite safe.' I decided not to tell her about the toast to overthrow kings. Instead, I tried to lighten the tone. 'He appreciates the importance of cultural activities in creating full citizenship and social cohesion. We need a public library in Newcastle. The campaign is growing stronger: there are plenty of subscription libraries but knowledge should be free. Cowen is prominent in the campaign, with Robert Spence Watson, Dr Rutherford and other local worthies.'

'Mmm, that's nice.' She was asleep, bless her. Almost eighty years old: so much had changed in her lifetime. As I watched her sleeping face, I thought of Tennyson's lines: 'The old order changeth, yielding place to new, and God fulfills himself in many ways.'

I knew then that it was time for me to move on, to commit myself to Joseph Cowen.

As the days passed, Mary grew weaker. I gave up my explorations and sat by her bedside reading, sometimes aloud though there was rarely any sign that she heard.

One afternoon, there was a knock and the maid came in.
'Miss Bowes? A letter for you.'
When I saw the postmark, I felt my heart contract and I opened the envelope with shaking hands.

Dear Miss Bowes
Delightful to hear from you, and I am most gratified at your request. I write in haste as I am about to leave for Paris, but upon my return in May, perhaps you would like to arrange to visit my studio in London to view the several versions of 'Love's Shadow' which I have produced since the return of Maisie, who I think you will agree has proved a most marvellous muse!
Yours in haste,
Fred Sandys

I looked up, dazed, my eyes burning. There came from the pillow a whisper of a word. 'Well?'

I reached for her hand where it lay upon the white coverlet, the skin transparent as a dried leaf: cold, delicate, light as gossamer. It lay across my palm like a feather.

I whispered, 'She has returned.'

I thought at first she had not heard, but then felt a faint stirring and her little finger curled around my own.

She died that night.

Chapter 34

On the day after Mary's funeral, I sat at the little desk in her bedroom and wrote a brief letter of resignation to Mr Hutt. In a separate envelope addressed to the Dowager Countess of Strathmore, I sent Poll a longer letter of explanation. It would be no surprise to her that I was leaving, but I wanted to explain, apologise and offer my reassurances that we would still see each other.

Then I wrote to Joseph Cowen. Although he knew who I was through my friendship with his father and my work at Winlaton Mechanics' Institute, I wrote a formal letter of application in which I expressed my admiration for his commitment to education and democracy in pursuit of peaceful social reform.

I rented one of a pair of sandstone cottages on Summerhill, a green bank rising steeply from the Tyne, and overlooking Cowen's Lower Brickworks. Across the narrow tree-lined valley of Blaydon Burn, I could see the edge of Winlaton on the top of the opposite hill. Pack-horses and wagons passed all day, coming from Hexham via the Lead Road and Path Head Watermill; I sometimes sat in the sunny front garden to watch the procession of new arrivals and pass the time of day.

The other cottage was occupied by a smith whose forge was at the back, reached by a narrow lane on the downhill side. He was always busy and the yard full of horses, carts and customers. I loved being in the centre of so much activity and due to my work at the Mechanics' Institutes in both Winlaton and Blaydon, I was known and accepted straight away.

The forge was built from the stone of an old field-wall that ran down the hill; beyond it were allotments, and beyond that, the grounds of Stella Hall, where the Cowen family lived.

When I started working as an assistant to Joseph Cowen, it was never entirely clear what my role was, but I was immediately plunged into the preparations for an enormous rally he was organizing. It was anticipated that twenty-five thousand artisans would march to the Town Moor. I have kept a copy of the speech that

Joseph gave that day. It never fails to move me, and it is a permanent reminder of the reasons I hitched my wagon to his cause:

"Gentlemen, this day's proceedings are the answer of the working men of Tyneside to the accusation that they are indifferent to the cause of political reform. When Mr Lowe, the next time he slanders the working men by accusing them of preferring a vicious gratification of their animal passions to their sense of duty as men and as citizens; when Lord Cranborne sneers at the artisans and ridicules the idea that they are made of the same flesh and blood as the titled idlers that now monopolise all the national honours; when Sir John Rolt strives to excite the timid fears of weak men and women by an appeal to some of the apocryphal terrors of the rising democracy, there will be three northern M.P.s who will be able to point to this meeting in Newcastle and to tell them that the accusations of one gentleman are false, that the fears of another are chimerical, and that the insinuations of the third are as unjust as they are ungenerous. Gentlemen, I know not how far these our opponents may feel disposed to give credit or to attach importance to the testimony of an individual who has had during the last sixteen or seventeen years no small intercourse with the working men of this district. How far they may be disposed to attach weight to that testimony I know not; but this I can say—that during that time I have known the working men of this district and of other parts of England intimately; I have mingled with them daily; I have met them as an employer; I have met them, too, in their efforts for political emancipation; I have been with them in the class-rooms of their Mechanics' Institute, in the committee-rooms of their industrial associations, and on the platforms of their temperance societies; I have been, too, within the sacred precincts of their domestic hearths; I have shared their joys and sorrows, listened to the recital of their wants and wishes, rejoiced with them in their successes, and mourned with them in their sufferings and struggles; and this I can say—the men who have slandered the working men, as the parties to whom I have just referred, are entirely in ignorance of the character of the artisan classes of this country. They know not their worth, and they are unable to estimate their virtues. Gentlemen, the working men have their faults like other men. There is no intelligent man—no

291

impartial and fair-dealing man—who would attempt to say that they are without their faults. But I have this to say - take numbers for numbers, and circumstances for circumstances, they are in every respect equal in morality and intelligence to the other sections of the community. "

As for his foreign activities, Joseph was always secretive and I rarely got to meet his visitors, many of whom were exiles from their own countries. I was well aware that parcels of leaflets were printed and bound at Stella Hall and smuggled into the consignments of bricks, gas-retorts and other fire-clay goods on their way to Europe, where he told me many people lived under repressive dynasties. Barrels of his firebricks destined for Danzig were packed with pamphlets and other publications banned from France, Austria, Italy and Russia.

The details of Joseph Cowen's part in it all were hazy to me, but I trusted and believed in him, in freedom of speech and the dissemination of ideas and information to working people everywhere. I was proud to be involved in such a laudable enterprise and I loved his clear-eyed optimism and dynamic personality.

I have to say I never really understood his preoccupation with Italian unification. Apart from his famous friendship with Garibaldi, I had heard rumours about the extent of his involvement with Joseph Mazzini: in fact, rumours about his friendship with the exiled Italian freedom fighter were the first indication that I could not be entirely devoted to Mr Cowen.

One night in January 1858, a bomb exploded at Paris Opera House, an attempt on the life of Louis Napoleon. It killed six innocent people and injured over one hundred more.

The day after the news, I was walking by the river when a man I didn't know said nastily, 'You'd best stay clear of Stella Hall for the time being. Your Mr Cowen looks likely to lose his precious liberty.'

'Why? What do you mean?'

'That bomb in Paris. Heads will roll.'

I said, 'What possible connection could Mr Cowen have to a bomb in Paris?' but a cold hand had gripped my heart.

'They say the casings were made at Cowen's and shipped out in firebricks.'

'I find that highly unlikely. Mr Cowen is an idealist. He would never be involved in violence against innocent people.'

'That's as maybe, but his friend Orsini would, and he's going to be executed.'

Now my blood ran cold. I had met Orsini when he'd been staying at Stella Hall. I'd been in the library transcribing a speech and the maid had run screaming down the stairs, thinking she had found the Italian guest dead in his bed. It transpired he had innocently blown out the flames on the gas lamps in his bedroom before he retired. The handsome, charming young man had been nearly asphyxiated. Although he made a full recovery, Mrs Cowen had been distraught and she would be heartbroken to hear this news. To think of him being executed: the thought was horrendous.

I hastened to Stella Hall and there was Joseph burning papers in the grate. I didn't have to ask, but I did.

'Do not concern yourself, Molly.'

'Tell me you were not involved in the making of the bomb?'

He did not falter: 'You should know by now that I do not share in the silly horror some entertain towards revolutionaries. Physical force is not the opposite of moral force. Physical force can be moral and justifiable.'

'I cannot agree. I am a pacifist.'

'Then we should speak no more on the subject.'

'But I respect you. I want to understand.'

'Molly, you are a pacifist and I am a pragmatist. Every situation is different. To my mind, there is no question that in some circumstances, violence is needed to achieve the principles of liberty and justice. Here in England, popular pressure can win extensions of liberty. In other countries, force may be what is required. I rely upon the judgment of men I have come to respect by virtue of their experience and their courage. I see you doubt me. Sit down, Molly.'

He stirred the ashes in the grate with the poker, put it back in its stand, brushed his hands on his trousers and went to his desk, where he unlocked a drawer and took out a file.

'It is easy to say you are a pacifist if your conviction has never been personally challenged. Italy has been for years divided and ruled by princes, dukes and despots. Ordinary people suffer under their rule, but must pay their taxes, accept their punishments and die under their banners. Garibaldi is fighting to establish a modern democracy. They must fight. Force is necessary: there is no other way for him to free his countrymen. I shall read you a letter from Garibaldi and perhaps you will re-examine your convictions.

He rummaged in the folder, eventually drawing out a piece of paper and opening it carefully.

Born and educated as I have been in the cause of humanity, my heart is entirely devoted to liberty, universal liberty, national and world-wide, 'ora e sempre.' England is a great and powerful nation; independent of auxiliary aid; foremost in human progress; enemy to despotism; the only safe refuge of the exile: friend of the oppressed; but if ever England, your native country, should be so circumstanced as to require the help of an ally, cursed be that Italian who would not step forward with me in her defence. Should England at any time in a just case need my aid, I am ready to unsheathe in her defence the noble and splendid sword received at your hands.

Yours always and everywhere.
Giuseppe Garibaldi."

'That is very touching, but I cannot countenance violence. In my youth, I spent time with members of the Religious Society of Friends and became convinced that pacificism is the only way. Blood will have blood. I cannot follow you in this, Joseph, and I no longer want to be involved, however innocently, in your political activities.' I stood up. 'I shall continue to teach in the Mechanics' Institute and help in the library, as I have always done. I bid you good day.'

It was a cold and dark January afternoon when I left Stella Hall, and it suited my mood. When I got home, I lit a fire and sat beside it for I know not how long, just staring into the flames. I had no regrets about leaving Stella Hall. To stoke up my convictions, I took down Masque of Anarchy from the shelf. When I reached the end, I closed the book with a sense of peace.

For the rest of that winter, I kept myself to myself by the fireside. I read widely, trudging to and from the library when the weather permitted. Sometimes, when I felt the urge to be creative or industrious, I did some sketching, I even baked some bread and a few modest cakes. I was quite content and I don't believe I was ever lonely.

When the warmer weather came, I walked further and higher, filling my lungs with the fresh air on the hilltops. Once I got as far as Hedley on the Hill. The light was fading before I realized how late it had become, so I stayed a night at The Feathers, feeling quite safe from male attention, masked in the safety of an aging face. I revel in the freedom.

I left Hedley on a bright spring morning and set off downhill towards Cherryburn, where I gazed at last upon the childhood home of Thomas Bewick, nestling on the south bank of the Tyne at Eltringham.

Upon being told that his grave was across the river in the churchyard at Ovingham, I paid a ferryman to row me over. Up beyond the tide-line, the river is still as it was in Bewick's day and my heart soared to see it. Nature has such resilience and the river cleanses and feeds and entertains as it always has and always will.

Returning home along the north bank, passing miners' terraces hugging the hillsides, seeing chimneys smoking and hearing trains steaming along the valley to Carlisle, I counted myself blessed that fate had brought me to Tyneside.

Chapter 35

When the autumn sun lit the hills with coppery light, I yearned to see Gibside in all its golden glory. The Hutts had been travelling that summer and I had promised to visit upon their return.

Poll's face was a picture when she saw me, and though I noted her frailty I could see she was full of excitement.

'Molly, How wonderful to see you! I have so much to tell! Sit, sit! I have sent for tea and I shall tell you all.'

Still with my large hands grasped in her small soft ones, I sat down and looked into her animated face.

'I have the most marvelous news! John and Josephine are seriously talking about building a museum! '

'In France?'

'No! Here in County Durham! You know what that means – they are coming home! They would surely live at Streatlam. My hopes are high indeed. We have had such a summer, I must tell you all about it! They have been here the whole time and Josephine and I are such good friends now! She is quite besotted with Gibside and she likes Streatlam well enough. We travelled to Scotland. We had house-parties. Josephine painted. She is very gifted, you know: one of her paintings has been accepted for the Academy Exhibition. We walked together and talked of all kinds of things. She is almost like a daughter to me. It seems unlikely there will be children, and that is of course a sadness. She is not in the best of health.' I kept my counsel. Mary Bowes had once told me that John was unlikely to be able to sire children as he had contracted an illness of an unspecified nature on his first visit to the continent as a young man.

'I am so happy for you, Poll.'

She looked at my face for the first time. 'I'm sorry. I do prattle on. I take it there is no news of your daughter? You would have told me if you had heard anything further from Frederick Sandys?'

'No. Nothing.'

'Come Molly. We used to be so close, you and I. Do tell me your news. Are you still living and working in Blaydon?'

'At the Mechanics' Institute, yes.'

Her face clouded.

'Your Mr Cowen...'

'I know what you're going to say, Poll. Please don't.'

She watched me over her teacup. Eventually she spoke. 'I have been selfish. I am excited and happy. I forget. I'm sorry.'

'There's nothing to be sorry for. I just don't want to talk about my work or Mr Cowen. It's good to see you, Poll.' I wanted to ask about her health. Beneath the animation, there was a pallor to her complexion and the whites of her eyes were tinged with yellow. 'Your letter implied you had a reason for wanting to see me as soon as you returned?'

She put down her cup and took a deep breath. I held mine.

'It is simply this. John's ideas about the proposed museum are in their infancy. Whilst I fervently hope they will come to fruition in my lifetime, I accept that they may not. But if I can believe that one day my son and his wife will have built a lasting legacy in his home county, I will die happy.'

I put down my cup and took hold of her hands, looking anxiously into her face. 'Come come, Poll. These are dark thoughts. You were so happy a moment ago.'

'I know. In truth, the museum idea was only aired once over dinner. I was unwise to let my over-excitement show and John withdrew. He would not speak of it again. It is his way.'

'He wants to make you happy, I am sure.'

'He would not be creating the museum for me, I know that, but of course he knows how much it would mean to me. It would mean he would be in England much more often. Now that the trains enable him to travel so swiftly between Paris and Streatlam...'

'Do you think he proposed the idea only to give you hope?'

'I did at first, and I cursed myself for gushing my enthusiasm. But Josephine saw my disappointment when he refused to elaborate. When we were next alone, she raised the topic herself.'

'So it is a real possibility?'

'Yes, I really think it is. They love each other so much, Molly. It quite brings me to tears of happiness that my boy should be so

297

loved. All the care he would otherwise have lavished on children, had he been so blessed, he gives to her. His whole concern is to make her happy.'

'And she? Does she make him happy?'

'She does. She blossoms in his presence. She makes him laugh: she teases him and challenges him and he loves her for it. Her tenderness and concern are moving to see.' Suddenly her eyes filled. 'It is all I want. For my boy to be happy.'

Suddenly I was looking through tears too. We held each other, our brows leaning together. I was startled by the pain I felt, not only for her and the prospect of losing her, but also for myself. For in truth I envied Poll her boy, his wife, their future. My own child was lost to me. I knew nothing of her fate and suddenly I could no longer bear it.

I loathe self-pity in others, and I honestly believe I have never indulged in it myself, but suddenly I was drowning in it. I got up and strode to the window to look out over the Derwent Valley while I struggled to master my feelings. I had no-one. It was my own fault, a consequence of my determined independence. Poll was not long for this world: I could sense it. I should have stayed here where I'd once felt I belonged. I should have helped Belle to care for Dorothy. I should have married Gabe – who knows, perhaps I would have had children, even grandchildren. Who would care if I simply vanished? When I died, the waters would simply close over my head and I would leave not a ripple.

I forced myself to focus on the real world as it was, out there in the valley, where life went on as it always would and progress was unstoppable. The banging and shouting, the sawing and jets of steam coming from the engines down there by the river – that would be the bridges being constructed. I'd heard that the route of the new Derwent Valley railway had finally been agreed after months of negotiations: the company had accepted that the tracks would cross the river twice so that the trains would not be seen from the Gibside estate. This place was an anachronism, but I loved it. Poll had all this, a husband, a son, a daughter-in-law, a vision of future legacy. I turned my self-pity into anger and bitterness and envy - far less painful, far easier to deal with and to swallow and to bury.

Poll sensed my distress and came to stand beside me, slipping an arm around my waist. It was as if she read my thoughts. 'Shall I tell you another of my hopes, Molly? You, I know, will understand. I hope that the beauties of this place will be preserved. Not for the enjoyment of a single family, but for everyone. It is, after all, a form of art to enhance the landscape through human endeavour.'

I turned to her. 'Do you think that would be possible?'

'I do. You and I have an understanding of the accident of birth and the meaningless of class. We have moved between them, as has Will. This place was built on vision, hard work and skill, like that railway. Gibside is a piece of art in its way, built by collaboration and based on mutual respect. It is the best of human endeavour, a kind of harmonic composition. It uplifts and feeds the spirit of all who see it. More people should have that pleasure.' She squeezed my waist and leant her head upon my shoulder.

'Oh Poll, we really are in melancholy mood, but there is comfort in this. Our own problems are as nothing when we consider the great tide of time. The Derwent will roll on into the Tyne. The Tyne rolls on into the sea, the waters mingle.'

'Yes, it is a comfort to contemplate.'

'May I ask you something, Poll?'

She nodded her assent, still looking out over the water-meadows towards the river.

'When John and Josephine finally join us in the great hereafter - not that I believe in its existence - what will happen to Gibside and Streatlam?'

To my surprise, she smiled a gentle and sorrowful smile. 'It will all revert to the Strathmores. I am sure that is partly why John wishes to build a legacy that is all his own. It is his intention that the museum will be an astonishing building. It will tickle him to know that whenever the Strathmore family visit their English estates, if they ever do, they will see a French Chateau rising out of the Durham countryside.'

'A French Chateau?'

'It is a secret. Josephine imparted it to me, but you must tell no-one.'

'I ...' in my mind's eye I saw the architectural drawings in a book I knew from this very library. My smile broadened. "What an astonishing and beautiful thing that will be! The incongruity!'

'And stuffed with treasures.'

'For the people?   For public enjoyment and education?' Tingles were running up and down my sides.

'Yes indeed.   And you, my dear Molly, can help this astonishing thing come to pass.'

Chapter 36

I returned to Summerhill in high excitement and wrote a letter to Joseph Cowen in which I tendered my resignation from all my duties at the Mechanics' Institutes with effect from Christmas. I delivered it by hand the following morning and returned home to begin to plan my art research. Before I met John Bowes as a prospective employee, I wanted to make sure I was worthy of the position.

After a lunch of boiled eggs from a neighbour's chickens and bread I'd baked myself, I was sitting on the bench by my back door when I saw a figure striding through the allotments towards me. It was Joseph Cowen. I had thought he was away from home.

I felt nervous: the full gaze of his attention was a formidable thing, and if he asked to come in, I knew that the floor around my desk was still scattered with drafts of my resignation letter.

But he was all smiles and lifted his hat to greet me. 'Good afternoon, Molly. It is a fine day! Would you care to walk with me up to the summerhouse? We don't need to talk if you would rather not. I need some fresh air and a sense of perspective on a knotty matter.'

I took my tray inside, closed the door and fell into step beside him. He began immediately, as I had known he would.

'You are sixty, you say in your letter. I would never have thought it.' He regarded me slyly out of the side of his eye. I didn't react, merely kept up my pace beside him on the steep hill. 'Not susceptible to flattery, I see.'

In answer, I smiled in what I hoped was an enigmatic way. In truth, I had not the faintest suspicion of which direction this conversation was going. I only knew I would stand firm against his powers of persuasion, should he choose to wield them.

'I shall miss you Molly.'

'I am not planning to leave Blaydon: I shall keep up my lease for the time being, as I explained.'

'You did not explain at all. But that's as maybe. You are determined, I see. Shall you continue your voluntary work in the library?'

'When my other work permits, as I explained.'

'Ah, your other work. Tell me about your work for Mr Bowes.'

I could not determine his tone, and despite our difference of opinion over the use of force, I feared his disapproval above all things.

'He has requested my assistance in a new endeavour.'

'An endeavour of what nature?'

'I'm sorry, Mr Cowen, but I need not trouble you with the nature of the enterprise. Suffice it to say that I am convinced that it is of an exceptionally noble and altruistic sort.'

There was no response and the silence continued for several minutes. It is a technique Joseph uses to great effect, although I have observed it does not work on everyone as well as it had always worked with me. Not this time, I resolved. My fear was that he would consider the amassing of an art collection an ostentatious indulgence and despise me for wanting to be involved in it.

Somewhat breathless, I was relieved to see that we had reached the peak of the hill and the glass roof of the summerhouse glinted in the afternoon sun. I looked out over the bend in the river towards Lemington. The conical towers of the glassworks sat neatly clustered and quietly industrious.

'Such a view! It never fails to restore me.' He sat down on the grass. 'We used to slide down here on tin trays.'

I considered several ways to answer, but settled on none of them. Instead, I sat down beside him and thought of the time Gabe and I had slid down this very hill, whooping and laughing in the snow. I had glimpsed him once or twice in the company of the widow who was his landlady. We had not spoken for years.

Once I felt Joseph was no longer waiting for me to elaborate on John's plans, I decided to tell him and be done with it.

'Mr Bowes and his wife are planning to build a museum in Barnard Castle.'

'Indeed?'

'A public museum. For everyone.'

302

'A laudable endeavour. I am glad to hear it.'

'You are?'

'Why yes, of course. I've a great respect for John Bowes. Fine fellow.'

I breathed out.

'I expect he feels guilty about having quitted public service so young. Strikes me as the kind of chap who wants to do good.'

'Yes, yes, he does.'

'We all do what we can in our own way. He had a theatre in Paris, did he not?'

'He did, yes.'

'We are planning a new theatre here in Newcastle. We shall call it the Tyne Theatre and we hope to build it on Westgate Road. It too will be for the people.'

'Indeed? I had not known of your interest.'

'Art, you say, for the people. Well that's marvelous.'

'You approve?'

'Why, of course I approve, Molly! Why would I not? You know of my belief in the importance of education: art has considerable capacity to expand and improve men's minds.'

'And they have invited me to supervise the inventory as the items begin to arrive from France.'

'You will do great good in this role: I am glad to hear it.' He stood up briskly, shook my hand and set off at a trot down the hill towards Stella Hall, calling over his shoulder, 'I wish you all the very best! Go forth to Barnard Castle and bring wonderful things to the people!'

The next day was a Friday and I woke with a sense of excitement: it took a few moments for me to locate the reasons for it. I spent the morning at the Mechanics' Institute teaching four young lead-workers to read. The lunch break I spent in the library, and then I called at the Co-op on my way home.

Having a new reason to visit the Post Office, I went in with hope and expectation in my bearing. The post-master was used by now to seeing my face at his counter. After so many months of disappointment, I had lapsed into the habit of asking the question with a simple wordless raising of my eyebrows. There had never been a letter from London or Norfolk, though he never tired of teasing me about the lover he thought I had lost.

Instead of the usual mute entreaty, I said, 'I am expecting an important letter. From France.'

'Oh aye? You won't be wanting this one then.' He waved a creamy envelope and was preparing to tuck it away back into the pigeonholes behind him, but seeing my suddenly stricken face, he stopped smiling and put it down on the counter. 'There you are pet. Hope it's the one ye've been waiting for.'

It was. I instantly recognized Fred Sandys' extravagantly looped handwriting. I snatched up the letter and backed into the corner of the office to open it.

Dear Miss Bowes

I must apologise profusely for the tardiness of my reply. I have been exceedingly busy of late with commissions, exhibitions and travelling. Added to which we have a new baby in the household. My time is not my own!

If you are still interested in purchasing a version of 'Proud Maisie', I currently have two: one a framed watercolour and the other an unframed study in coloured chalks. If you are planning a trip to London, I can arrange for you to view them here.

Alternatively, I shall be sending two large paintings to Edinburgh in the spring for an exhibition at the Scottish Academy. I may well decide to travel with them and bide a while in Auld Reekie, in which case I will spend a night at least in Newcastle.

If you would like to view these two small portraits, please confirm your continued interest and your preferred time and place.

I offer my assurances that I shall allow no other to see them until I have received your reply, so reprehensible has been my delay.

Yours, Fred Sandys.

A new baby in the household. My mind raced. Was it possible? I thought hard to separate what I knew from what I imagined. My thoughts were all in turmoil. His last letter had clearly stated that Maisie had returned and it had transmitted happiness. The two might well be related. Was it possible that the household to

304

which he referred was his and Maisie's? That they had a baby together, maybe more?

I bought paper, borrowed a pen and wrote my reply there in the Post Office, the faster to dispatch it.

Dear Mr Sandys
Thank-you for your letter and I accept your apologies: there was no need: you have been very busy. I would indeed be interested in purchasing a version of 'Proud Maisie' and would like very much to see any other portraits you have painted of the same model.
Since last we met, I have become directly involved in the art world: I will explain when next we meet, hopefully in Newcastle. Now that we have our own elegant railway station, you will find us quite the thing! I do not know when you were last here, but you will be entranced by the transformation in our town.
Congratulations upon your recent addition. I cannot recollect whether you were married when last we spoke, but if not, congratulations upon your marriage too. What is your wife's name?
I stopped, considered. This was too intrusive, too personal. I was a customer merely, one of many. I could not make personal enquiries about his wife and children in a letter. Nor should I express interest in the model for fear of seeming peculiar. The man barely knew me and might take fright. I re-wrote the letter, confining myself to a cool expression of serious intent, signed it, sealed it and gave it to the post-master without meeting his indulgent smile.

On my way home, I decided that I must do more to discreetly ascertain Fred Sandys' circumstances and try to find out whether Maisie really was the mother of his child. Thackeray was the obvious choice.

I had had occasional news of him since we had met at the Great Exhibition, and now that I was to be working closely with John Bowes, it seemed perfectly natural that we should renew our acquaintance.

I wrote a letter full of happy chatter: it flowed out of my pen. When it came to the end and I knew it was time to broach the subject closest to my heart, I stood up and walked about the room, my hands shaking.

Finally, I wrote:

I have heard from Fred Sandys at last. I had expressed interest in another portrait but received no response. It seems he has been exceptionally busy: I am glad to hear he took your advice about his strengths – I am sure he owes all his success to you! He also appears to have married and procreated since we met! I wonder whether you still see him? Has he married a model, I wonder? There was an actress he seemed smitten with, Miss Clive if I remember correctly. Perhaps it is she.

A reply arrived the following week. Bless him, Thackeray's letter was full of affection and went straight to the point, which of course he had perceived long ago.

You guess correctly. Miss Clive is now known in these parts as 'Mrs Neville' for reasons known only to herself and Sandys. She is the mother to a bevy of beauteous children in her own image.

It occurs to me, dear Molly, that your interest in Maisie is more than idle gossip. Do I startle you? No, I think not, for you and I always did understand each other. I have met Maisie in the flesh, as it were. Dressed demurely and with that astounding hair coiled into a bonnet. And do you know, the moment I saw her thus attired I saw you in her. I will not tease you Molly, for I suspect that I correctly divined the reason for your reaction when you first saw her image. The resemblance to your own face came to me then. Tell me what you intend to do. The situation is delicate, fascinating and worthy of a novel. (I am teasing. I love to think of you laughing, however indignantly.) If I can help you in any way, poor clod-footed mere male that I am, I am yours to command.

Years of self-control fell away from me in that instant and I cried until I could cry no more. The hope burnt me. It hurt me. I could not bear it. After I had exhausted myself of tears, I sat for I know not how long, starting into the empty grate, lost in a kind of trance.

Eventually, I stood up, washed my face and let down my hair. I lit a fire and sat before it, brushing the waves in the way I had always done, soothed by the repetitive stroking of my scalp and the

306

pleasure of seeing the waves of dark copper streaked with silver and gold.

At times, I thought I must master this hope, deprive it of air, dismiss it, for what if it proved false? The illusion that had kept me sane when I had chosen to believe so long ago, that my baby was safely in the care of a good family and living in affluent comfort in Scotland or France – I would have to face the fact that it had all been self-deception. All hope would be gone, forever.

And if Maisie really was my Charlotte? Did she have any inkling that she had been brought up by people not of her blood? Would she recognize me as I had her? Would she hate and despise me for failing to find her? Would she prefer her adoptive parents and reject me? Reject this alternative version of her truth? All those years! Oh, I could not bear it. I could not. I should have replied to Thackeray, but I simply did not know what to say. It was a cowardice I would live to regret.

Chapter 37

By Christmas, when there had been no reply from Sandys, I wrote to him again. It took me several drafts to convey a tone of cool enquiry when what I felt was overwhelming impatience, fear, frustration, anger and indignation, but I did it.

The whole of January was deep in snow and the world felt hushed, time suspended. My hopes were similarly muffled under layers of reason. Once again, I had achieved equanimity. I kept busy and tried not to think.

I knew from my enquiries at the Newcastle Art Academy that the Scottish exhibition was at Easter but I had been invited to an extended planning meeting which was to take place over two weeks at Streatlam Castle. John and Josephine would be there with some of their curatorial French staff, and we would be joined at different times by art dealers from London, Paris and the Netherlands.

One morning, swimming to the surface of consciousness from a deep and dreamless sleep, an inspired idea broke upon me and became a decision before I could quash it. I would write to Thomas Sword Good in Berwick-upon-Tweed.

I always have a notebook by my bedside: there was no excuse. I shuffled out of bed, the blankets wrapped round me, opened the curtains to look out on the melting snowscape, lit an oil-lamp and went back to bed to write my letter:

> *8 Summerhill*
> *Blaydon on Tyne*
>
> *Dear Thomas*
>
> *It is some years since last we met and I hope they have treated you well. I hear that you are long-since married: congratulations. It would be good to see you and perhaps to meet your wife if you are ever in Newcastle.*
>
> *I write to you on the matter that you know is nearest to my heart. If you are, by any chance, travelling to Edinburgh for the Spring Exhibition, there is something important you could do for me.*

Frederick Sandys will be exhibiting and he may well be there with his wife. I have a faint hope that his wife Maisie is my daughter Charlotte. There is so much I could say, but I beg you to keep this suspicion to yourself. If you are indeed planning to travel to Edinburgh and you could find a way of finding out about the lady in question without drawing attention to your enquiries, well, my gratitude will know no bounds.

If you have any news, I beg you to write to me at my own address above. For two weeks at Easter, I shall be at Streatlam Castle as the guest of John and Josephine Bowes, but directly upon my return on 15th April, I shall hasten to the Post Office here in Blaydon and hope to find there a reply from you.

The two weeks at Streatlam were a great pleasure in every way, and I even sometimes contrived to put the thoughts of Maisie out of my mind. It was revealed to us that a piece of land just outside Barnard Castle had been identified as ideal. Not wishing to reveal his identity for fear of inflating the price, John had employed an agent to negotiate the purchase on his behalf.

There was so much to learn, so many things to think of: until then, I had not fully appreciated what a great undertaking the Museum was to be. I had given a good deal of thought to the compilation of the inventory, and John was evidently surprised and pleased to discover my capabilities. Much of the subsequent discussion concerned not art but packing cases, wrappings, handling and storage. Whenever I found my mind wandering, I forced myself to concentrate on John's animated face and see Poll's flickering there. If only she had lived to see this.

I arrived back in Blaydon by train on 15th April and went straight to the Post Office. As I entered, a tall grey-haired gentleman came forward to greet me. It was Thomas.

'Molly! You look wonderful! I dreaded seeing your lovely face ravaged by time, but I need have had no fear – just look at you! And that green gown suits your skin tones so well!'

The post-master and his wife were standing side-by-side behind the counter beaming at me, clearly in the belief that they were witnessing long-lost lovers reunited. Which of course they were, I reminded myself.

He opened the door and let me pass through. I still had not spoken: I could barely move my feet, so overwhelmed was I with surprise and misgivings about what I might hear. Most of all, I dreaded the loss of hope.

He took my bag and linked his arm with mine, clamping it securely lest I fall, for he had no doubt perceived the colour draining from my face.

'Come, let us walk. There's a bench. Sit here, Molly. Here we cannot be overheard.' I sat down obediently, my legs weak and my heart fluttering.

'I have news. Sandys was indeed in Edinburgh and I contrived to meet him 'accidentally' at his club. He knows of no connection between us, but it was a precaution that turned out to be wise. I have in fact met him before but he doesn't remember. We spent a thoroughly enjoyable evening together, a group of artists partaking of fine whiskeys. I need not tell you that tongues were loosened.

'I blush to confess that there was a degree of banter about women: there always is when men are together and alcohol comes to the party. It transpires his wife is a stunner whose real name is difficult to ascertain. He calls her Maisie. In their neighbourhood of London, where they live with several children, they are known as Mr and Mrs Neville, though I doubt they are in fact married as I have heard that he has a wife in Norfolk from whom he has long been estranged.

'As to the origins of Maisie, her stage name was 'Miss Clive' and she still occasionally takes a part in a London theatre production, simply for the love of it. From what he said - and as I indicated, tongues were loosened - he is quite devoted to her and in thrall to her beauty and her wilfulness. Amongst her talents, he opined in his cups, is fluent French. It was a simple step to enquire and it transpires that she was indeed brought up in France, apparently born to a French mother, who still survives. But her father was a Scot, a formidable chap, not much liked. These are not the Blairs, by the way, but another Franco-Scottish family entirely. Catholics. They moved to France permanently when Maisie was three years old.'

I could not speak.

'As to the rest, how she came to be in a touring theatre troupe, I cannot say. But there is one thing more I must add to my account: I asked one question too many. Sandys abruptly got up and left. Mystified, the rest of us looked one to the other. "What was that all about?" I said. "One too many, I'll wager" said one of the group. "No, it's more than that," says another sagely. "He's been touchy about his wife since Thackeray's visit." I didn't understand the import of that, but I thought I should tell you. Have you any idea what he meant?'

I swallowed, and my voice came out more hesitant than I had intended. 'I … I have a suspicion. I think perhaps a clod-footed male has tried to help.'

'Whom do you mean?'

'William Makepeace Thackeray.'

'The art critic?'

'And noted novelist. Yes. The very same. He is a friend and not noted for his discretion. I fear he has told Fred Sandys of my suspicion and Sandys is alarmed. He might think me quite mad.'

'Or he might be justifiably afraid of losing Maisie.'

'Why would he lose her? They have children together.'

'I detect that Sandys is somewhat possessive of his wife, perhaps a little fearful of losing her. He had already indicated that she is not entirely satisfied with him or with her life in the suburbs. And remember, despite her profession, she is not without resources. If Thackeray has revealed your suspicions to him, he may have concealed them from her.'

'I had not thought of that. It is a possibility, as you say, and it would certainly explain why he never wrote to me again about the portraits I wished to view.'

'I have an idea. You must write to her directly. In case he sees the letter, I shall address the envelope so that he will not recognize your writing.'

'But the postmark? He will be immediately suspicious if it comes from Newcastle.'

'Then I shall post it from York, where I am headed directly.' He suddenly grasped my hands and knelt before me, as he had done all those years ago. Looking earnestly into my eyes, he said, 'Am I not the answer to all your prayers, sweet Molly? Marry me!'

I smiled and patted his hand. I felt quite calm now. 'You are married already, Thomas.'

'Oh yes, I quite forgot! It is your beauty bewitching me as it always did!'

I stood up. 'Come, we will go to the Mechanics' Institute. You can give an impromptu lecture on painting whilst I write my letter.'

8 Summerhill, Blaydon on Tyne

Dear Mrs Neville

We have never met, but I am acquainted with your husband. If when you have read this letter you want to know more about me, your husband's friend William Makepeace Thackeray will be happy to oblige.

What I am about to say may come as a shock to you. You might dismiss it as fancy and take me for a lunatic. It may indeed be fancy, but I will write it anyway.

Many years ago, in August 1819, my baby Charlotte was lost to me. The circumstances of her vanishing you may hear if you wish. The purpose of my letter is this: I believe that you might be my daughter. I base this upon nothing more than intuition. You may read this and discount it immediately. But if you have one iota of thought that it may be true, I beg you to contact me. I have no proof: I can offer nothing to support my belief. I attach no blame. I look for nothing, only my daughter. In all the intervening years I have never for more than a passing moment seen a child or a woman who I thought could be my daughter, but when I saw your portrait, first as the 'Weeping Magdalene' and then as 'Proud Maisie', I felt I knew with certainty.

After the first frantic months of searching, I lost heart. In time, I learnt to quench any flicker of hope, and I have found this to be the path to peace of mind. For the first time in over thirty years, I now have hope that I may see my daughter again. I have let it take light and burn in me. I cannot lose it again.

312

So here is a strange request on which to end. If you know with absolute certainty that it cannot be true, I beg you not to reply. I shall tell myself that the letter was lost or that your adoptive mother would be too distressed to be confronted with the truth. I shall tell myself that you yourself cannot bear to believe it. And I shall go on believing that you are in the world, a mother yourself, and happy and healthy and loved. And I shall be content.

With my sincere good wishes, Molly Bowes

Chapter 38

Answer came there none. The summer passed in a haze of distractions and by the time the seasons turned, I had settled into a kind of mellow acceptance. As I had promised, I formed in my heart and my imagination a peaceful belief that she was out there in the world, safe and loved and surrounded by her little ones.

I was kept busy in my dual life amongst the working people of Tyneside and the gathering glories of what would one day be the Bowes Museum: paintings, sculptures, furniture, ceramics, orange trees, a fawn, a donkey, a clockwork mouse... Josephine always had a fascination for automata, her father having been a clock-maker. She wrote to me of a marvelous thing she had seen at the Paris Exhibition: a life-size silver swan. It was not on the market at that point, but she told me she yearned for it, dreamt of it. To hear of its mere existence was a joy to me.

I never knew what to expect each time I opened a letter from John or Josephine: by the time the land was successfully purchased in 1865, there were hundreds of items in safe storage at Streatlam Castle.

Once a month, I would travel to Streatlam and take up residence in one of the opulent bedrooms. I spent my days supervising the arrival, checking and storage of beautiful valuable delicate artifacts. I walked to and from the Orangery, where many items were being stored, and I looked out over immaculate parkland. I have to say, I much prefer the natural beauties of Gibside.

William Hutt, now a widower and a member of the House of Lords, was rarely at home. There were rumours that he was planning to remarry and move to the Isle of Wight, where he had inherited property. The future of Gibside was again insecure, its treasures unattended, so I was asked to escort particularly precious items to Streatlam: Mary Eleanor's botanical cabinet, her mother's Rubens, Susan Ridley's porcelain.

I would take the train from Darlington to Newcastle and thence to Blaydon, return to my cosy cottage, swap my gown for more modest attire, and go to the Co-op. I entertained myself with the idea that I was like a female Jekyll and Hyde.

Occasionally my two worlds fused and those moments were precious to me: they galvanized both halves of my life. The most stark and moving moment of that nature was related to the Lancashire Cotton workers. The American Civil War stopped the supply of raw cotton and Lancashire's mills fell silent: cotton-workers were laid off and great suffering ensued. Joseph Cowen stood up and showed the country the universal spiritual community of manual labourers. In his newspapers, he repeatedly pointed out the links between the American slaves who lived in such terrible conditions and the English workers whose exploitation enslaved them to the mill-owners and their deafening machines.

In one edition of the Newcastle Chronicle was printed an engraving of a weaver. When I saw it, I immediately thought back to the Fallons and all the Lancashire weavers amongst whom I had lived so long ago. The engraving was entitled 'The Waiting Time' and it was by George Sandys. I felt a stab of pain when I saw his name.

I began to regret my determination to accept Maisie's silence. In the two years since I had sent it, I had several times had to stop myself going to London. I imagined various scenarios but the fear of rejection and denial kept me in the North East.

I do not believe in signs and portents, but something about the synchronicity of these things - the swan, the cotton workers, the Sandys engraving – made me feel that something indefinable was aligning. When I look back now, it seems fated, as though all the strands of my life were coming together on a great celestial loom.

The moment when it hit me most poignantly was at the funeral of my old friend Joe Cowen. Gabe was there, standing with other former Winlaton blacksmiths, a shrinking crew but all still fine well-built men. They stood in a line clasping their hats before them as Joe's coffin was borne past into St Paul's Church. Walking with other friends and colleagues of 'Sir Joseph', I passed the line of blacksmiths and caught Gabe's eye. You may think that I have become fanciful in my old age, but I firmly believe that a look passed between us that spoke of all that might have been.

The churchyard was packed, the doors all open: all of Blaydon and Winlaton mourned the passing of their finest son.

For me, in all the words I have heard him speak and seen him write, Joseph's speech about his father was his finest hour:

My father started life in humble circumstances, and he lived, by industry and integrity, to win for himself a fair share of this world's wealth. But he never allowed the mere getting of money, the adding of acre to acre, or house to house, to destroy his interest in public affairs.

In discharging his duty to his family he did not forget his responsibility as a citizen. He preserved to the end the ardent political interests of his youth, he maintained them faithfully to the last, and he died as earnest and advanced a Radical as he was when, fifty years ago, he marched at the head of his brother-blacksmiths to the famous gathering on the Town Moor.

It sometimes happens that a rise in a man's circumstances alters his political principles. That was not the case with the gentleman to whom I refer. There have been many men more learned in the knowledge of the schools, many men more brilliant but I can say that I knew of no man more conscientious in the beliefs that he entertained, and more consistent in enforcing them.

But all that wealth and all that power here can give will leave us all sooner or later; and everything, my friends, will soon be forgotten except the uses we have made of the opportunities for good that have been placed within our reach.

Chapter 39

After Joe's passing, a sense of my own mortality pressed upon me more urgently. I could not accept that I might go to my grave without knowing the truth about what had happened to my daughter. I must at least find a way of seeing Maisie.

The opportunity immediately presented itself. There was shortly to be a Newcastle Art Exhibition to raise funds for the town's Mechanics' Institute. It was moving to larger premises on New Bridge Street and funds raised by the exhibition were going to pay for the internal fittings. The exhibition was to be formed of new works by established artists and ones on loan from private collections.

I had an idea: it was daring, but as they say around here, 'Shy bairns get nowt.' I would write to John Bowes to let him know about the exhibition and suggest that he might like to offer a painting or two. Then I would make a special request: would he mind if I invited an eminent painter to stay at Gibside with his family? The gentleman in question was a friend of Thackeray as well as myself, the famous portraitist, Frederick Sandys.

When I received his assent, I wrote from Gibside, a carefully-crafted letter which made no mention of Maisie but flattered Sandys' ego and implied that the invitation came from John Bowes. Everyone in the art world knew about the collection that was being assembled in County Durham and every eminent artist wanted his work to be represented.

It took two weeks for the reply to arrive, but at last, there it was, a creamy glow on the library table.

Dear Miss Bowes,

It was with great pleasure that I received your letter. Please convey our gratitude to Mr Bowes for the generosity of his kind invitation. I look forward to meeting him, perhaps when he is next in London.

I have arranged for a large painting to be loaned to the forthcoming exhibition. (I should add that it was sold before it was completed, but the owner has agreed to allow it to spend a week at

Newcastle on its way to Scotland.) It should arrive by the beginning of August, in time to be included in the catalogue. I think you will find the subject of particular interest, Miss Bowes.

Mr Bowes' offer of accommodation at Gibside is most generous and in other circumstances we would have had no hesitation in accepting it. Unfortunately, if I am able to attend the opening, I will be unaccompanied. Maisie has been unwell: she is recently delivered of our tenth child and the circumstances of the birth in the wake of the loss of her own mother have left her incapacitated, as I am sure you will understand.

If I find myself in a position to travel to Newcastle for the opening ceremony, I look forward to meeting you there.

Kind regards
Fred Sandys

I hardly knew what to make of this letter: it was certainly very different from Sandys' previous communications, which had been chaotically presented, evidently hastily written and full of flourishes and ink blots. By contrast, this had clearly been executed with care, perhaps even drafted and re-drafted. And one sentence stood out: what could be the subject of the painting?

Of course I knew it could be any number of things that Sandys knew would be of interest to me: a portrait of Thomas Bewick or William Thackeray, Thomas Sword Good or the founder of the Newcastle Art Academy, Thomas Miles Richardson; it could be a painting made from the subjects of his woodcuts The Old Chartist or the weaver.

But deep at the bottom of all the imaginings with which I tried to distract myself was the suspicion that the subject was Maisie. And if that proved to be the case, what would it mean?

On Friday 2nd August, I travelled into Newcastle. I knew that the paintings would still be being arranged ready for the preview of the exhibition. When I entered the building to be greeted by a very young and attractive blonde receptionist, it made me smile to remember the chaos of that first exhibition forty years before.

'Miss Bowes! A pleasure. Have you come to see Mr Bowes's contributions in situ?'

'Yes, but I have another particular reason for calling in. Has the Frederick Sandys canvas arrived safely?'

The receptionist stood up, her face aglow. 'Why yes, and what a glorious thing it is! Would you like to see it?'

'I… What is the subject of the painting, could you tell me?'

'It is a Shakespearean heroine … what is the name, I cannot think. I do not really know Shakespeare's plays. I do go to the theatre, but I prefer the Tyne to the Theatre Royal…'

'Yes, yes, please show me the painting.'

She was just about to lead the way when she stopped and lifted a slender finger. 'Wait! I nearly have it! It begins with a P.'

I didn't need to think at all. My skin came alive. 'Perdita, the lost girl.'

I could barely breathe until I saw it. When my eyes at last found it in the second room - glowing gold, a foot square, intensely coloured – and I approached and looked at last upon Perdita, I exhaled slowly, my heart slowed and a deep calm spread throughout my being.

Her face was shown in profile, the shoulders forward, as though she was looking over her shoulder at someone approaching through the enchanted wood whose blossoms lit the dark background; skin luminous and tinged with gold; hair in the Grecian style, threaded with flowers, and flowing over her left shoulder in a cascade of russet curls; and across her chest a garland of laurel twined with flowers. There was vulnerability in the pale luminosity of skin, the exposed white throat, the flowers, the diaphanous muslin neckline of her dress, the slightly parted lips. But the set of that mouth, that strong chin, that long aquiline nose; the challenge and the fire in those limpid eyes: they spoke to me. I recognized myself in them.

I don't know how long I stood, rapt, before it.

'Miss Bowes?'

When I turned, I was still in a daze and it took me a moment to register that I was looking up into the face of Fred Sandys.

He smiled. 'I hoped I would see you here.'

I could not bring myself to speak.

He stood beside me then, gazing at the golden vision he had created. 'I am very proud of this. It conjures her up as she once was.'

My mind was all confusion, my heart strangely still. As she once was? Had she died? Was this what he'd come to tell me? Or was he merely telling me that he had used my story to inspire him, as Thackeray had done with Mary Eleanor's? Another man taking a woman's distress and making art from it, careless of the consequences?

Finally, I summoned my voice. My soul was curiously calm: I listened to myself speak as though it was someone else's voice. 'You are right to be proud of it, Mr Sandys. It has a powerful impact on me: Perdita's tale has always had a particular resonance.'

Musingly, he said, 'I think I successfully convey her spirit.' He looked at me and winked, 'For she is very spirited, my Maisie, alarmingly so. There have been times, Miss Bowes, when I feared I would lose her, and I simply could not bear it.'

I bit my lip and kept my silence.

'She is restless, you see. Motherhood is all very well, she tells me, but she wants more.'

When I still didn't reply, he went on, 'She has threatened to go back to France and establish an art school of her own.'

'And has she the means?'

'Yes. Her parents are dead: her brother is dead: the chateau is hers.'

'You are not married to her?'

'No. I have no claim, nor would I.'

I smiled. 'You would not dare.'

His smile was wry. 'No. You are quite correct. I would not dare.'

'So what is to be done?'

'I am hoping that we can find something in England that will bring Maisie happiness.'

'And fulfillment?'

'Yes, quite. Her word exactly.'

'Of what nature?'

'Maisie is bi-lingual. She has knowledge of the art world in France and England. I was hoping that perhaps you might be able to find a role for her in Mr Bowes' great enterprise.'

'And *why* would I help, Mr Sandys?'

He was looking over my shoulder at someone who had just come through the door and his eyes were filling with tears. 'Why, Miss Bowes? Because you are her mother.'

Epilogue

Today we saw an astonishing thing, my family and I. At first sight, it was marvelous enough: a life-size swan of exquisite beauty resting on a silvery-glass stream in which little silver fish seemed frozen in the act of sailing on invisible currents. We walked around it, this way and that, marveling at its intricacy, its lifelike pose, the intelligence in its eyes.

And then we settled into chairs as we were bid, and watched a man in a worsted apron fiddle about with spanners and screwdrivers, grumbling all the while.

And then John and Josephine came in - the foundation stone was laid today and the celebrations are to be crowned with a private demonstration for the family of the Museum's prize exhibit. The man in the apron has worked for weeks, we are told. It has been a major undertaking, almost impossible: it might not work. But woe betide the man if it does not work, for the children's faces are rapt with expectation.

And then the music starts and all chatter ceases, for isn't the stream moving? The water appears to be flowing, but how could this be? And – aaaah - the swan begins to move! And as it moves all human movement ceases: not even a blink will stir the air while this wonder unfolds.

She is preening herself! See? Her neck twists this way and that, elegantly swaying, worshipping her own beauty in the magic mirrored stream. She dips her head to catch and eat one of the small silver fish swimming below. Look! A silver fish wriggles in her beak! She swallows it! It is gone! But how can this be?

The music fades and stops. Held breath is exhaled into the room.

'Again! Again!' pipe little voices. 'Mama! Nana! Again!' Golden heads of curls rise and bob and wave. 'Again, again!'

John and Josephine look on, smiling their delight.

A thing of beauty is a joy forever.

Author's Note

If you've read *My Name is Eleanor*, you might have been astonished to hear that Stoney Bowes went on to have more children in prison. It seems incredible to us that whole families had to live in debtors' prisons; that debtors had to provide their own bedding, food and drink; that those who could afford it bought 'liberty of the rules', allowing them to live within three square miles; and that a man like Stoney would be allowed to seduce the seventeen-year-old daughter of a fellow prisoner of the King's Bench and rent a room to keep her in.

"A girl of perfect symmetry, fair, lively and innocent": you can read more about Polly Sutton's twenty-two years with Stoney in Dr Jesse Foot's account: there's a link on my website and a summary of the details relevant to this novel. After Stoney died, Polly and her five children were released; nobody knows what happened to them, and so I decided to make one of them the heroine of my story.

I'm from Manchester: hearing about the Peterloo Massacre was a political awakening for me. Molly's fictional life and adventures were always going to take her to St Peter's Fields on that fateful day in August 1819. How I was going to get her to Gibside, let alone involve her in the creation of The Bowes Museum, was a mystery to which I was sure someone at the Lit and Phil would provide a solution: thank-you, Bill Bower, whose casual observation that the iron-workers' village of Winlaton had had a library as early as 1819 was a turning point in the plotting of this novel.

Because of that revelation, I started reading about Winlaton, and then discovered that there was a huge demonstration in Newcastle in the wake of Peterloo. When I found out that the contingent of blacksmiths from Winlaton was led by Joe Cowen, it seemed fated. I can see Winlaton from my window, and the remains of Cowen's brickworks are a few yards from our front door; the grounds of Stella Hall adjoin our garden. From that point on, Molly was destined to live in my house, which was built as pair of cottages in 1855.

All the public characters, places and events in the novel are real, though I've used a bit of poetic licence with the dates. If you'd like to know more about any aspect of the history on which this novel is based, there's plenty of information on my website.

Acknowledgements

This is a work of fiction that borrows closely from history: a curious French knitting-doll of threads twined together. It is inspired by the wonderful people and history of Tyneside.

I have many people to thank, some of whom won't even know they've helped, so I'll start with the places I love and the people who care for them: The Literary and Philosophical Society of Newcastle upon Tyne; Gibside; The Bowes Museum; The Land of Oak & Iron Heritage Centre at Winlaton Mill.

Particular individuals attached to those institutions have kindly given invaluable help:

Bill Bower, Margaret Bozic, Roger Napier, Kay Easson, Caroline Grove and the staff of the Lit & Phil

Margaret Bozic and Richard Waldmeyer for their information about the Quakers

David Hepworth and the staff of the Local Studies Service at Newcastle City Library

David Butler, Peter Firth, Julie Hawthorn, Anthea Lang and Geoff Marshall of Gibside (National Trust)

Judith Phillips and Sheila Dixon of The Bowes Museum

Elspeth Gould of Seaton Delaval (National Trust)

The Land of Oak & Iron project, especially David Marrs

Winlaton, Sunniside and Swalwell Local History Societies

Susan Lynn, Dennis Shaw and John Terence Arthur

Peter Osborne and June Holmes of The Bewick Society

Carl and Jackie Haley of the Black Bull at Blaydon for running the best pub in the world, full of the best people and music of Tyneside, especially Pom.

Thanks also to all the friends and relatives who've helped and encouraged in any way, particularly the first readers: Margaret Bone, Sheila Nicholson, Kevin Boyle, Julie Walker, Vanessa Walker and Candida Giaquinto…and of course my special thanks to Kev for his boundless patience, love and support.

By the same author

Fiction

My Name Is Eleanor
Under the Spreading Chestnut Tree

Non Fiction

A People's History of Gibside
Tales of Derwentdale and the Extraordinary
J.W.Fawcett
Path Head Water Mill

Printed in Great Britain
by Amazon